PRAISE FOR RO D0462358

THE NEWS OF THE WORLD

"An exuberant, wise and wonderfully inventive evocation of the kinds of love and longing that never really go out of style. . . . It's a story like 'Life Before Science' that conveys best the blend of tragicomedy, sheer optimism, sharp perception, and almost manic energy that makes Carlson's work so distinctive—and so appealing." —Alida Becker, *Washington Post*

"There is in these stories a certain holiness bestowed on ordinary things, on ordinary lives, that is a powerful reminder of the late John Cheever."
—John Irving

"Wonderful. . . . This is a genuine collection, each tale separately coherent but also full of cross-references of tone, theme and image, so that the whole finally resonates as a novel would. . . . Carlson convinces us over and over again that he's just telling the truth, more than anything we'll read in the paper this morning or see on the tube tonight."
—Janet Burroway, *Philadelphia Inquirer*

"A demonstration of how much a skilled writer with a little passion and compassion can fit into the smallest of spaces. Very strong stuff."
—Madison Smartt Bell

"Carlson knows how regular guys feel, and writes about it thoughtfully, wittily, expertly. The 16 stories in this collection . . . have more dynamism than you'll find in ten other story collections put together."
—*Playboy*

"Marvelous. . . . Domestic love of a very rare homey and affectionate sort is alive and well in the work of a writer who has acquired the technique to depict such values and situations with absolute integrity. No sentimental gushing here. . . . I read Carlson's collection, racing from one good tale to the next, warmed by his familial passions in an otherwise wintry world." —Alan Cheuse, *Chicago Tribune*

"Quirky and thrilling. . . . His stories have something I've been hungry to hear, and his quiet, familiar style is so seductive, convincing, that I am led to believe that his ordinary people have elaborate, you could even say baroque, and not minimal lives; and they have speech too. A kind of friendly, naked, confidential prattle or ramble, not fancy but expressive and wide-ranging. . . . You'll want to read these stories as fast as you can, and hope for more." —Alice Bloom, *The Hudson Review*

"Carlson makes it all credible, amusing and very refreshing. . . . Most of [the stories] are models of economy, packing a great deal of joy-in-life into a few pages. . . . Even Carlson's sad stories are warm with love and humor." —Nancy Shapiro, *St. Louis Times-Dispatch*

"Ron Carlson has a lovely way with words. . . . Family life, its joys and its pitfalls, is a recurring theme in Carlson's work, but he handles this material in such a stunning variety of ways that his chosen theme always strikes the reader as new and fresh." —Phil Thomas, Associated Press

"Every story is hilarious and the characters pleasantly eccentric. . . . [The stories] are pithy and energetic and, often, ironic, but always with a touch of warm human emotion." —Lorna Gold, *Albuquerque Journal*

PLAN B FOR THE MIDDLE CLASS

"Wise and witty. . . . A lovely collection. . . . Carlson is a very funny writer indeed. . . . It is a generous author who creates a world at once so messy and loving." —Geoffrey Stokes, *Boston Sunday Globe*

"At their best . . . [the stories] tilt the world just enough to give us a sense of how much we need it to stand upright."
—Richard Eder, *Los Angeles Times*

"A gathering of tender and often humorous tales. . . . Ron Carlson is a brilliant comedic writer. . . . With its wildly humorous but truthful look at how much we can bend without breaking, *Plan B for the Middle Class* is a revealing—and sometimes unsettling—look at what we may really mean when we talk about 'family values.' "
—Maxine Chernoff, *New York Times Book Review*

"Ron Carlson . . . is a master of the quirky, bittersweet domestic story. . . . Funny and well-observed." —Mark Bautz, *Washington Times*

"Carlson plunges you into each universe, filling your mind with tactile detail and epigrammatic dialogue. Having crafted these careful, concentrated renderings of emotional states, he gets playful, spinning funky little tales. . . . The title story is a masterful and charmingly funny drama of dreams denied and dreams secured. Another splendid story collection by the author of *The News of the World*." —Donna Seaman, *Booklist*

"He does amazing things with astonishing economy. . . . Carlson restores to minimalism both its good name and its maximum punch." —Joseph Coates, *Chicago Tribune*

"These stories display an extraordinary craft and maturity of vision. . . . Carlson's range—from quotidian to surreal, encompassing everything in between—is astonishing. . . . Wonderful. . . . Ron Carlson has become a wizard of the short-story form." —Patty O'Connell, *Boston Sunday Globe*

"It is Carlson's sensibility as a perceptive, amusing and gracious storyteller that makes this collection so strong. . . . Everything we want from a story collection and just what we need." —Sheri Hallgren, *San Francisco Chronicle*

"There is substance and depth beneath the bizarre surface happenings. Mr. Carlson's range is remarkable, from the quirky to the affecting." —Bob Trimble, *Dallas Morning News*

"The wonderful stories in *Plan B for the Middle Class* mix outrageously funny observations with bittersweet meditations on mid-life." —R. K. Dickson, *Bloomsbury Review*

"Honest and honed narratives. In these stories Carlson has made reading about the modest life irresistible." —Nancy Zafris, *Cleveland Plain Dealer*

"I was entirely and happily in Carlson's thrall. The word 'happily' seems especially apt for this writer, who is a master of that rarity in contemporary fiction, the happy ending."
—Margot Livesey, *New York Times Book Review*

"A strange eclectic mixture of some of the funniest and saddest stories ever to cozy up together in one volume. Some stories are brilliant and deeply moving; others are wild and surreal. . . . Affirms both the breadth and depth of this writer's vision as well as the utter singularity of his voice." —Judith Freeman, *Los Angeles Times Book Review*

"Carlson's stories are authentic, honest, hilarious, and full of a kind of hard-won hopefulness. Again and again he achieves the perfect balance between understated humor and understated grief." —Pam Houston

"Pungent stories. . . . Hauntingly evocative."
—Margot Mifflin, *Entertainment Weekly*

"Ron Carlson hides the considerable art in his stories as well as anyone writing in English; he disguises it with humor, memorable language and likeable people. . . . Carlson is terribly funny without being unserious. . . . Carlson, however, *is* an artist, a deadpan chronicler of small-town tragedies, and, like Sherwood Anderson, the best kind of American writer." —Nathan Ward, *Newark Star-Ledger*

"These stories are imaginative, poignant, and funny."
—*Arizona Republic*

"Carlson produces clean and assured prose and animates familiar situations with imaginative twists, masterfully reported details and enough emotional honesty to fill a book twice this size." —*Publishers Weekly*, starred review

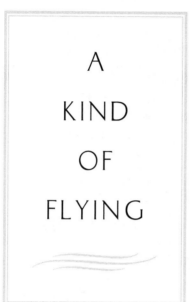

A
KIND
OF
FLYING

A
KIND
OF
FLYING

SELECTED STORIES

with an Introduction by the Author

RON CARLSON

W. W. Norton & Company
New York London

For Elaine

Copyright © 2003, 1997, 1992, 1987 by Ron Carlson

For information about permission to reproduce selections from this book,
write to Permissions, W. W. Norton & Company, Inc., 500 Fifth Avenue,
New York, NY 10110

Manufacturing by Courier Westford
Book design by JAM Design
Production manager: Anna Oler

ISBN 0-393-32479-6 (pbk.)

W. W. Norton & Company, Inc.
500 Fifth Avenue, New York, N.Y. 10110
www.wwnorton.com

W. W. Norton & Company Ltd.
Castle House, 75/76 Wells Street, London W1T 3QT

1 2 3 4 5 6 7 8 9 0

SC CARLSON

CONTENTS

FRIENDS OF MY YOUTH

I N 1982 I was remodeling our old house in Salt Lake City and feeling fine about it. It was an old house and needed repair. The inventory of things to do was thrilling: hinges, windows, shelving, painting. We'd left our teaching jobs at prep school after ten years in the east and were back in our hometown. My wife had taken a fine job as a technical editor with Sperry-Univac, and I was supposed to be writing a novel. But given a day, what was I going to do: type further into the dark or affix the new kitchen counter? The house was the biggest thing that had come between me and my writing, and I could feel it was going to be there for a while. Summer turned to fall and the inventory doubled. I was working alone (with our dog Max as company), replacing the wicked basement windows, tiling the laundry floor.

One day hauling trash to the landfill in my truck, I dropped a mattress off the elevated freeway there at Fifth South. This bothered me, of course, and I was generally bothered by not writing, but I tried to take satisfaction in my home repair. I continued cleaning, fixing, replacing until one day I found myself sitting on the cement carport floor beside the sawhorses on which lay the big front door. I was stripping the door, and I had taken a snootful of the powerful chemicals, and as dizzy as I'd been that year, I sat down. The good dog Max came up and nosed me in the face. From the workbench the radio broadcast a song, and I thought, "This is a terrible song." I wish I could remember the name of the annoying song, but I don't know the titles of ten songs. It was a man and he closed each stanza down with unrestrained wailing. He was as unhappy as I was. The dizziness you get from chemical stripper is not a joke, and most of an hour passed as I watched the light change in the larger world. I had some thoughts, among them: why are you stripping the door? I mention all this because that was the day that when I stood up, I went into the back room of our old house and sat at the typewriter and wrote the first draft of "The Governor's Ball," where the mattress flies off that one guy's truck.

I'm not saying there is a magic ingredient in paint stripper. I'm just saying I was at the end of my rope and I didn't know it until I sat down in that garage. I also will say that any writer who removes the front door from the house and then types a story is probably going to be working on a piece of fiction that has his attention.

I was going to write the narrative of losing the mattress as a letter to my folks, but I just let it go on. I've spoken about that story many times, about how I continued into it far past what I knew, and how the ending surprised me. A watershed moment in my life as a writer occurred when the homeless man asks if the mattress would fly out of the sky. I thought: that's right—he saw it. How I would have loved to see a mattress fly down from the elevated highway, but I didn't see it, he did. I wrote another story the next day and that story is also in this book. I wrote the tiny piece "Max" on the third day. Each of these stories surprised me in ways I wasn't used to. I was nervous, but typing. I had written and published two novels, and to be sure there were surprises in their writing, but this was something new. On my bulletin board was the tabloid headline, "Bigfoot Stole My Wife," and I read it for the thousandth time and for the first time thought, "That's no good. That had to hurt." I was living a life hoping every day that my wife would arrive home safely. I reread the headline, and I made ready to type that story.

I finished with the door, sanded it, and put four coats of lustrous Varithane on it (as well as the screen door frame), and they can be seen still shining today, if you know where to look. But my maintenance work moved into the avocation column, where it has stayed. In the twenty years since that season in Utah, I've written dozens of stories, but I have never stripped another door and, frankly, I never will. I don't think anybody should.

That first year the novel I'd been typing rose and disappeared like vapor. My kids arrived and I was glad the roof was right and tight and that the nursery had new carpet and paint. The boys changed everything I was thinking about. The two people in my novel were having trouble getting back together even though they loved each other, but who cared! We had kids! Agendas shifted like continents for me.

I wrote the stories "Life Before Science," and "Blood," and "Phenomena" and "Milk," in that house, on an IBM typewriter on a borrowed dining-room table. The snow seriously damaged our roof that winter, and I was true to my work, typing while workmen we could not afford swarmed around me. I was doing the one thing that John Gardner notes fiction writers must be able to do: live without guilt while their spouses support them. In December, we leased our vacant lot to a couple of kids who sold Christmas trees, and I wrote "The H Street Sledding Record." It had been my wife's father who had thrown manure on his roof years before. Our friend Karen Shepard was editing her monthly paper *Network* and she paid me a hundred dollars a story and then a hundred and five and then a hundred and ten. Carol Houck Smith at Norton who had been the editor on my first two books called. I thought she was going to inquire about the novel that I had not been writing, but she said of the stories I had sent her: *I think we have a book here.* I remember the call. Those stories became *The News of the World.*

In 1986 we moved to Arizona and I started teaching at Arizona State in a fine community of writers and students. I started "Plan B for the Middle Class" in our rental house on Yale Avenue and finished it in the house we bought in Tempe. The issues I faced then were the same for all writers who take teaching jobs. Universities are places where writers disappear. I had always loved to teach and I still find it an active investigation, and I fought the fight that teaching writers fight. I wrote after my classes were in place, running smoothly. Teaching, like home repair, takes time and it is a real thing. I wrote "DeRay" in that house on Alameda and finished "Hartwell" and started "Blazo." All my stories were taking names for titles.

I wrote "On the U.S.S. Fortitude," and smiled at my indulgence. You can hear my mother's voice in there. I gave the story to Bill Shore, of Share Our Strength, who sold it to *The New Yorker*, so Share Our Strength got the money and I got the credit, such as it was. We had the chance to go to New York and see my tabloid headlines produced at The Manhattan Punchline. "Bigfoot Stole My Wife" the evening was called, and it included the new monologue, "The Tablecloth of Turin." By now, also, Bigfoot himself had spoken in "I Am Bigfoot," and his monologue got everyone's attention when he stepped forward at the end and pointed at a member of the audience and said, "I'm watching your wife." We had the true honor of hearing Darren McGavin play the sheriff in a forty-minute version of "Phenomenon." When I look at it now, I hear his voice.

It rained on our vacation to San Diego and I bought a typewriter out of the local shopper from a ham radio operator in La Jolla for eight bucks and started "Sunny Billy Day." There isn't much rain in our lives, and it's important to jump on it, get all you can out of it. I finished that story on a picnic table on our small terrace in Arizona on that same typewriter. I kept that ten-pound Underwood there for a year, under a plastic dishpan when not in use. When the story appeared in *Gentlemen's Quarterly*, it was accompanied by my favorite illustration ever—those ballplayers at the Castaway. Then I went back into "Blazo" and wrote on it for a year. By the end the folder was two inches thick, and I'd cut more pages than were included. We parted friends, but that was the most work of any of my stories.

Though, again, I'd been sent out to write a novel, what I sent to

New York were these stories. I wrote "A Kind of Flying," that gives this book its title, as an assignment for National Public Radio. Susan Stamberg and George Garrett had cooked up the notion of a group of writers all writing stories that included a wedding cake in the middle of the road. I do love the song "El Paso," but I did not know until I was finished writing the story that the military base in that city is Fort Bliss. A few months later Elaine and I woke one morning in Colorado and heard me reading it on the radio. I collected these stories, and we put a blueprint from a school library on the front cover of the book and sent it into the world. The working title was *Plan B for the Middle Class*, a joke I'd concocted in honor of the world's worst movie: *Plan 9 from Outer Space*. A reference that one person, total, has acknowledged.

The next year, with my desk clear and a sabbatical staring me in the eye, certainly I would write a novel. I saw the Charles Laughton version of *The Hunchback of Notre Dame* and started a monologue about boiling oil, which became "What We Wanted to Do." I started "Zanduce at Second," with the longest sentences I'd ever written, and no story before or since stunned me more with its ending. I started "The Prisoner of Bluestone" with the sentence "There was a camera." and nothing more, thinking that I was writing a mystery, and that we'd see the film developed. I had a weird wrestling anecdote about Dr. Slime that I'd held for some years, and I kicked that out of bed and found the narrator, our stalwart baker, and I went back into his strange night with Betsy. "A Note on the Type" began as a private little joke for my printer friends and kept opening and opening. When Mrs. McKay arrived I wasn't even sure what I had, but I had that feeling of satisfying strangeness which I've learned to listen to. By the time I started "Oxygen," my plans for a novel were again upset, dislodged, vanquished. I think I knew that would happen. In the long story "Oxygen" I wanted to make a tough summer in a hot city for our guy; I wanted an unvarnished look at a kind of rite of passage. When I finished I saw that I had written my little novel in short-story clothing. That year also, I told a

Halloween story to my son's third-grade class. I told it as a court-room trial, and because all the players got to speak, I heard something that became the germ of "The Chromium Hook." A few years later, the guys who made the festival film from that story sent me a beautiful black corduroy jacket with "Spinard Institute" embroidered over the heart. It makes me wish I lived in a colder place.

I finished the last and title story in the book, "The Hotel Eden," at our cabin in Utah, far above Vernal, in the summer of 1996. I remember the day vividly. The story had turned on me, and my charismatic friend had become something else, and the last sentence surprised me again. I closed the file on my little Mac Powerbook. Max and I went out for a hike in the late day, and in the rocky glen a mile out we came across a coyote and her pups. I held Max's collar while the coyote herded her brood back into the tangle of sandstone and pine, and then we took those long strides across the big meadow in a circle toward home. You get to walk that way when you finish your book.

I smiled when I read what Wallace Stegner wrote in his collected stories about his first agent warning him, pointedly, about writing stories, saying that a short-story writer "lives on his principal, using up beginnings and endings." In a way I think she was right. None of these stories was free, and I worked at them, trying to give each its own believable world. It is an expensive endeavor. You don't get to reuse the sets. Maybe novels are the way to go. But right now I still have a few stories in the bank. I've written some stories since the ones in this book, and frankly, I'm writing a couple more these days. I've come to love the short story intensely. I have found some things out writing them. I'm grateful to W. W. Norton and to Carol Houck Smith, whom I met through the mail twenty-eight years ago, for gathering these pieces, all friends of my youth, into the present book. I hope they meet your approval.

Ron Carlson
Scottsdale, Arizona

From

THE
NEWS
OF
THE
WORLD

THE GOVERNOR'S BALL

I DIDN'T KNOW until I had the ten-ton wet carpet on top of the hideous load of junk and I was soaked with the dank rust water that the Governor's Ball was that night. It was late afternoon and I had wrestled the carpet out of our basement, with all my strength and half my anger, to use it as a cover so none of the other wet wreckage that our burst pipes had ruined would blow out of the truck onto Twenty-first South as I drove to the dump. The wind had come up and my shirt front was stiffening as Cody pulled up the driveway in her Saab.

"You're a mess," she said. "Is the plumber through?"

"Done and gone. We can move back in tomorrow afternoon."

"We've got the ball in two hours."

"Okay."

"Could we not be late for once," Cody said. It was the first time I had stood still all day, and I felt how wet my feet were; I wanted to fight, but I couldn't come up with anything great. "I've got your clothes and everything. Come along."

"No problem," I said, grabbing the old rope off the cab floor.

"You're not going to take that to the dump now, are you?"

"Cody," I said, going over to her window, "I just loaded this. If I leave it on the truck tonight, one of the tires will go flat, and you'll have to help me unload this noxious residue tomorrow so I can change it. I've got to go. I'll hurry. You just be ready."

Her window was up by the time I finished and I watched her haul the sharp black car around and wheel into traffic. Since the pipes had frozen, we were staying with Dirk and Evan.

The old Ford was listing hard to the right rear, so I skipped back into the house for a last tour. Except for the sour water everywhere, it looked like I had everything. Then I saw the mattress. I had thrown the rancid king-size mattress behind the door when I had first started and now as I closed the front of the house, there it was. It was so large I had overlooked it. Our original wedding mattress. It took all the rest of my anger and some of tomorrow's strength to hoist it up the stairs and dance it out the back, where I levered it onto the hood of the truck by forcing my face, head, and shoulders into the ocher stain the shape of South America on one side. Then I dragged it back over the load, stepping awkwardly in the freezing carpet.

The rear tire was even lower now, so I hustled, my wet feet sloshing, and tied the whole mess down with the rope, lacing it through the little wire hoops I'd fashioned at each corner of the truck bed.

There was always lots of play in the steering of the Ford, but now, each time it rocked backward, I had no control at all. My fingers were numb and the truck was so back-heavy that I careened down Fifth South like a runaway wheelbarrow. The wind had really come up now, and I could feel it lifting at me as I crossed the intersections. It was cold in the cab, the frigid air crashing through the hole where the radio had been, but I wasn't stopping. I'd worried my way to the dump in this great truck a dozen times.

The Governor's Ball is two hundred dollars per couple, but we went every year as Dirk's guests. The event itself is held at the Hotel Utah, and the asparagus and salmon are never bad, but holding a dress ball in January is a sort of mistake, all that gray cleavage, everyone sick of the weather.

I was thinking about how Dirk always seated himself by Cody, how he made sure she was taken care of, how they danced the first dance, when the light at Third West turned green and I mounted the freeway. As soon as I could, I squeezed way right to get out of everybody's way, and because the wind here was fierce, sheering across at forty miles per hour, at least. The old truck was rocking like a dinghy; I was horsing the steering wheel hard, trying to stay in my lane, when I felt something go. There was a sharp snap and in the rearview mirror I saw the rope whip across the back. The mattress rose like a playing card and jumped up, into the wind. It sailed off the truck, waving over the rail, and was gone. I checked the rear, slowing. The mattress had flown out and over and off the ramp, five stories to the ground. I couldn't see a thing, except that rope, snapping, and the frozen carpet which wasn't going anywhere.

The traffic around me all slowed, cautioned by this vision. I tried to wave at them as if I knew what was going on and everything was going to be all right. At the Twenty-first South exit, I headed west, letting the rope snap freely, as if whipping the truck for more speed.

The dump, lying in the lea of the Kennecott tailings mound, was strangely warm. Throwing the debris onto the mountain of trash, I could smell certain sweet things rotting, and my feet warmed up a bit. By the time I swept out the truck, it was full dark. I still had half an hour to make the Governor's Ball.

I hit it hard driving away from the dump, just like everybody does, hoping to blow the microscopic cooties from their vehicles, but when I got back to Ninth West, I turned off. I didn't want to go retrieve the mattress; it was nine years old and had been in the basement three. But I had lost it. I had to call Cody.

The first neon I ran across was a place called The Oasis, a bar among all the small industries in that district. Inside, it was smotheringly warm and beery. I hadn't realized how cold my hands were until I tried for the dime in the pay phone. The jukebox was at full volume on Michael Jackson singing "Beat It!" so that when Cody answered, the first thing she said was: "Where are you?"

"I lost the mattress; I'm going to be late."

"What?"

"Go along with Dirk; I'll join you. Don't let anybody eat my salmon."

"Where are you?"

"The mattress blew out of the truck; I've got to go get it. And Cody."

"What?"

"Behave."

It was not until I had hung up that I saw the dancer. They had built a little stage in the corner of the bar and a young girl wearing pasties and a pair of Dale Evans fringed panties was dancing to the jukebox. Her breasts were round and high and didn't bounce very much, though they threw nice shadows when the girl turned under the light. I sat in my own sour steam at the end of the bar and ordered a beer. My fingernails ached as my hands warmed. All the men along the row sat with their backs to the bar to see the girl. I sat forward, feeling the grime melt in my clothes, and watched her in the mirror.

When the song ended, there was some applause, but only from two tables, and the lights on the stage went off. The barmaid was in front of me and I said *no, thanks,* and then she turned a little and said, "What would you like, Terry?"

I realized that the dancer was standing at my elbow. Now she was wearing a lacy fringed pajama top too, and I could see that she was young, there was a serious pimple above one of her eyebrows. I didn't know I was staring at her until she said: "Don't even *try* to buy me a drink." I started to put up my hands, meaning I was no harm, when she added: "I've seen your kind before. Why don't you go out and do some good?"

The barmaid looked at me as if I had started the whole thing, and before I could speak, she moved down to serve the other end.

It was a long walk to the truck, but I made it. January. The whole city had cabin fever. She'd seen my kind before. Not *me*: my *kind*.

The old truck was handling better now, and I conducted it back along Ninth West to Ninth South and started hunting. I'd never been under that on-ramp before, except for one night when Cody took me to the Barb Wire, a western bar where we watched all her young lawyer friends dance with the cowboys. In the dark, the warehouses made their own blank city. It was eight o'clock. Cody and Dirk were having cocktails in the Lafayette Suite. She'd be drinking vodka tonics with two limes. Dirk would be drinking scotch without any ice. He would have the Governor's elbow in his left palm right now, steering him around to Cody, "You remember Cody Westerman. Her husband is at the dump."

I crossed under the ramp at Fourth West and weaved under it to the corner of Fifth, where I did a broad, slow U-turn across the railroad tracks to scan the area. Nothing. Two derelicts leaned against the back of a blue post office van, drinking out of a paper sack. I cruised slowly up beside them.

"Hi, you guys," I said. It was the first time all day I felt fine about being so dirty. They looked at me frankly, easily, as if this meeting had been arranged. One, his shirt buttoned up under his skinny chin, seemed to be chewing on something. The other had the full face of an Indian, and I was surprised to see she was a woman. They both wore short blue cloth Air Force jackets with the insignias missing.

"Have you seen a mattress?"

The woman said something and turned to the man.

"What did she say? Have you seen one?"

The man took a short pull on the bottle and continued chewing. "She said, *what kind of mattress is it?*" He passed the bottle to the woman and she smiled at me.

I thought: Okay. What kind of mattress is it. Okay, I can do this. "It was a king-size Sealy Posturepedic."

"King-size?"

"Yes: King-size. Have you seen it?"

He took the bottle back from the woman and nodded at me.

"You have? Where?"

"Would this king-size postropeeda fly out of the sky?" the man said. His eyes were bright; this was the best time he'd had all day.

"It would."

"What's it worth to you?" he said.

"Nothing, folks. I was throwing it away."

"You threw it all right!" the woman said, and they both laughed.

I waited, one arm on the steering wheel, but then I saw the truth: these two were champion waiters; that's what they did for a living.

"Where's the mattress? Come on. Please."

"It's not worth anything."

"Okay, what's it worth?"

"Two bottles of this," the man said, pulling a fifth of Old Grand Dad from the bag.

"That's an expensive mattress."

The man stopped chewing and said, "It's king-size." They both laughed again.

"Okay. It's a deal. Two bottles of bourbon. Where is it?"

For a minute, neither moved, and I thought we were in for another long inning of waiting, but then the woman, still looking at me, slowly raised her hand and pointed over her head. I looked up. There it was, at least the corner of it, hanging over the edge of the one-story brick building: Wolcott Engineering.

Well, that's it, I thought. I tried. Monday morning the engineers would find a large mattress on their roof. It was out of my hands.

The woman stepped up and tapped my elbow. "Back this around in the alley," she said. "Get as close to the building as you can."

"What?"

"No problem," the man said. "We'll get your mattress for you; we got a deal going here, don't we?"

I backed into the alley beside Wolcott Engineering, so close I couldn't open my door and had to slide across to climb out. The woman was helping the man into the bed of the truck, and when I saw it was his intention to climb on the cab of the truck to reach the roof, I stopped him.

"I'll do it," I said.

"Then I'll catch it," he laughed.

The roof was littered with hundreds of green Thunderbird bottles glinting in the icy frost. They clattered under the mattress as I dragged it across to the alley. For a moment, it stood on the edge of the roof and then folded and fell, fainting like a starlet into the cold air.

By the time I climbed down, they had the mattress crammed into the pickup. It was too wide and the depression in the middle formed a nest; the man and the woman were lying in there on their backs. "Two bottles," the man said.

"Don't you want to ride in front?"

"You kidding?"

The Ford's windshield was iced, inside and out, and that complicated my search for a way out of the warehouse district. I crossed sixteen sets of railroad tracks, many twice, finally cutting north through an alley to end up under the Fourth South viaduct. I heard a tap on the rear window. I rolled down my window.

"Could you please drive back across those tracks one more time?"

"What?"

"Please!"

So I made a slow circuit of our route again, rumbling over several series of railroad tracks. I adjusted the mirror and watched my passengers. As the truck would roll over the tracks, the two would bounce softly in the mattress, their arms folded tightly over their chests like corpses, the woman's face absolutely closed up in laughter. They were laughing their heads off. Returning to the viaduct, I stopped. The man tilted his chin up so he looked at me upside down and he mouthed: "Thanks."

I cruised around Pioneer Park, a halo frozen around each street-lamp, and eased into the liquor store parking lot.

"We'll wait here," the man told me.

Inside, I was again reminded of how cold I was, and the clerk shook his head looking at my dirty clothing as I bought the two bottles of Old Grand Dad and a mini-bottle for myself. He clucked as I dropped the change. My jacket pocket had gotten ripped pushing the mattress across the roof; the coins went right through. My hands were cold and I had some difficulty retrieving the money. When I stood, I said simply to the clerk: "These bottles are all for me. I'm going to drink them tonight sleeping under the stars and wake up frozen to Third West. You've seen my kind before, haven't you?"

Outside, I laid the bottles on top of my passengers, one each on their stomachs.

"Many thanks," the man said to me. "It was worth it."

"Where can I let you off?"

"Down at the park, if it's no trouble."

The woman lay smiling, a long-term smile. She turned her shiny eyes on me for a second and nodded. The two of them looked like kids lying there.

I drove them back to the park, driving slowly around the perimeter, waiting for the man to tap when he wanted to get out. After I'd circled the park once, I stopped across from the Fuller Paint warehouse. The man looked up at me upside down again and made a circular motion with his first finger, and then he held it up to signal: just once more.

I opened the mini-bottle and took a hot sip of bourbon. The park, like all the rest of the city was three feet in sooty snow, and some funny configurations stood on the stacks of the old locomotive which was set on the corner. The branches of the huge trees were silver in the black sky, iced by the insistent mist. There were no cars at all, and so I sipped the whiskey and drove around the park four times, slowly. It was quarter to ten; Cody would have given my salmon to Dirk by now, saying something like, "He's been killed on an icy overpass, let's eat his fish and then dance."

I stopped this time opposite the huge locomotive. I stood out beside the bed of the truck. "Is this all right?"

The man sat up. "Sure, son; this is fine." They hadn't opened their new bottles. Then I saw that the woman was turned on her side. Something was going on.

"What's the matter? Is she all right?"

"It's all right," he said, and he helped her sit up. Her face glowed under all the tears; her chin vibrated with the sobbing, and the way her eyes closed now wanted to break my heart.

"What is it? What can I do?"

They climbed over the tailgate of the truck. The woman said something. The man said to me: "We're all right." He smiled.

"What did she say?" I asked him.

"She said thanks; she said, *It's so beautiful. It's so chilly and so beautiful.*"

THE H STREET
SLEDDING RECORD

THE LAST thing I do every Christmas Eve is go out in the yard and throw the horse manure onto the roof. It is a ritual. After we return from making our attempt at the H Street Sledding Record, and we sit in the kitchen sipping Egg Nog and listening to Elise recount the sled ride, and Elise then finally goes to bed happily, reluctantly, and we finish placing Elise's presents under the tree and we pin her stocking to the mantel—with care—and Drew brings out two other wrapped boxes which anyone could see are for me, and I slap my forehead having forgotten to get her anything at all for Christmas (except the prizes hidden behind the glider on the front porch), I go into the garage and put on the gloves and then into the yard where I throw the horse manure on the roof.

Drew always uses this occasion to call my mother. They exchange all the Christmas news, but the main purpose of the calls the last few years has been for Drew to stand in the window where she can see me out there lobbing the great turds up into the snow on the roof, and describe what I am doing to my mother. The two women take amusement from this. They say things like: "You married him" and "He's your son." I take their responses to my rituals as a kind of fond, subtle support, which it is. Drew had said when she first discovered me throwing the manure on the roof, the Christmas that Elise was four, "You're the only man I've ever known who did that." See: a compliment.

But, now that Elise is eight, Drew has become cautious: "You're fostering her fantasies." I answer: "Kids grow up too soon these days." And then Drew has this: "What do you want her to do, come home from school in tears when she's fifteen? Some kid in her class will have said—*Oh, sure, Santa's reindeer shit on your roof, eh?*" All I can say to Drew then is: "Some kid in her class! Fine! I don't care what he says. I'm her father!"

I have thrown horse manure on our roof for four years now, and I plan to do it every Christmas Eve until my arm gives out. It satisfies me as a homeowner to do so, for the wonderful amber stain that is developing between the swamp cooler and the chimney and is visible all spring-summer-fall as you drive down the hill by our house, and for the way the two rosebushes by the gutterspout have raged into new and profound growth during the milder months. And as a father, it satisfies me as a ritual that keeps my family together.

Drew has said, "You want to create evidence? Let's put out milk and a cookie and then drink the milk and eat a bite out of the cookie."

I looked at her. "Drew," I had said, "I don't like cookies. I never ate a dessert in my life."

And like I said, Drew has been a good sport, even the year I threw one gob short and ran a hideous smear down the kitchen window screen that hovered over all of us until March when I was able to take it down and go to the carwash.

I obtain the manure from my friend Bob, more specifically from his horse, Power, who lives just west of Heber. I drive out there the week before Christmas and retrieve about a bushel. I throw it on the roof a lump at a time, wearing a pair of welding gloves my father gave me.

I PUT the brake on the sled in 1975 when Drew was pregnant with Elise so we could still make our annual attempt on the H Street Record on Christmas Eve. It was the handle of a broken Louisville

Slugger baseball bat, and still had the precise "34" stamped into the bottom. I sawed it off square and drilled and bolted it to the rear of the sled, so that when I pulled back on it, the stump would drag us to a stop. As it turned out, it was one of the two years when there was no snow, so we walked up to Eleventh Avenue and H Street (as we promised: rain or shine), sat on the Flexible Flyer in the middle of the dry street on a starry Christmas Eve, and I held her in my lap. We sat on the sled like two basketball players contesting possession of her belly. We talked a little about what it would be like when she took her leave from the firm and I had her home all day with the baby, and we talked remotely about whether we wanted any more babies, and we talked about the Record, which was set on December 24, 1969, the first Christmas of our marriage, when we lived in the neighborhood, on Fifth Avenue in an old barn of a house the total rent on which was seventy-two fifty, honest, and Drew had given me the sled that very night and we had walked out about midnight and been surprised by the blizzard. No wonder we took the sled and walked around the corner up H Street, up, up, up to Eleventh Avenue, and without speaking or knowing what we were doing, opening the door on the second ritual of our marriage, the annual sled ride (the first ritual was the word "condition" and the activities it engendered in our droopy old bed).

At the top we scanned the city blurred in snow, sat on my brand new Christmas sled, and set off. The sled rode high and effortlessly through the deep snow, and suddenly, as our hearts started and our eyes began to burn against the snowy air, we were going faster than we'd planned. We crossed Tenth Avenue, nearly taking flight in the dip, and then descended in a dark rush: Ninth, Eighth, Seventh, soaring across each avenue, my arms wrapped around Drew like a straitjacket to drag her off with me if a car should cross in front of us on Sixth, Fifth Avenue, Fourth (this all took seconds, do you see?) until a car did turn onto H Street, headed our way, and we veered the new sled sharply, up over the curb, dousing our speed in the snowy yard one house from the corner of Third Avenue. Drew took a real faceful of snow, which she squirmed around and pressed into my neck, saying the words: "Now, that's a record!"

And it was the Record: Eleventh to Third, and it stood partly because there had been two Christmas Eves with no snow, partly because of assorted spills brought on by too much speed, too much laughter, sometimes too much caution, and by a light blue Mercedes that crossed Sixth Avenue just in front of us in 1973. And though some years were flops, there was nothing about Christmas that Elise looked forward to as much as our one annual attempt at the H Street Sledding Record.

I THINK Drew wants another baby. I'm not sure, but I think she wants another child. The signs are so subtle they barely seem to add up, but she says things like, "Remember before Elise went to school?" and "There sure are a lot of women in their mid-thirties having babies." I should ask her. But for some reason, I don't. We talk about everything, *everything*. But I've avoided this topic. I've avoided talking to Drew about this topic because I want another child too badly to have her not want one. I want a little boy to come into the yard on Christmas morning and say: "See, there on the roof! The reindeers were there!" I want another kid to throw horse manure for. I'll wait. It will come up one of these days; I'll find a way to bring it up. Christmas is coming.

Every year on the day after Halloween, I tip the sled out of the rafters in the garage and Elise and I sponge it off, clean the beautiful dark blond wood with furniture polish, enamel the nicked spots on the runner supports with black engine paint, and rub the runners themselves with waxed paper. It is a ritual done on the same plaid blanket in the garage and it takes all afternoon. When we are finished, we lean the sled against the wall, and Elise marches into the house. "Okay now," she says to her mother: "Let it snow."

ON THE first Friday night in December, every year, Elise and Drew and I go buy our tree. This too is ritual. Like those families that bundle up and head for the wilderness so they can trudge through the deep, pristine snow, chop down their own little tree, and drag it, step by step, all the way home, we venture forth in the same spirit. Only we take the old pickup down to South State and find some joker who has thrown up two strings of colored lights around the corner of the parking lot of a burned-out Safeway and is proffering trees to the general public.

There is something magical and sad about this little forest just sprung up across from City Tacos, and Drew and Elise and I wander the wooded paths, waiting for some lopsided piñon to leap into our hearts.

The winter Drew and I became serious, when I was a senior and she was already in her first year at law school, I sold Christmas trees during vacation. I answered a card on a dorm bulletin board and went to work for a guy named Geer, who had cut two thousand squat piñons from the hills east of Cedar City and was selling them from a dirt lot on Redwood Road. Drew's mother invited me to stay with them for the holidays, and it gave me the chance to help Drew make up her mind about me. I would sell trees until midnight with Geer, and then drive back to Drew's and watch every old movie in the world and wrestle with Drew until our faces were mashed blue. I wanted to complicate things wonderfully by having her sleep with me. She wanted to keep the couch cushions between us and think it over. It was a crazy Christmas; we'd steam up the windows in the entire living room, but she never gave in. We did develop the joke about "condition," which we still use as a code word for desire. And later, I won't say if it was spring or fall, when Drew said to me, "I'd like to see you about this condition," I knew everything was going to be all right, and that we'd spend every Christmas together for the rest of our lives.

One night during that period, I delivered a tree to University Village, the married students' housing off Sunnyside. The woman was waiting for me with the door open as I dragged the pine up the steps to the second floor. She was a girl, really, about twenty, and her son, about three, watched the arrival from behind her. When I had the tree squeezed into the apartment, she asked if I could just hold it for a minute while she found her tree stand. If you ever need to stall for a couple of hours, just say you're looking for your tree stand; I mean the girl was gone for about twenty minutes. I stood and exchanged stares with the kid, who was scared; he didn't understand why some strange man had brought a tree into his home. "Christmas," I told him. "Christmas. Can you say 'Merry Christmas'?" I was an idiot.

When the girl returned with her tree stand, she didn't seem in any hurry to set it up. She came over to me and showed me the tree stand, holding it up for an explanation as to how it worked. Close up the girl's large eyes had an odd look in them, and then I understood it when she leaned through the boughs and kissed me. It was a great move; I had to hand it to her. There I was holding the tree; I couldn't make a move either way. It has never been among my policies to kiss strangers, but I held the kiss and the tree. Something about her eyes. She stepped back with the sweetest look of embarrassment and hope on her pretty face that I'd ever seen. "Just loosen the turn-screws in the side of that stand," I said, finally. "And we can put this tree up."

By the time I had the tree secured, she had returned again with a box of ornaments, lights, junk like that, and I headed for the door. "Thanks," I said. "Merry Christmas."

Her son had caught on by now and was fully involved in unloading the ornaments. The girl looked up at me, and this time I saw it all: her husband coming home in his cap and gown last June, saying, "Thanks for law school, honey, but I met Doris at the Juris-Prudence Ball and I gotta be me. Keep the kid."

The girl said to me, "You could stay and help."

It seemed like two statements to me, and so I answered them separately: "Thank you. But I can't stay; that's the best help. Have a good Christmas."

And I left them there together, decorating that tree; a ritual against the cold.

"HOW DO you like it?" Elise says to me. She has selected a short broad bush which seems to have grown in two directions at once and then given up. She sees the look on my face and says, "If you can't say anything nice, don't say anything at all. Besides, I've already decided: this is the tree for us."

"It's a beautiful tree," Drew says.

"Quasimodo," I whisper to Drew. "This tree's name is Quasimodo."

"No whispering," Elise says from behind us. "What's he saying now, Mom?"

"He said he likes the tree, too."

Elise is not convinced and after a pause she says, "Dad. It's Christmas. Behave yourself."

When we go to pay for the tree, the master of ceremonies is busy negotiating a deal with two kids, a punk couple. The tree man stands with his hands in his change apron and says, "I gotta get thirty-five bucks for that tree." The boy, a skinny kid in a leather jacket, shrugs and says he's only got twenty-eight bucks. His girlfriend, a large person with a bowl haircut and a monstrous black overcoat festooned with buttons, is wailing, "Please! Oh no! Jimmy! Jimmy! I love that tree! I want that tree!" The tree itself stands aside, a noble pine of about twelve feet. Unless these kids live in a gymnasium, they're buying a tree bigger than their needs.

Jimmy retreats to his car, an old Plymouth big as a boat. "Police Rule" is spraypainted across both doors in balloon letters. He returns instantly and opens a hand full of coins. "I'll give you thirty-one bucks, fifty-five cents, and my watch." To our surprise, the wily tree man takes the watch to examine it. When I see that, I give Elise four dollars and tell her to give it to Kid Jimmy and say, "Merry Christmas." His girlfriend is still wailing but now a minor refrain of "Oh Jimmy, that tree! Oh Jimmy, etc." I haven't seen a public display of emotion and longing of this magnitude in Salt Lake City, ever. I watch Elise give the boy the money, but instead of saying, "Merry Christmas," I hear her say instead: "Here, Jimmy. Santa says keep your watch."

Jimmy pays for the tree, and his girl—and this is the truth—jumps on him, wrestles him to the ground in gratitude and smothers him for nearly a minute. There have never been people happier about a Christmas tree. We pay quickly and head out before Jimmy or his girlfriend can think to begin thanking us.

On the way home in the truck, I say to Elise, "Santa says keep your watch, eh?"

"Yes, he does," she smiles.

"How old are you, anyway?"

"Eight."

It's an old joke, and Drew finishes it for me: "When he was your age, he was seven."

We will go home and while the two women begin decorating the tree with the artifacts of our many Christmases together, I will thread popcorn onto a long string. It is a ritual I prefer for its uniqueness; the fact that once a year I get to sit and watch the two girls I am related to move about a tree inside our home, while I sit nearby and sew food.

ON THE morning of the twenty-fourth of December, Elise comes into our bedroom, already dressed for sledding. "Good news," she says. "We've got a shot at the record."

Drew rises from the pillow and peeks out the blind. "It's snowing," she says.

Christmas Eve, we drive back along the snowy Avenues, and park on Fifth, as always. "I know," Elise says, hopping out of the car. "You two used to live right over there before you had me and it was a swell place and only cost seventy-two fifty a month, honest."

Drew looks at me and smiles.

"How old are you?" I ask Elise, but she is busy towing the sled away, around the corner, up toward Eleventh Avenue. It is still snowing, petal flakes, teeming by the streetlamps, trying to carry the world away. I take Drew's hand and we walk up the middle of H Street behind our daughter. There is no traffic, but the few cars have packed the tender snow perfectly. It *could* be a record. On Ninth Avenue, Drew stops me in the intersection, the world still as snow, and kisses me. "I love you," she says.

"What a planet," I whisper. "To allow such a thing."

By the time we climb to Eleventh Avenue, Elise is seated on the sled, ready to go. "What are you guys waiting for, Christmas?" she says and then laughs at her own joke. Then she becomes all business: "Listen, Dad, I figure if you stay just a little to the left of the tire tracks we could go all the way. And no wobbling!" She's referring to last year's record attempt, which was extinguished in the Eighth Avenue block when we laughed ourselves into a fatal wobble and ended in a slush heap.

We arrange ourselves on the sled, as we have each Christmas Eve for eight years. As I reach my long legs around these two women, I sense their excitement. "It's going to be a record!" Elise whispers into the whispering snow.

"Do you think so?" Drew asks. She also feels this could be the night.

"Oh yeah!" Elise says. "The conditions are perfect!"

"What do you think?" Drew turns to me.

"Well, the conditions are perfect."

When I say *conditions,* Drew leans back and kisses me. So I press: "There's still room on the sled," I say, pointing to the "F" in Flexible Flyer that is visible between Elise's legs. "There's still room for another person."

"Who?" Elise asks.

"Your little brother," Drew says, squeezing my knees.

And that's about all that was said, sitting up there on Eleventh Avenue on Christmas Eve on a sled which is as old as my marriage with a brake that is as old as my daughter. Later tonight I will stand in my yard and throw this year's reindeer droppings on my very own home. I love Christmas.

Now the snow spirals around us softly. I put my arms around my family and lift my feet onto the steering bar. We begin to slip down H Street. We are trying for the record. The conditions, as you know by now, are perfect.

SANTA MONICA

'M IN the King's Head at the end of Santa Monica Boulevard drinking my fourth pint of bitter wondering if maybe I should eat something and just go home. I'm sitting under the window watching one guy play darts against himself, and he's not very good. Judith called and said to meet, so I'll stay. The bitter is good; I haven't been here for a couple of months, so I might as well wait it out. If she doesn't show, maybe she's not in trouble after all.

I'm trying to make a catalogue in my head of all the pubs in Hampstead. It's been two years, but I remember the Three Horseshoes at the High Street, where we'd go and watch the teenagers pick each other up. Monday nights they had poetry readings upstairs. I remember one guy read poems with a dummy; he was a ventriloquist. And there was Sir Something who was ninety-six years old. He read from a book he had published at twenty and talked ironically between the poems about what a stupid young man he had been. It was hilarious, but at the end, he said something like he was glad they had asked him to read, but it was the saddest thing he could remember doing. He had to be helped to a chair. Late that spring they invited Judith to read, but we were packing by then for the return.

Across the street, there was the Bird in Hand, which was full of
worn-out working men, and down a block was the King of
Bohemia, which was warm and cozy, always half full of older married couples. The women had learned to drink. We had lunch in
there on Tuesday's, back in the nook by the aquarium. Across the
zebra from the Bohemia was King Henry the Fourth, which was gay
and way too small, but they had a little garden. All the men in velvet drinking John Courage, everybody's hands above the table,
moving. And then down the street, below the fish-market and the
newsstand and the doner-kabob shop, was the simplest pub of all,
the Rosslyn Arms, which was where we drank, where we met all the
American teachers, and where Gordon would get drunk and finger
each new necklace Judith wore—the smashed penny, the Parcheesi
tokens—pulling her as close as people get while talking to each
other. He was as big as a bear and would always get drunk and offer
to "bite her bottom," but he was harmless. He wasn't a writer. It was
in the Rosslyn Arms where I learned to play real darts, in fact,
where behind the bar, in one of the three cigar boxes, my best darts
sit right now.

I order another bitter from the girl, and I notice she's a pretty girl
about twenty-six, and I tell myself again: I've got to begin noticing
women, but by the time she returns with the pint, I've begun my
catalogue again, going way to the top of the High Street, at the corner of the heath, and I'm starting with Jack Straw's Castle. I'm trying to decide whether or not to include The Spaniards, where Judith
and I walked only one day, but we were too late for lunch and the
staff was all cranky. I feel a hand on my shoulder. Judith lifts my
glass and drains the whole pint until I can see her eyes closed
through the bottom of the glass.

"Hello, Douglas," she says. "Let's eat later." She leads me outside.

If we were strangers, or acquaintances, or anything less than what
we are, whatever that is, I would now ask *What's up?*, but we don't
talk that way. There is going to be some theater first, I see, as Judith
walks two steps ahead of me across the boulevard, through the park,
and down the winding steps to the beach. She's wearing a blue

oxford shirt under the brown baggy cardigan I bought her in Hampstead. She always wears clothes from the old days when she meets me.

There aren't many people out, since it's a gray day in February, but there is a brighter band of light on the horizon and a warm breeze comes off the sea. I walk behind Judith and kind of enjoy it; the air feels good and I'm full of beer. The light over the ocean makes it seem as if there is a lot of the day left. It's sunny for brunch in Hawaii. I swing my legs, stepping in every other of her footprints. It feels wonderful to move this way; she can take her time. I don't really want to hear about Reichert or the studio.

Judith walks in a forced jaunt, bunched a little against the weather, her fingers in her sweater pockets.

"You kind of walk like David Niven," I say to her back. I'm suddenly thinking this doesn't have to be a terrible interview; the beer has made me careless. She walks on. I let her go a little farther ahead, and then I follow doing crazy steps: five-foot leaps and then microsteps, inches apart. Backward steps, duck steps, and then a few real long side steps. She'll see this stuff on the way back.

We approach a couple who have committed themselves to a full-scale beach picnic. They are both sitting on a real checked tablecloth and we hear the man say "Voila!" to the young woman as he pulls a bottle of red wine from a large basket. He is wearing a dark sweater which I see has a large crimson "H" on the front. I've seen him in the story department at Paramount.

Judith stops. "Where are we going?"

As she faces me, I see the new necklace, a silver doodah of some kind. When she first came out, she wore a half pence and a New York subway token. When she finally moved in with Reichert, she made a string with six of my cigarette filters, painted turquoise, to make it look like it was my fault. She wants to show me this new one and holds it out. Taking it in my hand, I am as close to her as I've been in ten months.

"Pretty, right?" I see it is a smashed .38 cartridge. "I found it last week at the bottom of the swimming pool."

We start back, but I steer her higher along the beach. I don't want to see those tracks in the sand after all. "You want to go up to the pier?" I say. "You always like the pier."

"The guy back there, the Harvard guy," Judith says, now walking beside me, "he's at Paramount in the story department."

On the pier I finally ask her why she has the day off. She says that a rat has died in the office and they can't find it even though there are two carpenters taking all the video cabinets apart, and the smell is so bad that Reichert sent everybody home. "He's taking meetings at the house, telling everybody that they're so special he's meeting them in private. Today, it's Jamie Curtis. The smell is bad, but you get used to it. I just couldn't take those two stoned carpenters taking the doors off everything and chuckling their heads off."

We buy ten tokens and go into the arcade. She leads me down all three aisles of video games and then back to the booth where she says to the kid: "Don't you have any of the old games? Where's Space Invaders?"

All the games we've seen have "Mega" in the titles. The kid points out a Donkey Kong game in the corner which has seen a lot of use. Judith makes me go first and then she asks questions: "What do you think the point of this game is?" "Do you think the girl is even worth saving?" I'm trying to concentrate, but the little guy acts drunk. He can't decide which ladder to take, and Judith is beside me doing her show: "Do you think the guy really wants the girl?" I never get him above the second tier. The flaming barrel drops right on our heads.

Then, while she plays, she makes statements. She moves him expertly up the levels and says, "The guy could care less about the girl. He wants to get near the ape. He's just curious." She jumps two barrels at once and says, "See this, the guy only likes the outing; he loves to jump the barrels." He seems to run faster when she plays. Judith takes him all the way to the top three times, but when he reaches the girl, Judith steps back, hands off the controls, and lets the monkey grab them both and close the game. "It's fate," she says. "I'm not getting in the way."

As she starts another session, I slip away, out onto the pier and around to the restrooms. The bumper cars are empty. The kid in his booth sits hunched on the high chair, reading a hunting magazine. Reichert brought us out here when we had first moved. He had pointed at the kid in there and told me not to worry, there was plenty of work in California. Judith had laughed.

Later, after he'd hired Judith at the studio, she and I sometimes came out alone and stood at the end of the pier. It was like being on a great ferry headed west; she'd said that. She had liked California then. A lot of things were happening for her. We'd stand and let the waves break under us.

On the one trip we made to France from London, we'd gone out on the ferry deck in a gray drizzle, and she had said that the first thing she was going to do in St. Tropez was take her shirt off and sunburn her key onto her left breast. And, after a quick check that we were alone, she had opened her shirt, her nipples tight in the cold channel air, and placed the necklace in the spot. Two days later, she did just that, creating a little white shape that looked like that key for a long time. On the ferry that day, she had looked for a minute like a short blond figurehead; she'd said that too.

When I return, Judith is out on the pier rail. She holds up the last token and tells me that I'm not getting my last turn. I know that it will soon be another necklace. She has one like it with a Chuck E. Cheese token on it which reads, "In Pizza We Trust."

She puts the token in her pocket and turns to the sea. The day here is shot, the sun gone, the cloud cover a bald dusk, but in the far west that fuzzy line of light persists on the sea's edge.

"They're having brunch on the veranda in Waikiki."

"I'm as far West as I go." Judith says into the wind. "This is it for me."

I don't want to argue with her. It is a relief not wanting to argue. It is not my fault she came to California. I don't want to say that again. I don't want to attack Reichert or defend him or any of the dozen other people we both still see, all of them bright, well-educated, charming people, mostly young, and every one of them integrally involved in film projects that are hideous or silly. I won't argue. It is a relief. All I want is a beer. I want to push off this rail and walk back, swinging my legs, feeling my knees as we climb the steps, and go back across the street and have another beer.

"You think it's possible to write a good movie?" Judith says, turning to me.

"I think it's less possible than a year ago."

"Oh good, I can't wait until tomorrow."

I nearly say *Neither can I,* but that is exactly how we used to talk. I say: "Judith, let me buy you a pint of bitter and a sandwich."

"You think this is a good country? You think this is a livable country?"

I am not going to do this. "Judith, I can't go on without a pint," I say, stepping away from the rail. It is an old joke from London. I walk back to the first silver owl, as Judith calls the coin-operated binoculars on the pier.

Way out there I can see the guy from Paramount leaning back on one elbow drinking wine in the gray wind. Where do they learn that stuff? I close my eyes. I try to remember the name of the pub in Highgate across from Coleridge's grave. I can't get it. We walked there once on Easter, up through the cemetery where we stood before Marx's tomb, and now I'm trying to remember Marx's tomb: "Workers of the World Unite, ours is not to something something, but to change something." There was a green-headed mallard on every stone crucifer. Judith and I sat on a green bench in the park and argued about something. The ducks were all mating, walking in circles around us, and then we walked up to the pub which had been a real coach stop in the old days, and it's name was. I can't remember.

I can remember Judith, after she started writing for Reichert, coming home late in the car. She wouldn't come in the house. I would go out after a while and find her sitting in the Rabbit, listening to the end of a Jackson Browne tape. I should have known. It

was Reichert's tape: *Hold Out.* It was the Era of Maximum Smiling;
she called it that. She'd look up from the car and smile. "This is the
Era of Maximum Smiling," she'd say.

I wanted then to remind her that the Era of Quality Smiling was
when we could watch the kites on Parliament Hill on the heath,
when we could see all of London grumbling beneath us, when we
would smile at the idea of writing in California. But it was too late.
When a woman sits in the car listening to tapes, it's too late.

I walk almost to the second silver owl when Judith catches up. We
step back onto the continent, cross the beach, and by the time we're
at the top of the stairs, she's taken my arm. She doesn't speak except
to say, "David Niven's dead," as we cross the street and go into the
King's Head.

At the table, it starts. Her face, and I see again that it is a good
face, the only face, falls. When she leans forward to take her face in
her hands, I can see the silver cartridge again and all the little red
marks above her breasts where her jewelry has nicked her over the
years. I remember that after she'd shower it looked like a light coral
necklace there. "God, Doug," she says. "I don't know whether to go
forward or backward anymore." She's about to cry.

I feel the old numbness rise in my neck, the old bad confusion.
I'm glad the girl has brought the wonderful brown beer, and I lift my
glass in my hand. The beer is cool and sweet.

"Judith," I say.

"Doug, remember that bitch at the Spaniards who wouldn't serve
us because we were five minutes late for pub hours?"

"No," I say. There is no sense in starting. I could ask her now the
name of that pub at Highgate, the coach stop, Judith would remember. But: no.

The King's Head is empty now: four o'clock. By seven, every
English starlet on the coast will be in here. "Judith. Hey. Don't cry."
I push her glass across so it just touches her elbow. "Judith. Here.
Drink this. How about the turkey sandwich?"

She nods, her head in her hands.

"Don't cry," I say. "It's possible to write a good movie. It's a livable country. Judith, you are the most clever woman I ever met. But, you were right about that little guy. He doesn't want the girl. He wants to run back and forth. He wants to jump the barrels and not get burned."

OLYMPUS HILLS

I LEFT THE party early, finding my coat on the bed, surprising Karen and Darrel, who stood when I entered. "It's funny," I said, trying to ease their embarrassment, "but I know every coat in this pile." I lifted Cindy's rabbit fur jacket. "For five points. Careful: she does not wear this thing to work."

"Cindy," Karen said, her voice husky.

I had just left Cindy in the kitchen. She and Tom were sitting on the counter drinking tequila and having a heart to heart. Whenever people drink tequila, they always talk about it, the worm, a war story or two, and then maybe mushroom experience and it's a heart to heart. Cindy was wearing a white silk dress, sprayed with little red dots which turned out to be strawberries. I have been in these kitchens before and when Cindy hoists her bottom onto the kitchen counter and, nursing a tequila and lemon between her knees, starts telling drug experiences, it's just enough. Even Tom sitting up there by her looked a little spent. He's too big a guy to sit on a kitchen counter and look natural anyway.

Karen and Darrel had forgotten to let go of each other's hands and their faces were smashed red from all the kissing. They looked like the two healthiest people at the party. I was surprised, because I'd seen Karen with another guy from the firm, a programmer named Chuck who does our board overlays, at a dozen lunches in the last month. And I admired Darrel's ability to struggle in there with Karen, while we could all hear his wife, Ellen, singing along with Tommy James and the Shondells in the other room. It was a small house for Olympus Hills.

"Victor, Ted, Sharon, Tom, Ellen," I said, laying the coats aside, until I found the tan raincoat. "Lisa," I said, looking at it. The bed was a little archaeology of the party: all those layers of beautiful coats. Victor and his new leather flight jacket. Tom and his bright swollen parka. And Lisa's classy raincoat second from the bottom. She must have arrived early.

"My coat," I looked up and said to Darrel, and when I saw how embarrassed he still was, leaning there against the wall as if I was going to scold them, I added, "I'm leaving early. No problem." I patted my coat. "I'd say you've got an hour before another coat is touched. I'll close the door. Happy Valentines."

I didn't put my coat on in the hall, because I didn't want Ted or Sharon to make a fuss, to cry out, "Hal, you're leaving! Before charades! You can't leave before charades!"

I wanted to leave before charades. I'd played charades with this group before and it was worse than college. Victor, Ted, and about five others played solely to humiliate everyone. They would select unproduced plays from Gilbert and Sullivan, and then explode when people would claim to have not heard of them. "You ignorami!" I'd heard Victor scream. "You aborigines! Swinesnouts! This is incredible."

My wife, Lisa, could be wicked too. She would always write the sexiest titles she could, knowing that some woman on the other team, in the drunken spirit of camaraderie that sometimes waved over the group, would embarrass herself fully doing *How to Make Love to a Man* and be the talk of the office for a week. I remember in detail the vision of Cindy writhing before the group one night, clutching both her breasts with her hands, thrusting her pelvis at her team as if to drive them back on the couch. I don't remember the name of the literary work she was describing.

I wanted to slip through the living room as if I were getting some fresh air and then be gone. Lisa had come from work tonight and she had her own car; I'd see her at home later. There was a time when we had one car, and we used to go places together. It was a used silver Tempest, the car I had in graduate school. The original owner had applied zodiac stickers in circles on all the doors.

Lisa always claims to hate these parties. We'll be dressing at home and she'll wave the hairdrier at me, making predictions. "Karen will wear that blue mini and go after Lou. They'll have a clam dip diluted with sour cream. Generic sour cream. Did I say generic sour cream? Wayne will move in on me when I sit on the couch and tell me about his kids for two hours. He thinks that's the way you flirt. Ted will bring his oldies tape. Ellen will be the first one to sing. Tom will be the first one drunk. You'll get drunk too and come on to Cindy, and we'll have our little quarrel on the way home. Are you ready? Let's go."

And she used to be right. I would get drunk. I'd end up singing with Ellen and, later, making my three point five crass comments to some of the women. Wayne would do his sincerity routine for Lisa on the couch. He was no dummy; she was always the loveliest woman in the whole house. I'd end up in the kitchen, leaning against the counter with Cindy, sometimes leaning against Cindy and then the counter. It was a party, wasn't it?

That was then. Lisa wouldn't be right tonight, about me. February. It had been a long winter already: five, six parties since New Year's. No wonder Karen had been able to spot Cindy's coat. Too much snow, too much fog; by Friday night, no one wanted to go home. Everybody was kind of surprised suddenly to have money, but no one knew what to do about it. Most of us had Ted's oldies tape memorized the way you come to know an album; when a song ends, you know what's coming next. We knew what brand everyone smoked and who would lend you a cigarette gladly. We knew that Ted smoked Kools because he'd learned in college that no one would borrow them. We knew what everyone drank and how much. We knew where people would be sitting by eleven o'clock. I knew it all and I just wanted to go home. I was trying.

I eased by a group standing by the kitchen door, and edged around the two couples dancing to the Supremes. Ellen waved at me from across the buffet table with the breadstick she was using as a microphone. Baby Love. I could see Lisa sitting on the couch. She was smiling at Wayne who sat on the carpet by her knees. I know all her smiles and this was a real one. I had to thread between Victor and his new girlfriend to reach the door and then I was out in the snow.

Pulling on my coat, I walked down the trail in the falling snow, right into the deer. I didn't actually hit him, but by the time we both looked up we were at most three feet apart. It was a young male. He had a fine pair of forked antlers and a broad black nose, wet and shiny in the light from the yard lamp. I immediately backed up four or five steps to give him room, but he stood there, casually, looking at me. There were deer all over the city because of the snowfall, but I had never, ever, seen one this close.

I backed to the door, slowly, thinking to show someone. I forgot myself. I wanted Lisa to come out and see this guy. I wanted Lisa to come out and see this deer and come home with me. She could say, "We'll pick up my car tomorrow or the day after that," and steam up the dark with her laugh. I hadn't realized how lonely I was until I saw his face, his moist eyes, the bone grain of his antlers.

I pushed the door inward and said, "Hey, come see this deer." Cindy's face appeared in the opening. Behind her the party seemed to rage; Ellen was singing "Satisfaction," and the din of conversation was loud and raw and alien.

"What?"

"Look at this deer."

"What are you talking about?"

I let the door close and stepped back out. She followed me. "What are you talking about?"

"This deer." I turned and he was gone. I stepped to the corner of the house and was able to glimpse his gray back pass under a yard lamp two houses up.

"Right," Cindy said, taking my arm. "The deer." She lobbed her drink, glass and all, into the snowbank, and turned fully to me. Her mouth was warm with tequila, and I could feel the flesh of her back perfectly through the cold silk of her dress. She rose against me, ignoring the cold, or frantic against it, I couldn't tell which. It was funny there outside the party. When she went for me, I did nothing to stop her. I had made it outside, leaving early, but that was all I could do.

LIFE BEFORE SCIENCE

"Yeah. I know about babies."
—JOHN WAYNE
in *The Sands of Iwo Jima*

IN FEBRUARY, I drove Story to New Haven for the post-coital. It was Sunday, and if you want a definition of sterility, try downtown New Haven on the second Sunday in February. The clouds were frozen like old newspapers into the sky, and the small parking lot of the clinic was blasted with frozen litter too. I remember there were a pair of old work gloves in the ice. Looked like somebody trying to get out.

Dr. Binderwitz was meeting us on Sunday because Story had been keeping the basal charts for three months and we had to do the post-coital before Binderwitz, the most prominent fertility expert in the known world, flew off to Houston, Rio, Paris, and Frankfurt to deliver papers at conventions. It was a dark day and the doctor had all the lights in the clinic turned on. The doctor himself is one of the least healthy human beings I have ever met. He is a person who has literally spent years indoors, not grooming. When we shook hands, I was surprised at how soft his hand was, and up close, I could see that his hair was sprinkled with dandruff and larger particles I took to be bits of paper and pillow feather. So there we were with this force-ten genius, anxious to hear what he'd say.

The doctor took Story into the examination room, and I sat with a copy of *Sports Afield,* for a moment angry with the cover artist for making his rearing grizzly so predictable. He'd used all his light in the mouth, even spraying some white points of saliva, and that, coupled with the point of view (from below, as a victim) cancelled any real life or sympathy from the work. It was a cheap shot done in half a day by some ad illustrator. There was no setting for the portrait, except a single pine, and that had been drawn melodramatically small. It looked like a folded umbrella.

I was daydreaming. It was still early in the morning. Story had moved to me long before dawn and we'd made lost, unconscious love. It wasn't until after I'd rolled out of bed and stood under the shower that I realized we were participating in an experiment.

Story returned, calling me back to the doctor's office, and then Dr. Binderwitz himself shuffled in, carrying the small prepared slide. He had taken a smear from Story's cervix, and we watched as he positioned the slide under the microscope. Dr. Binderwitz studied the slide for a minute or two and then asked Story if she wanted to have a look. He told her what knob to rotate for focus.

Then it was my turn. By slowly rotating the control, I was suddenly able to see dozens, maybe hundreds of sperm swimming around. I could see the problem right away. "They're not all going the same way," I said. "Which is the right direction?"

It was a little joke, but the doctor said, "They're not supposed to. Do you see the ones with two tails?"

I bent to the eyepiece again and, after a moment I did see a couple of two-tailed sperm whipping around.

"Is that normal?"

"Sure."

"Well," I said, when the doctor was silent, "How does it look?"

"Normal. The sperm are alive. The medium is hospitable." To Story he said, "Call my office Monday and schedule a histogram early next month. I'll be back then."

TWO

SINCE IT was Sunday, there were Township Cocktails that night, this time at Annette and Hugo Ballowell's place on the big lake, Mugacook, right across from the college. It had been a long day, but Story was mayor of the town and there would be some skating on the lake later, so we went down.

It was at Township Cocktails at the Ballowells that February night that I first had a glimpse of what the next four months would hold for us. It was that night that I first saw the solution, the radical answers to this baby thing, though I didn't know it at the time, and it was that night when I came to understand there was a little more to the world than Dr. Binderwitz, even from his intellectual stratosphere, could see.

I don't really know how it happened, the specific point where I left my senses for . . . my senses. I was in a mild funk that had been solidifying over the last year or so as my painting dried up. McOrson was still selling a few every month in New York, but they were old paintings, some of them over two years and they were the skies, the landscapes at which I had become facile, and which I had come to loathe. The reality was simple: I wasn't painting and it hurt. So I wasn't really in a party mood, especially with all the driving, two hours to New Haven, two hours back, and now: cocktails.

Story dressed and drove us down and we ran into Gil Manwaring, the constable, on Foundry Road along the fish pond and he and his two men were parking cars. Story said no thanks and we parked it ourselves and walked four hundred yards in the icy brown dusk, carrying our skates.

The Ballowells' house is the biggest on Mugacook, the kind of place mistaken for an inn by forty cars every summer. Story and I immediately ran into Ruth Wellner, the county attorney, who had been a classmate of Story's in Boston and who was now Story's best friend in Bigville. Ruth and Billy were our age, and were in the first stages of chasing a baby down themselves. Ruth wanted children almost as much as we did, but she couldn't admit it. She played devil's advocate. Ruth used to challenge me: "You want children; *you* have them." She'd go on: "Why do we want kids? What are we going to do with children? Every time we want kids, we ought to get in the car and drive down to K Mart in Torrington. Stay half an hour and we'll get more parenthood than we bargained for."

Billy, whom I liked a lot and who is living proof that insurance agents are human beings too, sat on the arm of the couch wearing an expression the most prominent feature of which was its profound sperm-loss pallor. I winked at Billy and he nodded back stiffly, a gesture he'd seen a battle-weary soldier make in some World War II movie. I admired his courage and Ruth's. The feature of Clomid we all found most unique was the headache each dosage inspired, making intercourse impossible, an irony lost on the chemists.

There is something about women on fertility drugs, something I admire, I suppose, something that gives them an aura: larger than life. It's hard to explain, but it would be easy to paint. I stood to the side a little as Story and Ruth fell to rapt conversation, their voices the rich female timbre that by its very sound says: hey, we're calm here; something mature is transpiring. They could have been talking about the township or about the mysteries of estrogen; it was all music to me. I grabbed Billy's arm. "Let the wives talk, Billy," I said. "I'll buy you a cocktail."

Annette had a buffet that would have run twelve pages in *Ladies' Home Journal.* It started with a salmon the size of a dog and ended forty feet later with champagne and hot buttered rum. Luckily, Hugo was down at that end of the table sipping his scotch, and when I nodded at it he took us in the kitchen and poured us coffee cups full of Chivas, saying, "I never drank a party drink in my life. It's February and this," he held up his glass, "is scotch. Are you two going skating?"

And we did go skating, Hugo, Bill, and I. We had another cup of scotch and then clambered down with Hugo's hockey equipment, sticks and pucks. The moon had come out full and throwing down a couple of sweaters on one side and two hats on the other, we had a rink. For some reason we had constructed it such that the bonfire was at center ice, and the game was full of wonderful breathers while some hero stickhandled the puck back out of the embers. Then, finally, Bill himself skated full bore into the flames. He rolled out unhurt, but he had lost the puck fully in the fire and we stood around consoling him while it melted somewhere in the inferno.

"Showboat," Hugo said, smiling. He looked at me and said, "Remember the night Billy skated into the bonfire?" and he laughed, so sure and so happy to be on the spot as a memory was created, his party a success.

"And he did it showing off!" I said.

"And then he wanted more scotch," Billy said, getting up. "He lost the puck and then wanted more scotch. And none of your party drinks!"

Back at the mansion, the party had more than half fallen apart, but Annette and Story and Ruth were in the study grinding something over, so Hugo did pour us some more scotch. We stood around the kitchen like prep school kids when Hugo said, "Let me show you something."

Now, it's here, I guess, where I started to see again. We were all red-faced from the cold and warm from the scotch, and when Hugo ushered me in front of the telescope, it was time to see. He had lined it up so that the full moon filled the lens, and for a moment I was flooded with vertigo, my depth perception thrown away. Then it all twisted into a focus so sharp I winced. The moon, the ocher plains, the pale blue seas, and then like something scratching across my very eyeball, the geese. Canadian geese were flying across the moon. Four clipped the bottom. Two more, sliding. Silence. My heart in my neck. And then two full tiers, a double-winged vee of geese raking the moon, swimming into the heat which rose into my eye and blurred.

I stood away from the telescope.

"Did you see them? They must be three miles high!" Hugo took my arm. It was dark in his study. Billy bent to the eyepiece. I could hear the women murmuring below us in the den. "Do you know how far, how many miles they'll go tonight?"

And it was later, late into that Sunday night—Monday morning—that the seeing began in earnest. Story drove me home, and though it took a few minutes to rid her mind of township business, I achieved it, and we moved into the postures of lovemaking, and I saw her face, her eyes, her navel, and then just before my eyes rolled up into my head, I saw my three fingers coming over Story's shoulder, like three old men witnessing giants at play. Story kissed me and rolled into sleep. My eyes would not quit.

I walked through my house naked for a while, as is the right of any homeowner, ending up on the small brick porch onto the backyard with my father's Navy binoculars in my hand. The air was still and frigid, but I stood with the glasses on the moon. It was wonderfully clear to me there as the bricks froze my feet and my genitals shrank and numbed in the frosty night: sperm were swimming across the moon, and on the round world I had a lot to do.

THREE

FOR THREE months Story had been keeping the basal charts. When the alarm would sound, I would stumble to the bureau, shake down the thermometer and offer it to Story's sleeping face. She slept on her stomach with no pillow and for eighty days at least, that thermometer was the first thing she saw every day. She'd lie there while I said, "Okay, now, don't move. Two minutes and forty seconds to go. I'm watching you. You're moving. Please. Can you please lie still for two and a half minutes! Okay. I'm telling Doctor Binderwitz that your chart is a fabrication. Two minutes. Fine, fine, squirm around; do your calisthenics; see if I care." It would get down to 10–9–8–7–6–5 and I'd move around and find the glass tube snug in her sleeping mouth. I'd sit on her and announce: "Ninety-eight point nine. We're talking impending ovulation. We're moving into a period of massive fertility!"

She'd groan and say, "Get off me."

"You don't mean that."

Then, every other day, as part of our program, I'd throw my feet up in her side of the bed and she would pull me to her, moving from a warm sleep to the warm, insistent dreamarama lovemaking. She was always a morning person as far as sex was concerned, and it was a smooth, slow swimming which left us both wet eyed, awash, and stunned.

BIGVILLE IS a small college really, and they are glad to have me because they consider me not just an art teacher, but a *real* painter, that is, one who has two paintings in national collections and one who from time to time has a show on some second floor in New York and a carload of deans gets to go down and drink wine for an afternoon. No one knows I'm not painting, except Story, and as always, she treats me as if I've simply taken some well-earned time off for coffee.

I threw myself into my teaching with an organized enthusiasm that cautioned me. I made progress charts for each of my students, making notes on approaches, even encouraging the oppressive Mary Ann Buxton, who tried too hard to make Bigville into the finishing school she never attended. Her approach to painting was simple: it was something you owned, the way rich people own France during those cocktail parties on campus in the fall. They bought the experience, as if it were a stereo system or a fine meal. I noted happily that Mary Ann was doing less copying and more "emulation" of her neighboring easels. What I am saying is that I did what I could to make the spring into a positive sojourn for myself, despite the fact that my eyes were on fire, seeing things, and I knew that meant something would come of it. But as of March, I was not painting.

The ice on Mugacook began to rot, and sometime mid-month Fudgie Miller fell entirely through a section by the town wharf, ending the skating season for good. Fudgie, twelve, was one of the eight Miller kids who lived right across the road from us, and when Constable Manwaring drove Fudgie home wrapped in a blanket and shivering, he was received with the general joy and jumping up and down usually reserved for only children. I witnessed the crowd scene from my front porch, and I thought: that's it. That's what we're after right there. All right. Now all I need is eight kids.

Because of the headaches, we abandoned Clomid, that wonder-drug, and we drove back down to New Haven on a windy, tree-tearing day in late March for the histogram. The air was thick with rushing grit as we crossed the clinic parking lot, and a copy of the *Yale News* blew against my leg, the headline, as always: STRIKE!

Again I scanned the covers of *Sports Afield* in the waiting room, while the dye was injected through Story's uterus and up into her fallopian tubes. Each of the magazines I had selected bore covers of large fish (two trout and one bass) standing on their tails in a raw white splash. The bass was trying to spit out a salamander plug and each of the trout had an oversized Royal Coachman hooked in the corner of his mouth. I was surprised by how vital, kinetic, and primary each was, and they evoked in me sentiments usually tapped only by top forty hits from the fifties. I love art. Each painter had captured the look of death on a game fish face, and yet he left the viewer one small bright hope: the fish might get away.

Then the nurse came and took me to Story, dressed by now, and we watched the television monitor and the X-ray scan of Story's secret chambers. It was, by far, the best program I've ever seen on television. Story's tubes were clear and symmetrical, the shadow swelling at the end of each tube a bit like an antler in what the technician called the *fibrililium,* a word I had him spell.

We drove halfway home, up Route 8, before we understood that we felt bad. It was one of those half raw March days, the wind warm where it came around the sunny corner of a building and cold everywhere else. It blew Story's hair in her face as we came out of DeRusso's after a late lunch of hot Italian sausage for which they are famous. When she pulled her hair back, I could see that she was crying. In the car she said: "There's nothing wrong with us." She was right. She'd done the progesterone count twice and hers was *slightly* low, but nothing was wrong. My sperm count was *slightly* low, but still there were millions. Story's uterus was *slightly* tipped, but it shouldn't, in the doctor's words, present a problem. *Science,* I thought. Now there's a word. *Science.* We stopped at Outskirts, the little package store on the edge of Winstead for a roadkit of cold Piels light.

"Here," I said, handing Story a beer. "No ice, no twist of lemon, but a woman who is thirsty has nothing for tears." It was an old joke of ours and she smiled. But the rest of the way home, we felt bad. There was nothing wrong with us and we felt bad.

FOUR

I HAD class the day Story went down to New Haven for her cervical biopsy. I told her I'd cancel, but she insisted on driving down alone. It was the final day of watercolors, before we went on to Life Class with pencils and acrylics, and I had to put up with Mary Ann Buxton gushing about how much she had loved the medium and ya-da, ya-da about her plans to explore it further on her own this summer at her parents' place in Maine, the light there was so delicate and terrific, and la-di-da. I had to walk three easels away to get her to let up. I had to admit, however, she had done a fair job on the four birches that grew beside the Dean's garden. I see the four birches that grow beside the Dean's garden almost twenty times in a year in every possible medium, especially watercolor, and they have almost cancelled my ability to enjoy trees at all. Simply: I hate them. If I stay at Bigville, there will certainly come an evil night when I make their final rendering with a chainsaw.

By the end of class, I'd grown glum, worrying about Story, and I sulked through the easels like a panhandler. It makes you feel funny sometimes as a teaching artist to see your students march through their paces, their work not great, not bad, but *work* anyway: finished paintings. I went back to the four birches. I helped Mary Ann Buxton add a little more light to the upside of a dozen leaves, but I felt like a phony anyway. I needed to paint.

I was home by two and my funk had me nailed to a chair in the dark living room, unable to blink. Luckily, Billy Wellner came by. He'd been to lunch with Ruth and had three beers and didn't want to write any more policies that afternoon. We took off our shirts and played the World Series of one on one in my driveway: best of seven. For an insurance agent, Billy has a good jumpshot, but he rarely drives for the basket and he's all right hand. I beat him four straight and walked him to his car.

Across the street, Mudd Miller himself came onto his porch and began bellowing the names of his children. There were long pauses followed frequently by a name he'd already called.

Billy threatened a rematch and said, "Let us know how Story is."

Half an hour later, I heard the car in the driveway, but Story didn't come in. I found her sitting in the driver's seat, washed out and pale. She made a grim little smile. "I should have had you come," she said. "It's the only thing so far that's hurt. I could hardly use the clutch on the way home."

I took her in and put her to bed. "You're all slimy," she said.

"Sweaty. I'm all sweaty. Since I can't paint, I'm putting my energies into basketball. Does it hurt now?"

"Just a small fire. I think they used a fingernail clippers."

I called the Wellners. Ruth answered and I told her about Story and asked her to handle the Township tomorrow. Before hanging up I gave her the accurate score of this afternoon's basketball massacre. "Why is the world all women and *boys?*" she said. "You take good care of Story; I'll handle the office."

Later still, Dr. Binderwitz's secretary-assistant Michelle called and said that the biopsy showed nothing, that Story was all right. It was a great spring twilight, I could hear the one nightingale calling from

Mugacook, and the voices of children playing tag on the edge of the campus, but when I looked in on my sleeping wife, a powerlessness so profound swept over me that I felt my back knotting up. I wanted to shake her shoulder and whisper: "I'll solve this problem," the way a husband should about an incorrect billing or a loose window or a gummy carburetor. I leaned against the doorway that spring night, and I knew the truth: *I couldn't do anything about this.* I couldn't paint or make us have a baby. I could throw a jump shot in from the corner, but as Ruth said, that is a matter for boys.

Story slept. The examination had told us again: she was all right. I folded my arms and felt them tingle with a tension that was new to me; I know now it was the blood sense that I was getting closer.

FIVE

BIGVILLE HAS, just as it has a Volunteer Fire Department, a volunteer baseball team, which is one of the oldest institutions in the township. And one of the customs that has grown up with our team is that the mayor throws out the ball for the opening game, which is always played at home against New Hartford.

At one in the afternoon on the day after her laparoscopy, Story stood up on the first row of the silly little bleachers in Bigville Park and threw a brand new Bradley baseball to Mudd Miller, who plays catcher for the ball team. He was standing inside the baseline, so it was a fine toss by a woman who had just twenty-four hours prior had a laparoscopy. In fact, when Mudd came over ceremoniously to hand Story back the baseball, he commented that she had more on the ball than any mayor in his fifteen years catching.

Ruth sat with us, being solicitous of her friend Story; she let me know just with her posture that Story's discomfort was somehow all my fault and that she, Ruth, was fundamentally alarmed that a person of my caliber would even try to impose his twisted gene pool onto another generation. Besides her motto about all the kids at K

Mart, she always said to Story, while I was in the room; "Why would you want a child, when you're married to one?" However, there was a look of genuine concern on the county attorney's face today, so I could take her cheap heat and watch the ballgame.

During a laparoscopy, a probe is inserted near the navel and searches the fallopian tubes for obstructive material, primarily known as endometriosis. Dr. Binderwitz had been able to tell us that the search had shown nothing, no obstruction. Story's tubes were clear. The operation left a tiny wrinkled scar under her navel, as if to underline it, an emphatic italic of her beauty.

The field was full of townspeople, tradesmen, and friends. Billy was straightaway in right field. Mr. Cummings from the food center was at second base, and one of the deans from the college was on the mound.

The baseball game was tight until the top of the ninth when a bearded man who works in the Sinclair in New Hartford hit a change-up over the old railroad trestle scoring three runs. Bigville couldn't match that, and after the game, Story and I walked the mile home.

"What are we going to do?" Story asked.

"Find a better pitcher; move the dean to the outfield."

She grabbed me around the neck in a mock wrestling hold. I tried to duck out, restrain her arms.

"Careful, one of us just had an operation." I took her hand and we walked on. "Is that the last test?"

"Yes," she said. "And there's nothing wrong with us." The two of us kicked stones along the old road, like two teenagers walking home from school. It was full May, two weeks past even the last cold rain, and the blossoming trees drooped into our path. I could see four men dragging the diving raft toward the lake down at the Grove. Tomorrow, Sunday, some lucky ten-year-old would climb the twenty red rungs on that wooden platform and commit the first cannonball into Mugacook for the summer season.

"What do we do?" Story whispered.

"Keep our chins up." I said. "Interact sexually . . . and . . ."

"What?"

"I don't know. Something else. It'll come to me. Something else."

Story took my arm. "I love you," she said. "I'm sorry we can't have children, but I still and will always love you."

WHEN YOU hold a woman you know quite well, press her softly into, say, a mattress, one hand under her neck, the other on the swelling of her hip, her skin so smooth as to seem forbidding and inviting at the same time, if she moves once, say to reach under your arm and to pull you forward, your mind will go right on by progesterone counts and histograms into a warm lyric zone where it will disappear in a dandy stinging swelter.

In such a swelter, my limbs lost in Story's, one night in May, at a moment when my eyes were about to roll away, I again saw my three fingers come creeping over Story's shoulder; and in the blurred proximity of the warm moment, they looked like the same three blank-faced old men arriving to witness our coupling. At the time I thought it was an odd vision for such a crucial time, but it was the beginning of an odd era, a time when cause–effect would take on new meaning, when order, sequence, science would whirl away.

That night when we rolled apart, I first dreamed of moons and geese and drowning, and then sometime late in the night I saw a perfect and vivid vision:

A man wearing a turquoise steerhead with jeweled horns does a low, steady hop around a campfire, swinging a stone phallus on a gold chain and singing with the insistent drums: HAH-MAH, LOH-LAH, HAH-MAH, LOH-LAH! He stops. He twists a glass vial of some thin red nectar onto the flames. They reach up in a hissing flash and light the area. In the new flare, the man thrusts his painted hand into the abdomen of a splayed chicken, tosses the entrails out in a splash, and begins—as the fire crawls back down to the logs—to read the throw, fingering the shiny organs apart as his shiny eyes begin to fill with the future.

I won't say much about the next few days, except that I did not start painting. I spent all my free time between morning and afternoon classes in the library and the library annex. With the good weather, the buildings were empty, all the undergraduates gone outside to court, and my research was simple. After I exhausted the campus libraries, I went down to Bigville Memorial, built of hewn granite and given to the town by Hugo Ballowell's great grandfather. I spent more than one day there, in fact, I used up the rest of May, not even looking up as the light changed at midday or in the evening, and I ended up in a corner of the basement. I found everything. The two volumes I selected had to be catalogued before I could take them home. *The Dark Arts* and *Life Before Science.* Together they weighed twelve pounds. Mrs. Torrey looked at me as if I was unhinged while I waited for her to write the library cards, but the heft of those books as I hauled them down to my studio seemed the first real thing in my quest. At last, I thought, I am finally doing something.

SIX

I ROWED the boat into dark Mugacook. Okay. Okay. Okay. Now. I've done all my homework. The first sperm to reach the ovum is the only one to enter. Of the millions of sperm sent out, only hundreds reach the ovum, and only the first to touch it enters. Upon entering, he swells and bursts, spilling the twenty-three chromosomes he's been carrying. That part is beyond me.

I rowed the old red rowboat and said aloud, "Okay, okay, okay."

When I perceived I was in line with the lighted church spire in town and the dozen lights of the Ballowell main house, I rowed toward town another five pulls and shipped the oars. It *felt* like the middle of the lake, but I didn't know; it was dark. I picked up the basketball, my old Voit. I'd scored layups on ten driveways in four states with this ball. I felt the ball in my hands. It was a little flat, but I mounted it on my fingertips for the shot, feeling the old worn nubble, and sent it up in a perfect arc, rocking the old wooden boat a bit more than I meant to. I grabbed the gunwales to keep from going in the dark water myself, and I heard the satisfying *bip!* of the ball's splash.

The sperm's journey is the equivalent of a three-and-a-half-mile swim, so I was going to have to swim from the town beach over to the boathouse and then head for the middle. I rowed back. I pulled the heavy boat up on the sand, dragging it well clear of the water, and I undressed, putting my clothing over the bow. Then I curled onto the cool sand and tried to grow quiet. I was too excited. I could feel, smell, sense the whole round lake lying beside me, and somewhere in the middle, the basketball. I squeezed my eyes shut in joy. This is it. I could feel a warmth in my shoulders and in the backs of my legs; this was really working.

But I'd left nothing to chance. Tomorrow, the garlic would arrive, and I'd pick up the jade. I had ordered the chickens and the birdseed and the rice. I'd become part of a process that had me in its sweep, and in a second, I was on my feet, yipping like a monkey as I rushed in four long strides right into the warm waters of Lake Mugacook.

The medium of the water enveloped, moved me. I was flying, floating, gliding. The trees along the water's edge drifted by as if the lake were quietly turning for me, taking me with it. I closed my eyes as I swam for minutes at a time. By the time I took my first real breath—or so it seemed—I looked up and saw the square white face of the boathouse smiling at me. Behind me, in the middle of this huge lake, the deepest lake in Connecticut, was a basketball. I turned, kicking hard, headed right for it. I imagined the other millions of sperm swimming behind me, wandering, loitering, taking the wrong turn into Cookson Swamp or Succor Brook, drowning in the acid at the top of the vagina, their tails being eaten by antibodies.

I swam for a long time. It became real swimming, my arms finally heavier than the water, and I could hear myself breathing, blowing water out. It was a big lake. When I crawled to where the middle might have been, I sighted the church spire, a lighted sliver over the town. I turned to line up with Ballowells' lights.

There were no lights.

I stood in a treadwater position and swiveled. No lights. Ballowells had gone to bed. Ballowells had turned out every one of their seventy thousand lights and they had gone to bed. I had no idea where I was. For a while I was under the water, which I did know, and I came up several times saying the word "Okay!" spitting like a seal. Across the lake I could still see the white line of the church spire. It was a mile and a quarter to the rowboat, then through the grove, down the pond road a half mile, across Route 43, and up the steps into the church. My knees ached like burning rubber.

I was under, then way under, and then up for air. Each time I cracked the surface my "Okay!" had more water in it, and finally I couldn't even hear the word. This was not a hospitable environment. I went into my drown-proofing moves, but I kept going down too far and had to kick to mouth air. Something touched my toe, something small, but it was enough. I panicked. The antibodies were eating my tail. In a frenzy of side straddle hops, side strokes, leaping waves, I called "Whoa!" and went down.

The water played a lugubrious synthesizer tone in my ears as I fell freely through the thermoclimes past two, three zones of colder water. Small hot squiggles crawled across the inside of my closed eyes. I was swaying back and forth wonderfully. It was like the time I was playing one on one with Billy Wellner at his house. We were playing around his pickup and I perfected a shot where I would drive around the rear of the truck and then lean back into the fence and throw a set shot up off the board and through the hoop. I made the shot nine times in a row and beat Billy 22–2. All he could say was, "You're wrecking the fence."

Then.

Then I touched the basketball, and it was in one hand, then both hands, and my knees closed around it too, as we bobbed past forty-six million stars in outer space.

THE VOICE behind the flashlight said, "Get up." It was our constable, Gill Manwaring, I could tell, and he was trying to sound real tough. Story herself had hired Gill as constable.

"You better get up, fella."

I lay still, wrapped around the ball, in the same fetal position in which I must have washed upon this shore. He hadn't recognized me. His boot ran up under my kidney. "Up!"

In a voice I recognized as Raymond Burr's, I said, "Hey, Gill." I rose, not unlike a cow would, a piece at a time, and looked into the flashlight. "What time is it?"

"Dan?"

"Yeah." I stood facing him, holding the ball nonchalantly in front of my private parts. He lowered the light and I came to understand there was a personage standing behind Gill.

"You all right?"

"Yeah," I said. "Late night swim got away from me. Can you take me around to my boat? It's at the grove." My eyes adjusted by steady, painful degrees in the starlight, and I could see that this was the three acre front lea of the Ballowells', and that Annette Ballowell was backing steadily toward her dark and significant mansion.

It wasn't until I sat my bare ass on the seat of Gill's Rover that I lifted the ball onto my lap and saw the disturbing and exciting truth: it wasn't the same ball. It wasn't my ball at all.

SEVEN

THE NEXT morning when I removed the thermometer from Story's mouth, she looked up at me. "It's the deep end you're over, isn't it."

I read the thermometer with new intensity. "Ninety-seven point seven."

"Why don't you just paint household objects until it takes. You'll get it. You'll see it again. School will be out this week, and you can just take some time."

"I'm going to do that. I'll be all right." I nodded and heard the angry little tides inside my ears. "I'm going to paint everything."

When Story left for Town Hall, I burst into action. I didn't have

class until four, so I ran to the studio barelegged in my Sears robe
and stretched three canvases, 60 by 60, my shrunken hands atrem-
ble. I could feel the heat. I was in motion; I couldn't do it fast
enough. I had one palette wet under cellophane and without changing it a bit, I started in.

The volleyball that had saved my life in the confidential waters of
Lake Mugacook ten hours before was a Sportcraft Professional
Model manufactured in New Castle, Pennsylvania. In postal blue
magic marker script along one seam was the name: Allen. Luther
Allen was a retired broker who clipped coupons on his lakefront
property in town. His children and grandchildren came up from
New York and New Haven on weekends.

On the first canvas, I broadbrushed the curve of one side in ver-
milion. I had to hold my head cocked a certain way as the lakewater
gurgled up and down my eustachian tubes. Many times when I
changed positions, water ran out of my ears. I worked fast because I
figured I had two hours tops before Story ran into Gill Manwaring
and I'd get a phone call. If I could grab a secure start on three canvases, it might testify to my equilibrium. But as my hands moved
across the paintings, working all three in one stroke, then one for
twenty minutes, I wondered. They didn't look like volleyballs as we
know them.

So many times the magic in painting transpires in the twelve
inches between the palette and the canvas, and your head, hand, or
heart better get out of the way. I felt that warmth in my arms now,
and I tried to proceed with caution or reason or passionless purpose,
but I might as well not have been there. This was not the way I used
to paint. I ran from the studio several times, whenever my neck
would get too sore, and I dressed a piece at a time, retrieved the
hammer, all my roofing nails, the butcher knife. My garlic was arriving at noon.

When the phone did ring, Story simply said, "What's going on?"

"Story, I've got a start on three good pieces. Can I call you back?"

"Dan, what's this with Gill?"

"Don't worry. Don't worry. Don't worry. I'll tell you later. All about it. I gotta go." And I did go. I found myself an hour later in the studio, one canvas finished, the others running to a close. The first looked like nothing, like a rose moon in a blue blanket, I don't know, but God it thrilled me! Some of the edges floated like folded velvet; I'd never done that before. I'd never seen it done before! This was no landscape that I knew. The whole time I'd been in the studio, I'd only had two thoughts. One was simply a picture of Story's face as she hung up the phone: that worry. The other was so profound it powered me through the day. I wanted, more than anything, for my children and grandchildren to come visit and play volleyball on the lawn. The picture made sense and gave reason to everything in my life.

The garlic man, not a farmer but Cummings from the Food Center, had to come all the way through the house and he startled me, appearing at the studio door. I hadn't heard him for all the water in my ears.

Cummings was also the butcher, and as he stood at my studio doorway in his bloody apron, he seemed one of the Fates come to abbreviate me at last.

"I've got your garlic," he said, and the first glorious strains of the herb drifted my way.

"Good!" I must have said it a little too loudly as Mr. Cummings stepped back and raised his hands in self-defense. To assure him that I meant no harm, I placed my brush and palette aside and asked him in to see what I was doing. He folded his arms over his apron and browsed my canvases, nodding steadily. The spectacle of the three huge canvases, flashed and spiraled with those strange colors, and the volleyball sitting on the table behind them seemed to confuse Mr. Cummings, but his nodding quickened. His assessment was only "Yep," followed by seven or eight small "Yep, yep, yeps." It didn't strike me until we had unloaded two hundred pounds of garlic onto the front lawn, that Mr. Cumming's yepping had been identical to the sad and final pronouncements of a doctor whose suspicions have been confirmed.

When he left, I didn't hesitate. I took up my hammer and jammed my pockets with the short galvanized roofing nails, and wondered why the opinion of one of the most prominent village tradesmen didn't bother me; why in fact, I took his incredulity as encouragement; why, in fact, I felt absolutely encouraged by everything in the world: the flat noon light, the impending thundershower, Mudd Miller's black Honda motorcycle leaking oil on his driveway across the street. Oh, I just breathed it all in and began tacking the garlic to my own sweet home.

I framed all the doors in garlands first, in case there wasn't enough garlic, tapping the nails through the center of each bulb, spacing them three fingers apart. Then I ringed the windows, the basement windows, and the storm cellar door. The oil each clove gave its nail slathered down my wrists to the elbows, but after twenty minutes, I couldn't smell a thing. It all gave our house a fuzzy, gingerbread look, not unbecoming and kind of festive. By the time I finished, I was high, high with a new taut certainty that I was unquestionably on the right track, and high with a sort of major garlic sinus dilation. My eyes felt poached.

I ran to the studio to retrieve my car keys, but was again arrested by the three paintings and worked for a furious moment on the third. This "volleyball" was becoming more elongated than the other two and looked like, I'll say for now, a rose setting sun in a green and ocher sky. But something told me that when I looked into the canvas I wasn't looking all the way to the horizon. Something was trying to get out; I love that sense. When the phone rang, I came to and strode out to my old Buick. I sat still in the driver's seat for a moment, listening to the phone ringing. It sounded like a vague, intermittent alert for the future going off in garlic house.

In my book, *Life Before Science,* it said:

Garlic and garlic substitutes were often used by tribes in Africa, Asia, Australia, and England to heat a childless domicile. The huts were festooned with fresh garlic once a month, and the man and the

woman wore garlic in various forms sewn into a garment or on a
string around the neck, or crushed into the hair. Some tribes were
known to use a garlic mattress, which was rumored to have never
failed. In many societies the smell of garlic was synonymous with
fecundity.

EIGHT

YOU LAY yourself open to attack by a powerful creeping chagrin if
you drive miles away from home one fine afternoon, as I did, guided
only by your overwhelming desire to have children and by a lurid,
illustrated half-page advertisement from the back pages of the scur-
rilous local shopper *The Twilight Want Ads.* Just the tabloid illustration mocked me: a crude wood block print featuring, or so it said,
Mrs. Argyle, "Gypsy Wizardress, Alchemist, Seer, and Tax Advisor,"
her face seemingly radiating small lightning rays of power and—
what I took to be—understanding.

So I set my mouth against the thorough feeling that I was a fool,
and I followed the directions Mrs. Argyle had given me over the telephone, driving toward the village of Boughton, where I had never
been.

The interview that followed, in the woody turnout three point
four miles from Boughton, with Mrs. Argyle, is still a mystery to me.
Her rusty Ford van was there along with the two jade talismans
hanging from the rearview mirror. I stood around for a while, trying
to look innocent, and then finally I put two hundred dollars on the
seat, as I'd been instructed in our call, took the necklaces, and left.

Driving home was a different matter. Cruising the rural roads in
Connecticut after twilight in the early summer, past farmers' fields
and the little roadhouses, their pink Miller Beer signs just beginning
to glow in the new darkness, with two *guaranteed* jade talismans in
my pocket, I began to swell with confidence and good cheer. I sang
songs that I made up (with gestures) and grinned like an idiot. I

never saw Mrs. Argyle at all. I motored toward Bigville, my mouth full of song, the jade glowing at my side.

At garlic headquarters, my house, Story was waiting. I could see my sweet mayor and Ruth Wellner, my favorite county attorney, having Piels Light on the rocks with a twist in the living room. Piels beer is the only thing Story drinks, always on ice with a twist, and I had come to see the brown bottles with their cadmium orange labels as little symbols of pleasure and ease, perhaps celebration. But this time as I walked through the kitchen and saw the bottles standing on the counter, I don't know, I was worried. Our normal life was amazing; why did I want to tamper with it? But then I thought: okay, if this is what I have to do to create another human being, to have a son or daughter with whom to play catch and Scrabble, and to show Picasso and Chagall, and to teach how to fish and to cook a good garlic sauce for spaghetti squash, someone to send to the fridge for another beer and who will chase his sister through the house with a pair of scissors and to lend the car keys to and to ground for two weeks for being late for some ridiculous curfew and to spend two hundred thousand dollars on and to leave all my stuff to, my collection of Monster Magazines, my hand-tied flies, my railroad watch, though it is broken, and someone to fake-right, go-left past for the hoop, and to paint a thousand versions of before I die, then okay, I'll do it. I entered the living room.

Ruth Wellner gave me the hardest ride with her eyeballs I'd ever had. "Hi, everybody!" I said. "How's the township?"

Story smiled at me, which is great about her. She always smiles at me at first. Then, of course, she said, "What's going *on*, Dan?" I thought for a moment that she had read my mind or had seen the two lumps of jade in my pocket, but then she went on: "What have you done to the house?"

"Oh! Yeah." I hadn't thought of an answer, especially in front of the county attorney. "It's a conceptual piece I'm trying."

"Garlic?"

"This one's garlic." I said, wishing I'd grabbed a beer. "It's been done with apples." I nodded, believing what I'd said myself. "It's only a temporary piece," I explained, waving my hands as a kind of truce. Ruth leaned back and shook her head imperceptibly, a subtle gesture they all learn in law school which means: "I don't believe a word of it, you lying bastard." But Story smiled at me again, a new smile this time, the ancient smile of women who know their men.

"You missed your class, you know."

"Oh, sure," I said affirmatively. "Sure, sure. That's wonderful." And it was wonderful in my crazy head. I could see my students waiting for the keys to unlock their lockers, grumbling and then drifting away. Mary Ann Buxton would have drifted right to the department chairman's office to offer him most of an earful, but it was wonderful. I smiled. I put my hand over the two charms in my pocket and I realized that I was moving through the most centered and affirmative period of my life. And though I couldn't see them all clearly, there were still things to do.

NINE

IN THE morning, I placed the thermometer in Story's mouth and sang three minutes from the theme song of *High Noon,* making the "Do not forsake me, oh my darling!" really mournful, and then read the little gauge: "Ninety-seven point nine. Or ninety-eight flat, I can't tell."

I felt an almost impossible intensity, an anticipation that ran me with chills. All my magic was aligned for tonight, all my preparations.

"You're in a . . . mood," Story said cautiously, giving me an odd side glance.

"Good night's sleep," I said trying to suddenly appear mature. I stood and the song rose into my throat. "On this our we-e-edding day-ay!" I sang and headed for the bathroom.

In the shower steam rose around me rife with garlic, the very smell of babies hovering in the air. There was nothing wrong with us. Tonight was the night.

Story came into the bathroom just in time to hear the best rhyme in my song:

> "He'd made a vow while in state prison,
>   Vow'd it'd be my life or his'n!"

"Oh, this garlic!" she yelled. "This garlic has got to go!"

"Tomorrow," I answered. "Just one more day."

"You know what Ruth thinks?"

"That she could get me off with insanity?"

"That you're having an affair."

I poked my head outside the shower curtain and stared at Story. She was naked, brushing her teeth, and the way she bent to the sink burned across my heart. "What?"

Story tapped her brush and looked up. Such a smile. "You're not having an affair. You've got your secrets, but you're not having an affair."

Before Story left for the office, I grabbed her lapels and said, "Listen, try this: get the township business out of your head, okay? If you have to, delegate some authority, make a new committee, but get it out of your head. And Story."

"Yes, sir?"

"Come home alone. No Ruthless Ruth. No complicated preoccupations. Just you. Seven o'clock."

"Is there something I should know, Dan?"

I showed her my palms and waved one up at the garlic doorway fringe. "You know it all already. I'll see you at seven."

She gave me a funny, get-well-soon look, and I thought what it must be like for the mayor to be married to a wizard-master of the dark and light arts, but I also thought: *it's worth it.* She'll go and worry about me for thirty-five minutes, until township troubles hit the fan, and it's worth it.

After Story had left, I ran up to the campus for my ten o'clock life class, arriving just in time to let Tim, our model, in early. An irrepressible townie, he sits for the group bareassed in a buckskin jockstrap on a wooden stool, one knee drawn up to his chest, his heel on the stool seat. As he passed by me to go change clothes, he said: "One more time! Tomorrow I'm in Virginia Beach, and," he pointed at me and smirked, "art class is history."

I had forgotten: it was the last day of school. I was surprised and for the first time in weeks, time became real. My students filed in around me, and I had to smile; this was certainly a waking dream, but a good dream.

Mary Ann Buxton was waiting for me as I drifted among the easels. Seated directly behind Tim, she had drawn an incredibly precise version of the stool and had skipped up and drawn his shoulder axis and neck.

"Where were you yesterday?" she said. "The studio class, all nine of us, waited forty-five minutes. Is this what we pay tuition for?"

I wanted to say: Truce; it's the last day of school. Cease further hostilities. But I did say: "I'm sorry, Mary Ann; I was away." Before she could start again, I interrupted her with this whisper: "Mary Ann. What's he going to sit on?" I pointed to the blank space on her paper where his ass should have been. "Don't be shy," I said. "This is art." I couldn't stop myself; I winked. "Go ahead, really."

I was in a daze the whole hour. The volleyball at home. I couldn't see a thing but the ball and the three paintings emerging in my mind. I wandered the studio muttering, "Good, good," to everybody, even Mary Ann Buxton and her feathered fluffy version of Tim's posterior. It was a tangible relief when Tim himself stood up, stretched, and said, "Okay. That's my twenty bucks. Anybody looking now pays overtime."

Oh, Bigville! You sweet township! What I did the rest of the day was seen through eyes blurred by heat and vision. I shook hands with my fine young painters and headed out, running across campus, gathering a hundred stares in my wake. If any dean had been looking out the window, I would have received a letter.

At home, I retrieved the ten-pound bag of rice and the fifty pounds of birdseed from the basement and spread them in a blinding flurry of thrown handfuls across the backyard, and incidentally my hair, the roof, and the raingutters.

I went to see Mr. Cummings at the Food Center and he had my two chickens, that is, their innards, and he handed me the plastic pail without a look, my eccentricity gone ordinary in his eyes. At home, crackling across the birdseed and rice, I tossed gloopy handfuls of the intestines, et cetera, around the yard. I stripped off my shirt and made circles on my belly with the blood. I bent and tried to read the throws. I'm not sure what they said, but they looked authentic. I went into the basement and drew on the furnace room walls with charcoal briquets: sperm entering the egg, wiggling tails, hash marks of excitement, seven stars, the blistered moon. When I came back upstairs, blinking into the light, I saw Buster and Sadie, Mudd Miller's two dogs, rolling on their backs in the chicken guts. It dismayed me at first until I remembered that Sadie had already thrown three healthy litters of five puppies each, and I debated whether to go out and writhe around with them for a while.

The doorbell rang, and it turned out to be Mary Ann Buxton, in her traveling clothes, her little Volvo packed to the windows, still running on the driveway. She looked at me in a three-part glance: my charcoaled face, my bloody belly, and then, stepping back slowly, the aboriginal whole. There was nothing I could do.

"Hello," I said.

"Mr. Baldwin," she said finally. "Thank you for the help and encouragement in art this year. I've learned a lot. It was one of my favorite classes, and in appreciation, I brought you this little present."

It was a prepared speech or she wouldn't have gotten through it, and she managed a "Thank you and good-bye," handing me something and backing down the stairs with a look of frenzied relief on her face. She was glad to have left the car running.

I looked in my hand. It was her painting of the four birches near the Dean's garden. My eyes burned inexplicably, and I went back into the house and sat on the floor in the hallway for a moment. Mary Ann Buxton had squatted outdoors for three days frowning at this canvas, chewing her lip, and it was a good painting, two steps beyond representational. I looked at it for five minutes, as if I was counting the strokes. Those damn trees. I love those trees.

In my studio, my three paintings rose to me like live things. I buried my heart into the third and final canvas. I didn't look up again until I heard Mudd Miller on his porch calling the names of his children, the ones he could remember. Oh, it was a bellow full of love! I looked at myself, covered with blood and paint and charcoal, my face a savage smear in the mirror. "Oh, Bigville," I moaned aloud. "It's all going to work."

I showered and began to cool down. I called the office and Ruth Wellner said the meeting would go another hour. I stood in the dining room looking out through a window ringed by garlic at my yard littered with chicken waste, rice, and birdseed, and I had the momentary thought: "You fool, you've ruined your own home." But it was a fleeting doubt and to quash it, I did an errand. I drove the Sportcraft volleyball over to Luther Allen's and left it with the groundskeeper.

Story did not arrive home until after ten. I had roamed the house for a while, cruising my new paintings with a hot, fond confusion. I liked them even if I didn't know what they were. Finally I settled in the living room with Mary Ann Buxton's four birches propped against the mantel where I could see them, and *Life Before Science* on my lap. In the new darkness, the volume put my legs to sleep and I followed soon thereafter. It was a heavy book.

I was dreaming of Dr. Binderwitz scolding me, pointing his unwashed finger in my face, when Story woke me, bumping me softly with her leg. "Hey," she said. "Did you eat?"

I checked my watch: ten-thirty. "What happened?"

"Want some chicken?" she said. "I brought you some chicken."

So we ate cold chicken and drank Piels Light on the rocks at the kitchen table like two characters in a good short novel while I woke up and Story gave me the details of the meeting.

As Story told me the tale, she laughed and ate chicken and we drank cold beer, and the moment in the kitchen light reminded me in a primal way of why and how much I loved her.

"I'm painting again," I said.

"I knew you would." She reached and took my forearm.

"Wait here," I told her, and I rose and fetched my two jade friends from the bureau. I put one around her neck and one around my own. Chin down, Story examined her necklace.

"You need to wear it tonight, while we . . ."

"Interact sexually?"

I nodded.

"Well, you are dear, aren't you," she said. "Confused, but dear."

"Can you get the township out of your head long enough to conceive a baby?"

"Come here," she said. "Come get me."

WE DIDN'T make it to the bedroom. She started playing Eva Marie Saint in *On the Waterfront* and sliding down the hall doorframe, her arms around my neck, and by the time we were on our knees, no one was playing anymore, or rather, now we were playing in earnest. Several times we stopped and shifted to gain leg room, and we rolled, twice, three times, I don't know, but then we were under the piano in a pane of moonlight, and I don't know, her flesh, her breath, I was on my back and I could see the round moon just like an egg sliding down the blue-black tube of the sky. We were gathering the pieces as she held me, three hundred million coiled swimmers in a garlic sea, and in a rush that grabbed my throat like a fist, they were flying.

The first thing I saw when I took my mouth from Story's was the grouping of my three fingers over her white shoulder, those three bald men come to greet us, but then as my eyes rinsed once more I saw them again and this is when I saw it all: they weren't three old

men at all, but three babies I had seen somewhere before. My eyes
filled. Three babies. I had painted these guys for the last week, each
on a canvas of his own.

Story reached her arm around my neck and turned on her side.
"Are you going to get us a blanket?" she said. "Or shall we go to bed?"

I got her the quilt. In my study the only light came from the children. Not one: three. I painted until blue dawn and they focused like
photographs: three babies. From my window I could see the sun
about to burst over Mugacook Mountain; the trees stood out in
chromosomal pairs. My heart was swimming. I could see the children, do you see? In her arms. One. Two. Three.

BIGFOOT STOLE MY WIFE

HE PROBLEM is credibility.

The problem, as I'm finding out over the last few weeks, is basic credibility. A lot of people look at me and say, sure Rick, Bigfoot stole your wife. It makes me sad to see it, the look of disbelief in each person's eye. Trudy's disappearance makes me sad, too, and I'm sick in my heart about where she may be and how he's treating her, what they do all day, if she's getting enough to eat. I believe he's being good to her—I mean I feel it—and I'm going to keep hoping to see her again, but it is my belief that I probably won't.

In the two and a half years we were married, I often had the feeling that I would come home from the track and something would be funny. Oh, she'd say things: *One of these days I'm not going to be here when you get home,* things like that, things like everybody says. How stupid of me not to see them as omens. When I'd get out of bed in the early afternoon, I'd stand right here at this sink and I could see her working in her garden in her cut-off Levi's and bikini top, weeding, planting, watering. I mean it was obvious. I was too busy thinking about the races, weighing the odds, checking the jockey roster to see what I now know: he was watching her too. He'd probably been watching her all summer.

So, in a way it was my fault. But what could I have done? Bigfoot steals your wife. I mean: even if you're home, it's going to be a mess. He's big and not well trained.

When I came home it was about eleven-thirty. The lights were on, which really wasn't anything new, but in the ordinary mess of the place, there was a little difference, signs of a struggle. There was a spilled Dr. Pepper on the counter and the fridge was open. But there was something else, something that made me sick. The smell. The smell of Bigfoot. It was hideous. It was . . . the guy is not clean.

Half of Trudy's clothes are gone, not all of them, and there is no note. Well, I know what it is. It's just about midnight there in the kitchen which smells like some part of hell. I close the fridge door. It's the saddest thing I've ever done. There's a picture of Trudy and me leaning against her Toyota taped to the fridge door. It was taken last summer. There's Trudy in her bikini top, her belly brown as a bean. She looks like a kid. She was a kid I guess, twenty-six. The two times she went to the track with me everybody looked at me like how'd I rate her. But she didn't really care for the races. She cared about her garden and Chinese cooking and Buster, her collie, who I guess Bigfoot stole too. Or ate. Buster isn't in the picture, he was nagging my nephew Chuck who took the photo. Anyway I close the fridge door and it's like part of my life closed. Bigfoot steals your wife and you're in for some changes.

You come home from the track having missed the Daily Double by a neck, and when you enter the home you are paying for and in which you and your wife and your wife's collie live, and your wife and her collie are gone as is some of her clothing, there is nothing to believe. Bigfoot stole her. It's a fact. What should I do, ignore it? Chuck came down and said something like well if Bigfoot stole her why'd they take the Celica? Christ, what a cynic! Have you ever read anything about Bigfoot not being able to drive? He'd be cramped in there, but I'm sure he could manage.

I don't really care if people believe me or not. Would that change anything? Would that bring Trudy back here? Pull the weeds in her garden?

As I think about it, no one believes anything anymore. Give me one example of someone *believing* one thing. I dare you. After that we get into this credibility thing. No one believes me. I myself can't believe all the suspicion and cynicism there is in today's world. Even at the races, some character next to me will poke over at my tip sheet and ask me if I believe that stuff. If I believe? What is there to believe? The horse's name? What he did the last time out? And I look back at this guy, too cheap to go two bucks on the program, and I say: it's history. It is historical fact here. Believe. Huh. Here's a fact: I believe everything.

Credibility.

When I was thirteen years old, my mother's trailer was washed away in the flooding waters of the Harley River and swept thirty-one miles, ending right side up and nearly dead level just outside Mercy, in fact in the old weed-eaten parking lot for the abandoned potash plant. I know this to be true because I was inside the trailer the whole time with my pal, Nuggy Reinecker, who found the experience more life-changing than I did.

Now who's going to believe this story? I mean, besides me, because I was there. People are going to say, come on, thirty-one miles? Don't you mean thirty-one feet?

We had gone in out of the rain after school to check out a magazine that belonged to my mother's boyfriend. It was a copy of *Dude,* and there was a fold-out page I will never forget of a girl lying on the beach on her back. It was a color photograph. The girl was a little pale, I mean, this was probably her first day out in the sun, and she had no clothing on. So it was good, but what made it great was that they had made her a little bathing suit out of sand. Somebody had spilled a little sand just right, here and there, and the sand was this incredible gold color, and it made her look so absolutely naked it wanted to put your eyes out.

Nuggy and I knew there was flood danger in Griggs; we'd had a flood every year almost and it had been raining for five days on and off, but when the trailer bucked the first time, we thought it was my mother come home to catch us in the dirty book. Nuggy shoved the magazine under the bed and I ran out to check the door. It only took me a second and I hollered back *Hey no sweat, no one's here,* but by the time I returned to see what other poses they'd had this beautiful woman commit, Nuggy already had his pants to his ankles and was involved in what we knew was a sin.

If it hadn't been the timing of the first wave with this act of his, Nuggy might have gone on to live what the rest of us call a normal life. But the Harley had crested and the head wave, which they estimated to be three feet minimum, unmoored the trailer with a push that knocked me over the sofa, and threw Nuggy, already entangled in his trousers, clear across the bedroom.

I watched the village of Griggs as we sailed through. Some of the village, the Exxon Station, part of it at least, and the carwash, which folded up right away, tried to come along with us, and I saw the front of Painters' Mercantile, the old porch and signboard, on and off all day.

You can believe this: it was not a smooth ride. We'd rip along for ten seconds, dropping and growling over rocks, and rumbling over tree stumps, and then wham! the front end of the trailer would lodge against a rock or something that could stop it, and whoa! we'd wheel around sharp as a carnival ride, worse really, because the furniture would be thrown against the far side and us with it, sometimes we'd end up in a chair and sometimes the chair would sit on us. My mother had about four thousand knickknacks in five big box shelves, and they gave us trouble for the first two or three miles, flying by like artillery, left, right, some small glass snail hits you in the face, later in the back, but that stuff all finally settled in the foot and then two feet of water which we took on.

We only slowed down once and it was the worst. In the railroad flats I thought we had stopped and I let go of the door I was hugging and tried to stand up and then swish, another rush sent us right along. We rammed along all day it seemed, but when we finally washed up in Mercy and the sheriff's cousin pulled open the door and got swept back to his car by water and quite a few of those knickknacks, just over an hour had passed. We had averaged, they figured later, about thirty-two miles an hour, reaching speeds of up to fifty at Lime Falls and the Willows. I was okay and walked out bruised and well washed, but when the sheriff's cousin pulled Nuggy out, he looked genuinely hurt.

"For godsakes," I remember the sheriff's cousin saying, "The damn flood knocked this boy's pants off!" But Nuggy wasn't talking. In fact, he never hardly talked to me again in the two years he stayed at the Regional School. I heard later, and I believe it, that he joined the monastery over in Malcolm County.

My mother, because she didn't have the funds to haul our rig back to Griggs, worried for a while, but then the mayor arranged to let us stay out where we were. So after my long ride in a trailer down the flooded Harley River with my friend Nuggy Reinecker, I grew up in a parking lot outside of Mercy, and to tell you the truth, it wasn't too bad, even though our trailer never did smell straight again.

Now you can believe all that. People are always saying: don't believe everything you read, or everything you hear. And I'm here to tell you. Believe it. Everything. Everything you read. Everything you hear. Believe your eyes. Your ears. Believe the small hairs on the back of your neck. Believe all of history, and all of the versions of history, and all the predictions for the future. Believe every weather forecast. Believe in God, the afterlife, unicorns, showers on Tuesday. Everything has happened. Everything is possible.

I come home from the track to find the cupboard bare. Trudy is not home. The place smells funny: hairy. It's a fact and I know it as a fact: Bigfoot has been in my house.

Bigfoot stole *my* wife.

She's gone.

Believe it.

I gotta believe it.

I AM BIGFOOT

THAT'S FINE: I'm ready.

I am Bigfoot. The Bigfoot. You've been hearing about me for some time now, seeing artists' renderings, and perhaps a phony photograph or two. I should say right here that an artist's rendering is one thing, but some trumped-up photograph is entirely another. The one that really makes me sick purports to show me standing in a stream in Northern California. Let me tell you something: Bigfoot never gets his feet wet. And I've only been to Northern California once, long enough to check out Redding and Eureka, both too quiet for the kind of guy I am.

Anyway, all week long, people (the people I contacted) have been wondering why I finally have gone public. A couple thought it was because I was angry at that last headline, remember: "Jackie O. Slays Bigfoot." No, I'm not angry. You can't go around and correct everybody who slanders you. (Hey, I'm not dead, and I only saw Jacqueline Onassis once, at about four hundred yards. She was on a horse.) And as for libel, what should I do, go up to Rockefeller Center and hire a lawyer? Please. Spare me. You can quote me on this: Bigfoot is not interested in legal action.

"THEN, WHY?" they say. "Why climb out of the woods and go through the trouble of 'meeting the press,' so to speak?" (Well, first of all, I don't live in the woods *year round,* which is a popular misconception of my life-style. Sure, I like the woods, but I need action too. I've had some of my happiest times in the median of the Baltimore Belt-route, the orchards of Arizona and Florida, and I spent nearly five years in the corn country just outside St. Louis. So, it's not just the woods, okay?)

WHY I came forward at this time concerns the truest thing I ever read about myself in the papers. The headline read "Bigfoot Stole My Wife," and it was right on the money. But beneath it was the real story: "Anguished Husband's Cry." Now I read the article, every word. Twice. It was poorly written, but it was all true. I stole the guy's wife. She wasn't the first and she wasn't the last. But when I went back and read that "anguished husband," it got me a little. I've been, as you probably have read, in all fifty states and eleven foreign countries. (I have never been to Tibet, in case you're wondering. That is some other guy, maybe the same one who was crossing that stream in Northern California.) *And,* in each place I've been, there's a woman. Come on, who is surprised by that? I don't always steal them, in fact, I never *steal* them, but I do *call them away,* and they come with me. I know my powers and I use my powers. And when I call a woman, she comes.

SO, HERE I am. It's kind of a confession, I guess; kind of a warning. I've been around; I've been all over the world (except Tibet! I don't know if that guy is interested in women or not.) And I've seen thousands of women standing at their kitchen windows, their stare in the mid-afternoon goes a thousand miles; I've seen thousands of women, dressed to the nines, strolling the cosmetic counters in Saks and I. Magnin, wondering why their lives aren't like movies; thousands of women shuffling in the soft twilight of malls, headed for the Orange Julius stand, not really there, just biding time until things get lovely.

And things get lovely when I call. I cannot count them all, I cannot list the things these women are doing while their husbands are out there in another world, but one by one I'm meeting them on my terms. I am Bigfoot. I am not from Tibet. I go from village to town to city to village. At present, I am watching your wife. That's why I am here tonight. To tell you, fairly, man to man, I suppose, I am watching your wife and I know for a fact, that when I call, she'll come.

THE TIME I DIED

I READ a lot. I mean: I read *everything*. I always have. It used to really drive Grant crazy. My whole side of the bedroom was a hazard: stacks of pamphlets, magazines, papers, paperbacks, and about four dozen hardback books which I received from my book club and the library. But I love to read. Grant would say, "What's in that damn book, anyway?" But he really didn't want to know. I know this because several times I answered him. "Honey, this book is about Bud Sackett trying to deliver cattle to Santa Fe . . ." or "The woman in this article says she lost forty pounds of ugly fat by chewing each bite thirty-one times. . . ." But before I could finish the explanation, Grant was in the other room cranking the channels like he was trying to start an outboard motor.

I read a lot of trash. I do. I read *The Realms of Twilight Tabloid News of the World* from cover to cover. I've read all the stories about people coming back from the dead, and all twenty-one people have said about the same thing: there's that white room and some floating and their relatives and most of the time some music. I have also read some fine books, such as *Madame Bovary*, the biography of Dorothy Kilgallen called *Kilgallen,* which my book club sent me, and a large book called *The Gulag Archipelago,* a book which scared the devil out of Grant. "What language are you reading now?" he said.

Maybe I read too much. But I always felt it was better than drinking too much or chasing around. Later, that is what Grant got into. I suspected he was having troubles, and then I found out when he gave me herpes two. It's a virus. He stopped coming home. I really started reading.

I was reading fourteen hours a day. In one day I read *Are You a Genius?, Great American Mystery Stories* (the whole volume), *The Book of Lists II,* and *Frankenstein,* which turned out to be different than I had ever thought. It was during this heavy reading period that Susan, my maid of honor, my best friend from high school, since before high school, called, and that led to how I died and why I'm in the hospital now.

Susan has a great attitude. She got married in high school to Andrew Botts, one of the most popular guys in our class, and then about three years ago, Andrew split. He's in California now, but Susan never let it get her down. She smiles about him like she knew it all along.

She used to call me up and talk, and then sometimes I'd have her over for dinner with Grant and me. Grant didn't like her, because he couldn't figure her out; but it was okay, because he would eat and then go in the other room and crank the channels, and Susan and I would talk for three hours. In fact, I'd rather be with Susan, talking, than alone reading in bed. She's a crazy woman and always has a new story about some new man in her life and what he's trying to get her to do now. She can laugh way down in her throat for about a minute without taking a breath.

So, when she called the last time she said she had heard about Grant leaving, and she laughed and said, "That's the real facts of life, Linda," which was exactly what she said at my wedding. Anyway, she said I was definitely going to stop reading for one night and go out for a night with the girls. I had been reading back through a stack of *The Realms of Twilight Tabloid News of the World* at the time, and didn't want to go, because I was reading a pretty good series on UFOs, which have already picked up fifty-four people who have never been seen since and who are living better lives somewhere, according to their relatives and sometimes according to the sheriff. I was also rereading about the twenty-one people who had died and come back. Their stories all matched perfectly even though some of their stories were in different issues. It is their stories which really bother me, because now I have died and I *know* that there are twenty-one people who have fooled and lied to *The Realms of Twilight Tabloid News of the World.* But, when Susan called, I decided to close the papers and go out. Sometimes Susan can be just the wild thing I need.

When she picked me up in her Pinto, she told me we were going to a Daycare Fund Raiser at the Redwood Club, and that there would be a male stripper, and she laughed and blew cigarette smoke all over the windshield. I have read about male strippers in at least five magazines. The women all had good things to say in the articles, and in the pictures, the women looked like they were having a good time.

It was twelve dollars at the door, and the woman stamped our hands with a little purple star. The Redwood Club is just a big barroom with a real low sparkling ceiling. Susan knew a lot of the women there and we joined a table with three of her friends near the front. We had been drinking a little vodka in the car, and we had some more, and it was just flat fun being half high out of the house with a room full of women who were just roaring and carrying on.

There were actually two strippers. The first guy was announced as Rick. He came out to a record, the Supremes singing something, and he was very serious about removing his brown silk shirt, and then his brown silk pajama bottoms or whatever they were, and then he played a coy game of thumbs with his G-string for the rest of the song. The second and final song for Rick was The Four Seasons singing "Big Girls Don't Cry." He came stepping between the tables like a stretching cat, and Susan actually reached out and stuffed a dollar bill inside his jock along with all the other dollars hanging there like a bouquet.

I'm a buns person. Why that is, I don't know. But buns can start me up. I loved the arch of Rick's rear, and when he finally stripped off the G-string and flopped his petunia before us all, Susan and the girls went wild! Susan was laughing and bouncing in her seat and reaching for what she was calling "that banana." But Rick was a professional; I could tell by the way he kept just beyond an arm's length.

Then there was a very funny vodka intermission with everyone groaning and laughing and snorting and Susan laughing and asking me wasn't I glad I came, and you know, I was glad. Not because of Rick's buns, but because of a warm feeling I had. I really liked Susan and her attitude and the fact that she was a friend of mine.

In high school, when we were juniors, she stopped me after homeroom one morning in the spring and took my arm tightly and walked me down to her locker, smiling so her eyes nearly shut, and she told me she was going to get married. "You're the first person I've told," she said to me. "And you're the only person. Do me a favor," she laughed, "break it to our dear classmates." And then she said, "You know why we're doing it?" And she laughed so hard she dropped a book and could hardly get through her own answer, which she had to whisper: "To give the baby a father!" Then she straightened herself out and lifted her chin like a queen and walked off down the corridor, turning once to announce: "The facts of life."

Now, I'm no good judge of penises. Grant had one, I'm sure. He must have, I think. But the next stripper, Doug, made it clear from his entrance on, that he was out to set new standards for us all. Susan was crazy for him. He would back way up then open his shirt and stride toward the audience as if he was going to jab us all with that heavy G-string. Everyone would scream when he did that. Susan couldn't stop laughing. She did yell: "What have you got in there anyway, Dougie?" And everybody thought the same thing: that is not all him. Susan would yell, "What is that, a shoe?" and the Redwood Club would just go nuts. But at the end of the third song

(Doug stretched his strip to three records), which was Elvis singing "My Way," we all found out the truth. He turned his back on us and flexed his buns in a way that almost made me shudder, and he flipped his G-string into the fourth row, another eruption of screaming, and he rotated to us revealing the most god-awful THING— and that is the right word, "THING"—in the whole world. It looked like a hammer. The place exploded. There was more screaming than if there'd been a fire. He lobbed it around for a good while, and I'm sure people passing by in cars could hear The Redwood Club rising off the earth. It's lucky for me I like buns, I told Susan, or I would have embarrassed myself. A lot of women did.

After that session died down, we plunged outside and the fresh air really made us drunk. Susan hopped on the hood of her car and leaned against the windshield. The sky was full of stars. It was funny sitting there. I thought: all these stars, are they out every night? I'd never seen the stars before. We sat on her car and drank a little more vodka. Susan had been sweating and the hair over her face was wet in a little fringe. She was smiling, kind of wicked, like she knew things were going to be like this all along. After a while, she said, "You know, all this entertainment has made me kind of hungry. Let's go eat."

We went over to Rose's, where I'd never been at night before, and the place was empty except for Leo, Rose's husband, who served us two Burrito Specials and cold beer. God, it was fun sitting there at night, like being girls. When Leo would bring another beer, Susan would keep her head down, her eyes under her eyebrows going to his crotch, and then back to my eyes, and we'd laugh until we couldn't even eat. It was like we had this great big secret on all men.

Grant had never liked to go out to dinner with me. I always liked to read the whole menu, every word. For me it's part of the pleasure of dining out. Grant liked to order the same thing all the time: spaghetti or burgers. He'd order and I wouldn't be through reading Column A. I loved to read phrases in some of the places like "nestled amid french fries aplenty" or even "smothered with onions." I

always ordered the item which was the most well written. I don't
need to tell you what Grant thought of that.

The rest of the night with Susan happened a little too quickly. We
were driving down Front Street and we hit the hill a bit fast, and
Susan couldn't make the corner. That part went slow. We drifted
wide in the turn, and when the tire hit the island between the four
lanes, I looked at Susan, and she was still smiling like this was all
expected. The Pinto wouldn't straighten up. It rose over the island
and gently and quietly steered into the deserted lobby of the
Cambert Hotel. Grant and I spent our wedding night at the
Cambert Hotel, and as the glass doors burst and I saw the front desk,
I knew I was going to die. There was no sound. The last thing I felt
was my back coming through my chest, and I was dead.

Now, this is the real part: it was not a white room. I did not float
above a white room. There was no white room into which my relatives floated one at a time. Do you see? There was no white room.
It was not a room at all, but a tiny cave, black as black, no light
whatsoever. No relatives drifting in to hug me. I felt like I'd been
hammered in the little cave, and there was a pair of sunglasses
underneath my right hip, poking me. It really hurt. I could feel the
cave wall with my hands and the wall was damp and cold, and I
could tell I was stuck. There were piles and piles of old shoes on top
of me and *there was no music.* I listened for a long time and there
was a little noise, it was a distant rasping, muffled by all the shoes,
and it sounded like a fork on a pie plate. Then it was quiet for I
don't know how long. I couldn't move and I couldn't go to sleep.
But there was no music. I waited and waited, just feeling those sunglasses under my thigh, and I thought any minute I might hear
Susan laughing or see some person in a white robe coming to greet
me. Nothing. I was smothering under all those shoes in a dark cave,
rubbing my fingertips up and down the walls feeling the slime, and
I did this for a long time. I mean, up to what I thought was three
or four weeks. Nothing. And I came to know that this was it: I was
dead, that's all. I wished I had something to read. But even if I'd had

something, it was too dark. I did get kind of mad at those twenty-one liars who had made money spinning fibs to *The Realms of Twilight Tabloid News of the World.*

Later I heard some quiet chipping noises, like someone putting cups away. Then in the quiet dark, I realized that I was going to come back from the dead. All that happened was this: the rock became softer and I stretched my legs through it and pushed my hands through it and reached around and removed that damn pair of sunglasses jabbing my butt and the shoes floated away and I leaned my head back into the soft putty-like rock and I was in this bed. A moment later Dr. Fergus came in and used his little flashlight on me.

Later still, Grant came by and brought me some magazines and said some words while I lay very still and squinted at his crotch.

So, all I want to say is this. I've read those goddamned liars in the papers, and I'm here to tell you there's no white room. I crashed into the lobby of the Cambert Hotel, where I spent my wedding night, and I was killed along with my best friend since before high school, Susan McArgul. And after being dead for three and a half weeks my time, and almost four minutes your time, I was allowed to return from being dead. Susan McArgul didn't get to return. Now, those are the real facts of life.

PHENOMENA

FIRST OF all, I'm not one of these people who ever wanted to see a UFO, an unidentified flying object. I have never wanted to see an unidentified anything. The things in my life, I identify; that's good with me. I'm not one of these people who is strange or weirded-out over unexplainable phenomena. I don't want any phenomena at all, and we're lucky in Cooper, because there isn't much phenomena. About the time there is a little phenomena, I identify the phenomena and throw them in jail.

I'm the sheriff.

So I'm not a weirdo. Things happen sometimes and I do my best. My name is Derec Ferris, and I've traced the Ferrises back all the way to Journey City, near the border, and there isn't a weirdo in the whole bunch. Now, I'm the sheriff; you notice I didn't say I'm the law around here. Whitney used to say he was the law around here. That was when he was sheriff. I can tell you exactly when he stopped saying that. Four years ago in September. We were together in his car late one night after coffee at The World, and we nailed this speeder right down from the high school. A rented Firebird, gunmetal gray. Actually we flashed him on the curve of Quibbel's Junk Yard and it took us the whole mile of town to slow down.

We pulled him over in front of Cooper Regional, where Whitney and I had been Cougars for four years together. It was about two in the morning. Whitney put his hand on my arm and went up to the Pontiac. I could see he was working up his sarcastic rage; he used to say that eighty percent of being a good sheriff was acting. Anyway, he starts: "Who do you think you are, endangering the lives of the citizens of Cooper by whipping through here at eighty-two miles an hour?" And the guy goes: "I'm Dan Blum, and I'm late. Who do you think you are?" Whitney loves that, an opening. "I'm Whitney Shields and I'm the law around here." Well, Dan Blum, as his name actually turned out to be, thought that was the funniest thing he'd ever heard, and after a little chuckle, he said, "Say, that's great. So, it's your wife that sleeps with the law." That comment seemed to confuse Whitney, even though he slapped the guy for seventy-five big ones, and he never said that about being the law again.

That was, like I said, four years ago, and since then Whitney's in-laws have had troubles outside Chicago, and he and Dorothy, who was also a Cougar with us, and whom I had also known for forty-one years, moved over there, and they might as well be on another world for all I hear from them. This is all to say, I'm not the law. I'm fifty-five years old and I've lived in this county all my life, except for fourteen months when I lived in Korea employed by Uncle Sam. My name is Derec Ferris and that's who sleeps with my wife.

The fact is, I'm still surprised that Whitney left. I mean, where is he? I still expect to see him squashing his stool at the counter at The World every time I walk in there. Hell, he grew up here along the river just like I did; he and I and Harold were the three musketeers. We worked for Nemo at Earth Adventure two summers in high school, and we gained four hundred and forty-four yards passing as Cooper Cougars in 1949, setting a record that stood until 1957. Then: poof! he's gone, and I'm sheriff. I've got his car and everything. It still smells like him.

I don't want to talk about it. At all. What I want to talk about is the Unidentified Object that has come into my life, the whole unidentified flying object day, so that you can see I'm not a phenomena weirdo; I'm only Derec Ferris, the sheriff here in Cooper.

First of all, I'm not going to give you any theory, because I don't have any. And I don't want any. Where did it come from? I don't care. I've been here in Cooper all my life and it might have come from over in Mercy or even Griggs. It kind of looked like something from Griggs. I don't care. It was a UFO. It might have come from Korea; try to tell me that's on this earth. And why did it come? *Please.* I'm going to give you the day, the whole day, and—really— nothing but the day.

First thing: Sarah calls. She says we received a card from Derec; that's our son, same name. He works for a textbook publisher in Palo Alto, California, and he's a painter. Paints pictures. Well, it's a little news, because we haven't seen him in five years, and we don't get that much mail. Every time I drive by Cooper Regional I think about him, though. Even then when he was in high school refusing to play football, he said he couldn't wait to get out of here, Cooper, and go to California. Which he did. I feel bad about it, and I miss him, but I figure it this way: at least somebody got what he wanted.

Sarah says that Derec is going to have a show. Well. I don't know what that is, and she explains that it is a show of his paintings and it is good news. She wants to go. She is excited on the telephone. I tell her great, but there's a radio call coming in, I'll talk to her later, and I hang up. I thought: I want to go, too.

I want to go and hold down my stool at The World and drink my gallon of coffee, but Arvella the dispatcher says it's something from Nemo out at Earth Adventure, a bear attack or something. So I lock up and I drive out to Earth Adventure.

On the way out I'm thinking about Derec and his show, and I'm kind of blue thinking about what he ever thinks of his old man. Did you ever do that, wonder what your grown kids think of you? The times you tried, the times you didn't try. No matter who you are, I think, you still want your boy to be like you. Derec *is* like me, with his ears, and he's got the build, but the rest . . . I don't know.

Old Earth Adventure is about on its last legs. If you didn't know where you were going, I doubt you could find the place. The two terrific signs Nemo put up before Harold, Whitney, and I worked for him are all peeled to hell, and a Chinese elm has taken the best one, the one with the dinosaur peeking over at the boatload of people. You can still see the profile of the dinosaur poking up above the sign, but you can't read a word through the bushes.

It turned out not to be a bear attack. I knew it wouldn't be. Nemo's bear, Alex, hasn't been awake for about two years. It turned out to be Monty, the old cougar, who must be forty now and who's lost most of his hair and teeth and whose skin sags off his bones like it was somebody else's suit; Monty had fallen out of a tree and broke his hind leg on the hood of some tourist's Ford. By the time I arrived, Monty had already dragged himself into the women's restroom and he was growling in the corner like an old man getting ready for his last spit. His poor old rheumy eyes were full of tears. Hell, I'd known him from a kitten when they found him west of Mercy at the Ringenburgs', crying in the barn being harassed by a dozen swallows. I'd fed that cat a lot of corndogs the summer I was seventeen and worked the boats.

So I kept guard by the women's room door, so nobody would get a surprise, while we waited for Doctor Werner to come out from town. The guy from the Ford was arguing, or trying to argue, with Nemo about the damage and the scare and the hazard, and all Nemo would do was point at me and say, "There's the sheriff." But the guy wasn't coming near me or the shack where Monty was dying. Finally he left and the vet pulled up in his black van. I stayed with him while he drugged the big old cat. Then Werner and Nemo had a little talk outside while I watched Monty's tongue loll farther and farther out of his mouth. Just above him in the stall, somebody had carved "Kill All Men" in uneven printing.

When the two men came back they had decided that this was it for Monty, and Werner said he'd haul him off. But Nemo said no, said to put him to sleep right there in the women's room, so Werner did. Monty, who was already asleep, didn't even quiver.

Then Nemo and Werner argued about money for a while, Nemo trying to give the doc a twenty and the doctor not even looking Nemo in the face, saying, "No way, Nemo, not this time. No charge." They pushed that twenty back and forth twenty times like two men in a restaurant, and finally the vet climbed in his van and headed out.

Nemo stood there with his twenty still in his hand in the middle of the dirt road and said he was pretty close to it this time. If he lost any more animals, Earth Adventure would have to close. You couldn't charge people four bucks a car to drive along a half mile dirt road to see one bear sleeping in a way that showed his worn out old ass, a plastic tiger Nemo had gotten from the Exxon station in Clinton, six peacocks, and four hundred geese. "It was different with a mountain lion," he said. "Monty was *something*."

Old Nemo. I told him not to worry, he still had the underground canal trips, but that wasn't too good either, since the boats—the same boats I worked—are in pretty bad condition. One sank last summer out from under a family from Mercy. It was lucky for Nemo the boat went down just outside the tunnel, where the water is only a foot deep, or he'd have had genuine legal action.

So I stood there with old Nemo, looking around at Earth Adventure crumbling in the weeds. I could see it clearly: the closed sign across his gate next summer. After a while, he thumbed his overall strap and went to get an old canvas mail bag and started filling it with the round white rocks that he uses to line the paths.

"Can I help you, Nemo?" I said, and he opened the bag.

"Right here," is all he said.

So I lifted Monty, who must have weighed ninety pounds, and Nemo helped guide him into the bag. He cinched the tie and started dragging the bag toward the canal. When we got there, he wanted to put it in one of the boats, and by the time I'd helped him do that, I was committed. He climbed in the bow of the old peeling boat and there was that seat in the stern. I found one paddle in the weeds and took my place. The boat was so weathered and shot I couldn't tell which one it had been; it could have been mine once.

When I was seventeen, we came out here—Whitney, Harold, and I—and Nemo hired us piecework. We each had a boat and we got seventy-five cents a tour. In those days Nemo had a little dock strung with Christmas lights, and summer nights it was great. There was a popcorn stand right there too, so people could feed the ducks, all those mallards tame as barnducks in the bright water. We'd tear the tickets and Whitney would feed them to the ducks whenever he ran out of other bad jokes.

I'd get five people in my boat, and I'd pole off. "These are the natural wonders of Cooper," I'd say as we entered the cave. "They were formed a million million years ago. They have found albino perch in these waters and there may still be creatures as yet undiscovered beneath us. The legend is that a trip through this wonder makes you five years younger or five years older depending on how you've treated your mother and father. Please keep your hands inside the boat."

Now Nemo perched on his seat, his knees together, as I steered us out into the cool dark of the cavern. I hadn't been in here for years. I used to have to come down and chase teenagers out and break up their beer parties, but it wasn't too hard, because I knew my way around. There in the quiet dark with Nemo, I could almost hear Harold doing his romantic version of the tour for his boat. It was like singing. Or Whitney kidding with the passengers, laughing and telling off-color jokes, "Keep your hands inside the boat, not there, buddy. Lady, keep your hands to yourself; just because it is dark there is no need to turn into an aborigine." The passengers in his boats would laugh and call back and ahead and go "Wooo-woooo!" And at the other end, Whitney always got the tips.

For me it was a job. I was saving for a car that turned out to be a used 1939 Buick. For Harold, it was romantic, each little trip got him a little. He believed it; he even painted a name on his boat: The Santa Maria. For Whitney, it was fun.

And then later, after I met Sarah, we all used to stay around almost every night, make a tour or two. Stop in the middle, bump around in the boats. It smelled nice then, like sand and willows, before the water treatment plant went in and raised the temperature. The five of us would take a boat in. Whitney and a date, Sarah and I, and Harold. Whitney would start on his spiel about how no virgin had ever emerged from these caverns, and he would let Sarah and me off midway on the limestone ledge, and then he'd take Harold to the far end where Harold would sit with his guitar and just play and play. Sometimes he'd sing, "Stormy Weather" or "Pennies from Heaven." Sarah and I would eat the popcorn and talk about high school or the families who came to Earth Adventure. We could hear Whitney hauling around in the boat, saying, "Come on; come on," to some girl from Mercy, a waitress, or somebody he'd picked up that night. He and I were clearly different that way. I never touched a girl casually in my life, not to this day. Whitney never touched them any other way. And I guess, Harold never touched one at all. I don't know. Anyway, they were great nights.

When Nemo and I passed the ledge, he lifted his hand and looked ahead. There was one rock column and then we could see the end, the rough triangle of light that opened on the river.

"This is good right here," he said.

He started to stand, but I motioned him down, and I got up and took hold of the bag. I set it carefully on the gunwale and looked at Nemo. All I could see against the light was his silhouette, and it didn't move. I waited. He didn't say anything, so I set the bag out and let the water take it.

NOW, REMEMBER, this is the day of the phenomenon. I went back to the jail and filed the report and by then it was lunchtime. I went over to The World and had the liver and onions for an hour. All that reminiscing had me hungry.

It was Monday, like I said, and so I knew they'd have a workout at the high school. I parked across the tennis court with the radio on in case Arvella came up with something, and watched practice. Well, here it was only the second week of school, still summer really, so I knew no one would be breaking his back, but still, I was disappointed when one of the coaches blew the whistle and the practice fell apart and the kids sauntered off toward the gym. I had been dreaming a little, but I still didn't see anything that was going to beat Griggs. For a minute I thought of the sheriff going over to the two coaches and giving them a word to the wise. But: nope.

It made me a little sad, sitting there in the car after the field had emptied. Football. As great as it was for Whitney and me, football was one of the first things Derec and I argued about. I couldn't understand why he didn't want to play, but after I saw that he really didn't want to, I let it go. I didn't care if he played or didn't; it wasn't worth fighting over. But I don't think he ever understood that. I think to the day he left Cooper he thought I was disappointed. As a man, sometimes, I find there are some things I can do nothing about. The words just won't line up in my mouth.

I went down to The World for my evening coffee until it was dark and then I got the call from Arvella, the only other call that day. Somebody was injured out to the Passion Play Center. I have a call or two out there every summer. Somebody gets a snakebite behind the stage or a flat settles on somebody's foot as they're shifting scenery in the dark. But this time I was a little worried because Arvella said, as she was signing off, that she thought it was Harold Kissel. And Harold is now pushing three hundred pounds and if he missed a step out of his trailer or fell off the apron, it would be serious.

I've been told that every community has a Harold Kissel, my old friend. I doubt it. He'd moved to Cooper with his mother when we were in tenth grade and for two years everybody thought he was from New York, and he didn't tip his hand about it either. His manners were amazing. I mean it was amazing that he had any, because I guess, none of the rest of us did. But he had a hat, a dark derby sort of hat and he'd tip it, and he'd hold doors for about everybody, and the things he'd do with his napkin even in The World were worth watching. It's funny, but he never took much guff for any of it, everybody just kind of knew him: eccentric. That's why I liked him and why he was the only friend I had who wasn't on the football team.

He wasn't allowed to go to Korea either, which was a relief for just about everybody in town, because by that time, the year after we graduated, everybody liked Harold in their own way. While I was gone, he started and became director of the Cooper Players and was just known for that. He was the theater. Sarah wrote me about the productions. She helped sew costumes, even the curtain for the stage at the old Episcopal Church.

When I came back from Korea, which is a cold place mostly, Sarah and I were married in the Lutheran Church, and Harold was one of the ushers along with Whitney who was also best man. The first year I was a deputy, Harold's mother died, and he went away. Sarah was real worried. She and Whitney's wife, Dorothy, had been in two plays by then. They kind of starred in *Arsenic and Old Lace* as the aunts. You should have seen Sarah as an old lady. I told her right then that I'd love her my whole life, because even with white hair and big gray lines all over her face, she was too pretty to stand. Oh, and they were also in *Julius Caesar* after that. They were two Roman soldiers, which was pretty goofy in my opinion, but it was okay, because about nine people total saw that deal. So when Harold's mother passed away, Sarah was worried. There was a lot of talk. The Playhouse, as they were calling the church, had added a lot to Cooper, especially in the winter, and people said it would be a shame to lose it.

Where he went for four years, nobody knows. I know that, because he never told me. Some say he finally went to New York and there was a rumor about his going to France or Africa. No clues. When he came back, he had the beginnings of the fat and he looked worn. Hell, we all do. He had a meeting of the old Cooper Players and announced that what this town needed was "a passion play."

That was thirty years ago. The passion play has become the biggest thing about Cooper really. People say, "Have you been over to the Cooper Passion Play?" It's a real institution. Every summer thousands of people see Harold play the life of Christ, and I've seen it quite a few times myself. The local joke is that whenever anybody says Jesus H. Christ, the H. stands for Harold.

He's real good in all the parts where he's among the children and disciples. He knows how to walk and he's got great hand movements, but the part which everyone remembers, the part which has been told across the counter in The World ten thousand times is when the music starts and the lights go out. The last thing you see is Mary Magdalene and the others on their knees weeping and praying and then the darkness in the amphitheater, just the sky with all our stars, sometimes the moon on a little cloud cruise, and the music real low and sad along with the sound effects of some hammering.

Then, Harold climbs those stairs behind the cross and steps out and places his arms on the crossbars, his head hung down at the perfect angle, and pow! the spotlight puts everybody's eyes out with the white circle of Jesus on the cross: you can feel the chilly waves of goose bumps cross over the whole audience. Even his bald spot jumps at you in the scene like a halo. I remember listening to his voice in the Earth Adventure Caverns as he sang, "Stormy Weather," and I know he's just a man with the God-given ability to give others the chills.

The cross had come down while Harold was setting his arms up on the crossbar. The cross was old and Harold was heavy. The old timber leaned over and ripped out of the stage like a tree in a storm. They said it sounded like a bomb. Harold had hit the stage hard and there was blood and make-up blood everywhere. He wasn't moving. The cross had clobbered Bonnie Belcher who was playing Mary Magdalene and a high school girl from Mercy, but they were both okay, just lots of blood. They hadn't moved a thing. Feely told me they were afraid they would break his back. So, I had it all right there. I thought this is what happens: Whitney is gone, dead to me, and now Harold is killed.

I knelt over him, but I couldn't feel a pulse and I couldn't tell if he was breathing. In that loincloth he looked like a great big dead kid, a two-year-old. By this time I was crying, or tears were just coming, I don't know. And I didn't care. I had to get Feely and Jerry—who plays Judas—to help me lift the cross off Harold and we dragged it back and dropped it off the rear of the stage. Then I heard this noise. Clapping. Out there in the dark, about half the audience still waited to see what was going to happen to Jesus now. It must have looked pretty strange to see the sheriff bending over him. And it was strange for me too; I couldn't see the people at all.

I was scared. We wrestled Harold into the ambulance and he never made a noise, not a gurgle or a groan. Then Jerry shut the doors and Boyce drove away. Jerry turned to me and said, "You better say something, Derec. The people aren't leaving." There I was out there in the dark talking to Judas in his nightgown, Jerry Beemer, who is going to be the assistant manager at the Dairy Creme in Griggs all his goddamned life, and he is instructing me as to what I had better do. And what really made me boil, on top of being sick and scared, was that I knew he was right. I went back up onto the stage in the lights and stood in front of the blood stain and said, "He's going to be all right, folks. You can go home now. And be careful driving. Those of you parked to the side can slip back to 21 through Gilmers' place, even though it is the entrance."

It was real quiet for a second, but then I heard the shuffling, and the families sorted themselves out and went off in the dark.

ON THE WAY home I didn't want to see another thing. I didn't want to see the UFO. I'd seen enough for one day already. I just wanted to see Sarah. It was after one in the morning and I just wanted to see her. She'd be asleep, which was good because I didn't want to go over anything again. I try not to tell her any of what goes on with my work; it's all either ridiculous or hideous—who wants to hear that? If she asks me about something, I try to wait and let it pass. I can wait.

There's a lot inside a man that never gets out; I don't understand that or pretend to understand it, but if women ever knew that those waits, those times that I stir my coffee, twenty times right, twenty times left, were just full, full of the way a day crams my heart full, if women knew how much was in a man, they'd never let up. But there's nothing I can do about it. The worse something is, the deeper I keep it. That's the law.

If Sarah won't let it go, if she gets on me, I have a simple strategy:

I turn and ask when she's going to have that rummage sale and get rid of some of the junk in the garage and the basement. That'll start her. She's a woman who has saved everything she's ever had in her hand. I won't go into it, but she has a box of egg cartons once touched by her Uncle Elias and they remind her of him. Actually, they do me too.

Anyway, I don't tell her all the ugly details of being sheriff. And I especially didn't want to tell her about Harold and how he fell and killed himself. All I want to do is see her there sleeping and to crawl into the bed by her.

It was 1:20 A.M. I was driving home and I was a tired man.

Now get ready. At 13 and 30, where I turn for home, there at Chernewski's Tip-a-Mug, I saw the UFO. It sat down in the road right in front of me. Actually, I heard it as I slowed for the four way. There was a clanking—awful—like a pocket knife in the drier. I mean a real painful sound, some machine about to die, and then: *whomp!* The whole contraption dropped onto Route 30, hard as a wet bale.

At first I thought a combine had turned over; I didn't know what was going on. I couldn't see it too well. It just sat there clanking and hissing. I could also hear it spitting oil on the pavement; honest to god, this UFO was a wreck. I stood out of the car. I could see all the terrible plumbing caging several gray oil drums and rusty boxes, and lots of little ladders, some missing rungs. The wiring ran along the outside of the heavy ductwork, taped there by somebody in a hurry.

Then the smell hit me. It had been burning oil and something else, something like rubber or plastic. The fumes were thick, billowing off one side just like the train wreck over at Mercy when the asphalt truck got creamed last winter.

I was going to go up to the thing to see if anybody was hurt, but the way it was settling, jumping around like a winged duck, and banging, I was afraid it would all give way and fall right on me.

Besides, about then I saw the alien. A door slammed open right then, falling out like the gate on the back of a pickup. And I stood there in the dark while the alien climbed down.

Now the alien, the alien. The alien looked a lot like my boy, Derec. To me, the alien looked like my son. It was a kid about twenty-three years old wearing a sleeveless white T-shirt with the words JOHN LENNON on the front. He wore greasy green surgical pants and tennis shoes. No socks. He jumped onto Route 30 and walked past me this close and looked in the backseat of the car. Then he folded his hands like this, across his chest like he was confused. Then he looked in again and put his hands on top of the car like this, like he was waiting to be frisked or just thinking it all over. I don't know what he'd expected to be in the car, but it wasn't there. Then I found out. He looked at me, and this is going to sound like a weirdo, like some airbrain who likes these encounters, but he looked in that moment just like Derec. He said to me, "Where's Harold?"

Well, I was a little surprised by that. I didn't know what to say. And I didn't have to say anything. He skipped past me again, walking just like Derec, bouncing a little in those tennis shoes, and he climbed back up in that crazy rig. He had to slam that tailgate hatch or whatever it was four times to get it to stay closed, and the last time I heard glass break and sprinkle onto Route 30.

I stepped back, watching all the time. The UFO cranked itself up into a frenzy, the hissing made me squint. He had it revved up and shaking, just a raw sound for three or four minutes, more than any engine I know could take. Then it jumped, and that's the right word: *jumped,* ten feet straight up, and it came down again hard, really shaking, and then it jumped and hovered up over Route 30. As it climbed up a little ways, I could see a small propeller on the under carriage—and the oil was dripping onto that and it sprayed me a good one going by. After I couldn't see the UFO anymore or hear it, thank God, or smell it, all I could hear were the crickets and the buzzing of Chernewski's Tip-a-Mug neon sign with that silly cocktail glass tipped and fizzing the three green bubbles, and all there was left on the road was the worst oil spill you'd want to see. I went over to it and it was oil all right, dirty oil that hadn't been changed in five or six thousand miles of hard driving, and I found all these pieces of glass. Looks like some kind of Mason jar. And I found this one bolt. It's left-handed. The oil stain is still out there—over both lanes, for you to see for yourselves. You can't miss it: four or five gallons—at least.

That was the UFO.

I WAS A boy in this town. And now I am a man in this town. A lot of things happen some days. Somebody'll die and there'll be a mattress in the backyard. Some kid driving a hard hangover and an asphalt truck won't see a train and there'll be smoke clear to Griggs. And some days nothing happens. The flies won't move five inches down the counter in The World. Some days things happen, and some days nothing does, but at the end of each I have to lie down. I lie by Sarah, the collector of treasures, in our bed which is surrounded by rooms full of the little things of our lives. She still has the ticket stubs from the game with Mercy, our first date, and they too sleep in some little box in some drawer in our house. I lie by Sarah in my place on earth, and slowly—it takes hours—I empty for the earth and turn to prepare me for the next thing, another day.

Sarah is in the bed under the covers in the shape I will always identify. Her form is identifiable. "The hospital called," she says. She's awake. I button my pajamas and don't answer. I don't want to get started. I don't want to get started on Harold and go over the whole thing. I climb heavily into bed. "Delores called from the hospital." I weigh nine hundred pounds; sleep is coming up around my eyes like warm water. "Delores called from the hospital. She said Harold is going to be all right."

I float in the bed by my wife Sarah's side. I know she is going to go on. "I made reservations for Palo Alto, for Derec's show. We're going next Thursday, so get the time off. You want to go, don't you?"

"Yeah," I say. "Yeah." Sleep rises in me like sweet smoke. It is late here in Cooper. It kind of feels late everywhere. Maybe it is just late for me. My son Derec. We're going to Palo Alto, California. We're going to fly out there.

MILK

THEY ALMOST fingerprint the children before I can stop them. Phyllis is making a rare personal appearance in my office to help me with a motorcycle injury claim, and I want to squeeze every minute out of her, and I'm taking no calls. We all call Phyllis "The Queen of Wrongful Death," which is the truest nickname in the firm. She likes being a hard case, and she's lording it over me a bit this morning, rereading a lot of the stuff that I'd summarized for her, when Tim buzzes and says Annie's on the line.

I almost wave it off. She probably wants to meet for lunch and today there's going to be no lunch, because I want to get this motor-cycle case buttoned up so we can take the twins on a picnic this weekend. Now that they can walk, our house is getting real small. But it's not lunch. Annie's voice is down a note or two, stern, as she says she and my mother are going to take the boys down to Community Fuel, where there is another fingerprint program today. I listen to Annie tell the story and watch Phyllis frowning through the file. My mother read about the program in the paper and with so many children abducted and missing, etc. etc. etc. Annie closes with *I know what you think, but this is something we should do for your mother's sake.*

I don't say anything.

"Jim?" Annie says.

"Ann. You said it. You know what I think. *No way.* Not the twins. Not for my mother. Not for anybody."

"She's coming over to get us in half an hour."

"Ann," I say again. "Take her to lunch, but do not fingerprint the boys. Okay? Under no circumstances. That's all."

"It's no big deal . . ."

"Tell my mother that."

"I'm going to tell your mother that you're terrified and unable at this time to do the right thing."

When I hang up, Phyllis looks up. At thirty-four she wears those imperious half glasses, which, in a drunken moment at the firm barbeque last summer, she admitted to me are just part of her costume, "dress to win"; and I admit now that they intimidate me.

"Fingerprints?" she says. "Are the twins being booked?"

"It's that I.D. program at Community Fuel. My mother wants to take the kids."

"And . . . ?"

"My kids are not being fingerprinted. I'm not caving in to this raging paranoia. It's a better world than people think."

Phyllis takes off her awful glasses and lets them drop on their necklace against her breast. "And you're not scared in the least, are you?"

WHEN I come home from work, Lee and Bobby laugh their heads off. It has become my favorite part of the day. I peek into the kitchen and say, "Oh-oh!" and they amble in stiffly in their tiny overalls, arms up for balance. They start: "Oh-oh!" as I pick them up and they laugh and laugh as we do our entire repertoire of sounds: *Dadda, Momma, Baby,* and the eleven or twelve other syllables, as well as a good portion of growling, humming, meowing, mooing, and buzzing. When I whistle softly through my teeth, they hug me hard to make me stop.

They are fraternal twins. Bobby has a lot of hair and a full face.

Lee, though he probably weighs the same, twenty-two pounds, seems slighter, more fragile. Ironically, Bobby cries more and easier. They can lie on a blanket with fists full of each other's hair, and only Bobby will fuss. They each have four and a half teeth and they call each other the same name: *Baby.*

Tonight I lift them up and the laughing intensifies as I tote them into the living room where Annie is picking up the blanket and toys.

She starts right in: "Well, boys, it's Daddy, the Rulemaker."

"Annie . . ."

"The lawgiver." She holds the bundle in her arms and stands to face me. She goes on in a gruff voice: "*No fingerprints. Not in this house! Not for anybody!*"

Bobby and Lee think this is wonderful and they laugh again. Each has a good hold on my hair and their laughing pulls my scalp in two directions. Annie comes right up to the boys and makes a mock frown, her nose against mine. She growls. "*Not even for my mother!*" She kisses me quickly and disappears into the boys' room. The boys snap around to watch her and the hair pulling brings tears to my eyes.

Annie's got me. We've been married nine years, and it's been a good marriage. We've grown up together really, and only since the boys have arrived have I started with this rule stuff. Annie and I used to go crazy after visiting our friends Stuart and Ruth and their kids. Everything was rules. *No baseball in the backyard. No jackets in the basement. No magazines in the kitchen. No loud talking in the hall. No snacks during homework.* We promised then never to post rules. Driving home from their house, Annie and I would make up rules and laugh until we'd have to pull over. *No hairdryers in the bathtub. No looking out the window while someone is talking to you. No peeking at the answers to the crossword puzzle. No shirt, no shoes, no service.* And Annie even gave Ruth one of our ridiculous lists, typed up as a joke (their lists were typed and posted on the refrigerator door), but Ruth did not think it was that funny. She said, "Wait until you have kids."

And now I have both kids in my arms when Annie comes back into the room. "Call your mother," she says, taking Lee from me and putting him in his high chair. "She wants to know why you're not looking out for the best interest of your children. Put Bobby in his chair before you call, okay?"

WE'VE BEEN through this all before, but I can see this week is going to be worse. I watched the news programs on television and saw the troops of children being fingerprinted. I made it clear from the beginning that we did not want to do that. Annie watched my opposition grow over the weeks, realizing that this was probably the biggest disagreement in our marriage.

"I don't understand you," she said. "You're a lawyer, for Petes' sakes. You like things nailed down. What's the problem?"

But she said it as: what's *your* problem? I watched the children, many babies, being fingerprinted. I couldn't express what my problem was.

And my mother wanted to know why, in light of all the missing children and the recent abductions, why wouldn't I do it *for their sake*.

"Because," I had explained to her at last, at the end of my patience: "Because the only use those prints will ever have is in identifying *a body*, okay? *Do you see?* They use them to identify the body. And my children will not need fingerprints, *because nothing is going to happen to my children*. Is that clear?" I had almost yelled at my mother. "We don't need fingerprints!"

Then my mother would be hurt for a few days and then silent for a few days, and then there'd be another news story and we'd do it all again.

Annie tried to intervene. "Stop being a jerk. It's not a big deal. It's not going to hurt the boys. They'll forget it. Your mother would feel better."

"No."

"Why not?"

I don't know how many times we had some version of that conversation, but I do know that once I took Annie's wrist and raged
through the house like the sorry creature I can be at times, pointing to the low surfaces, "Because, we've got fingerprints! Look!" I
made her look at the entryway door and the thousand hands
printed there, at the car windows, and the front of the fridge, and
finally the television, where a vivid hand printed in rice cereal made
Tom Brokaw on the evening news look like he was growing a beard.
"We have fingerprints. And I love these fingerprints. We don't need
any others."

All Annie said was, "Can I have this now?" She indicated her
arm. I let her go. She shook her head at me and went in to check
on the boys.

AND THERE was the milk.

I wanted Annie to change milk. We had been getting the Hilltop
green half-gallon cartons. Then they started putting children on the
back panels, missing children. Under the bold heading, MISSING,
would be two green and white photographs of the children, their statistics printed underneath: date of birth; age; height; eyes; hair;
weight; date missing; from. . . . The photographs themselves
assumed a lurid, tabloid quality, and everytime I opened the fridge
they scared me. I'd already seen ads for missing children on a weekly
mailer we receive which offers—on the flip side—discount coupons
for curtain and rug cleaning, optical services, and fast food, primarily chicken. And in Roy's Drug one night I dropped the Archie
comic I was going to buy for the boys (to keep them from ripping
up our art books), when I saw two missing children inside the front
cover. It was all getting to me.

One night late, I went into Smith's Food King and turned all the
Hilltop milk to the back panel so sixty children stared out from the
dairy case. I started it as a statement of some kind, but when I
stepped back across the aisle and saw their group sadness, all those
green and white poor resolution smiles, wan even in the bright Food

King light, I lost my breath. I fled the store and sulked home and asked Annie if we could buy another brand.

When I told her why, when I told her about the two kids taking a little starch out of the world for me when I opened the refrigerator at two A.M. to grab Bobby a bottle, those nights when he still fusses, Annie just said *No.*

TONIGHT AFTER I have the fifteenth version of my fingerprint call with my mother, I am out of tolerance, reason, generosity, and any of their relatives. I never swear in the company of my mother, and as I sit down in the kitchen and watch Annie spoon the boys their macaroni and strained beef, I think perhaps I should. I might not have this knot in my neck. There on the table is the Hilltop milk with somebody's picture on the back.

I don't know why, but I start: "Annie, I don't want this milk in the house."

She's cool. "And is there a reason for that, oh powerful Rulemaker?"

"I've told you the reason. I'm not interested in being depressed or in having my children frightened by faces of lost souls in the refrigerator."

Annie says nothing. She spoons the macaroni into Bobby's open mouth. After each mouthful, he goes: "mmmmnnnnn!" and laughs. It's something I taught the boys with Milupa and bananas, but Lee's version is softer, almost a sigh of satisfaction.

"What is the point? There is no point in publishing these lurid photographs."

"They're not lurid."

"What's the point? I am supposed to study the carton, cruise the city, stop every child walking home from school: *is he missing? would he like to go home now?* Really, what? I see some girl playing tennis against the practice wall in Liberty Park, am I supposed to match her with my carton collection of missing children?" I've raised my voice a little, I can tell, because Annie looks narrow-eyed, stony.

She hands me the spoon for Lee, who is smiling at me for yelling. Annie rises and takes the milk and puts it in the refrigerator. "Missing children don't get to play tennis," she says quietly, wiping Bobby up and putting him on the floor. Bobby goes immediately to the one cupboard I haven't safety clipped, opens it, and pulls a large bottle of olives onto his foot.

He watches the bottle roll across the floor and when it stops against the stove, he looks up into my face with his beautiful face and he starts to cry.

"Bobby's first," Annie says, plucking him from the floor. "Bobby's first in bed tonight!"

When she carts Bobby off, I let Lee out of his chair. I hand him his bottle out of the fridge and he takes it with both hands as if it were an award. He starts to walk off, then realizes, I guess, that Mom isn't here and he doesn't really know where to go. So, he looks up at me, a child who resembles an angel so much it is troubling. Then Annie is behind him, lifting him away, and I am left alone in the kitchen.

I wipe up the chairs and the floor and cap the macaroni and strained beef, but when I put them away, I see that green Hilltop milk carton.

"You want to close the fridge?" Annie is behind me.

"No, look. Look at this."

"Close the fridge door."

"Look!" I point at the child, his green and white photograph so grim in the bright light of the fridge.

I take one carton of milk out and close the fridge. I read aloud: "MISSING: Name: Richard Tarrel. D.O.B.: 10/21/82. Age: 4. Height: 2 feet 8 inches. Eyes: blue. Hair: light brown. Weight: 27 pounds. Date missing: 6/24/86. From: Omaha. . . ." I mean to make a point by reading it, but the *twenty-seven pounds* gets me a little, and by the time I read *Omaha,* I stop and sit down and look across at Annie. She looks like she is going to cry. She looks a lot like I have made her cry again.

She firms her mouth once and shakes her head as she stands up to leave the room. "Nebraska," she whispers. "Omaha, Nebraska."

I SIT at the kitchen table listening to Bobby and Lee murmuring toward sleep in their room, and I look at little twenty-seven-pound Richard Tarrel. Even in the poor quality photograph, he is beautiful, his eyes huge and dark, his lips pouted in a coy James Dean smile. There is no background in the photo, but I've been to Omaha. I can imagine the backyard somewhere out near 92nd Street, the swingset, the young peach tree Richard's father planted this summer, after the man at the nursery told him that though it was small, there would be peaches next fall.

THE NEXT morning, I've got the day trip to Denver, the quick deposition, and back on the nine o'clock. Annie is cordial to me in the morning, well, stern. I have a cup of coffee and pick at some of Bobby's scrambled eggs. Annie doesn't offer to have the whole gang drive me to the airport, which would have happened if we weren't fighting. I feel bad about it, kind of flat, but the boys will not have their fingerprints taken. I do not believe in it and it will not happen. Not my boys. It's a rule.

The flight over is rocky. The plane pitches heavily up the slope and then down, across the mountains to Denver. Sitting in the window seat of my row, one empty seat away, is a pale blond girl. I'm trying to fill in all the forms so I can maybe make the early plane tonight, but she stops me. I have to study her. She huddles to the window, her fragile face poised there, watching the unchanging grayness. Her Levi's are worn and the red plaid bag she clutches on her lap is years old. Her shirt is a blue stripe dress shirt that could have never, ever fit her; it is five sizes large. She sits in a linty, dark blue serape. I can't stop myself from looking at her. Date of Birth: 1969. Age: 17; Height: 5 feet 9 inches; Eyes: brown; Hair: light blond; Weight: 120; Date Missing. . . .

The girl turns her face to me in the bouncing airplane and speaks, her lips barely moving: "Don't," she says. "Please. Just don't."

My deposition is a witness to a motorcycle accident, a sophomore in psychology, and I meet him at the University Union in Boulder just after noon. In our hour, I learn: both children moved to avoid the cycle, but they moved different ways and one, the victim, our client, was hit and injured. My witness was driving pizza delivery behind the motorcycle and saw it all. Daylight. Sun to his back. A simple story. After the witness leaves for class, I sit in the modular furniture mesmerized for a while by the young people streaming around me.

There are children everywhere. All the way down the highway from Boulder to Denver, I see them alone and in groups, kicking along in the gravel. They all seem to need haircuts. I check my watch: two o'clock on a school day. Why isn't anybody where he's supposed to be? I think about our case; it's a given. I wonder what help the settlement will be to the parents of the hurt girl. I try to make the equation in my mind. We'll ask for six hundred thousand and get two. The girl's eleven years old and has one complete knee and six-tenths of the other. Let's see: she'll have that limp for sixty-eight years, if she lives her statistic. That's three thousand dollars a year not to walk like everyone else, or play soccer, I guess, or tennis. I ditch my rental car at the Avis curb, and think: what a strange man I'm becoming. What's happening to me?

The six o'clock is full so I hit the little sky-lounge near the gate and have a Manhattan. I used to love having an hour or two to ransack the magazines and have a Manhattan, my little joke living in the West, but now it's not much fun. There seems some urgency about getting home. I can't really settle down. I want to get home.

SOMETIMES, DRIVING home alone in the last two blocks before our house, a feeling descends upon me like a gift. It is as if a huge door opens and I can breathe differently, see the entire scope of our lives, and it makes me unreasonably happy. It makes me want to rush into the kitchen and sweep Annie up and cry: *forgive me, forgive us, let's never quarrel again, we have everything.* I don't know where the feeling comes from or how real it is, but I have it tonight as I turn into the driveway.

My mother's white Seville is parked to one side, something I didn't really want to see, but there's our house standing like a house in a story, an entire happy little world. The kitchen windows are beautiful yellow squares and a blue glow in the two small windows out front means they're watching television.

I vow to go in cheerfully and join them, open a beer, chat openly with the two women about everything. This fingerprint thing doesn't have to be such a big deal. We can agree. We can face the future without unreasonable fear.

In the kitchen, two blue Community Fuel Folders spill across the table. On the cover of each is a large white fingerprint the size of a head of lettuce. Underneath the print, it says: COMMUNITY I.D./PROJECT FINGERPRINT. I can hear the women talking in the other room under the television noises. I open the first folder and there it is in Annie's printing: Bobby Hensley. Date of Birth. Age. Weight. Hair. There is an empty square: place recent photograph here. And below: the ten smudges of Bobby's fingers.

I reach two bottles out of the fridge, one Nuk, one yellow nipple for Lee, and slip them inside my sportcoat. I tiptoe into the boys' room. Lee is asleep in a knot of blanket; Bobby lies on his side with his thumb loosely in his mouth experimenting with sounds: *doya, doya, moya.* He looks up at me calmly and smiles and then rolls to a crawl and stands in his crib. I pick him up and park him in a shoulder and then lift Lee like a melon under my forearm. I sweep the boys noiselessly through the kitchen and out to the car.

I am calm enough to strap them in their car seats, Lee asleep in the back and Bobby on the seat next to me in the front. I coast back down the driveway before starting the car, and I am on the road half a block before I pull the lights on.

"Ba," Bobby says as we pass a city bus in front of East High. "Ba."

"Bus," I say, the first word I've said aloud since my plane landed. "That's right. It's a bus."

The streets are luminous, wet and shiny, ticketed with early leaves, and our tires make the friction I have always loved to hear after rain.

So the streets whisper darkly as we slow at each bright intersection, the flaring Seven-Elevens, the flat white splash of a gas station. Then it is dark again, and we are driving.

Lee starts to squeak, which means he will babble for a while and then cry. He's a little tongue-tied and is gradually tearing the cord underneath by stretching his mouth in low squalls which becomes real crying after about a minute. I stop at the light at Fourth and State and give both boys their bottles.

We turn left onto State and head south, cruising by the jillion colored lights the kids love. In the rearview mirror, I can see Lee settled now in his seat. He has learned to balance the bottle on the carseat arm-tray, so his hands are free. Right now, they extend off to each side, palms up, and Lee opens and closes his hands slowly as he watches them and sucks on the bottle.

Bobby has his head tipped right to witness the spectacle of neon from the bars and motels, the bright dragon above the Double Hey Rice Palace, the pulsing tire in front of Big O. He has his bottle clutched in both hands and set hard in the side of his mouth like a cigar.

WHEN I was a boy I remember that my father would always pick up babies in restaurants. We'd go to Harmon's on North Temple about every other Sunday as a treat. My brother and I always had the gorgeous shakes, strawberry and chocolate, too thick for the straw, my mother always wore one of her three pretty dresses and patted our faces with the corner of her napkin, and my father would always spot a baby three tables away. He would simply rise and go over to the little family and pick up their baby and bring it over to our table and talk to it, asking did it want to be ours and things like that, just loud enough for the parents to hear. I remember the parents always smiling, perhaps an older sister craning her neck to see where the baby had gone, and my father dipping a spoon into my strawberry shake for the child. Sometimes he'd keep the baby on his lap for half an hour, showing off, sometimes, he would return it right away, the baby squirming in his arms, fighting for a last glance at my strawberry shake. My father gave forty kids their first taste of ice cream at our table, and no one seemed to be scared of anything.

"NAMMA," BOBBY says, lifting his bottle over the seat and dropping it. He places one hand on the window and says it again, "Namma."

Somewhere out in this garish Disneyland of light, he has spotted a bear, and now he wants "Namma," his bear, actually a stuffed toy raccoon. Namma is the one who taught us all *peek-a-boo* and *Where's-your-nose.* In my haste leaving the house, I have forgotten Namma.

In the backseat, Lee is again asleep, his arms limp at his sides, his bottle still protruding from his mouth.

"Namma," Bobby says, turning to me.

"Namma," I say back to him, and he smiles. We will have to go home. Namma is at home peeking out of a corner of the crib. Bobby is still smiling at me coyly, waiting for me to say something else, so I sing his favorite song: "The Lion Sleeps Tonight."

"Ooh Wimoweh. Wimoweh, O Wimoweh . . ." I sing, nodding my head so Bobby will nod his too. "In the jungle, the quiet jungle, the lion sleeps tonight. . . ."

Tired, he leans his head back against the car seat and watches me sing, his open-mouth grin never changing. I do a lot of extra "*O Wimoweh*"s, and the song ends somewhere in Murray. Bobby has closed his mouth now; his eyes are next. I look at my watch: ten to twelve; and I realize that this is the latest I've been out since the boys were born, and people are everywhere. We better go home.

I do a U-turn in the bright, crowded parking lot of a Seven-Eleven. A lone teenager leans against the phones, smoking a cigarette. He wears a Levi's jacket and a blue bandanna around his neck. I look at his face, the eyebrows almost grown together, the pretty lower lip. Date of Birth: 1971; Age: 15; Height: 5 feet 7 inches; Weight: 125; Eyes: blue; Hair: dark brown; Date missing: I don't know. On the milk carton there will be a date, but as I glance back at the boy, I can only see that it looks like he's been out in the night a long time.

Three blocks later, Bobby's asleep. It's late. The traffic is thick and bright. I pass a twenty-four hour Safeway and the parking lot is full. Behind me the headlights teem. A man cruises by us smoking a cigarette in a large Chevrolet. Two couples on motorcycles, the girls holding on, their faces turned out of the wind into their boyfriends' backs. A new station wagon, three girls bouncing in the front seat. Two boys in a Volkswagen bug, their elbows out the window as if summer weren't really over.

At home Annie has checked on the children by now and found them gone, and she has found my valise, and she has given my mother another drink and calmed her down. She knows I'm coming home. We have been safe all our lives. We've traveled: London, Tokyo, Paris, where we saw a diplomat shot down the block from us. Annie has broken her leg skiing. Our Cherokee was totaled by a street department truck two summers ago. We have always felt safe until the boys arrived, and now I am afraid of everything.

I start to sing. We're locked in, the windows are up. These are my boys. I sing softly: "Ooh Wimoweh. Wimoweh, O Wimoweh, Wimoweh," and on, even at a stoplight. I can feel people looking at me, and I lower my face onto the back of my hand on the steering wheel. It's so late. What is everybody doing up so late?

BLOOD
And Its Relationship to Water

THE NOISE Eddie makes when he first wakes for his two A.M. feeding is closest to a fanbelt slipping, a faint periodic squealing, which like a loose fanbelt doesn't signal an emergency; it just means that if not looked to soon, there is going to be real trouble. In Eddie's case, if we linger in our bed too long, the sound becomes a wail similar to that of straining power steering in some late-model Fords. Some Fairlane will try a U-turn on a side street and you hear that low scream near the front axle.

At six weeks, Eddie's also developing a strange growl that he uses primarily when we try to burp him; it is as if he's trying to fake one so as to get back to the bottle. And at night sometimes, as the fanbelt slips into the power steering wail, he'll throw in a little growl as counterpoint, just to show us he's beginning to do things on purpose.

He also has a four-note nasal coo, which is the sweetest noise ever created. He coos whenever the bottle is plugged in his mouth, and sometimes he coos for a moment or two after he's eaten, as his eyes roll sleepily back in his lids.

We know his every peep, every soft snort (he has two), and we listen to him and study these noises because like any parents, we take them as signs of life. We go to the crib at all hours and listen for the feather breath, the muted sigh, some small sound. But we are also keen because Nancy is looking for a sign of love. She hangs on his every glance, tic, start; he's smiled a couple of times now and when he has, Nancy has called me into the room where she stands with his little head in her hands, while she sobs and sobs. "He smiled," she says. "He smiled at me." She has fallen in love with Eddie so profoundly that our house seems a new place, and she needs some small sign of love in return.

I know she's going to get one, but she is not so sure. Eddie came to our house in the arms of my lawyer's wife, Bonnie, when he was two days old. Bonnie, who has four children of her own, was weeping, and repeating again and again: "He's so beautiful, so perfect." It was the moment of transfer that changed Nancy, utterly. She had been cool. She had been hopeful, surely, but also steady and reasonable, and then when Bonnie put Eddie in Nancy's arms, it was as if the infant carried 50,000 volts of some special electricity. Nancy sat down with her eyes on his little face, and her mouth became a scared line. I stood there wishing she would just cry instead of looking like she was about to start crying.

And it's been that way for six weeks. A solemnity has crept into our lives as my wife, the dearest soul I know, waits to see if this adopted child will love her. Hey, I've talked to her, and obviously, logic has no place in the deal. So my wife listens to the baby and watches his face the way astronomers stare into the deepest heavens for the first sign of a new star.

TONIGHT, WHEN Sam came over, in fact, was the first time Nancy has relaxed enough to drink a beer, and I think by the time he left after midnight, she'd had four. Sam loves kids and just the way he held Eddie and how obviously happy he is for us to have a baby put Nancy at ease.

I brought a chair in from the dining room and we sat in the

kitchen and Sam tried to remember when Robbie and Juney were babies. He told a funny story about how Rob wouldn't stop crying at night and the doctor had told them just to let him cry. But a neighbor, suspecting child abuse, had called the police. It had happened twice. Now Robbie is fifteen and works for me weekends, mowing the lawn and washing the cars. He lives with his mother.

After his ten o'clock bottle, Eddie went to bed, bunching himself on his arms and knees like a bug. When I returned to the kitchen, Nancy had opened another beer and had her feet up under herself on the chair. Sam had opened the window and pulled out his cigarettes. Something was up.

Well, with our old friend Sam, it's always Vicky. They've been divorced over three years, but he feels that she still conducts her life around a massive and undiminished hatred for him. "It's no Sun Valley this summer," he said, blowing smoke like a strong secret out the window. He smokes differently since we've gotten the baby. "It's her option, as always, and she says that she and Jeff are taking the kids to San Diego for five weeks after the Fourth. She's known since Thanksgiving about my time off and my plans to let Juney learn to ride, but all of a sudden, she's got this craving to take the kids on her honeymoon. Rob and Juney are acting funny, like it was my fault, like if I'm really their father why don't I just make it happen."

Sam lifted an empty beer can and deposited his cigarette, tilting the can to extinguish the butt. I remember Vicky smirking when he did that; she always called him a "bo-ho," her joke for *bohemian*.

"Rob sure is getting to be a handsome young man," Nancy said.

"Now that is undisguised flattery," I said to Sam. "He looks just like you." And Rob does. What is most affecting, however, is that Rob *walks* just like Sam, and when we play one on one in the driveway, Rob has the same fake-left-go-right move that Sam uses. I haven't told him about it yet, because with my age, I need the little advantage.

"I wonder if Eddie will look like us," Nancy said, hugging her knees in her chair.

"He already does," Sam said. "The poor little guy has that problem already." He reached for his cigarettes, showed them to us. "How we doing with the smoke?"

"You're all right, Sam. None's blowing in here," Nancy said.

"I look more like my father than my brother Tim does," Sam said, lighting up and shaking the match in front of the window opening. "Tim's even six inches shorter than both of us." He laughed. "I think it pisses him off."

"It sure forced him to become an outside shooter," I said. I reached behind Nancy into the fridge. "Beer?"

"One more, then I gotta go," Sam said. "Last hearing on the rate hike tomorrow; the public defender better be sharp."

"Tim's not adopted," Nancy said, taking the beer from me. "Is he?"

"No. He and Irene came along after Mom and Dad had adopted me and Carrie."

I took a chance. "Nancy's a little worried, Sam." I said. "How . . ."

"How do you feel about *your* parents?" Nancy said.

Sam looked up, his face confused, and then he looked over at Nancy, huddled on her chair. His face rose into a large grin. "You're kidding," he said. "Nan, you're worried? Come on. She's kidding, right?" Sam leaned on his elbows toward Nancy. "Well, don't worry. He's your little boy and he'll always be your boy. Look at me. I love my parents and I love my kids; it's my wife I can't abide." Sam laughed and stuck the cigarette back in his mouth. "She's the one who grew up to hate me."

Sam stood up. "I gotta go. Thanks for the beer. I'll call you late tomorrow and give you the play by play of the hearing."

"What will you do if you can't take the kids to Sun Valley?"

"Plan two. Stay around here. Drink beer with you guys. Teach Eddie about women and how to ride a bike."

"Go on," Nancy said. "You're not finished. What's the punchline?"

Sam shrugged and opened the door. "Once you learn to ride a bike, you never forget."

After Sam left I asked Nancy if she felt better.

"Sam's a good guy," she said. "And I should probably drink more beer; this is the first time my back has let go since the baby got here."

"What about this. You go to bed and I'll listen for the baby," I said, clearing the counter.

"My son," she smiled briefly hugging me, her head against my chest. "Please listen for my son."

IT WAS twelve minutes after two when the fanbelt began to squeal, just a short touch and then another, then the real sound of a fanbelt slipping. I mean, it is so close I could tape it and convince people of car trouble. Nancy was out so cold with the worry and fatigue of six weeks that in the half light we have from the hall she could have been the definitive photograph of sleep deprivation.

You see a kid that small in his crib and it looks like someone sleeping on a jailhouse floor and you don't wonder about *any* sound he may make. I slipped my hand under Eddie's head just as the fanbelt was rising into power steering trouble and we ducked quickly into the kitchen. He quieted for the ride into the new room, and the quick flash from the fridge door turned his head in curiosity for the moment that allowed me to retrieve the bottle and stick it in the warmer. Since we'd had the baby, I'd become used to standing naked in the kitchen at night with Eddie in my arms.

The standing-zombie fatigue was worst the third week and now in the sixth it had settled to just my eyes and knees, a low burning. My head rocked slightly and I kept my eyes closed, drifting through the routine.

While Eddie was still too amazed at being whisked around to cry, I changed him, and when I pulled the heavy wet diaper away from under him, he swam happily in the air for a moment, punching softly into the dark. By the time I had him powdered and diapered, he was squealing again, each breath a wonderful, powerful compression, focused and building.

In the kitchen, the bottle was ready. I found it without reaching twice, unplugging the warmer as an afterthought, the kind of motion that in ten years I would forget I had committed a thousand times. With a quick flip I had milk on my wrist, and then of all the easy connections and coincidences in the universe, the baby's mouth found the nipple easiest of all. And as I walked around my own house naked as they say Adam was, holding my son, I heard cooing, edged by a kind of purring slurp, and one or two real, honest deep breaths.

In the dark living room, I sat in the corner of the old couch, holding Eddie, and listened until he snorted two or three times and then gasped, a sharp little gasp, and I knew that two ounces were down, and we could try for a little air. I stood him against my chest and patted his back while he squirmed and growled, his head bobbing in search of the bottle. Then he grew quiet, which always is a good sign. He stood, head away from my body, as if he was listening for something, and then it came: a belch, a good two-stage belch, which he delivered partially in my ear and which sounded exactly like a lawn mower coming around the corner of a house. After that, his head bobbed some more, poking me about the face, and he was ready for more dinner.

I had already fallen asleep twice during the feeding, but sometime during the second burping, Eddie really woke me up with his head. He was bumping against my face softly, working his mouth like a little fish, whining a little bit, when I felt him swing back into space. I had a good hold of him, so I wasn't too worried, when *wham!* his forehead hammered my nose. I saw a quick flash and my eyes filled with tears that burned and burned. I must have started or moved somehow, because I felt Eddie wet me right through the diaper leg, which—out of a kind of misguided concern—I always leave a little loose.

Eddie was fussing and I stood and walked him around the room for a minute, too tired to change him, too tired to go to bed. My head felt strange, kind of empty. And finally I gave up in the middle of our second lap and sat back on the couch. Leaning there I burned with fatigue, wet and warm, and headed toward three o'clock.

Once or twice I thought about getting up, drying us off, and going back to bed, but my head was light and I was tired to the bone. Eddie began to sleep there on my chest, evenly against me, each breath a bird wing in the night sky. I pulled the TV quilt over us and leaned back into warm sleep myself.

It's funny about love, about how you think you're in love or how you may think you know your capacity for love, and suddenly somebody like Eddie comes along and shows you whole new rooms in your heart. I never thought Nancy would be nervous about making this baby belong to us; and when I saw that she was, that she wanted fiercely for him to be ours in every way, I started getting nervous, because I didn't know how to help her.

When I woke there was crying. This was no gentle revving of the small engines of crying. This was roaring, and then I opened my eyes and it was Nancy. She had a hand on my forehead and all I could see in her face was her open mouth in a gasp so full of horror and fear as to seem counterfeit. Her eyes were wide, crystalline, unblinking. In the late dawn light, she looked as though she had bad news for me.

Then I looked down. Eddie lay on my chest in a thick mess which included the blanket, both my hands, my side, and a good portion of the couch cushion. It was blood. I reached up and felt the crust of blood on my neck and chin. My head ached slowly, a low-grade ice-cream headache, and I felt my swollen nose with my fingers. All the time, I realized, my other hand had been feeling Eddie sleep.

"It's okay, Nan," I said in a thick voice. "I had a bloody nose." She sat on her heels next to me, her hands now clasped in her lap, her lower lip clipped fast in her teeth. "Eddie's okay. He's still sleeping, see?" I tried to lift Eddie up just a little to show his breathing face to her, and when I tried that, I realized we were stuck. My nose had bled over everything, blood that would be on the couch for generations, and now a thin layer of blood had glued Eddie to my belly and chest.

When you lie naked in an empty bathtub with your son attached to your abdomen by the stickiness of your very blood, and your wife gingerly sponges you apart with lukewarm water, there is a good chance you too will wake the baby. Eddie opened his eyes in the warm wash of water and lifted his head, as he's learning to do. His eyes tracked the strange space, while Nancy squeezed water between us, and then he saw his mother and made the most extraordinary gesture of tilting his head in recognition, his mouth pursing comically as if to say, *Please, Mom, spare me this indignity.*

And she did. With a noise of her own, something between a sigh and a cough, Nancy reached down for her child. His body awash with blood and water, Eddie hopped into his laughing mother's arms. There was no question about it this time: he put his arms around her laughing neck and, in a happy, bucking hug, he grabbed her hair.

MAX

M AX IS a crotch dog. He has powerful instinct and
insistent snout, and he can ruin a cocktail party faster
than running out of ice. This urge of his runs deeper than any training can reach. He can sit, heel, fetch; he'll even fetch a thrown snow-
ball from a snowfield, bringing a fragment of it back to you
delicately in his mouth. And then he'll poke your crotch, and be
warned: it is no gentle nuzzling.

So when our friend Maxwell came by for a drink to introduce us
to his new girlfriend, our dog Max paddled up to him and jabbed
him a sharp one, a stroke so clean and fast it could have been a box-
ing glove on a spring. Maxwell, our friend, lost his breath and sat on
the couch suddenly and heavily, unable to say anything beyond a
hoarse whisper of "*Scotch. Just scotch.* No ice."

Cody put Max out on the back porch, of course, where he has
spent a good measure of this long winter, and Maxwell took a long
nourishing sip on his scotch and began recovering. He's not athletic
at all, but I admired the way he had folded, crumpling just like a
ballplayer taking an inside pitch in the nuts. It wasn't enough to
change my whole opinion of him, but it helped me talk to him

civilly for five minutes while Cody calmed the dog. I think I had seen a sly crocodile smile on Max's face after he'd struck, pride in a job well done, possibly, and then again, possibly a deeper satisfaction. He had heard Cody and me talk about Maxwell before, and Max is a smart dog.

Maxwell, his color returning, was now explaining that his new girlfriend, Laurie, would be along in a minute; she had been detained at aerobics class. Life at the museum was hectic and lovely, he was explaining. It was frustrating for him to be working with folk so ignorant of what made a good show, of counterpoint, of even the crudest elements of art. Let alone business, the business of curating, the business of public responsibility, the business in general. I was hoping to get him on his arch tirade about how the average intelligence in his department couldn't make a picture by connecting the dots, a routine which Cody could dial up like a phone number. But I wasn't going to get it tonight; he was already on business, his favorite topic.

The truth is that Maxwell is a simple crook. He uses his office to travel like a pasha; he damages borrowed work, sees to the insurance, and then buys some of it for himself; he only mounts three shows a year; and he only goes in four days a week.

Cody came in for one of her favorite parts, Maxwell's catalogue (including stores and prices) of the clothing and jewelry he was wearing tonight. Cody always asked about the clerks, and so his glorious monologue was sprinkled with diatribes about the help. Old Maxwell.

When his girlfriend, Laurie, finally did arrive, breathless and airy at the same time, Maxwell had all three rings on the coffee table and he was showing Cody his new watch. Laurie tossed her head three times taking off her coat; we were in for a record evening.

Maxwell would show her off for a while, making disparaging remarks about exercise *of any kind,* and she would admire his rings, ranking them like tokens on the table, going into complex and aesthetic reasons for her choices. I would fill her full of the white wine that all of Maxwell's girlfriends drink, and then when she asked where the powder room was, I would rise with her and go into the kitchen, wait, count to twenty-five while selecting another Buckhorn out of the fridge, and let Max in.

THE STATUS QUO

I T WAS a tough time and she didn't know why. One of those
times that *develops* like a storm front, slowly, imperceptibly; you
run to the store a few times, drive your boys to piano and tennis for
a few years, and suddenly you look up and something's tough, *something* hurts.

Changes had already begun before Glenna saw Jim in the tub.
She's already changed radio stations, switching from KALL and its
forced adult glee to someplace in the sevens, a station she didn't even
know the name of that played raw, vaguely familiar rock and roll.
And she played it loudly, driving around in the Volvo. Glenna would
come out of Seven-Eleven with a coffee and she could hear the music
vibrating the running car. And she found herself going to movies
alone in the afternoon. One day she went to see *Micki and Maude*
at the Regency and though she knew it was one of the worst pictures
she had ever seen, she couldn't help feeling for the characters, losing
herself in the wash of images. On the way home, she stopped at the
Upper Crust and had a cup of cappuccino sitting in the corner facing the wall, pretending she wasn't from Salt Lake at all, that she
didn't have a son at East and one at Bryant, that her husband wasn't

an accountant, that, somehow, there wasn't *something* bothering her heart at all.

It was when she arrived home that she saw Jim in the tub. She had driven home in a rush of Iron Maiden songs and found another *New Era* in the mail, a magazine her mother subscribed to for her, and it had been the limit. She took it, gathered the three others that sat politely on the coffee table and threw them in the garbage beside the patio. Tyler, the family's sheepdog, came bounding from his nap; if Glenna was moving this fast, it must mean play. He jumped up on her. It was bad timing. She swiped him across the ears with her fist, almost screaming: "Get away from me!"

In her state, near tears, she cut through the boys' bathroom to reach her bedroom, and that's when she saw Jim, her fifteen-year-old, lying in the soapy water. He was reclining, his Walkman earphones clamped on his head. The little machine sat beside the tub on a towel.

On seeing his mother march through, Jim started and said, "Mom?" way too loud in a tone that implied: *What's the matter?*

Even then it was too late. Glenna sat on her bed and thought: something's wrong. The image rushed her closed eyes: her son's long body floating, his white belly, his navel, the dark hair below in the soapy water. She couldn't figure it out, but she was mad, really mad. She was mad because her son had hair growing on his body.

She wanted to accuse Lance, her husband. "Did you know our son has pubic hair! Is this something you've arranged?" She sat on the edge of the bed and rocked back and forth slightly. She felt tragic and silly at the same time; she felt betrayed.

It didn't let up. Mark came home late from Bryant, and though Glenna had calmed herself, she still jumped him: "Where have you been? Feed your damn dog!"

"Mom," Mark said, sliding into one of the kitchen chairs. "I've got to talk to you."

Mark was in a little trouble at school. He was halfway through his tale about the vice principal, when Jim came down the stairs dressed in his McDonald's uniform.

"Where are you going?" Glenna asked him.

"Mom," Jim said, opening his palms to model his outfit. "I'm going out to do drugs. What do you think? You know I work tonight. Carl's picking me up. He's out front right now. See you at eleven."

She turned back to Mark. He had "Oreoed" the vice principal's car, and he and three other boys had had to stay and wash the car, and they were going to be in detention the rest of the term, thirty minutes after school *every* day. Lance, her husband, walked in. He saw the looks on their faces and asked, "What's up?"

Glenna looked at Lance with the very look that said: "You're the author of all this misery." And she brushed by him on her way upstairs. What she did say was, "I'm sick of it. I'm sick of them. No more boys. No more dogs. You handle it."

That night, as a surprise to Lance, Glenna came on as a tigress. She covered his mouth every time he tried to speak, insisting that they just make love *her way.* At times it was strangely rough. Afterward, Lance rose on an elbow and asked, "Glen? Is there anything the matter? Glenna?"

Glenna knew something was happening. She found herself trying to remember the lyrics to Boston and Twisted Sister songs. She even knew she was self-conscious when she went to Nordstrom and bought whole outfits of Guess and Camp Beverly Hills. She wore her Guess sweatshirt around the house without a bra. Late one afternoon she stood at the sink singing, "I Want to Know What Love Is" along with Foreigner on the radio. She could see the stupid dog, Tyler, sitting in the backyard watching her, his head cocked to the side in what looked like sympathy. In the evenings, she noticed that her sons avoided her when possible.

LANCE AND GLENNA went to cocktails at the Weymans'. The Weymans' children were grown, out of college, and lived in other cities. The Weymans were the oldest couple in the neighborhood. While Glenna looked forward to the party, she needled Lance about it, saying, "Oh yes, another gathering of the stodgy status quo."

"They're nice people, Glenna."

"They could get over that with the proper help."

It was a rather large gathering. The Weymans' house was filled. Glenna didn't know many people there, most were from the University. This was the party for Dr. Weyman's retirement. She left Lance with a group he played tennis with and scouted onward into the den, where she found her friend Mimi.

"Ah, basic black," Mimi said, nodding at Glenna's dress. "Your credo still is 'safety first,' right?"

Glenna liked Mimi, and seeing her, she was tempted to confess her pain, ask her, "Mimi, is there something happening to you?" But there was just enough jealousy to prevent it. Mimi was four years younger, richer, and—Glenna thought—more clever. The two made fun of their husbands for a moment. Mimi had names for them: "Ordinary Lance" and "Dull Don," but when she looked through the archway, Lance was leading a small conversation and he looked handsome and animated. Don leaned against the mantel talking to two attractive women, members of the history department.

"Want to get stoned?" Mimi asked.

They went out the side door and sat in Mimi's Audi. It was cold in the car and the two passed the joint back and forth in silence. Glenna looked through the windshield at the ice hanging from the Weymans' garage. Finally, Mimi announced: "This is your life, Glenna!" Glenna looked at Mimi placidly and felt the panic of having another person read her mind. Then Glenna watched in alarm as Mimi said something Glenna knew she was going to say. Glenna felt she could see each word fall from Mimi's mouth, and Glenna felt how they lined up in the air and were at once right *and* obscene: "I saw Jim the other day," Mimi said. "He's quite a hunk."

Glenna snapped: "You stay away from my son!" And though she meant it and intended it as a grave warning, the two women began to laugh, to howl uncontrollably, laughing until there seemed no more air in the car. Glenna's stomach hurt from laughter and her jaw ached, when she turned in slow motion and saw the close-up of Lance's face outside her window. "Ahhhhhhhh!" Mimi screamed as she too saw the face, and the laughter tripled.

"Honey," Lance said to the closed window. "Honey, come in before you catch cold."

A moment later Lance was introducing Glenna to Jim's French teacher, Mr. Van Vliet. "I've always wanted to learn French myself," Glenna said, interrupting the compliment Mr. Van Vliet was making about their son. "Do you do any private tutoring?"

Sunday afternoon, Glenna sat alone on the kitchen table with her feet on a chair, nibbling Saltines, staring at Tyler out in the backyard. She had sent Lance, Jim, and Mark off to her mother's house.

"Why is Mom not going?" Jim had asked.

"Your mother has her reasons."

"And tell her to stop sending me magazines *and* do not bring back any clippings she's saved. I've had it with that stuff," Glenna had said.

"You've had it with a lot of stuff," Mark had said.

"That's enough, Mark."

"Well, Dad, it's true!"

"Let's just go. Let's just go to Grandma's," Jim had said.

"I'm bringing back the clippings," Mark had called from the front door. "I'm bringing them all!"

She had watched them climb into the car. Mark was still upset, Jim resigned, Lance dutiful. She had heard Jim say, as he pushed Mark into the backseat, "Forget it, big guy, she's having a little trouble with her *heritage*."

Glenna nibbled the crackers and rolled her eyes again, remembering his words. *Heritage,* for chrissakes. She stood, and Tyler in the backyard responded by standing too and waving his tail.

"No way," Glenna said to him, and moved to turn the radio on.

Mark arrived home from school just as Glenna was leaving for her first appointment with Mr. Van Vliet. Mark was doing better in school. The vice principal's car was okay; the Oreos hadn't damaged any of the paint. The vice principal had even admitted to the boys that in a way, a harmless prank could be funny. Mark stood on the front walk and watched the Volvo back down the driveway. Glenna saw him watching her. She rolled down her window. He just looked at her.

"Well?" she said finally. "What is it?"

"Mom," he said calmly, walking down to the car. "You're always running. I don't care that you don't talk to me. You're mad at me maybe. But Tyler's the family dog. You ought to be nicer to Tyler." In the cold air, his breath rose on both sides of his face. They looked at each other.

"I'll see you later," Glenna said to her son. "I'm late."

MR. VAN VLIET met Glenna at the door. "Can I get you something? Some coffee?"

"No coffee," she heard herself say. "But I'll take a drink."

As soon as he went into the kitchen and Glenna sat down, she felt like a fool. "French? I'm going to study French?" A flame of panic touched her throat.

Mr. Van Vliet returned with two coffee cups. "White wine. There's no other choice." Glenna tried to picture this man teaching her son's class, fussing over the roll, scolding a daydreamer.

The apartment was modern, primarily white. A framed poster centered each wall announcing exhibitions of paintings in French. Stolen on summer sabbatical, she thought.

"Now," he sat down on a stool by the counter, "what makes you want to study French?"

Her throat constricted again, but she managed: "Oh . . . I've always wanted to. This seems like a good time for me." Then in her flooding nervousness a picture flashed in her mind. She was standing at cocktails with Mimi, saying, "Oh, yes, I'm taking French. It's *wonderful*." Glenna looked up at Mr. Van Vliet and said, "I'm not sure. If my son can learn it, can't I?"

"He's a good kid," Mr. Van Vliet said. "You did something right, something special to have such a good kid."

Glenna tried to sip the wine, but it tasted all wrong and she placed the cup on the end table.

Mr. Van Vliet smiled at her and said, "I'm sorry."

"No, it's fine wine, really. I'm just not sure if I have the discipline to study, to . . ."

"French can be a drag," he interrupted her. "Thank you for coming. I'm glad to see you, but you don't need French. You don't need a French tutor. You've got great kids."

Three days later, Glenna went to McDonald's. She parked next to the building where she could see Jim through the window. He was the tallest of the counter help. She saw him nodding amiably at the customers as he took their orders. She saw him flip the pencil and catch it and slip it behind his ear. Glenna sat in her car for twenty minutes watching the two little girls behind the counter with Jim smile and laugh and flirt with him. One took his nametag and pinned it on her shirt. Glenna put her hand to her face and felt herself smile. She turned off the radio and drove home.

LANCE PLANNED a party. "It's what we need for these winter blues," he said to her.

"I haven't got the winter blues."

"Well, say I do. Come on. Let's have some people over."

MARK AND JIM served the party. Lance and Glenna invited everybody they knew from work, the neighborhood, parents of their sons' friends.

"You boys look nice," Glenna said to her sons. They stood in the kitchen in their church pants and red vests. She reached and adjusted Jim's tie. "It's hard to get it straight because it's so narrow," she said.

"Want me to wear a tie, Mom?" Mark asked.

"No, I don't," she said, putting her hands on his shoulders. "I never want you to wear a tie." She looked closely at his face. "How old are you?"

"Eleven," he said.

"Going on five," Jim said, smiling.

"You boys know to serve . . ."

"From the left, Mom. Don't worry. Your family will not embarrass you."

AN HOUR later, the house was full. The Weymans. Robb Van Vliet came with Maria Del Prete, a Spanish teacher at East. Mimi arrived without Don.

"Mimi!" Glenna greeted her friend.

"Ah, the status quo in action. How's the party?"

"Fair. Nobody's stoned yet. Where's Don?"

"Dull Don will not be here."

Jim appeared at Mimi's left shoulder with a tray of shrimp. "From the left, properly, comes the shrimp. Madam, care for any?" he said.

"Hi, Jim," Mimi said. "None for me. I married one."

"Tut-tut," Jim said. "Your mouth! The way you talk." He moved away.

"He's so grown up," she said to Glenna.

Glenna looked at her friend, and without really thinking said, "We all are." The words seemed tangible in the air. Across the room she saw Mark hand Mrs. Weyman a glass of wine. For the first time she saw that he had the same fine shoulder-back posture as Lance, and then Lance was at her side, his arm around her.

"No drugs, ladies. There are children present." He kissed Glenna on the cheek.

Mimi made a little face. "I need a martini," she said moving away.

The party swelled into all the main floor rooms, shifted, and then sometime after midnight settled back into the living room where Lance was restoking the fire.

Robb Van Vliet and his companion, Maria Del Prete, had hooked up with Mrs. Weyman and Glenna, and they sipped brandy and

laughed like old friends as Mrs. Weyman told stories about disas-
trous faculty parties at the University. Her tales wove back through
the fifties and she told them each as little histories that held her lis-
teners rapt. Glenna found herself again conscious of a kind of happiness, and she pressed her fingers to her lips as she smiled. It felt so
good to laugh. When Mrs. Weyman finished the episode of "The
Department Chairman and the Ice Bucket," Maria Del Prete said,
"We don't have anything like that at our Christmas potlucks."

"This wicked woman is telling tales out of school," Mr. Weyman
said. He had come up behind his wife's chair. "Don't deny it. I can
tell by the scandalized look on everyone's face."

"I haven't started on you, dear. Don't worry."

Moments later, Robb Van Vliet rose and Maria Del Prete joined
him. He told Glenna, "It's not too late to sign up for Spanish." He
quickly held up his hand and said, "Just kidding. Thanks for the
party. It was fun. You have nice friends."

GLENNA AND LANCE walked their last guests, the Weymans,
home. "It's the first time we've been the last to leave a party in thirty
years," Jack Weyman said.

"And it was a ball," Virginia said. The four of them stood in the
street in front of the Weymans' in their coats talking for almost half
an hour. Finally, Jack Weyman shook Lance's hand and Glenna gave
Virginia a quick hug.

"We're going to San Diego Thursday," Jack Weyman said. "For a
month. See if you can't get down for a long weekend. It's been a
tough winter, and we'd love to have you."

Walking back, Glenna took Lance's arm. "That was fun. It *was* a
ball. A good party."

"The Weymans are interesting people." Lance said.

"I want to see more of them."

"Really?"

"What do you mean, *really?*"

"They don't seem your . . ."

"They are!" Glenna said. "Call him tomorrow and tell him we'll come down in a week or two."

When they arrived home, Lance and Glenna found the boys doing dishes. "Wrong house," Lance said. "We've got the wrong house, Glen."

"Thanks, boys," she said. "Good work at the party. I don't know what I'd do without you." She walked to the patio door, still in her coat and went out into the backyard. Lance joined the boys in the dish assembly line. "She meant that, guys."

"Is she feeling better?" Mark asked.

"Check it out," Jim said, pointing a soapy cup out the kitchen window. There Glenna sat on the edge of the deck with her arm around Tyler. Tyler had his head on her shoulder. Her fur coat made it look like two dogs breathing into the icy night.

"It's a good sign," Mark said. "But I'm not convinced until she starts wearing her bra around the house. I'd like to bring some friends over again one of these years."

From

PLAN B
FOR
THE
MIDDLE
CLASS

HARTWELL

Ｔ HIS IS about Hartwell, who is nothing like me. I have sometimes told stories about people, men and sometimes a woman,
who were like me, weak or strong in some way that I am or they
shared my taste for classical music or fine coffee, but Hartwell was
not like me in any way. I'm just going to tell his story, a story about
a man I knew, a man not like me, just some *other* man.

Hartwell just didn't get it. For years he existed, as the saying goes,
out of it. Let's say he wasn't alert to nuance, and then let's go ahead
and say he wasn't alert to blatancy either. He was alert to the
Victorian poets and all of *their* nuances, but he couldn't tell you if it
was raining. This went way back to when he was in college at the
University of Michigan and everybody was preparing for law school
taking just enough history, political science, things like that, but
Hartwell majored in English, narrowing that to the Victorians, which
could lead only to one thing: graduate school. As a graduate student,
he was a sweet guy with a spiral tuft of light hair that rose off his head
like fire, who lived alone in a room he took off campus and who read
his books, diligently and with pleasure, and ate a steady diet of the
kind of food eaten with ease while reading, primarily candy.

When I met him, he had become a sweet, round man, an associate professor of English, who taught Browning and Tennyson, etc., etc., and who brought to our campus that fall years ago his wife, Melissa, a handsome woman with broad shoulders and shiny dark hair cut in a pixie shell.

I say "our campus" because I too teach, but Hartwell and I couldn't be more different in that regard. I know what's going on around me. I teach rhetoric and I parse my students as well as any paragraph. My antennae are out. I can smell an ironic smirk in the back row, detect an unprepared student in the first five minutes of class, feel from the way the students file out of class what they think of me. Hartwell drifts into his classroom, nose in a book, shirt misbuttoned, and reads and lectures until well after the bell has rung and half the students have departed. He doesn't know their names or how many there are. He can't hear them making fun of him when they do it to his face while handing in a late paper, whining his name into five sarcastic syllables, *Pro-fess-or Hart-well,* and smiling a smile so fake and sugary as to make any of us avert our eyes. He is oblivious.

This was apparent to me the first time I met him with Melissa at the faculty party that fall. The effect of seeing them standing together in the dean's backyard was shocking. Anyone could see it: they wouldn't last the year. As I said, she was attractive, but as she scanned her husband's colleagues that evening it was her eyes, her predatory eyes, that made it clear. Poor old Hartwell stood beside her, his hair afloat, his smile benign and vacant, an expression he'd learned from years alone with books.

Melissa shopped around for a while, and by midterm she was seeing our Twentieth-Century Drama professor, a young guy who had a red mustache and played handball. It took Hartwell the entire year to find out about the affair and then all of summer session to decide what it meant. Even then, even after he'd talked to Melissa and she to him and *he'd* moved out of the little house they were buying near the college, even then he didn't really wake up. The students were more sarcastic to him now that he was a cuckold, a word they learn as sophomores and then overuse for a year. Watching that was hard on me, those sunny young faces filing into his office with their million excuses for not being present or prepared, saying things that if I heard them in my office would win them an audience with the dean. Things I wouldn't take.

I, however, am not like Hartwell. There isn't a callow hair on my head. I am alert. I am perspicacious. I can see what is going on. I've become, as you sense, a cynical and thoroughly jaded professor of rhetoric. My defenses are up and like it or not, they are not coming down.

It was in the period just after Melissa that I became friends with Professor Hartwell. Our schedules were similar and many afternoons at four-thirty we fell into step as we left the ancient Normal Building where we both taught. Old Normal was over a hundred years old, the kind of school building you don't see anymore: a red block structure with crumbling turrets, high ceilings, and a warped wooden floor that rippled underfoot. I'd walk out with Hartwell and ask him if he'd like to get a coffee. The first time I asked him, he said *what* and when I had repeated the question, he looked at me full of wonder, as if I'd invented French roast, and said, "Why, yes, that sounds like a good idea." But, of course, with Hartwell that was the way he responded every time I asked him. He was like a child, a man without a history. His experience with Melissa certainly hadn't hurt him. He thought it was odd, but as he said one day, over two wonderful cups of Celebes Kolossi at the Pantry, about the drama teacher, "He had vigor." But we primarily talked shop: semantics. Hartwell was doing a study of Gerard Manley Hopkins, and I offered my advice.

I wasn't surprised during this time to see him occasionally lunching with Melissa. He was the kind of man you could betray, divorce, and then still maneuver into buying you lunch.

But our afternoons together began to show me his loneliness. He was as seemingly indifferent to that feeling as any man I'd ever met, even myself in the life I have chosen, but more and more frequently during our conversations I would see his eyes narrow and fall upon a table across the room where a boy and a girl chatted over their notebooks. And when his eyes returned to me, they would be different, and he would stand and gather his books and go off, a fat fair-haired professor tasting grief. He never remembered to pay for his coffee.

THEN THE next thing happened, and I knew from the very beginning what to make of it. When you fall in love with a student, three things happen. One: you become an inspired teacher, spending hours and hours going over every tragic shred of your students' sour deadwood compositions as if holding in your hands magic parchment, suddenly tapping into hidden reservoirs of energy and vocabulary and lyric combinations for your lectures, refusing to sit down in class. Two: the lucky victim of your infatuation receives a mark twice as high as he or she deserves. Three: you have a moment of catharsis during the denouement in which you see yourself too clearly the fool, a realization that is probably good for any teacher, because it will temper you, seal your cynicism and jade your eye, and make you sit down once hard and frequently thereafter.

The object of Hartwell's affections was a girl I kind of knew. She had been in my class the year before, and she was a girl you noticed. Ours is a small midwestern college and there are a dozen such beauties, coeds with the perfect unblemished faces of pretty girls and the long legs and round hips of women. These young creatures wear plaid skirts and sweaters and keep their streaming hair in silver clips. They sit in the second row and have bright teeth. They look at you unseeing, the way they've looked at teachers all their lives, and when one of these girls changes that glance and seems to be appraising, you wear a clean shirt and comb your hair the next day.

That was what gave Hartwell away: his hair. I met him on the steps of Normal and he looked funny, different. It was the way people look who have shaved beards or taken glasses, that is, I couldn't tell what was different for a moment. He simply looked *shorter.* Then I saw the comb tracks in the hair plastered to his head and I knew. He had been precise about it, I'll give him that. After a life-time of letting his hair jet like flame, wildfire really, he had cut a part an engineer would have been proud of and then formed the perfect furrows across the top of his head and down, curling once to disap-pear behind the ear. If you'd just met him, I suppose, it didn't look too bad. But to me, god, he looked like the concierge for a sad hotel. He had combed his hair and I knew.

There were other signs too, his pressed shirt, the new tie, his loafers so shiny—after years of grime—that they hurt the eye. He was animated at coffee, tapping the cover of the old maroon anthol-ogy of Victorian poetry with new vigor, and then the *coup de grâce*—one afternoon at the Pantry, he picked up the check.

Hartwell was teaching a Hopkins-Swinburne seminar at night that term and the girl who was the object of his affections, a girl named Laurie, was in that evening seminar. When Hartwell began to change his ways, I simply noticed it. It was none of my business. One's col-leagues do many things that one doesn't fully appreciate or under-stand. But Hartwell was different. I felt I should help him. He had not been around this particular block, and I decided to stay alert.

I could see, read, and decipher the writing on the wall. This shrewd pretty schoolgirl was merely manipulating her professor to her advantage. I knew she was an ordinary student from her days in rhetoric, an officer in Tri-Delta sorority who wore a red kilt and a white sweater and who spent more time choosing her blouses than studying verb phrases, and now she was out for poor Hartwell.

I changed my office hours so I could be around when his class broke up, which was about nine P.M. Tuesdays and Thursdays, and I saw her hang around my old friend, chatting him up, always the last to leave and then stroll with him, and that is the correct word, *stroll,* down the rickety corridor of Normal, the floor creaking like the fools' chorus. She would laugh at the things he said and toss her hair just so and squeeze her books to her chest. And Hartwell, well, he would beam. From the door of my office I could see the light beam off his forehead, he was that far gone.

In most cases these things are not really very important, some passing infatuation, some shrewd undergraduate angles to raise his or her grade point average, some professor's flagging ego takes a little ride, but I watched that term as it went further and further for Hartwell. The shined shoes were a bit much, but then at midterm that spring, he showed up one day in gray flannel slacks, his old khakis and their constellations of vague grease stains gone forever. And I could tell he was losing weight, the way men do when they spend the energy necessary to become fools.

Melissa, his ex-wife, now uneasily married to our drama professor (who had since developed his own air of frumpiness), came to my office one day and asked me what was going on with Hartwell. I hadn't liked her from the beginning, and now as she sat smartly on the edge of the chair, her short carapace of hair as shiny as plastic, I liked her even less, and I did what I am certainly capable of doing when required: I lied. I told her that I noticed no difference in her former husband, no change at all.

I knew with certainty that there was danger when one afternoon in April he leaned forward over his coffee and withdrew a sheet of type paper from the pages of his textbook. It was a horrid thing to see, the perfect stanzas typed in the galloping pica of his office Underwood, five rhyming quatrains underneath the title "To Laurie." It was fire, it was flower, it was—despite the rigid iambic pentameter—*unrestrained.* It was confession, apology, and seduction in one. I clenched my mouth to keep from trembling while I read it, and after an appropriate minute I passed it back to him. He was eager there at the table in the Pantry, beaming again. He had begun to beam everywhere. He wanted to know what I thought.

"It is very, very good," I told him quietly. "The metaphors are apt and original, and the whole has a genuine energy." Here I leaned toward his bright face. "But Hartwell. Don't you ever, under any circumstances, give this to a student."

"I knew it was good," he said to me. "I knew it. Do you see? I'm writing again."

"Do not," I repeated, "give this to Laurie. You will create a misunderstanding."

"There is no misunderstanding," he told me, folding the poem back into the old maroon book. "It is a verity," he said. "I am in love."

As everyone knows, there is nothing to say to that. I stirred my coffee and saw from how high an altitude my friend was going to fall.

APRIL IS a terrible month on a campus. This too is a verity. Every pathway reeks of love newly found and soon to be lost. It is one of the few times and places you can actually see people *pine*. The weather changes and the ridiculous lilacs bloom at every turning, their odor spiraling up the cornices of every old brick building in sight, including, of course, Old Normal. Couples lean against things and talk so earnestly it makes you tired. Everywhere you look there is some lost lad in shirtsleeves gesturing like William Jennings Bryan before a coed, her dreamy stare a caricature of importance. This goes on round the clock in April, the penultimate month in the ancient agrarian model of the school year, and as I walked across campus that spring, I kept my eyes straight ahead. I didn't want to see it, any of it.

OF COURSE, Hartwell and I couldn't be more different. That's clear. But I had a sensation after he'd left that afternoon that reminded me too strongly of when I had my troubles, such as they were. Years ago, a lifetime if you want, a student of mine became important to me. She wasn't like Hartwell's Laurie—at all—her name isn't important, but it wasn't a pretty name and—in fact—she wasn't really a pretty girl, just a girl. She came to my notice because of an affliction she carried in her eyes, a weight, a sorrow.

This is not about her anyway, but about me in a sordid way. I saw what I wanted to see. What I needed to see. She was frail and damaged somehow and I was her teacher. Well, who needs details? It was

the same story as all these other shallow memories, some professor
off balance and a young person either willingly or unwillingly the
victim or beneficiary of it all. My student, this strange girl, received
an A for B work, and I waited for her to pick up her term paper a
week after the semester ended. Let me explain this to you: there was
no reason for me to be on campus, sitting in my office in Normal
Hall, no reason whatsoever. I had my door cracked one inch and I
waited. Tuesday, Wednesday, Thursday, Friday. On Friday afternoon
I was still on the edge of my chair. Just having her paper (which I
read and reread, held in my lap as I waited) was enough, and
undoubtedly, it would have powered me through the weekend. I am
the kind of professor who is in his office more Saturdays and
Sundays than he will ever admit. On Friday evening, when I was
preparing in my routine way to leave and go home, she came. I
heard a step on the stair, the first step which was not the janitor's
step, and I knew she was coming. How long could it have taken
between the sound of those beautiful footsteps and their pausing at
my opened office door? Twenty seconds? Ten? Whatever the time, it
was the eon between my young and my old selves. I had a chance,
as the old scholars put it, to know my tragic flaw. Not that I'm any
more than pathetic, and certainly not tragic, but I came to know in
that short moment that I was a fool and that I was about to join a
legion and august company of the history of all fools. The girl came
to my door and paused and then knocked on the open door. She
acted surprised to find me there. She acted as if she expected to
retrieve her paper in a box outside my door. I told her no, that I had
it. I handed it to her, still warm from my lap. She nodded and
averted her eyes and said something I'll never forget. "This was a
good class for me," she said. "You made it interesting." And then she
turned and touched the rippled floor of Normal Hall for the last
time. Without her paper and with no reason to be on earth on
Friday night, I became a fool, and in a sense the guardian of fools.

Like Hartwell.

But what could I do? This Laurie was as shrewd as any I'd seen come along. She not only accepted his poem—she'd commented on it. I'd quizzed him on what she had said, but he'd just smiled until his eyes closed, and shook his head. He was so far gone that I had to smile.

But Laurie hadn't stopped there. With no reason whatsoever, she had invited him to the Spring Carnival. There was no reason to do this. She'd already won her victory. Hartwell was absolutely incandescent about it. He was carnival this and carnival that. I should come, he said. Oh go with *us,* he said. It was as if they were engaged. I told him no. It was a sunny spring afternoon in the Pantry, too hot really to be drinking coffee, and I told him no to go ahead, but for god sakes be careful. If you want to know the meaning of effete, just say *be careful* to a fool in love. My advice didn't get across the table.

The Spring Carnival on our campus is a bacchanalian festival. It is designed with clear vengeance: victory over winter has been achieved and this celebration is to make sure. Years ago, it was held on the quad and consisted of a few quaint booths, but it has grown, exploded really, to the point where now every corner of campus is covered with striped tents and the smell of barbecued this and that clouds the air. I haven't been in years.

But. Hartwell's invitation was tantalizing, and then it was all tripled by something that happened the last week of classes. I was packing my briefcase in my office in Normal when the door opened. There wasn't a knock or a hello, the door just swung open and Hartwell's Laurie was hanging on it, half out of breath, her blond hair swinging like something primeval. "Oh, good," she said. "You're here. Listen, Downey," she said, using my nickname without hesitation, "Hart and I are going to the carnival and he mentioned you might like to go. Please do. You know it's Friday. We're going to eat and then take it all in." Hartwell's Laurie looked at me and smiled, her tan cheeks not twenty-two years old. "It's going to be fun, you know," she said and closed the door.

Well, an interview such as that makes me sit down, and down I did sit. I took the old old bottle of brandy out of my bottom drawer, a bottle so old my father had bought it in Havana on one of his trips, and I had half an ounce right there. Downey. I was jangled. So she and Hartwell called me Downey, when they called me anything. The prospect of being talked about set part of me adrift.

To the carnival I went.

But I didn't go with them. I told Hartwell that I might see him at the carnival, but to go ahead. It was the last week of classes and I had a lot to read. Friday afternoon I was plowing through a stack of rhetoric papers when—outside my window—I heard the Gypsy Parade, the kazoos and tambourines that signal the commencement of festivities. A feeling came to me that I hadn't had in years. I had heard this ragtag music every spring of every year I'd been in Normal Hall, but this year it was different. It called to me. I felt my heart begin to drum, and I put down my pen like a schoolboy called outside by his mates. It was the last Friday of the school year and I was going to the carnival.

Part of all this, naturally, was a sympathetic feeling I had for Hartwell. Laurie had invited him to the carnival, after all. I was—and I'll admit this freely—happy for him. At the corner I stopped and bought a pink carnation and pinned it to my old brown jacket and I thrust my hands into the pockets and plunged into the carnival. The crowds of shouting and laughing merrymakers passed around me in the alleyway of tented amusements. It was just sunset and the shadows of things ran to the edge of the world, giving the campus I knew so well an unfamiliar face, and I had the sense of being in a strange new village as I walked along. Bells rang, whistles blew, and a red ball bounced past. I saw Melissa, Hartwell's former wife, on the arm of one of our Ph.D. students, eating cotton candy. By the time I'd walked to an intersection of these exotic lanes, I had two balloons in my hand and it was full dark.

I bought some popcorn and walked on beneath the colored lights. Groups of students passed by in twos and threes. They didn't see me, but I know that I had taught some of them. I felt a tug at my arm then and it was Laurie, saying, "Downey. Great balloons!" She had Hartwell by the other arm.

"Yes," I said, smiling at both of them and tugging at the two huge balloons. "They're big, aren't they?"

Hartwell was in his prime. He looked like a film actor and confidence came off him in waves. He wore a new white flannel jacket and a red silk tie. "They're absolutely grand!" Hartwell said. "They're the best balloons in this country!"

Laurie pulled us over to a booth where for a dollar a person could throw three baseballs at a wall of china plates. The booth was being managed by a boy I recognized from this semester's rhetoric class, though he wouldn't make eye contact with me.

"I want you two to win me a snake," Laurie said, pointing to the large stuffed animals that hung above our heads.

"Absolutely," Hartwell said, reaching in his pocket for the money. Hartwell was going to pitch baseballs at the plates. It was a thrilling notion—and when he broke one with his final throw, that was thrilling too.

"Well," I said. "If we're going to ruin china, I'm going to be involved." I paid the boy a dollar and threw three baseballs, smashing one plate only.

We stayed there awhile, acting this way, until on my third set, I broke three plates, and the boy, looking as shocked as I did, handed me a huge cloth snake. It was pink. Hartwell was right there, patting my back and squeezing my arm in congratulation, and I imagine we made quite a scene, Laurie kissing my cheek and smiling as I handed her the prize. I'll say this now: it was a funny feeling there in the green and yellow lights of the carnival—I'd never been patted on the back before in my life. I am not the kind of person who gets patted on the back, which is fine with me, but when Hartwell did it there, calling out "Amazing! Magnificent!" it felt good.

We floated down the midway, arm in arm after that, until I realized we had walked all the way down to Front Street, which is the way I walk for home. I said good night to them there, Hartwell and I bowing ridiculously and then shaking hands and smiling and Laurie kissing my cheek lightly one more time and calling, "Good night, Downey!" I turned onto Front Street and then turned back and watched them walk away, Laurie tightly on Hartwell's arm. They stopped once and I saw them kiss. She put her hand on his cheek and kissed his lips.

As I moved down Front Street, the noises of the carnival receded with every step and soon there was just me and my two balloons in an old town I knew quite well.

It is not like me to enter houses uninvited. I have never done it. But I was in a state. I can't describe the way I felt walking home, but it was about happiness for Hartwell and a feeling I had about Hartwell's Laurie. I had begun to whistle a lurid popular tune that I'd heard at the carnival. This should tell you something, because I do not whistle. And when I came to Old Tilden Lane, where all the sorority houses are lined up, I turned down.

I'd been to all of the Greek houses at one time or another. Each fall, the shiny new officers invite some of the faculty out to chat or lecture or have tea in the houses, and we do it when we're younger because it counts as "service" toward tenure or we're flattered (we're always flattered), and I had done my canned "English Department" presentation at Tri-Delt years ago.

I found Tri-Delta, halfway down the winding street tucked between two other faded mansions. It was almost ten o'clock. The lights were on all through the house and the windows and doors thrown open. I walked up the wide steps and into the vestibule. Everyone was at the carnival at this hour and I felt an odd elation standing in the grand and empty house.

This was among the strangest things I have ever done as a college professor—wander into a sorority house. But I did. I went through the living room and up the wooden stairway to the second floor and I went from door to door, reading the nameplates. The doors were all partially open and I could see the chambers in disarray, books scattered on the beds and underthings on the floor. The hallway smelled musty and sweet, and the doors were festooned with collages of clippings and photographs and memorabilia so that many times I had to read the notes to discover whose room it was. It was kind of delicious there in the darkened hallway, sensing that hours ago a dozen young women had dressed and brushed their hair in these rooms.

At the end of the corridor, on a dark paneled door, there were several sheets of white typing paper, and I saw instantly that this was Laurie's room, even before I went close enough to read any of it. It was, of course, Hartwell's poetry. The poem I had seen was taped there, along with five others he had typed and not shown me. Now, however, each was scrawled with red-ink marginalia in the loopy, saccharine handwriting of sorority girls. Their comments were filthy, puerile, and inane. Obscene ridicule. My heart beat against my forehead suddenly, and my eyes burned. Through her open door, I saw Laurie's red plaid kilt on the floor next to a black slip. I felt quite old and quite heavy and very out of place.

I fled. I rattled down the stairway, taking two steps at a time, and across the foyer and back into the night. A couple, arm in arm, were coming through the door. They were drunk and I nearly knocked them over. I recovered and hurried into the dark of Old Tilden Lane, where I found something on my hand, and I released the two balloons.

I am a man who lives in six rooms half a mile from the campus where I teach. I like Chopin, Shostakovich, Courvoisier, and Kona coffee. I have a library of just over two thousand books. After these things, my similarities with Hartwell end. He has his life and I have mine, and he is not like me at all. We are lonely men who teach in college. I'll give you that.

DERAY

ONE THING led to another. Liz and I started fixing up our place before the baby came. First the nursery and then wallpaper in the hall and new carpet and then new linoleum and new cabinets in the kitchen and then a new small bay window for the kitchen; and it was through this new window that we would look out upon the lot and silently measure the progress of the weeds.

I was ready to use August to lean back and do a little reading, but you get a woman and an infant standing in a tidy little bay window looking out at a thorny desert and seeing a grassy playground, and you get out the grid paper and sharpen the pencils and start making plans.

A dump truck unloaded nine yards of mountain topsoil. I took delivery of eighteen railroad ties and four hundred and fifty used bricks. I tiered the garden with three levels of ties and laid a brick walkway along the perimeter. I dug the postholes and stained the redwood before I assembled the fence, and then, when I nailed the boards in place—just so along the string line on top—that's when my plan became apparent from the window. It would be a little world, safe, enclosed, where my daughter, when she got around to walking, would tumble in the thick green grass.

It was a dry summer and I'd wait until late in the day when the house could throw its shadow on the project and then I'd plunge out into the heat. Our pup, Burris, wouldn't even go out with me. I was only good for two hours, and then I'd stumble into the house, dehydrated, a crust of dirt on my forehead, my shirt soaked through. Burris would lift his head from the linoleum and then go back to sleep.

Evenings while my strength held, I marched around the yard, pulling my old stepladder loaded with four cinder blocks, leveling the topsoil. I would drag it in slow figure eights through the thick dirt with the rope cutting at my chest like a crude halter. And it was during this time, during my dray-horse days, that my neighbor DeRay would cruise in on his cycle and come to the fence and say, "Hey, good for you, Ace. I'd give you a hand, but I've already got a job. But you know where you can find a beer later."

So I started going over there when I'd feel the first dizziness from the heat. I'd drop the rope and pick my wet shirt away from my chest and walk next door and visit with DeRay.

IF I told you that DeRay was a guy who was on parole and loved his motorcycle, it would be misleading, though he did have a big blue tattoo of a skull and a rose. He wore size-thirteen engineer boots and a biker's black cap, greasy as a living thing. In the evenings he arrived home, proud as a man on a horse, yanking the big Harley back onto its stand, and throwing his right leg back over the bike purposefully to come to the ground and stand as a body utterly capable of trouble.

But the picture needs qualification. For instance: it wasn't actually parole. It was *like* parole. Once a month DeRay saw a guy at social services to state that he had not been in any bars. He could not go into a bar for another four months, because he used to be in barroom fights. He would go to biker bars and when a fight would start, he would fight. It was his personality, they told him. He knew none of the people in the fights and the fights weren't about him in any way, but his personality—when it was exposed to a fight, especially indoors—dictated that he fight too. So, it wasn't parole. And he did have that tattoo on the inside of his right forearm, but unless he stopped to show it to you it was hard to tell there was a rose. It looked like a birthmark.

He showed it to me one night on his front porch. Evenings were cool there and that is where he and Krystal sat on an old nappy couch and watched the traffic and drank beer. They drank exactly five six-packs every night, he told me, and—at first—thirty cans seemed a lot, and I worried that there might be a fight, but I came to see that DeRay generally slowed down over the evening, climbing off the porch in those big boots to move his Lawn Jet, or to pack another six beers into the Igloo. Some nights he stood and talked to the traffic. If he started talking like that while I was around, I stood and quietly left. It was his business.

The thing about DeRay that cannot be minimized was his love for his motorcycle. It was a large Harley-Davidson with a beautiful maroon gas tank and chrome fenders. The world was ten miles deep in the reflections. The way he listened to it when he first kicked the starter; the way he kept it running—silent—when he drove away in the morning as if man and machine were being sucked into a vacuum, disappearing down the street; the way he dismounted with clear pleasure—these things showed his affection.

Once Liz was out in front of our garage putting Allie in the stroller when DeRay came up and plucked the baby from her, saying, "Come on over here, baby, check these wheels." He put Allie on the seat of the huge motorcycle and she broke into a real grin. She could see her face in a dozen shiny places. "See," DeRay said to Liz, "she loves it. It won't be long." He called to the porch: "Hey, Krystal, check this out!"

Krystal appeared and leaned over. "Oh, right, DeRay. She's a real mama. She's your new mama, all right."

I watched it all from our new kitchen window, and seeing DeRay there holding the baby on the Harley, I thought: There's the center—the two most loved things on the block.

Both DeRay and Krystal were somewhere in their forties. She was a lean woman who looked good in tight jeans. In the face she resembled Joan Baez, perhaps a little more worn—and her nose was larger, pretty and hawklike at the same time. Her long reddish hair was wired with some gray and she usually wore it all in a bandanna. She told me she was one of four women who were on line crews in the entire state. She made it sound like a lot of fun. I'd sit on their porch, my head full of bubbles anyway with yard fever, dirt, and cold beer. One of my calves would start to tremble, and I imagined if I worked with Krystal she'd always be telling me what to do, like a mother, and I would do it. Her lean face seemed hard and affectionate. It had seen a lot of traffic, that was clear. From the corner of the porch, I could see my new kitchen window—Liz in there moving around the high chair.

One night when I was at DeRay's, Krystal went inside where we could hear her on the phone. "Her in-laws," DeRay told me. "Old Krystal's had herself a couple of cowboys."

Later, we were just talking when out of the blue he said, "What's the worst thing you ever did?"

I knew that he was going to make some confession, a theft or beating a woman, some threat he'd made stick. He looked hard that night, his face vaguely blue in the early-evening gloom.

"I don't know," I said. "Burn down the ROTC Building." It was an old joke. I was on the roof of the building the night it burned, but I was only peripherally involved in the crime.

"Oh, arsony," DeRay mocked. "That's terrible."

I drank from my beer and went ahead: "What's the worst thing you ever did?"

"What you're doing now."

"What?" I sat up. "What am I doing?"

"Dragging dirt around. Putting in a yard."

"Oh," I said. "I hear that. It's torture."

"No you don't. You don't even know," he said. "I've had three houses. How old do you think I am?"

"I don't know. Forty-five?"

"Forty-nine." He rocked forward and threw his beer can out with the others. "I've had three families, for chrissakes. And that doesn't even count this deal here." He gestured over his shoulder where Krystal was on the phone. He snapped another beer open and grimaced over the first sip: "I mean, I put in some lawns."

"That's a lot of work," I said.

"Nah." He waved it off. "You can't even hear me. But listen, when you dig for the sprinklers, rent a trencher. You won't be sorry."

And DeRay was right. There is nothing better after an unbroken plain of manual labor than to introduce a little technology into the program. The trencher was beautiful. The large treaded tires measured the line exactly and the entire mechanism crawled across my yard like a tortoise. The trench was carved as if with a knife, straight sides and a square bottom exactly eight inches from the surface. All the other feats of the past year, the room in the basement, the kitchen window, my straight fence, vanished before this, the first stage of my sprinkling system. That night I worked way beyond my usual quitting time. When I finally looked up, I saw the yellow light in the kitchen; the world was dark.

This is when DeRay opened the gate and came up and took the handlebars of the trencher out of my hands and conducted it to the end of the line. It was the last ditch. He surveyed the yard and switched the machine off. "Yeah, it's a good, simple machine," he said. "Load it up and come over for a beer."

I stayed at their place until almost eleven. I didn't count as I left, but I knew there were more than thirty empties on the lawn. DeRay receded from the conversation and Krystal told me about her first husband, who was in a mental health facility in Denver, a chronic schizophrenic. She filed to divorce him while he was in the hospital. "He was as crazy as you get to be," she said. "I still keep in touch with his mom and dad in Oklahoma City. He was a dear boy,"

Krystal said, "but he couldn't keep two things together and his jealousy cost me three jobs."

When I went home all the lights were off. I took my clothes off in the garage as always and padded in. Liz was in bed watching television. I could hear people laughing. I turned on the bathroom light, and Liz said, "How're the Hell's Angels?"

"You've been watching too much Letterman." I came to the bedroom door.

"You've been outside this house since four o'clock. We had a lovely dinner."

"Oh, now we're going to fight about dinner?" I could feel the rough cuff of dirt around my neck and I hated standing there dirty and naked.

"We're going to fight about whatever I want to fight about."

"Look, Liz. Don't. I've been in the yard. We want the yard, right?" I felt the closeness of the rooms; it was suddenly strange to be inside. "I've got to take a shower," I said.

"Where are you?" she said before I could turn. It was a tough question, because I was right there full of beer, but she was on to something. It was August and I wasn't looking forward to school starting. I shrugged and showed her my brown arms. She looked at me and said, "Let it go, if you like. Just let the yard go."

I BOUGHT the controls for the sprinkling system. Opening the boxes on my lap and holding the timer compartment and the bank of valves was wonderful. The instruction booklet was well written: simple and illustrated. I took the whole thing over to DeRay and showed him.

"Yeah," he said, turning the valves over in his hand. "They've got this thing down to the bare minimum and there's a two-week timer." I knew he was a union machinist for Hercules Powder Company, and in the four months he'd been my neighbor he'd told me that three different deals he'd worked up had gone into space on satellites. "You're going to be the King of Irrigation with this thing."

Though Liz didn't like the idea, I put the control box on the guestroom wall downstairs. It took me two six-packs. She said it didn't look right, a sprinkler system timer box on the guestroom wall. I said some things too, including the fact that it was the only wall I could put it on. She just shrugged.

I finished at three o'clock in the morning. I went out in the garage and filled the spreader and spread the lawn seed all across the yard first one way and then the other in a complete checkerboard just like it said on the package. It was quiet in the neighborhood and I tried to step lightly through the raked topsoil. There was no traffic on the streets and the darkness was even and phosphorescent as I walked back and forth. It seemed like the time of night to spread your lawn seed.

The next morning, Liz woke me with a nudge from her foot. I was asleep on the floor in the nursery. "Who are you?" she said.

"We're all done," I said. "The yard's all done."

"Great," she said, carrying Allie into the kitchen. "Looks like we drank some beer last night. Did we have a good time? I think you've caught a little beer fever from your good buddy next door. This is being a hard summer on you."

Very late that night, Burris began barking and Allie woke and started crying. "What is it?" Liz said from her side of the bed.

"Nothing. It's okay," I said. There was a strange noise in the house, a low moan in the basement, which I understood immediately was the water pipes. I went to Allie and changed her diaper. She was awake by that time so I carried her into the kitchen, where Burris was jumping at the window. I had set the system to start at four-thirty, which it now was, and outside the window the sprinklers, whispering powerfully, sprayed silver into the dark. I sat down and Allie crawled up over my shoulder to watch the waterworks. Burris stood at the window on two legs humming nervously. I swallowed and felt how tired I was, but there was something mesmerizing about the water darkening the soil in full circles. A moment later, the first bank of sprinklers shrank and went off and the second row sputtered and came on full, watering every inch I'd planned. It was a beautiful thing.

There were five banks, each set for twenty minutes, and when the last series—outside the fence—kicked on, I saw a problem. The heads were watering not only my strip of yard, but the sidewalk and part of the street. Along the driveway, they were spraying well over my strip, and DeRay's motorcycle was dripping in the gray light.

I stood so sharply that Allie whimpered, and I took her quickly in to Liz and laid her in the bed. I put on my robe and grabbed a towel, and I went outside. It was a little after five and I wiped down the bike until the towel was sopping, and then I used the corner of my robe on the spokes and rims, and I was down on my knees when I heard voices and two high school girls in tennis clothes walked by swinging their rackets. It was full light. I looked up and saw Liz in the kitchen window. Her face was clear to me. There was grit in my knees and my feet were cold.

"I'm going to have to adjust those last heads," I told her when I went inside.

"Why don't you make some coffee first," Liz said. She was sitting at the table. Allie was back in her crib asleep.

"You want to talk about what's going on?" Liz said. I poured coffee into the filter and set it on the carafe.

"There's too much pressure this early," I said with my back to her. "We soaked DeRay's motorcycle."

"You're taking care of DeRay's motorcycle now?" she said. "You're going to get arrested exposing yourself to schoolgirls."

After a long tired moment of standing staring at the dripping coffee, I poured a cup while it was still brewing and set it in front of my wife. "Look, Liz, everything's fine." I opened my hand to show the kitchen, the window, the yard. "And now the grass is going to grow."

That evening there was a knock at the kitchen door just after six. Liz answered it and when she didn't come back to watch the news, I went out and found her talking to DeRay on the back porch. "Hello, Ace," he said to me.

"DeRay has invited us to . . ." Liz smiled. "What is it, DeRay?"

"They're testing one of our engines and I've got passes. We could make it a picnic."

Liz looked at me blankly, no clue, so I just said, "Let's do it. Sounds good. This is one of your engines?"

"We did some work on it. It's no big deal, but we can go up above the plant in the hills and get off the homestead for a while, right?"

"Right," I said, looking at Liz. "A picnic."

THE SATURDAY of our picnic dawned gray—high clouds that mocked the end of summer. I offered to make the lunch, but Liz nudged me aside and made turkey sandwiches and put nectarines and iced tea and a six-pack of Olympia in the cooler along with a big bowl of her pasta salad. When I saw the beer I realized that she was going to do this right by the rules and then when it turned into a tragedy or simple misery or some mistake, she would have her triumph. She had never bought a six-pack of Olympia before in her life.

At eleven, we met DeRay and Krystal in our driveway. She was wearing a bright blue bandanna on her head. DeRay lifted his orange ice chest into the back of our Volvo and said, "Now follow us."

Before we were down the block, Liz said, "We're not driving like that."

"It's his right to change lanes," I said, moving left. "He's using his signals."

"We've got a baby in the car."

"Liz," I said, "I know we've got a baby in the car. And we're following DeRay out to Hercules Powder for a picnic. This is going to be a nice day."

As it turned out, DeRay made the light at Thirteenth and we didn't. He disappeared ahead, the blue bandanna on Krystal's head dipping in front of two cars in the distance, and they were gone. We sat in silence. Allie was humming as if she had something to say and would say it next. There was no traffic on Thirteenth at all. How long is a traffic light? I've never known.

When the light turned green, Liz said: "Just let us out."

"Good," I said. "Where would I do that?"

"Right here," she said.

Without hesitation, instantly, I pulled against the curb. The sudden stop made Allie exhale with a high, sweet squeal. "Is this good?" I said.

Liz looked at me with a face I'd never seen before. She unlocked her door and unbuckled her seat belt.

"Wait," I said. I knew I was out of control. "I'll drop you at Claire's. Shut your door."

She snapped her door closed, but did not refasten her seat belt. I wheeled sharply back onto the street and dropped three blocks down to her sister's house. I jumped out and ran around to the baby's door and lifted her out. I kissed her and placed her in Liz's arms and went back around to my door. I didn't want any more talking. It was like the things I've done when I was drunk. Before I could measure anything, I was back on the access headed for West Valley.

I just thought about driving, how I would pass each car, dip right, reassume my lane, and head out. When I entered the freeway, I hammered the Volvo to maximum speed. I hated this car. It had always been too heavy and too slow.

DeRay waited for me at the main gates of Hercules, the plant situated alone on the vast gradual slope of the west valley. There was a guard at the gate, and DeRay waved me through, grinning, and then he and Krystal shot past me through the empty parking lot and under the red-checked water tower to the corner of the pavement where they dropped onto a smooth dirt road that wound up the hill. Powdery dust lifted from their tires and they led me up the lane and around into a small gravel parking area where there were already four blue government vans. Off to the side about twenty people, about half of them in military khaki, stood in the weeds. DeRay parked his bike and came over to where I was getting out of the Volvo.

"Where's the wife?" he said, looking in. "Is the baby here?"

"No, they decided to go to Liz's sister's."

"Oh hell, that's too bad. This should be good."

We carried the coolers and a blanket to a high spot in the dry grass and spread out our gear. "Who are those guys?" I asked.

"The staff and some guys from Hill Air Force Base."

"Is it okay to have a beer?"

"That's why we brought it." He reached inside the orange Igloo for the cold cans and handed me a beer. Krystal wasn't drinking.

DeRay walked down a few yards to look at the bunker a half mile below. I had forgotten the view from out here. I could see the whole city against the Wasatch Range and each of the blue canyons: Little Cottonwood, Big Cottonwood, Millcreek. On the hill I could see the old white Ambassador Building, two blocks from my house, and I could imagine my yard, the fence.

Krystal was staring out over the valley. "Your wife didn't want to come to the country?" she said. I could tell that she knew all about it.

DeRay came back. "It's all set. In twenty minutes, you're going to hear some noise." He pointed to the bunker. It'll fire south. They'll catch this on the university seismograph as a two-point. What'd you bring to eat?"

We broke out the sandwiches and the salad. DeRay sat down on the blanket, Indian-style, his big boots like furniture beneath him, and ate hungrily. "Hey, this is good," he said, pointing his fork at the pasta salad. "Nothing like a picnic." He drained his beer and tossed it over his shoulder into the tall grass. "Just like home," he said. While we ate, DeRay had waved at a couple of the guys by the vans, and later when we were cleaning up the paper plates, one man walked up to us.

"How does it look?" DeRay asked him as they shook hands.

"Good, Ace. We've got a countdown."

DeRay introduced us to the man, Clint, and we all stood in a line facing the bunker. "In a minute you are going to see thirty seconds of the largest controlled explosion in the history of this state," DeRay said to me and winked. "We hope."

A moment later I saw the group near the vans all take a step backward and then we saw the flash at the earthen mound become a huge white flare in a roar that seemed to flatten the grass around us. It was too bright to look at and hard to look away from, and the sound was ferocious, a pressure. I found myself turning my head to escape it, but there was no help. Clint wore sunglasses and was staring at the flash itself. He wasn't moving. Round balls of smoke rolled from the flame and began to tumble into the air, piling in a thick black column. Krystal watched with her head tilted. She was squinting and her mouth was open.

When it stopped, it stopped so suddenly it was as if someone had closed a door on it, and the roar was sucked out of the air and replaced by a tinny buzzing which I realized was in my ears.

"Jesus Christ," Krystal said.

The people by the vans were kind of cheering and calling and several of them turned and pointed at DeRay happily.

"Congratulations, Ace," Clint said and shook DeRay's hand again. "It was beautiful."

"Yeah, right," DeRay said. "Now on to phase four."

Clint walked down to where the group was boarding the vans, and two more guys came up and shook DeRay's hand, and then the four vans packed up and drove carefully down the dirt road out of sight. I was watching the smoke cloud twist and roll silently in the sky, thick as oil. You could see this from our house. I wondered what Liz was doing, what she had told her sister. My ears simmered. With the vans gone this seemed a lonely place.

"That was your rocket?" I asked him.

"Fuel feed. I'm the fuel feed guy."

I looked at him. "I thought you were a machinist."

"That's all it is, really." He pulled out another beer and sat on the cooler. "Just like this can. Same problem. You've got to keep the beer under pressure—two or three atmospheres. But you've got to cut the top here so I can open it with one finger. How deep do you score it? Figure that out and your problems are history." He lifted the tab and the beer hissed. He took a long swig and shrugged. "Oly's a good beer, right? We're having a fine picnic here. Am I right?"

Krystal walked toward us, arms folded.

DeRay said, "Hey, let's not head out yet." He stood. "Ace, you feel like riding the bike? I feel like a little ride." He turned to the woman. "You okay, Krystal, if we run up the hill for a minute? You can have some more of that great macaroni salad."

He started the Harley and I climbed on behind him. "Your wife is some cook. I'm sorry she missed this."

We cruised slowly down the road and through the lot. I was thinking about Liz and I felt bad and I could feel it getting worse. And it was funny, but I wanted it worse.

When we hit the highway, DeRay turned and said, "My second wife could cook," and he jammed the accelerator and we were lost in the wind, going seventy up the old road toward Copperton, slowing through Bingham and then hitting it hard again, winding up the canyon using both sides of the road. It didn't matter. The air was at me like a hatchet and I'd watch the yellow line drift under the bike on one side and then another. At the top, the gate to the mine was closed. The mine had been closed for years.

DeRay pulled up to the gate and I felt the dizzy pressure of stopping. "I come up here all the time," he said. "After work I just drive up. Push the gate." The chain was locked, but it opened three feet. He conducted the motorcycle under the chain easily. Near the pit, we sped up a paved incline and circled into the parking lot of the old visitors' center.

The structure was weathered. The back walls of the shelter held poster-size framed photographs of the mining operations: a dynamite blast, the ore train in a tunnel, one of the giant trucks being filled by a mammoth loader. DeRay had gone to the overlook and was leaning on the rail staring out at the vast rock amphitheater. The clouds above the copper mine were moving and shredding. The wind was chilly. "You want to bring the bike in?" I asked him. "We're going to get wet."

"Forget it," he said.

"I hope Krystal gets in the car."

"That woman knows what to do in the rain." He stood and pointed at four deer that walked along the uppermost level of the mine. "Check that."

"What are they looking for?" I said. The animals had made some kind of mistake.

DeRay leaned on the rail and said, "You know that Krystal's leaving."

"What?"

"Yeah, she has to go. Her crazy man is on leave. He's out. They weren't really divorced. You can't divorce someone who's crazy. Something. She's going out to his folks.'"

"I didn't know. Hey, I'm sorry."

"Come on, what is it? She has to go," he said. DeRay rubbed his eyes with a thumb and forefinger. His face in the dim light looked blue, the way it did some nights on his porch. When he looked up, he said, "Hey, look at you." I reached up and felt my hair standing all over. "You're going to want to get a cap." DeRay lifted his and snugged it on my head. "Why don't you take it for a spin? Go ahead, down the road and back." He waved at the motorcycle and his tattoo in the gloom looked like a wound.

I said, "Krystal's a good woman."

"Oh hell," he said. "They're all good women."

"Things happen," I said.

He turned to me. "No they don't. I know all about this. Things don't *happen*. I'm an engineer. One thing leads to another. Listen. You're a nice kid, but that fence around your place won't stop a thing. What are you, thirty?"

We could smell the rain. It felt real late. It felt like October, November. When you have a baby, you have to put in a lawn. You're supposed to build a fence. There's no surprise in that. I am like every other man in that.

"That was some rocket," I said. I could taste trouble in my mouth and I felt kind of high, like a kid a long way from home. "I'm sorry Liz didn't see it. It won't be easy to describe."

DeRay pointed again at the deer and we watched as they tried to scramble up the steep mine slope. It was desperate but so far away that we couldn't hear the gravel falling. They kept slipping. Finally, two made it and disappeared over the summit. The two left behind stood still. "Hey, don't listen to me," DeRay said. "I'm just squawking. We should have brought some beer."

I went out and mounted the Harley. It came up off the stand easier than I thought and started right up. I sat down in the seat and looked over at DeRay as the wheels crept forward. I could sense the ion charge before rain. We were definitely going to get wet. Just a little spin.

DeRay was right. He had been right about the trencher and he was right about one thing leading to another. I am not the kind of person who stays out in bad weather, but there I was. I lifted my feet from the pavement and felt it all happen. It was a big machine, more than I could handle, but I could just feel it wanting to balance. It began to drift. I'd never felt anything like it before. There were accidents in this thing. I would just take it down to the gate and right back up again.

BLAZO

WHEN BURNS arrived in Kotzebue, they were shooting the dogs. He'd never been to Alaska before and it
seemed without compromise. Weather had kept him in Nome for
two days, where he'd seen a saloon fire. He'd been across the street in
a shop buying chocolate and bottled water, and the eerie frozen
scene mesmerized him. As the flames pulsed from both windows in
the sharp wind and the crews sprayed water which caked on the
wooden structure instantly as ice, the patrons emerged slowly, their
collars up in the weather, drinks in their gloved hands. Burns wasn't
drinking. He sipped water and ate chocolate in his hotel room, listening to the wind growl. Then the short hop over to Kotzebue was
the roughest flight of his life, the plane pitching and dropping,
smacking against the treacherous air. Burns could hear dogs barking
in the front hold and they helped. It's a short flight, he thought, and
they wouldn't crash with dogs.

In Kotzebue, Burns waited in the small metal terminal until a wiz-
ened, leather-faced Inuit came up to him and grinned, showing no
teeth, and lifted his suitcase into the back of an orange International
pickup. Burns followed the man and got into the truck. The cab was

rife with the smell of bourbon and four or five bottles rolled around Burns' feet. The man smiled again, his eyes merry, and drove onto the main road of the village, where they fell behind the sheriff's white truck. There were two men in the back with rifles riding in the cold. Kotzebue was gray under old drifts but the wind had ripped the tops from some of the banks and spread new whiter fans of snow across the road. The high school was letting out and three-wheelers and snow machines cruised along the road, both sides, and cut the corners at every crossroad.

Suddenly, the two men in the sheriff's truck stood and raised their rifles, shooting into a field behind the buildings. Each shot twice and then they quickly clambered out of the vehicle as it stopped. One of the men fell to the ice and got back up and followed his partner running into the field.

"What's going on?" Burns asked, but his driver only squinted at him and shook his head slightly. Burns could see the two men standing over a dark form in the snow. He saw one of them shoot again. The man behind the wheel of the sheriff's truck lifted a hand, but Burns's driver did not wave back.

Two streets later, the orange International turned into a narrow off street and stopped in front of an ice-coated trailer. The man unloaded the suitcase and held out four fingers. The way he tapped them made Burns understand.

"Miss Munson will be back at four?"

The man nodded and reached behind Burns and opened the trailer's door. Whiskey, Burns thought, as he watched the man return to the truck and drive off. A thick drift of whiskey moved with the man. As Burns lifted his bag and turned to the iced steps, a black Newfoundland on a chain rose from a doghouse half buried in the snow, shook, and looked up expectantly. It took Burns a moment to recognize the dog, and then he knelt down and ran his hand through the fur. "Molly, you pup," he said. "You grew up." There was a muffled clamor from the roadway and Burns turned to see a passenger fall from a three-wheeler, slide along on his back for ten yards, then climb back on behind the driver. It had begun to snow faintly in the early afternoon, and the tiny dots of frozen snow were sparse in the gloom. Burns scratched the dog again. "Molly," he said. "What happened to Alec?"

In the close warmth of the trailer, Burns again found himself craving food. The cold left him ravenous. In Nome after his daily walks he would fall upon his stash of chocolate like a schoolboy. And now, he barely took time to hang his gear in the small mud room and sit at the table in the kitchen before he was stuffing the candy into his mouth. It was amusing to be so aware of his body after so many years.

There was a stomping, felt more than heard, and Burns saw light in the entry as the door opened and closed. "Hello!" a man's voice called, and a large bearded man in a blue military parka came into the kitchen, pulling off his glove and extending a hand to Burns. "You picked one hell of a week," the man said, shaking Burns' hand. "Glen Batton. I'm the Forest Service here, and," he added in another tone, "a friend of Julie's."

Burns said his name and Glen Batton went ahead with the weather report about a new Siberian front moving in. "If it cleared, I'd fly you out to Kolvik myself. As is, you'll be lucky to get down to the Co-op for candy." Batton pointed to the candy wrappers on the table. "I'm sorry about your son."

Burns nodded.

"You're from Connecticut."

"Yes. Connecticut."

Glen Batton put his glove back on. "Well, listen, I just wanted to introduce myself and offer my services, though that may be useless. How long are you here?"

"I'm not sure," Burns said. "I need to get out to Kolvik."

"Well, you won't do that," Glen said, moving back to the door. "But have a nice visit. I'll probably see you Friday at the hospital party."

"Why are the police shooting the dogs?"

"Strays," Batton said. "Too many loose dogs raising hell with the teams. Count the dogs in this town sometime." He turned to leave, but came back into the room. "Hey, listen. You may need to know a couple of things." Batton brushed the parka hood off his long hair, "Look, what happened to Alec is a bad deal, but it happens all the time. People don't understand this country. They think they can handle it, but you can't handle it."

"I see," Burns said.

"And I should tell you this." Glen Batton looked quickly away and back. "Julie is a little fragile about this whole deal. Your visit a year after it all happened. We've talked about it. I don't know what your plans are, but you may want to step lightly."

"I will."

"If it gets tight, you can always bunk with me or at the hotel."

"Thank you. I'll remember that," Burns said, holding Glen's look until the bearded man turned and left. Now he wanted a drink, blood sugar or no blood sugar; Burns could feel the call in his gut, his heartbeat, the roof of his mouth. He went to the sink and drew and drank three glasses of water.

BURNS HEARD a fuss outside and then the clatter of claws on the linoleum of the entry and the Newfoundland came bounding in and burrowed his nose into Burns' hand where it hung beside the easy chair in which he slept. He had sat down to read in the small living room and sleep had taken him like an irrefutable force. Now a woman appeared in the entrance, and that was Burns' first thought: She's not a girl. He had last seen his son Alec six years ago when he had graduated college in New Haven. Burns had expected his wife to be a girl. Julie removed her knee-length lavender parka and the white knit cap and shook her hair, smiling at him. Without meaning to, Burns stared frankly at her in her white nurse's dress. It was the first surprise he'd had since he'd been in Alaska: Julie was a woman, a tall woman with pale blond hair that fell below her shoulders. He stood and took her hand.

"What are you smiling at?" she said, and smiled. "Sit down, Tom.

I'm going to call you Tom, okay? I'm glad you're here. How was your flight?" Burns felt things shifting. First all the hunger, and then the nap taking him like a kid, and now this woman in white.

"I fell asleep," he said. "Sorry."

"It's too warm in here." Julie went to the thermostat. "That's the one thing about Alaska. It's too warm all the time. There's no such thing as a little cold. They keep the hospital at eighty degrees. It reminds me of Manhattan that way." She sat on the couch and took off her shoes. "Alec talked about you quite a lot. And so did Helen, but you're quite different than I pictured."

"Oh?"

She stood up, her dress rustling. "You want a drink?"

"Water's fine."

"That's right. I knew that. Sorry." Burns watched her splash some Wild Turkey into a plastic tumbler. "Okay, I'll be right back. I've got to get these stockings off. Yes, from Helen I imagined you'd be a bit wrecked or frumpy, you know, dirty overcoat, greasy hair."

"Bottle of tokay?"

"I'm kidding, but your ex-wife can be a bit severe."

"Helen is a woman with a memory."

Julie went down a short hallway where Burns could see the edge of a bed. When he saw her dress fall upon the bed, he stood and moved to the kitchen sink, poured a glass of water, and tried to see out the frosted window. He felt agitated. He pressed the glass against his lip. He was deeply hungry again and he felt funny about falling asleep. Napping wasn't his custom, but the sweet closed warmth of the trailer and the wind heaving at the structure, rocking it faintly, had just taken him. He had been doing things by will for ten years now, since the first week after his forty-second birthday, and he was known as a measured man who had placed the remaining components of his life back together purposefully. He was a man who didn't feel things instantly, and now there was this person, Julie, whom he instantly felt quite wonderful about, and suddenly his mission seemed strange and he felt far from home.

She returned in a worn pair of brown corduroys and a simple

white turtleneck. His room was at the other end of the trailer, and as she laid out some towels, Burns couldn't take his eyes from her.

"Blazo picked you up all right?" she said.

"The talkative soul? The whiskey person?"

As she moved about the room, showing him the bureau and the electric blanket control and the closet, he studied her long arms, her wristwatch, her short, unpolished fingernails, the small gold necklace, the rise of her collarbones under the fabric of her pullover.

"He can't talk. He drank some heating fuel years ago. Blazo. He drank some Blazo and doesn't talk, but he's a gem. He is the mechanic to trust in this village."

Julie had pale green eyes and a faint spray of freckles across her nose and forehead. Burns put her at about thirty. He felt like a teenager sneaking looks at her breasts. He hadn't seen a woman in a turtleneck sweater for twenty years. There was an angry red scar on her neck protuding from her shirt, which stunned him at first, and then he realized it was a violin mark. Alec had had one.

Burns heard two concussions from outside and then two more, the distant snapping of gunfire. He held on to the sink and felt the wind pull at the trailer and he thought: Don't touch her. Don't you touch this woman.

FOR DINNER Julie had a white cloth on the kitchen table and Burns tried to eat slowly. "I appreciate your putting me up like this," he said. "I'm genuinely sorry we haven't met until now."

"Tom, don't start apologizing. I mean it. This is Alaska, there isn't room." Julie looked at him squarely. "I understand about the wedding and Alec did too. Believe me. And you were right not to come. It was Helen's show really." She sipped her bourbon, then lifted a finger from the rim and pointed at him. "I'm not kidding."

"I just want to see where he lived out there, where he . . . I missed so much, and now I just want to see what it's like here."

"This is what it's like, dark and windy, lots of accidents."

"I spoke with Helen before I came and she simply wanted you to know that she would love to hear from you and that if you ever needed anything she would help. She was quite sincere."

Julie placed her glass carefully on the table. "I know. We've spoken about the funeral. He wasn't my husband anymore, of course. We were only married the one year. And I hadn't seen him for months. I tried to handle everything I could at this end, but I couldn't go down to the states and get all involved in a world which wasn't there anymore. You went out?"

"I did," Burns said. "I finally went to something."

Burns ate slowly, his hunger a fire that had him on the edge of his chair. He felt oddly alert. "Who found Alec?"

"Glen reported the cabin burn on his return from a caribou count, and the Search and Rescue went out from here. You can see Lloyd tomorrow, the sheriff. It was his men."

They were quiet for a while, Burns eating and watching Molly, chin down on the living-room rug, watch him. All of these things had happened, Alec's wedding, divorce, death, in half a dog's life.

"So, you're Thomas Burns," Julie said, smiling again. "It is just a little weird to see you."

"That's the way everybody seems to be taking it."

"Well, Glen is convinced you're a cop." She pointed at his clean plate. "Still hungry?"

"No," he lied. He stood and set his dishes in the sink. "Is there need for a cop?"

She joined him at the counter and spoke softly. "No. It's an unhappy story, but we've got all the cops we need." She stopped him from clearing the table. "Come on, I'd better take you down to the Tahoe before my students get here. All visitors go to the Tahoe. The largest bar in the Arctic Circle. Even though you don't drink, it's a good walk, and next week in Darien, you can say you've seen it once, tell stories."

OUTSIDE IN the heavy wind, Burns and Julie shuffled along the hard snowpacked roadway. The dark was gashed by several flaring arc lights above the armory and the high school, new brick buildings built with the first oil surplus money. Several vehicles passed them at close range, snow machines and three-wheelers bulleting by, and as Burns shied from them, he bumped Julie several times, saying, "Sorry, I'm not used to this."

"It's all right. They're not either," she said, pointing to the way the small vehicles cut the corners at every intersection, their paths running across open yards and slicing very close to the buildings. The drivers wouldn't slow down at all around these shortcuts. Burns cringed watching them disappear. They'll be killed, he thought. They'll crash head-on with someone coming the other way and be killed. He and Julie didn't speak in the pressure of the cold. They stopped several times to pick things from the roadway: a scarf, a big leather mitten, and at the corner where they turned for the bar, a loaf of bread, still soft. He found such litter alarming, but Julie only smiled and told him simply, "Bring it along."

The Tahoe was a large metal building which looked like a one-story warehouse. Julie led him up the iced steps and across the wide porch into the big barroom. Inside the door, in the dark, one booth was stacked high with miscellaneous gear: sweaters, hats, and gloves. Julie told him, "Put your treasures right there. It's the lost and found." The vast room was gloomy and crowded. As Burns's eyes adjusted, he saw that the booths were full of Inuit, and though the room was warm and redolent of cigarettes and fur, few people had taken their coats off.

"What would you like?" Julie said.

"I'd like a vanilla shake," Burns said. "This country has got me starved. But I'll take a soda water, anything really."

It was not an animated bar. Burns could see four school board members who were on his flight standing at the bar, talking, but they were the loudest group. The dark clusters of natives huddled around the tables and booths in the room spoke quietly if at all. Even the pool players moved with a kind of lethargy. Burns stood by the end of the bar, his stomach growling as he thawed. He'd been in lots of bars and this was possibly the largest. In the old days, after martinis at his club, he'd hit every hole in the wall on the way to Grand Central, eventually taking the last train to Connecticut, the ride as cloudy and smeared as the windows. He hadn't been a sloppy drunk; he'd been a careful drunk. The word was "serious"—for everything he'd done, really. He was a serious young man, who had married seriously and become a serious attorney, who drank seriously and became a serious drunk. The mistakes he made were serious and now, in the Arctic Circle, he thought of himself in the Tahoe as a serious visitor on a serious mission who did not drink and took his not drinking seriously. He knew how he was perceived and it was a kind of comfort for Burns to have the word to hold on to.

"Welcome to Alaska," Julie said, handing him a glass of sparkling water. "There are no limes." She touched his glass with her own.

"I'd worry if there were."

"You don't drink," she said, sipping her whiskey. "Smart man."

"No. Alec I'm sure told you. I got smart a little late." He sucked on his lip and nodded at her. "I've missed a lot. I'm an *old* man."

"Not quite." She smiled and touched his glass again. "And it is a world of accidents, believe me. Someone just dropped the bread, right? And on the way home we'll find the peanut butter. Lots of things get dropped." She looked at his face appraisingly. "You're still a smart man." Julie waved a hand out over the room. "How do you like the Tahoe, the hub of culture on the frontier?"

"It's big. I spent a lot of time having stronger drinks in smaller places."

"You're a lawyer."

"I am. I was a good lawyer years ago. Now I'm simply highly paid: probate on the Gold Coast. Did Alec say he'd forgiven me for it?"

"Alec always spoke of you in the best terms. You taught him how to sail?"

"One summer a long time ago. I wasn't around much."

Someone, a figure, fell out of a booth across the room and two tablemates stood and lifted the person back into place.

"Will you stay here?" Burns asked her. "In Kotzebue?"

"I'm a nurse. There's a lot of call for that here. I've got a life—and I've got my students."

The walk back to the trailer again awakened in Burns a huge hunger. He had the same feeling he always had when he spoke of his past, honest and diminished, but now he mainly felt hungry. The wind was in their faces and they leaned against it, talking, while Burns felt the chocolate bar in his pocket. Julie spoke of meeting his son their year at Juilliard. "I wasn't their kind of musician," she said, punching the words into the wind. "I was lucky. I'd been lucky with the competitions really. And I didn't really care for all the work. It was nonstop." They could hear dogs barking out in the fields where the teams were staked. Julie took his arm and turned into the narrow, icy lane where her trailer stood. "I like to play—I teach and I still play—but at Juilliard, well," she faced him in the cold dark, her face luminous, "too many *artists*."

Inside the trailer, Julie's three students plucked at violin strings tuning their instruments. She introduced them to Burns: Tara, Mercy, and Calvin, native kids all about twelve. They sat serious and straight-backed in the living room for the lesson while Julie began leading them through the half hour's exercises. Calvin's eyes kept going sideways to Burns, and Burns could see they were all self-conscious, so he stood and started for his room. Julie stopped and came to him. "Can I get you anything?"

"No, thank you," he said. Taking off his coat had made him impossibly tired. "I'll see you in the morning."

As he climbed into bed he could hear the sliding harmonies of the four violins rise and fall. Alec had started the violin when he was six, the year Helen had taken him and gone back to Ohio, and years later when Alec finished Juilliard, he had gone to Alaska to teach. Burns had never contacted his son when he was studying in New York. In those days guilt had slowed everything Burns did. He had moved his practice to Connecticut by then, and three times Burns had taken the train into the city and walked by the music school, slowing enough to hear the strains of piano or French horn from a window.

And then as if scolded by the music, he hurried away. He couldn't cross the street and go in. Now Burns cringed at his cowardice.

Under the heavy blankets in his room, as the wind moaned over the trailer, Burns listened to the violins. He'd eaten his chocolate and was tired to his bones. He could feel the structure moving in the weight of the gusts. It was like being aboard ship.

Later he had heard voices, their timbre, something almost angry, and then he felt the door shut, and the rushing quiet took him again.

BURNS WOKE in the bright morning and heard the white wind. He was disappointed as he wiped at the frost on the inside of his window to see the storm outside, but there was something else: all this weather. He liked this odd place, big on the earth and full of weather. He'd had the same feeling on certain days sailing off St. Johns: the ocean could be a big, unknowable thing there, indifferent to anybody's plans.

Julie had left him a map on the table, a pencil grid of the village with arrows to the sheriff's office and his phone number. At the bottom it said, "I'll be back at five—and then I'd better take you to the hospital party, so everyone can meet the mystery man. It's at seven. J." Beside it was a large sweet roll, which Burns wolfed down with a mug of the cold powdered milk from the fridge. Standing there in his pajamas in the kitchen drinking the thick, cold milk, Burns grinned. He felt like a kid. He was grinning. Powdered milk was better than he had imagined.

Outside, marching sidelong into the killer wind, Burns felt the cold only in his exposed forehead and then not as cold, but as a constriction, a tight band of pain. He walked with his head turned for protection into his parka hood, and the drivers of the snow machines who roared past also drove with their heads turned. It made him stop and move aside several times. He saw several more mittens in the snow, but didn't pick them up. The day, the world, was all wind, even the rustle of his coat was lost in the gale.

The sheriff's office was two long blocks past the Tahoe in a small complex of state and federal buildings, one-story brick cottages linked by covered walkways. The sheriff was waiting for him, but after they shook hands, Burns had to sit down for a moment and rub his forehead while the aching subsided. He'd sat behind his own desk just like this, rubbing his head, unable to talk to some client as a low wave of nausea rinsed through. In those days, while he tried to poison himself with it, drinking pernicious amounts of gin every night, his clients never knew, his business never quivered. When he went down, they didn't find him for a week, and when Helen came to the hospital, she simply said to stop it, that she was fine and would be, but that killing himself would make it worse for everyone. "You've broken me," she said. "I'm taking the baby and going home." And that was that. He was two weeks in the hospital, having almost lost toes to frostbite, and when he came out, he moved the office to New Canaan, dropped everything but probate, and knew—essentially— and this had nothing to do with the drinking—that his life was over. Helen had already taken Alec back to Ohio, where her mother had lived, and a few years later she married Charley, an attorney in Chagrin Falls.

The sheriff's name was Lloyd Right, a man all in khaki, whom Burns liked right away. "Mr. Burns," he said, taking Burns' coat and pointing out the easy chair, "now tell me exactly the objectives of your visit to the frozen north."

He nodded through the tale, his jaw in his fist, and then when Burns finished, Lloyd Right stood and went to the three-drawer file in the corner and pulled out a folder. "It doesn't appear as if Glen Batton or anybody else is going to be able to lift you out there." Right went back to his desk and sat down, placing the folder squarely in front of him. "This weather has been tight for a week, and it's a pity, not that there's much to see, but I understand too well the importance of just being at the scene." Right dialed the phone and then hung up. It rang and he picked up and said, "Jerry, bring us two coffees." He looked at Burns. "You want some coffee, don't you?"

"I do."

"Anyway, Julie told me about you and about Alec's mother. These things are always bad. What I can do for you is tell you what I know, let you read the file. It was an accident, you can tell his mother that. We don't have any photos. But Julie had been by his place and she can describe it to you. You could tell the family that you went out there, that—"

"No, I couldn't," Burns said. "I couldn't do that. You understand. I am the family. I could tell Alec's mother I was here and saw this file and that I spoke to you."

The deputy came in with the coffee, setting the two mugs on the sheriff's desk and backing out. While the office door was open, another officer came in, the cold on him like an odor, a rifle in his hand. "Lloyd, they've seen the stray out at the foothills. You coming?"

"Take Bob. Call me in half an hour," Right said. When the men had left, the sheriff sipped his coffee. "We've got one goddam stray left, and he's a smart one. What a lone dog can do to a staked team. You don't want to see it. Some of our teams are worth thousands; two teams are going down for the Iditarod next month. Do they hear about the Iditarod in Connecticut, Mr. Burns?"

"They do," Burns said. "You don't think I can get out to Kolvik?"

"I don't. It's too bad. I've been to the site. Alec lived about two miles from the village, south, in the low hills. The cabin had been totally consumed." The sheriff stood and came around his metal desk, sitting on the edge of the short bookshelf near Burns. "You know, even before he left here, something had happened to Alec," he said. "He had a breakdown or something. This is not in the report. But he began acting strange. You can ask Julie about it. We were sorry about it here. What he had done for the music program in the high school in two years was wonderful, and when he dropped out and moved out there sixty miles, well, everybody felt bad. But we see this kind of thing here. A guy moves out and then further out and moves, if he can, to what he sees as the end of the road, the edge, and either he lives there or he doesn't, but he doesn't come back."

Lloyd Right went back and sat behind his desk, working his

closed eyes with his fingers for a moment. He went on, "You figure it. He was a fine musician. So, he moves out to Kolvik and starts a trapline. It was just above the cabin in a draw. That's where they found the body. It was a classic case of freezing to death, I mean, he'd taken off his clothes and they were scattered around. It's very common, Mr. Burns, and I would think it's important that you know this was an accident, not suicide. He misjudged the time and was out too long." Lloyd Right stood again and drained his coffee. "We found the dog out there with him. Julie has her."

ON THE way home, Burns felt his mouth dry with hunger and he went into the small Co-op and bought a bag of chocolate bars. Outside a man had fallen on the steps and Burns and a woman helped the man climb back up. Burns took the back street to Julie's, the wind now pushing him along the pathway. There were fewer close calls with snow machines here, and he ate the candy and walked slowly, his hands thrust deeply into his parka pockets. Then a strange thing happened that scared him so badly he involuntarily ducked and nearly fell. At first Burns thought something had hit him, but then he saw the light change, a sunflash that settled on the village for a second dropping thick blue shadows on the sides of things. It was painfully bright. The sun was out. In the sky Burns could see the contours of individual clouds. Stay there, he thought. Just stay there.

THE PARTY that night was held in the hospital recreation room, a small square room lined with blue vinyl couches. The hospital was obviously an old wooden military building that had been superficially redone. There was a new checkerboard linoleum floor, but wooden-framed windows lined each wall. Julie took Burns by the arm and they went around to everybody in the room, thirty or so people: Julie's head nurse, Karen; Lloyd Right and his wife; both deputies; several nurses and two doctors (both women); Glen Batton; the high school principal and his wife; a dozen teachers there; the school board members whom Burns recognized from his flight; a social counselor named Victor (the only Inuit at the party); some guys from the National Guard; and part of the airport staff. Burns wasn't very comfortable. He'd slept all afternoon and his feet hurt and his face felt swollen. But he was keen, too, because the weather had changed—there was talk of a clearing. Jets were coming in from Nome tomorrow.

He stood by the buffet table and ate strips of the salty ham while he filled a small paper plate with deviled eggs. He felt a bit foolish, but he could not move away from the buffet table, eating handfuls of the chips and dip and mixed nuts, nodding at people with his mouth full, smiling, absolutely out of control. When one of the airport personnel came up and said, "So, you're not a cop," Burns just smiled at him too and shook his head, popping another of the tangy eggs into his mouth.

There was a slide show. One of the nurses had been in the Grand Canyon the past summer and showed slides of her river trip. They were good slides, not professional, but full of steep purple rock and shadow. Burns stood behind the couches during the presentation, eating carrot sticks and drinking 7UP, and the Grand Canyon on the hospital wall, the foaming brown river, the two huge yellow rafts, and the travelers in their bikinis and sunglasses all gave him a kind of spin and he finally stopped eating and sat down.

"You're from Connecticut," a woman next to him said. It was Karen, the chief nurse. In the near-dark he saw that she was about his age, a brunette with an aquiline nose, like a pretty schoolteacher.

"Yes, I am," he said. The slide changed and everybody laughed: four naked people holding hands ran toward the river.

"Which one is you, Leslie?" Glen Batton said.

"Dream on, Glen," the projectionist said.

The woman next to Burns, Karen, whispered, "Before we were transferred, we lived in New London for ten years."

Lake Mead appeared as a blue plate under a pale sky. It was the first slide that had a horizontal theme and then the lights clicked on and there was applause. "This year," Leslie said to the group, "we're going to the Everglades and the Keys."

Glen Batton, who had been sitting with Julie, said, "Well, keep your clothes on around the alligators, Leslie."

"That wasn't me."

"Don't listen to him," Julie said. "He's been in Alaska too long."

People were standing up and moving the couches against the walls now, and suddenly the lights went down and a tape began to play a Beatles song that Burns knew, but didn't know the name of, and three couples began to dance. Burns went to the window and holding his hand against the pane, he saw the stars.

"The weather's clearing for a spell." One of the deputies had come up to him.

Burns looked at the man. "Did you find that dog?"

"Not today, but we will."

"How often do you have to do this?"

"Not twice a year. Usually just spring. A lot of dogs are let loose. It's a bad deal."

"Come here," a man said from behind him, taking his arm. It was the counselor, the Inuit, Victor. "I'll show you something." He led Burns past Karen and down the hallway and out the side door into the cold. "Check this." The man pointed over the roof where Burns saw a finger of yellow light run up the sky and fade followed by two pale pink ones that shifted like something seen through a depth of water.

"I've never seen them before," Burns said to the man. His breath rose as white mist.

The man smiled. "Alec hadn't either," he said. "I'm sorry for what happened. He was related to you?"

"He was my son." Now a greenish white washed up the sky and flared in sections as if cooling.

"He was too smart for this place," the man said.

"What do you mean?"

"What would keep him here? All the white guys with their dog teams? Alec was a genius, right? He must be what a genius is."

"Possibly," Burns said. The cold had gone through him and become a pressure in his neck. Now the pink was back, shooting like a crazy beacon into the black.

"You're staying with Julie?"

"Yes," Burns answered, and alerted by something in Victor's voice he added, "Why?"

"Nothing," Victor said, looking up, his hands thrust deep in his pockets. "I could never figure them. Alec and her."

"I see," Burns said. For a moment the sky was black. "She's so . . ." Burns opened the sentence hoping the other man would finish it. He wanted this information.

"I don't know. I shouldn't talk. You'll see that not much up here is what it seems, but they didn't fit. She's too sociable. Maybe that's what I mean."

Suddenly a canopy of blue light came up the sky and then shredded and disappeared.

Someone took Burns' arm and he felt a body next to him. "Aren't you freezing?" Karen said. She shivered against him, hugging his arm with both hands. "It's twenty below." Burns put his arm out and around the woman.

"Do you know what happened to him?" he said to Victor.

"I don't. I took him hunting once, his first year here, before he moved out. He was good people. I never saw somebody so swept away by this place. He loved it all. He was an intense guy all around."

Karen shifted her position, running her arms around Burns' middle and burying her head in his shoulder. "It's cold!" she said, laughing. The night continued to convulse above them, a huge panorama revolving across the horizon. The sharp dry cold sized Burns' skin, his face. The food and the slides were all gone. He was awake.

"What's the weather tomorrow, Victor? Could a person fly somewhere?"

"We'll get one day," Victor said. "Tomorrow you could fly anywhere you want."

INSIDE, KAREN kept his arm, the cold now real in the warm room. Most of the people at the party were dancing, and Burns saw Glen Batton and Julie moving slowly to the music, another song he knew but couldn't identify. He didn't know the name of five songs in the world. It was a wonder to him; he didn't know any songs.

Karen asked him if he wanted to dance and he smiled and said he had to go. She led him back to the coats, which were in the dark entry hall. She handed him his parka, and the way she looked at him, frankly, without any real pity, led him to do something he hadn't done in ten years. He leaned to her and put his free hand around her back and kissed her. She embraced him fully, but without anything frantic, and the dark of the hall and the smell of the coats made him feel like a boy again and now too he was full of resolve about tomorrow as he held her there, lifting her against him. He liked feeling her body and she shifted twice against him, moving so their legs were interwoven, and he heard her moan in the shifting coats, and he did not let go. Then he heard his name. Glen was saying his name.

"Excuse me," Glen said, coming down the dark hallway. They had disengaged by the time he spoke again. "Julie asked me to tell you that I'm willing to take you out to Kolvik tomorrow." Glen was looking at Karen. "The weather's supposed to clear."

"I appreciate that," Burns said. "Are you sure?"

"The weather is going to be splendid." Julie had come up behind him. She saw Burns putting on his coat. "Where are you going?"

"I thought I'd get some rest. Deviled eggs, the Grand Canyon, the northern lights . . . this is a lot for an old man."

"He'd never seen the lights before," Karen said, squeezing Burns' arm.

"Here," Julie said, taking his arm from Karen. "I'll go with you."

"No, please," he said. "I know the way. Please. Stay."

Julie retrieved her coat and pushed Glen back to the party. Karen stood around until she saw that Julie was serious about leaving, and then she took both of Burns' hands and reached up and kissed him quickly, drifting back to the party herself. As he opened the door for Julie and pushed out into the white night, Burns saw Batton watching them.

The night was now still, the first stillness Burns had felt in Alaska, and he felt the weight of the profound chill, the northern sky fringed with erratic blooming light. "Her husband ran the armory here," Julie said. "He was killed loading freight two years ago."

"She stayed."

Julie looked at him. "People stay," she said. "You come out, you don't go back." Julie held his arm all along the crunching snowy road and they didn't speak further, but fell into step like the oldest of friends, and Burns let the night and the cold disappear and he imagined that she was thinking what he was thinking: that tomorrow he would see where Alec died.

AT JULIE'S trailer, the lights were on and two little boys sat at the kitchen table in their stocking feet drawing with crayons. "Well, hello, Timmo," Julie said. "How are you?" Neither boy looked up, but Burns could see their eyes looking around. "Is this your cousin?"

Timmo nodded.

"Well, good. What's he drawing?" The cousin turned his paper a bit so Julie could see the two figures on the sheet. Burns looked at the two brown smudges. The boy traced a line from one to the other. "This is you shooting a caribou, isn't it," Julie said. "And it is very good." The boys smiled to each other. Julie opened the cupboard and put out a plate of graham crackers and poured two glasses of milk. "Now, Timmo," she said, looking at her watch, "at eleven, you must go home." She looked up at Burns. "This is Timmo and his cousin No Name." At this the boys giggled. "Timmo is an artist who comes over some nights. His mother is in the Tahoe." Burns stood there in his coat. He wanted one of the crackers. He wanted them all. He smiled at the beautiful native boys. What a day. He had been warm and cold and hungry. This was all so new.

Julie took her coat off and came over to him. "We'd better go to bed," she said. "You've got a big day ahead, and if we don't leave the room, they'll never eat the crackers."

THE NEXT afternoon, in the low white angle of sunlight, Burns walked out to Glen Batton's place, a trailer behind the Forest Service buildings. The light was terrific, knifing at Burns, and he squinted behind his sunglasses.

In the small yard he slipped and fell, and climbing awkwardly back up, saw that he had stumbled across the hindquarters of a caribou lying in the snow. "That's the freezer up here," Glen Batton said from the doorway. "Fresh meat all winter. Hop in the truck, I'll be right there."

Batton seemed in a good mood, quite happy to show Burns all he knew about the small airplane, which was tethered—along with a dozen others—out on the frozen sea. A runway had been freshly bladed through the drifts along the waterfront, and Batton talked Burns through all the preparations he made, taking off the heavy insulated blanket over the motor, checking the oil, freeing the flaps. He had Burns help him push the plane forward a foot, cracking the icy seal between the skis and the snowpack. He opened the passenger door and pointed out the emergency gear under the seat, the food, the cross-country skis, and then he pointed to a small orange box in the back of the small cargo space and said, "Don't worry about that, Mr. Burns. That will start signaling on impact."

And Glen was chatty on the way over to Kolvik, talking to Burns—over the intercom—about his work with the Forest Service. They flew up the river in the sunshine, Batton pointing out the moose and caribou. He explained that for the caribou counts he usually took one of the secretaries and that Julie didn't like that. "Did you ever have a spat with your wife, Mr. Burns?"

"A spat?"

"You know, where she's jealous over something you're doing, although you're totally innocent."

"I guess, sometimes," Burns said, his voice distant on the inter-

com, sounding small, like what it was: a lie. Helen had never fought
with him, never complained. She had been a sweet, happy, confident
woman who had—even in their extremity—never fought with him.

"Yeah, well, Julie . . ." Batton said. "That's why she left last night
and went home early with you." Batton pointed ahead, where a
small herd of caribou moved across the frozen river. "What am I
going to do, land out there and screw Denise?"

A haze had come up, like bright smoke, and the plane rippled
across the changing sky. Burns was concentrating, trying to see the
country as Alec might have seen it.

"We take a lunch and stop for lunch," Glen Batton went on. "But
that's lunch. People eat lunch. Right?"

The rest of the flight was different from what Burns could have
foreseen. He couldn't get Glen to put down in Kolvik. They came
upon the small toss of cabins which was Kolvik and Burns' heart
lifted, but then it all changed quickly. There was no strip near the
small village, of course, and Glen explained that it wasn't safe to land
in the snow so soon after the recent storms. He made one pass by the
clearing near where Alec's cabin had been and laid down a pair of
tracks with the skis, but then circling he explained to Burns—
through the noisy intercom—that it was too soft, too dangerous.
Shoulder to shoulder with Glen Batton in the front seat of the smallest plane he'd ever been in, Burns asked again if they couldn't possibly try to land.

"No can do, Mr. Burns," Batton said, his voice tiny through the
receiver, sounding miles away. "Too deep, too soft. No one else has
been out either. That's where he lived"—Batton dipped the passenger wing steeply and pointed—"below that hill." There was no sign
of anything in the perfect snow. They made one more broad circle
over the area, seeing several moose in the valley where Alec supposedly had trapped, and then they headed west toward home. Burns
felt the little plane rattle in the new headwind, the door flexing
against his knee more than it had for the flight out, and he felt a disappointment that replaced hunger in his gut. He'd been so close. He

could have jumped from the plane and landed in the drift. From the air, the place where his son lived had looked like all the other terrain they'd seen: snowy hills grown with small pine. Alaska gave up its stories hard. He'd learned nothing.

They had flown quite low on the way out, but now Glen was taking the plane up to three and then four thousand feet. The sun was obscured in the west in a thick roseate mist. Burns was silent, mad at first, feeling cheated, and then resolved simply on what he now knew: he would ask Blazo.

"You spoke to the sheriff," Batton said.

"I did." Even Burns' own voice sounded remote on the intercom. "He was a help."

"And now you've been to Kolvik."

"Not quite, Glen. I've flown over it."

Batton ignored him, resetting some instruments, finally saying, "Did you ever see Russia?"

"I never have."

Batton leveled the plane at five thousand feet and turned it slightly, squinting through the windshield. "You know, it's funny your being here. I wouldn't have walked across the street for my old man and here you've come all the way north to see where your kid died." Burns said nothing. "There." Glen Batton pointed at a faint solid form below the sunset. "That line. That's Russia."

Burns could see the landfall that Batton had indicated, dark and vague beneath the fading rosy dusk, and as the little aircraft was bumped and lifted, he could sense the curvature of the earth from this height. Flying into the lost light made him feel again the sorrow he'd lived by for so long. The little plane descended in rocky strokes, lurching and gliding through the darkening frigid night. The men did not speak, but when the lights of Kotzebue glimmered on the horizon, a settlement in the void, Glen Batton spoke to the airport and then said to Burns: "Look. I know he was your son and he was a good kid, but the end was no good. He was a pain in the ass for everybody. Nearly drove Julie crazy."

Burns just listened. He wasn't mad anymore. He didn't want to argue. The lights of the village grew distinct and Batton circled out over the frozen ocean showing the town as a sweet Christmas decoration, a model, the pools of lamplight on the snowpacked streets.

"And now you're here, starting it all up again. You ought to get the flight to Anchorage tomorrow before this next weather really hits, and let Julie get on with her life."

Burns could see an orange bonfire on the hill at the edge of town and the dark forms of sleds descended the slope. Batton banked sharply, moving for the first time all day with an undue haste, and then leveled, and as the icy runway approached Burns felt the bottom drop out. The plane dipped suddenly, wrenching him up against his seat belt, where he floated for a second before slamming down. His head hit the windscreen and the edge of the console and then he felt the plane riding hard on the ridged ice, shaking him to the spine.

Batton ran the plane to the end of the runway and then wheeled it around to the tie-downs. "Sorry about that," he said. "It's always a little rough, but we hit her pretty hard that time."

Burns' hand was in the blood on his hairline and he could feel the welt rising where his forehead was split.

"You okay?" Batton asked, turning off the plane and climbing down.

"What'd you do to him, Glen? What did you do to Alec?"

With the earphones off everything sounded flat. Batton was fastening the fixed cables to each wing. Burns opened his door and jumped down onto the ice and moved away from the plane. He was dizzy and there seemed to be blood everywhere. Head cuts were like faucets; he'd had plenty playing hockey.

Batton was struggling with the insulation blanket for the engine. "You bleeding?" he said. "Let me see that."

"Were you after Julie before Alec moved?" Burns said.

Batton stopped fastening the snaps on the cover and came around to Burns. It was clear he wanted to hit him. The two men stood between the plane and the pickup on the rough sea ice. "Look," Batton said. "You're a smart guy. Julie said you went to Yale."

"Glen," Burns said, "I didn't come up here for trouble. I came up here to see what Alec saw, something for myself. And now I want to know what you did to him."

Glen came up to Burns and took a handful of his parka shoulder. In the icy light, Burns could see his face, angry and tight, and he felt himself being lifted. He didn't care. He was bleeding. He didn't care what Glen did. Burns saw Batton's eyes flicker over the things he was going to do and then focus on him. "Get in," Glen said finally, letting go of the coat. But Burns backed past the truck and into the dark toward the mounds of ragged plate ice between himself and the village.

NOT TEN minutes later, Burns found himself on a dark side street disoriented and full of the old dread. He'd just walked and something—the cold, the gash on his head, the iron hardness of the packed roadway, the glimpse of the earth growing dark—had let it all gather in his heart. For years he had thought that the weight of it, the darkest part, was his drinking. He'd wake somewhere sick and feel it around his chest like a cold hand and not be able to swallow. But after he stopped drinking, it didn't lift. It didn't come every day, but when it came as it had tonight, it hit with a force that left him weak.

On their holidays when he and Helen would go to St. Johns, he was drunk by noon, usually, rum was such an easy thing to drink. You could drink it in anything, coffee, juice. You could drink it in milk, for chrissake. You could take warm mouthfuls right from the bottle.

You could drink vodka and bourbon from the bottle too, but not in balmy weather. In the islands it was rum. Manhattan was gin. Airplanes were gin too, the stiff chemical push in the face. Clients were scotch, something that bit and then slid in Burns, he could drink scotch for weeks. He had done it. But his rules were his rules:

Manhattan was gin; St. Johns was rum; clients were scotch; and he drank vodka and bourbon those nights when the rules began to float. It was vodka the time he tried to die.

Now Burns felt the goose egg on his forehead. The blood had stopped, but the flesh was too tender to touch. He looked around and couldn't find a landmark. Four or five buildings, warehouses or churches, stood over him. He wasn't sure of the way he'd come and he couldn't tell north from south. He felt drained. He turned around searching for a clue, even a snowbank to sit on, but he could only see how much, how very much, of his own life he had missed.

Between buildings he thought he caught sight of the bonfire on the hill, and then someone took his arm. He looked down at Blazo, his grin showing the missing teeth, a man who by the wrinkles in his brown face could have been a hundred. With a firm grip on Burns' arm, Blazo marched him to the corner, out of the shadows, and pointed at the sledding fire.

"I saw them sledding," Burns said, but Blazo pointed again. A flare of powdery red light rose in the sky and then dissolved as a wave of yellow swelled and faded. "This place," Burns said. He felt dizzy. "These nights. This place is something else." He stepped away from Blazo. "Thanks," he said. "Julie's place is that way, right?"

Blazo nodded. He seemed to be examining Burns' face.

Burns started down the street and then hesitated. "I need to get to Kolvik. Soon. I need to see where Alec Burns lived, where he had a trapline. South of town."

"He was your boy," Blazo said.

Above them, the sky was relentless, the random vast armatures of colored light wheeling up and then vanishing, sometimes printing themselves from nothing on the darkness like bright stains. "He was," Burns whispered. The cold air cut at his nose as he breathed, and he could feel his pulse aching in his wound. "You can talk," Burns said.

"Not really." Blazo quickly pointed down the snowpacked lane, and Burns saw a figure trotting swiftly under the lamplight, a dog, some kind of husky, moving as with purpose. "But we'll go out there," Blazo said. "Tomorrow morning. It's going to snow, but we'll get half a day of good weather."

THE TRAILER was dark. Burns opened the door quietly and heard a strange sound which he then recognized as the violin. He felt the warmth and it made him catch his breath. He almost wept.

As he passed through the mud room without removing his coat, he felt Molly's nose fit into his palm in the dark. His legs were trembling. Julie was playing something sharp, full of energy and angles, it filled the space completely, and Burns saw her as he passed through the living room. She sat on the ottoman in her underwear, playing by the light of two candles. He saw the shine of sweat on her forehead and breastbone, and then he was in his room, suddenly warm himself and pulling at his coat and sweater.

There was a knock at his door, and Julie was there, tying her robe. "Hi," she said. "Sorry about that. . . . What's all this blood?"

"Nothing," he said. He was sitting on the bed. "You play very well."

Julie took his chin in her hand and pulled at the cut with a thumb. "Oh, yes, it's nothing," she said. "Looks like Glen hit you with an ax."

"It was an accident," Burns said quietly. On the warm bed, with his head in a woman's hands, he felt himself letting go. Julie was standing very close. He was a serious and controlled man, and he clenched his jaw, but his eyes welled.

"I'm going to have to stitch this closed, Mr. Tom Burns, or you'll return to the East Coast with a genuine Alaskan tattoo." And in a moment she came back with a warm wet cloth and a small kit. "You want something to eat?"

"No," he said. "I'm all in." He could feel his voice unsteady. "We didn't make it. Glen couldn't land."

Burns leaned back and looked at Julie and he saw her read his face. She stood beside him and put her arm around his neck. Burns held perfectly still. "What are you doing in Alaska? I'm not so sure this is a good idea for you." She began dabbing at his forehead with the cloth.

Then Burns' head began to ache and he could feel her working at the skin with the black thread. He was pulled into the open front of her robe where freckles rose from her cleavage in warm, vertiginous constellations inches from his face and he could smell her skin and the sweet Wild Turkey on her breath. His right ear was full of dried blood and his hearing came and went. He had both of his hands on her hips and he could feel her moving against him, the warmth and pressure of her legs.

"Are you all right," Burns whispered.

He heard her say, "I know what I'm doing."

He had a high hollow feeling and his mouth tasted sweet and dry the way it did before a drunk, and Julie cinched each stitch with three short tugs and this became part of the litany, her shifting breasts, the freckles riding there, his eyes half closed in the warm room, and the steady and expected tug-tug-tug. He ran his hand inside her robe and lifted his face to kiss her. She kissed him back, pausing for a moment to move the dangling needle on its black thread out of their way. She came over onto him on the bed. "Isn't this why you've come?" Her eyes fixed him as she continued to move with each word: "Isn't it?" Burns could feel the needle riding in his ear now and Julie lifted it away. "Watch out for me. I'm not what you think."

"What do I think?"

"You think I'm some coping person. A nurse. Something. I don't even know anymore what they do in your world, but here we take comfort where we find it. Glen came after me like a dog in heat. It's like that, Tom." Julie moved against him and Burns knew she could feel that he was aroused. "I'm like that."

"No you're not," he said. Even as he heard the words, he realized he didn't know what he was saying. He'd decided who she was yesterday, standing in her kitchen. The whole journey to Alaska had seemed mad to him at first, but once he was committed, he'd decided what he would see. He had written a kind of scenario without knowing it and now it was coming undone. It was a long moment for Burns, as if he had dived into the ocean and was waiting to turn and ascend. He was airless and without will.

Julie had lifted herself and was looking into his eyes, waiting for something. She looked much older here, harder. When he didn't move, she said, "You really don't get it, do you?"

"What? What is it?" he said to her. "What am I missing? Did Glen hurt Alec?"

"You're hard to believe, Tom," Julie said, rolling off him and standing by the bed. "You're too old to be that innocent." She took his head in her hands once again, but she held it differently. "Yes, Glen hurt Alec. So did I. So did this place. And probably you did too. Alec went mad. He did. But when he moved out there, Glen didn't help him. I know that. They hated each other by then, you can tell that. I knew he wouldn't land with you. I'm trying to be honest here. What happened would have happened. Glen didn't kill Alec."

"He didn't save him."

"That's what I'm telling you, Tom." Julie stood back, tugging sharply at the thread in Burns' forehead, and she looked at him frankly. "None of us did."

BURNS WAS walking in the snow. So this is where it was, he thought. He tried to see the valley as Alec might have, and began picking his way across the meadow. The surface of the snow was crusted and his snowshoes only cut a few inches with each step. He worked into a warm rhythm of small steps up the incline, breathing into the gray afternoon. It was wonderful to move this way after being on the snow machine all day. The clouds had come down and Burns felt the air change as he marched. It lifted at him somehow, not a wind but some quickness that was sharper in his nose, and it grew darker suddenly and he saw the first petals of snow easing down around him.

At the top he turned, breathing hard, and put his hands on his hips to rest. He felt the old high thrill in his chest just like the winter days at Yale, the flasks in the stands at the rink, and crossing campus at midnight wired tight with alcohol, his coat open to the sharp tonic of the air. Now his head was almost against the somber tent of clouds and below him the snow fell as it does at sea, ponderous and invisible at once, disappearing except where it fell on his sleeves, his eyebrows. The snow was falling everywhere.

His knees burned faintly as he stepped along the crest of the hill and descended into the draw where Alec had trapped. Here the small pines were thicker and there were game trails in the snow between the clumps of trees.

The year he quit drinking, that June, he and Alec had sailed from Martha's Vineyard to the Elizabeth Islands and an exhilaration had set in that Burns remembered keenly. Alec had been on loan from Helen. They had anchored off the islands and swum the hundred yards to shore and then lain on the deserted sand, laughing and panting, and the boy had said to him, "This is it, Dad. This is the best day of my life." Burns thought at that time: I am as close to being happy as I will ever be. And he did feel happy, proud to be a good sailing coach and pleased to have captured the Elizabeth Islands on the most beautiful day in the year, but the other thing was always with him. He didn't say it before they stood and began to swim back, but Burns had decided that day to live. He would live.

Halfway up the draw, Burns stopped. This was it. He fell back in the snow, flinging out his arms. He lay there and let his heart pound him deeper. He could hear it crashing in his ears. The pin-dots of snow burned across his forehead, and his arms and legs glowed. Julie was right about Alaska: it was too warm. Burns closed his eyes. This was where Alec died. When he opened them, he stared up into the falling snow until he felt the lift of vertigo. The roaring silence was nicked by a new sound now, the snow machine buzzing closer and then—as he felt the snow fix and himself rise into the sky, weightless—a face appeared above his head.

"Right," he said to Blazo. "I'm coming. One more minute." He caught Blazo's look and added, "Don't worry. I'll get up."

"You and me," Blazo said. "We've been gone a long time already." Blazo's face disappeared, and Burns felt himself again sink into the snow. It was pleasant here, lonely and floating, and Burns stopped trying to sort his thoughts. He was hungry, and pleased to be hungry again. He could feel his feet. His blood seemed very busy. Something had a grip on him. He thought, the world has got ahold of me again. He drew a breath, the air aching in his chest, and he said, "Alec." His voice sounded sure of something. "I've been in the snow here, Alec," he said into the sky. "I've lain on my back in the snow."

ON THE
U.S.S. FORTITUDE

S OME NIGHTS it gets lonely here on the U.S.S. Fortitude. I wipe everything down and sweep the passageways, I polish all the brass and check the turbines, and I stand up here on the bridge charting the course and watching the stars appear. This is a big ship for a single-parent family, and it's certainly better than our one small room in the Hotel Atlantis, on West Twenty-second Street. There the door wouldn't close and the window wouldn't open. Here the kids have room to move around, fresh sea air, and their own F/A-18 Hornets.

I can see Dennis now on the radar screen. He's out two hundred miles and closing, and it looks like he's with a couple of friends. I'll be able to identify them in a moment. I worry when Cherry doesn't come right home when it starts to get dark. She's only twelve. She's still out tonight, and here it is almost twenty-one hundred hours. If she's gotten vertigo or had to eject into the South China Sea, I'll just be sick. Even though it's summer, that water is cold.

There's Dennis. I can see his wing lights blinking in the distance. There are two planes with him, and I'll wait for his flyby. No sign of Cherry. I check the radar: nothing. Dennis's two friends are modified MIGs, ugly little planes that roar by like the A train, but the boys in them smile and I wave thumbs up.

These kids, they don't have any respect for the equipment. They land so hard and in such a hurry—one, two, three. Before I can get below, they've climbed out of their jets, throwing their helmets on the deck, and are going down to Dennis's quarters. "Hold it right there!" I call. It's the same old story. "Pick up your gear, boys." Dennis brings his friends over—two nice Chinese boys, who smile and bow. "Now, I'm glad you're here," I tell them. "But we do things a certain way on the U.S.S. Fortitude. I don't know what they do where you come from, but we pick up our helmets and we don't leave our aircraft scattered like that on the end of the flight deck."

"Oh, Mom," Dennis groans.

"Don't 'Oh, Mom' me," I tell him. "Cherry isn't home yet, and she needs plenty of room to land. Before you go to your quarters, park these jets below. When Cherry gets here, we'll have some chow. I've got a roast on."

I watch them drag their feet over to their planes, hop in, and begin to move them over to the elevator. It's not as if I asked him to clean the engine room. He can take care of his own aircraft. As a mother, I've learned that doing the right thing sometimes means getting cursed by your kids. It's okay by me. They can love me later. Dennis is not a bad kid; he'd just rather fly than clean up.

Cherry still isn't on the screen. I'll give her fifteen minutes and then get on the horn. I can't remember who else is out here. Two weeks ago, there was a family from Newark on the U.S.S. Tenth Amendment, but they were headed for Perth. We talked for hours on the radio, and the skipper, a nice woman, told me how to get stubborn skid marks off the flight deck. If you're not watching, they can build up in a hurry and make a tarry mess.

I still hope to run across Beth, my neighbor from the Hotel Atlantis. She was one of the first to get a carrier, the U.S.S. Domestic Tranquillity, and she's somewhere in the Indian Ocean. Her four girls would just be learning to fly now. That's such a special time.

We'd have so much to talk about. I could tell her to make sure the girls always aim for the third arresting wire, so they won't hit low or overshoot into the drink. I'd tell her about how mad Dennis was the first time I hoisted him back up, dripping like a puppy, after he'd come in high and skidded off the bow. Beth and I could laugh about that—about Dennis scowling at his dear mother as I picked him up. He was wet and humiliated, but he knew I'd be there. A mother's job is to be in the rescue chopper and still get the frown.

I FROWNED at my mother plenty. There wasn't much time for anything else. She and Dad had a little store and I ran orders and errands, and I mean ran—time was important. I remember cutting through the Park, some little bag of medicine in my hand, and watching people at play. What a thing. I'd be taking two bottles of Pepto-Bismol up to Ninety-first Street, cutting through the Park, and there would be people playing tennis. I didn't have time to stop and figure it out. My mother would be waiting back at the store with a bag of crackers and cough medicine for me to run over to Murray Hill. But I looked. Tennis. Four people in short pants standing inside that fence, playing a game. Later, I read about tennis in the paper. But tennis is a hard game to read about at first, and it seemed a code, like so many things in my life back then, and what did it matter, anyway? I was dreaming, as my mother was happy to let me know.

But I made myself a little promise then, and I thought about it as the years passed. There was something about tennis—playing inside that fence, between those lines. I think at first I liked the idea of limits. Later, when Dennis was six or so and he started going down the block by himself, I'd watch from in front of the Atlantis, a hotel without a stoop—without an entryway or a lobby, really—and I could see him weave in and out of the sidewalk traffic for a while, and then he'd be out of sight amid the parked cars and the shopping carts and the cardboard tables of jewelry for sale. Cherry would be pulling at my hand. I had to let him go, explore on his own. But the tension in my neck wouldn't release until I'd see his red suspenders coming back. His expression then would be that of a pro, a tour guide—someone who had been around this block before.

If a person could see and understand the way one thing leads to another in this life, a person could make some plans. As it was, I'd hardly even seen the stars before, and now here, in the ocean, they lie above us in sheets. I know the names of thirty constellations, and so do my children. Sometimes I think of my life in the city, and it seems like someone else's history, someone I kind of knew but didn't understand. But these are the days: a woman gets a carrier and two kids in their Hornets and the ocean night and day, and she's got her hands full. It's a life.

And now, since we've been out here, I've been playing a little tennis with the kids. Why not? We striped a beautiful court onto the deck, and we've set up stanchions and a net. I picked up some rackets three months ago in Madagascar, vintage T-2000s, which is what Jimmy Connors used. When the wind is calm we go out there and practice, and Cherry is getting quite good. I've developed a fair backhand, and I can keep the ball in play. Dennis hits it too hard, but what can you do—he's a growing boy. At some point, we'll come across Beth, on the Tranquillity, and maybe all of us will play tennis. With her four girls, we could have a tournament. Or maybe we'll hop over to her carrier and just visit. The kids don't know it yet, but I'm learning to fly high-performance aircraft. Sometimes when they're gone in the afternoons, I set the Fortitude into the wind at thirty knots and practice touch and go's. There is going to be something on Dennis's face when he sees his mother take off in a Hornet.

CHERRY SUDDENLY appears at the edge of the radar screen. A mother always wants her children somewhere on that screen. The radio crackles. "Mom. Mom. Come in, Mom." Your daughter's voice, always a sweet thing to hear. But I'm not going to pick up right away. She can't fly around all night and get her old mom just like that.

"Mom, on the Fortitude. Come in, Mom. This is Cherry. Over."

"Cherry, this is your mother. Over."

"Ah, don't be mad." She's out there seventy-five, a hundred miles, and she can tell I'm mad.

"Cherry, this is your mother on the Fortitude. You're grounded. Over."

"Ah, Mom! Come on. I can explain."

"Cherry, I know you couldn't see it getting dark from ten thousand feet, but I also know you're wearing your Swatch. You just get your tail over here right now. Don't bother flying by. Just come on in and stow your plane. The roast has been done an hour. I'm going below now to steam the broccoli."

Tomorrow, I'll have her start painting the superstructure. There's a lot of painting on a ship this size. That'll teach her to watch what time it is.

As I climb below, I catch a glimpse of her lights and stop to watch her land. It's typical Cherry. She makes a short, shallow turn, rather than circling and doing it right, and she comes in fast, slapping hard and screeching in the cable, leaving two yards of rubber on the deck. Kids.

I take a deep breath. It's dark now here on the U.S.S. Fortitude. The running lights glow in the sea air. The wake brims behind us. As Cherry turns to park on the elevator, I see that her starboard Sidewinder is missing. Sometimes you feel that you're wasting your breath. How many times have we gone over this? If she's old enough to fly, she's old enough to keep track of her missiles. But she's been warned, so it's okay by me. We've got plenty of paint. And, as I said, this is a big ship.

SUNNY BILLY DAY

THE VERY first time it happened with Sunny Billy Day was in Bradenton, Florida, spring training, a thick cloudy day on the Gulf, and I was there in the old wooden bleachers, having been released only the week before after going 0 for 4 in Winter Park against the Red Sox, and our manager, Ketchum, saw that my troubles were not over at all. So, not wanting to go back to Texas so soon and face my family, the disappointment and my father's expectation that I'd go to work in his Allstate office, and not wanting to leave Polly alone in Florida in March, a woman who tended toward ball players, I was hanging out, feeling bad, and I was there when it happened.

My own career had been derailed by what they called "stage fright." I was scared. Not in the field—I won a Golden Glove two years in college and in my rookie year with the Pirates. I love the field, but I had a little trouble at the plate. I could hit in the cage, in fact there were times when batting practice stopped so all the guys playing pepper could come over and bet how many I was going to put in the seats. It wasn't the skill. In a game I'd walk from the on-deck circle to the batter's box and I could feel my heart go through my throat.

All those people focusing on one person in the park: me. I could feel my heart drumming in my face. I was tighter than a ten-cent watch—all strikeouts and pop-ups. I went .102 for the season—the lowest official average of any starting-lineup player in the history of baseball.

Ketchum sent me to see the team psychiatrist, but that turned out to be no good, too. I saw him twice. His name was Krick and he was a small man who was losing hair, but his little office and plaid couch felt to me like the batter's box. What I'm saying is: Krick was no help—I was afraid of him, too.

Sometimes just watching others go to bat can start my heart jangling like a rock in a box, and that was how I felt that cloudy day in Bradenton as Sunny Billy Day went to the plate. We (once you play for a team, you say "we" ever after) were playing the White Sox, who were down from Sarasota, and it was a weird day, windy and dark, with those great loads of low clouds and the warm Gulf air rolling through. I mean it was a day that didn't feel like baseball.

Billy came up in the first inning, and the Chicago pitcher, a rookie named Gleason, had him 0 and 2, when the thing happened for the first time. Polly had ahold of my arm and was being extra sweet when Billy came up, to let me know that she didn't care for him at all and was with me now, but—everybody knows—when a woman acts that way it makes you nervous. The kid Gleason was a sharpshooter, a sidearm fastballer who could have struck me out with two pitches, and he had shaved Billy with two laser beams that cut the inside corner.

Gleason's third pitch was the smoking clone of the first two and Sunny Billy Day, my old friend, my former roommate, lifted his elbows off the table just like he had done twice before and took the third strike.

It *was* a strike. We all knew this. We'd seen the two previous pitches and everybody who was paying attention knew that Gleason had nailed Billy to the barn door. There was no question. Eldon Finney was behind the plate, a major league veteran, who was

known as Yank because of the way he yanked a fistful of air to indi-
cate a strike. His gesture was unmistakable, and on that dark day last
March, I did not mistake it. But as soon as the ump straightened up,
Sunny Billy, my old teammate, and the most promising rookie the
Pirates had seen for thirty years, tapped his cleats one more time and
stayed in the box.

"What's the big jerk doing?" Polly asked me. You hate to hear a
girl use a phrase like that, "big jerk," when she could have said something like "rotten bastard," but when you're in the stands, instead of
running wind sprints in the outfield, you take what you can get.

On the mound in Bradenton, Gleason was confused. Then I saw
Billy shrug at the ump in a move I'd seen a hundred times as roommates when he was accused of *anything* or asked to pay his share of
the check at the Castaway. A dust devil skated around the home
dugout and out to first, carrying an ugly litter of old sno-cone papers
and cigarette butts in its brown vortex, but when the wind died down
and play resumed, there was Sunny Billy Day standing in the box. I
checked the scoreboard and watched the count shift to 1 and 2.

Eldon "the Yank" Finney had changed his call.

So that was the beginning, and as I said, only a few people saw it
and knew this season was going to be a little different. Billy and I
weren't speaking—I mean, Polly was with me now, and so I couldn't
ask him what was up—but I ran into Ketchum at the Castaway that
night and he came over to our table. Polly had wanted to go back
there for dinner—for old times' sake; it was in the Castaway where
we'd met one year ago. She was having dinner with Billy that night,
the Bushel o' Shrimp, and they asked me to join them. Billy had a
lot of girls and he was always good about introducing them around.
Come on, a guy like Billy had nothing to worry about from other
guys, especially me. He could light up a whole room, no kidding,
and by the end of an hour there'd be ten people sitting at his table
and every chair in the room would be turned his way. He was a guy,
and anybody will back me up on this, who had the magic.

Billy loved the Castaway. "This is exotic," he'd say. "Right? Is this

a South Sea island or what?" And he meant it. You had to love him.
Some dim dive pins an old fishing net on the wall and he'd be in
paradise.

Anyway, Polly had ordered the Bushel o' Shrimp again and we
were having a couple of Mutineers, the daiquiri deal that comes in a
skull, when Ketchum came over and asked me—as he does every
time we meet—"How you feeling, kid?" which means have I still got
the crippling heebie-jeebies. He has told me all winter that if I want
another shot, just say so. Well, who doesn't want another shot? In
baseball—no matter what you hear—there are no ex-players, just
guys waiting for the right moment for a comeback.

I told Ketchum that if anything changed, he'd be the first to
know. Then I asked him what he thought of today's game and he
said, "The White Sox are young."

"Yeah," I said. "Especially that pitcher."

"I wouldn't make too much out of that mix-up at the plate
today. You know Billy. He's a kind that can change the weather."
Ketchum was referring to the gray preseason game a year before.
Billy came up in a light rain when a slice of sunlight opened on the
field like a beacon, just long enough for everyone to see my roommate golf a low fastball into the right-field seats for a round trip.
It was the at-bat that clinched his place on the roster, and that gave
him his nickname.

"Billy Day is a guy who gets the breaks." Ketchum reached into
the wicker bushel and sampled one of Polly's shrimp. "And you
know what they say about guys who get a lot of breaks." Here he
gave Polly a quick look. "They keep getting them." He stood up and
started to walk off. "Call me if you want to hit a few. We don't head
north until April Fools' Day."

"I don't like that guy," Polly said when he'd left. "I never liked
him." She pushed her load of shrimp away. "Let's go." I was going
to defend the coach there, a guy who was fair with his men and kept
the signals (steal, take, hit-and-run) simple, but the evening had
gone a little flat for me too. There we were out to celebrate, but as

always the room was full of Billy Day. He was everywhere. He was in the car on the way back to the hotel; he was in the elevator; he was in the room; and—if you want to know it—he was in the bed too. I knew that he was in Polly's dreams and there he was in my head, turning back to the umpire, changing a strike to a ball.

The papers got ahold of what was going on during the last week of March. It was a home game against the Yankees and it was the kind of day that if there were no baseball, you'd invent it to go with the weather. The old Bradenton stands were packed and the whole place smelled of popcorn and coconut oil. Polly was wearing a yellow sundress covered with black polka dots, the kind of dress you wear in a crowded ballpark if you might want one of the players to pick you out while he played first. By this time I was writing a friendly little column for the *Pittsburgh Dispatch* twice a week on "Lifestyles at Spring Training," but I had not done much with Billy. He was getting plenty of legitimate ink, and besides—as I said—we weren't really talking. I liked the writing, even though this was a weird time all around. I kind of *had* to do it, just so I felt useful. I wasn't ready to go home.

It was a good game, two-two in the ninth. Then Billy made a mistake. With one down, he had walked and stolen second. That's a wonderful feeling being on second with one out. There's all that room and you can lead the extra two yards and generally you feel pretty free and cocky out there. I could see Billy was enjoying this feeling, leaving cleat marks in the clay, when they threw him out. The pitcher flipped the ball backhand to the shortstop, and they tagged Billy. Ralph "the Hammer" Fox was umping out there, and he jumped onto one knee in his famous out gesture and wheeled his arm around and he brought the hammer down: OUT! After the tag, Billy stood up and went over and planted both feet on the base.

"What?" Polly took my arm.

Ralph Fox went over and I could see Billy smiling while he spoke. He patted Ralph's shoulder. Then Fox turned and gave the arms-out gesture for safe—twice—and hollered, "Play ball." It was strange, the kind of thing that makes you sure you're going to get an explanation later.

But the ballpark changed in a way I was to see twenty times during the season: a low quiet descended, not a silence, but an eerie even sound like two thousand people talking to themselves. And the field, too, was stunned, the players standing straight up, their gloves hanging down like their open mouths during the next pitch, which like everything else was now half-speed, a high hanging curve which Red Sorrows blasted over the scoreboard to win the game.

Well, it was no way to win a ballgame, but that wasn't exactly what the papers would say. Ralph Fox, of course, wasn't speaking to the press (none of the umpires would), and smiling Sunny Billy Day only said one thing that went out on the wire from coast to coast: "Hey guys, come on. You saw that Mickey Mouse move. I was safe." Most writers looked the other way, noting the magnitude of Red Sorrows's homer, a "towering blast," and going on to speculate whether the hit signaled Sorrows's return from a two-year slump. So, the writers avoided it, and in a way I understand. Now I have become a kind of sportswriter and I know it is not always easy to say what you mean. Sometimes if the truth is hard, typing it can hurt again.

There were so many moments that summer when some poor ump would stand in the glare of Billy's smile and toe the dirt, adjust his cap, and change the call. Most of the scenes were blips, glitches: a last swing called a foul ticker; a close play called Billy's way; but some were big, bad, and ugly—so blatant that they had the fans looking at their shoes. Billy had poor judgment. In fact, as I think about it, he had no judgment at all. He was a guy with the gift who had spent his whole life going forward from one thing to the next. People liked him and things came his way. When you first met Billy, it clicked: who is this guy? Why do I want to talk to him? Ketchum assigned us to room together and in a season of hotel rooms, I found out that it had always been that way for him. He had come out of college with a major in American Studies, and he could not name a single president. "My teachers liked me," he said. "Everybody likes me."

He had that right. But he had no judgment. I'd seen him with women. They'd come along, one, two, three, and he'd take them as they came. He didn't have to choose. If he'd had any judgment, he never would have let any woman sit between him and Polly.

Oh, that season I saw him ground to short and get thrown out at first. He'd trot past, look back, and head for the dugout, taking it, but you got the impression it was simply easier to keep on going than stop to change the call. And those times he took it, lying there a foot from third dead out and then trotting off the field, or taking the third strike and then turning for the dugout, you could feel the waves of gratitude from the stands. Those times I know you could feel it, because there weren't many times when Billy Day took it, and as the season wore on, and the Pirates rose to first place, they became increasingly rare.

Sunny Billy Day made the All-Stars, of course. He played a fair first base and he was the guy you couldn't get out. But he was put on the five-day disabled list, "to rest a hamstring," the release said. But I think it was Ketchum being cagey. He wasn't going to gain anything by having a kid who was developing a reputation for spoiling ball games go in and ruin a nice July night in Fenway for fans of both leagues.

By August, it was all out: Billy Day could have his way. You never saw so much written about the state of umping. Billy was being walked most of the time now. Every once in a while some pitcher would throw to him, just to test the water. They were thinking Ketchum was going to pull the plug, tell Billy to face the music, to swallow it if he went down swinging, but it never happened. The best anybody got out of it was a flyout, Billy never contested a flyout. And Ketchum, who had thirty-four good years in the majors and the good reputation to go with them, didn't care. A good reputation is one thing; not having been in the Series is another. He would be seventy by Christmas and he wanted to win it all once, even if it meant letting Billy have his way. Ketchum, it was written, had lost his judgment too.

I was writing my head off, learning how to do it and liking it a little more. It's something that requires a certain amount of care and it is done alone at a typewriter, not in the batting box in front of forty thousand citizens. And I found I was a hell of a typist; I liked typing. But I wasn't typing about my old roommate—at all. I missed him though, don't think I didn't miss him. I had plenty to say about the rest of the squad, how winning became them, made them into men after so many seasons of having to have their excuses ready before they took the field. Old Red Sorrows was hitting .390 and hadn't said the word "retirement" or the phrase "next season" in months. There was a lot to write about without dealing with Billy Day's behavior.

But, as September came along, I was getting a lot of pressure for interviews. I had been his roommate, hadn't I? What was he like? What happened to my career? Would I be back? Wasn't I dating Billy Day's girl? I soft-pedaled all this, saying "on the other hand" fifty times a week, and that's no good for athletes or writers. On the topic of Polly I said that we were friends. What a word. The papers went away and came out with what they'd wanted to say anyway: that Billy Day's old roommate had stolen his girl and now he wouldn't write about him. They used an old file photograph of Billy and Polly in the Castaway and one of Billy and me leaning against the backstop in Pittsburgh, last year, the one year I played in the major leagues. Our caps are cocked back, and we are smiling.

During all this, Polly stopped coming to the games with me. She'd had enough of the Pirates for a while, she said, and she took a job as a travel agent and got real busy. We were having, according to the papers, "a relationship," and that term is fine with me, because I don't know what else to say. I was happy to have such a pretty girl to associate with, but I knew that her real ambition was to be with Billy Day.

The Pirates won their division by twenty-eight games, a record, and then they took the National League pennant by whipping the Cardinals four straight. With Billy talking the umps into anything he wanted, and the rest of the team back from the dead and flying in formation, the Pirates were a juggernaut.

It took the Indians seven games to quiet the Twins, and the Series was set. Pirate October, they called it.

The Cleveland Press was ready for Billy. They'd given him more column inches than the Indians total in those last weeks, cataloguing his "blatant disregard for the rules and the dignity of fair play." Some of those guys could write. Billy had pulled one stunt in the playoffs that really drew fire. In game four, with the Pirates ahead five-zip, he bunted foul on a third strike and smiled his way out of it.

As one writer put it, "We don't put up with that kind of thing in Cleveland. We don't like it and we don't need it. When we see disease, we inoculate." As I said, these guys, some of them, could write. Their form of inoculation was an approved cadre of foreign umpires. They brought in ten guys for the Series. They were from Iceland, Zambia, England, Ireland, Hungary, Japan (three), Venezuela, and Tonga. When they met the press, they struck me as the most serious group of men I'd ever seen assembled. It looked good: they knew the rules and they were grim. And the Tongan, who would be behind the plate for game one, looked fully capable of handling anything that could come up with one hand.

Polly didn't go out to Cleveland with me. She had booked a cruise, a month, through the Panama Canal and on to the islands far across the Pacific Ocean, and she was going along as liaison. She smiled when she left and kissed me sweetly, which is just what you don't want your girl to do. She kissed me like I was a writer.

So I went out alone and stayed in the old Hotel Barnard, where a lot of the writers stay. It was lonely out there in Ohio, and I thought about it. It was the end of a full season in which I had not played ball, and here I was in a hotel full of writers, which I had become, instead of over at the Hilton with my club.

I was closing down the bar the night before the Series opener when Billy Day walked in. I couldn't believe my eyes.

"I thought I'd find you here," he said.

"Billy," I said, waving the barman to bring down a couple of lagers. "I'm a writer now. This is where the writers stay. You're out after curfew."

He gestured back at the empty room. "Who's gonna write me up, you?" He smiled his terrific smile and I realized as much as I had avoided him for eight months, I missed him. I missed that smile.

"No," I said. "I don't think so." Our beers came and I asked him, "What's up?"

"It's been a rough season."

"Not from what I read. The Pirates won the pennant."

"Jesus," he said. "What is that, sarcasm? You gonna start talking like a writer too?"

"Billy, you've pulled some stunts."

He slid his beer from one hand to the other on the varnished bar of the Hotel Barnard. And then started to nod. "Yeah," he said. "I guess I did. You know, I didn't see it at first. It just kind of grew."

"And now you know."

"Yeah, now I know all about it. I know what I can do."

"So what brings you out on a night to the Hotel Barnard?" I pointed at his full glass of beer. "It's not the beer."

"You," he said, and he turned to me again and smiled. "You always knew what to do. I don't mean on the field. There was no rookie better. But I mean, what should I do? This is the Series."

"Yeah, it's the Series. If I were you, I'd play ball."

"You know what I mean. Ketchum wants me to use it all. He doesn't care if they tear down the stadium."

"And you?"

"I don't know. All my life, I played to win. It seems wrong not to do something that can help your team. But the people don't like it."

I looked at the clouds crossing the face of Sunny Billy Day, and I knew I was seeing something no man had ever seen there before: second thoughts.

"These new umps may not let you get away with anything."

"Kid," he said to me, touching my shoulder with his fist, his smile as wide and bright as the sun through a pop-up, "I've been missing you. But I thought you knew me better than that. I've lived my life knowing one thing: everybody lets me get away with everything. The only thing I ever lost, I lost to you. Polly. And I didn't even think about it until she was gone. How is she?"

"I'd get her back for you if I could," I said, lifting my glass in a toast to my old friend Billy Day. "Polly," I told him, "is headed for Tahiti."

BILLY WAS right about the umps. They looked good, in fact, when they took the field and stood with their arms behind their backs along the first-base line, they looked like the Supreme Court. The people of Cleveland were ready for something too, because I noted in the article I wrote for the *Dispatch* that the squadron of umpires received a louder ovation when they took the field than the home team did. Everybody knew that without an iron heel from the umps, the Indians might as well take the winter off.

Okay, so it was baseball for several innings. Ohio in October smells sweet and old, and for a while I think we were all transported through the beautiful fall day, the stadium bathing in the yellow light and then pitching steeply into the sepia shadow of the upper decks. See: I was learning to write like the other guys.

Sunny Billy Day hadn't been a factor, really, walking twice and grounding a base hit into left. It was just baseball, the score two to one Cleveland in the top of the eighth. Now, I want to explain what happened carefully. There were seventy-four thousand people there and in the days since the Series I've heard almost that many versions. The thirty major papers disagreed in detail and the videotapes haven't got it all because of the angle and sequence. So let me go slow here. After all, it would be the last play of Sunny Billy Day.

I wasn't in the press box. The truth is that the season had been a little hard on me in terms of making friends with my fellow reporters. I'd had a hundred suppers in half-lit lounges and I don't think it came as a surprise that I didn't really care for the way they talked—not just about baseball, for which they had a curious but abiding disdain. And I'm not one of these guys who think you have to have played a sport—or really done anything—to be able to write about it well. Look at me—I was good in the field, but I can't write half as good as any of the guys I travel with. But sportswriters, when they are together at the end of the day, a group of them having drinks waiting for their Reuben sandwiches to arrive, are a fairly superior and hard-bitten bunch. You don't want to wander into one of these hotel lounges any summer evening if you want to hear anything about the joy of the sport. These guys don't celebrate baseball, and really, like me, they don't analyze it very well. But they have *feelings* about it; I never met a man who didn't. That's why it's called the major leagues.

Anyway, I don't want to get going on writers and all that stuff. And don't get me wrong. Some of them—hell, most of them—are nice guys and quick about the check or asking how's it going, but it was October and it was all getting to me. I could see myself in two years, flipping my ash into somebody's coffee cup offering a weary expert's opinion. So I wanted to sit where someone might actually cheer or spill a little beer when they stood up on a third strike or a home run. Journalists are professionals, anyone will tell you this, and they don't spill their beer. I ended up ten rows behind third in a seat I paid for myself, and it turned out to be a lucky break given what was going to happen.

With one out in the top of the eighth, Billy Day doubled to right. It was a low fastball and he sliced it into the corner.

On the first pitch to Red Sorrows, Coach Ketchum had Billy steal. He's one run down with one out in the eighth, a runner in scoring position, and a fair hitter at the plate, and Ketchum flashes the steal sign—it's crazy. It means one thing: he's trading on Billy's magic all the way. When I saw Ketchum pinch his nose and then go to the bill of his cap, which has been the Pirate's steal sign for four years, I thought: Ketchum's going to use Billy any way he can. The pitch is a high strike which Sorrows fouls straight back against the screen, so now everybody knows. Billy walks back to second. I have trouble believing what I see next. Again Ketchum goes to his nose and his cap: steal. The Cleveland hurler, the old veteran Blade Medina, stretches and whirls to throw to second with Billy caught halfway down and throws the ball into center field. He must have been excited. Billy pulls into third standing.

Okay, I thought, Ketchum, you got what you wanted, now *stop screwing around.* In fact, I must have whispered that or said it aloud, because the guy next to me says to my face, "What'd I do?" These new fans. They don't want to fight you anymore, they want to know how they've offended you. Too much college for this country. I told him I was speaking to someone else, and he let it go, until I felt a tap on my shoulder and he'd bought me a beer. What did I tell you? But I didn't mind. A minute later I would need it.

Sorrow goes down swinging. Two outs.

It was then I got a funny feeling, on top of all the other funny feelings I'd been having in the strangest summer of my life, and it was a feeling about Ketchum, and I came to know as I sipped my beer and watched my old coach walk over to Billy on the bag at third that he was going to try to steal home. Coach Ketchum was the king of the fair shake, a guy known from Candlestick to Fenway as a square shooter, and as he patted Billy on the rump and walked back to the coach's box, I saw his grin. I was ten rows up and the bill of his cap was down, but I saw it clearly—the grin of a deranged miser about to make another two bucks.

Billy had never stolen home in his career.

Blade Medina was a tall guy and as he launched into his windup, kicking his long leg toward third, Billy took off. Billy Day was stealing home; you could feel every mouth in the stadium open. Blade Medina certainly opened his. Then he simply cocked and threw to the catcher, who tagged Billy out before he could decide to slide.

Ketchum was on them before the big Tongan umpire could put his thumb away. For a big guy he had a funny out call, flicking his thumb as if shooting a marble. I have to hand it to Billy. He was headed for the dugout. But Ketchum got him by the shirt and dragged back out to the plate and made him speak to the umpire. You knew it was going to happen again—and in the World Series— because all the Indians just stood where they were on the field. And sure enough after a moment of Ketchum pushing Billy from the back, as if he was some big puppet in a baseball suit, and Billy speaking softly to the umpire, the large official stepped out in front of the plate and swept his hand out flat in the air as if calming the waters: "Safe!" he said. He said it quietly in his deep voice. Well, it was quiet in Cleveland, do you see? I sat there like everyone else looking at the bottom of my plastic glass of beer and wishing it wasn't so. Seventy-four thousand people sitting in a circle feeling sour in their hearts, not to mention all the sad multitudes watching the televised broadcast.

Then my old coach Ketchum made it worse by hauling Billy over to touch the plate; Billy hadn't even stepped on home base yet. Just typing this makes me feel the ugliness all over again.

But then the real stuff started to happen, and, as I said, there were no good reports of this next part because of everybody looking at their shoes, programs, or their knuckles the way people in a restaurant read the menu real hard when a couple is arguing at the next table. But I saw it, and it redeemed Sunny Billy Day forever to me, and it gave me something that has allowed me, made me really, get out my cleats again and become a baseball player. I'm not so bad a writer that I would call it courage, but it was definitely some big kick in the ass.

What happened was, halfway back to the dugout, *Billy turned around.* His head was down in what I called *shame* in my report to the *Pittsburgh Dispatch,* and he turned around and went back to home plate. Ketchum was back at third, smug as a jewel thief, and he caught the action too late to do anything about it. Billy took the ump by the sleeve and I saw Billy take off his cap and shake his head and point at the plate. We all knew what he was saying, everybody. The ballpark was back, everyone standing now, watching, and we all saw the big Tongan nod and smile that big smile at Ketchum, and then raise his fist and flick his thumb.

Oh god, the cheer. The cheer went up my spine like a chiropractor. There was joy in Ohio and it went out in waves around the world. I wrote that too. Not joy at the out; joy at order restored. It was the greatest noise I've ever heard. I hope Billy recognized the sound.

Because what happened next, as the Cleveland Indians ran off the field like kids, and Ketchum's mouth dropped open like the old man he would become in two minutes, surprised everyone, even me.

When the Pirates took the field (and they ran out joyfully too— it was baseball again), there was something wrong. The Pirates pitcher threw his eight warm-up pitches and one of the Cleveland players stepped into the box. That is when the Irishman umping first came skittering onto the field wheeling his arms, stopping play before it had begun, and seventy-four thousand people looked over to where I'd been staring for five minutes: first base. There was no one at first base. Sunny Billy Day had not taken the field.

I wish to this day I'd been closer to the field because I would have hopped the rail and run through the dugout to the clubhouse and found what the batboy said he found: Billy's uniform hung in his locker, still swinging on the hanger. I asked him later if he got a glimpse of a woman in a yellow dress, but he couldn't recall.

AND NOW, this spring, I'm out again. I'd almost forgotten during my long season in the stands how much fun it was to play baseball. I still have a little trouble at the plate and I ride my heartbeat like a cowboy on a bad bull, but I want to play, and if I remember that and hum to myself a little while I'm in the box, it helps. The new manager is a good guy and if I can keep above .200, he'll start me.

Oh, the Indians won the series, but it went six games and wasn't as one-sided as you might think after such an event. Ketchum stayed in the dugout the whole time, under heavy sedation, though I never mentioned that in my stories. And I never mentioned the postcards

I got later from the far island of Pago Pago. I still get them. Sometimes I'll carry one in my pocket when I go to the plate. It's a blue-and-green place mainly, and looks like a great place for a lucky guy and a woman who looks good in summer clothing.

Sunny Billy Day was a guy with a gift. You could see it a mile away. Things came his way. Me, I'm going to have to make my own breaks, but, hey, it's spring again and it feels like life is opening up. I'm a lot less nervous at the plate these days, and I have learned to type.

THE TABLECLOTH OF TURIN

*A man, anywhere from forty to sixty, comes onto the stage. He wears
glasses, a white shirt with the sleeves rolled up, wool slacks, and shined
black shoes. Under his arm he carries a folded tablecloth. It is very
large. He is also carrying a folding desk lamp, a pointer, and a packet
of other small gear. The man, Leonard Christofferson, pins the tablecloth
to the backdrop, sets up the desk lamp to illuminate the tablecloth, lifts
the pointer, and steps toward the audience.*

THIS IS the seventy-first public appearance of the famed
Tablecloth of Turin. My name is Leonard Christofferson, and
the tablecloth and I have been traveling for almost three months
now. I am an insurance investigator by trade from Ann Arbor,
Michigan, but I've pretty much let that all go. After all, it is my
tablecloth, and it is my wish to share it and show it to as many folks
as I can.

In the last three months, I've met with a lot of skepticism about
the authenticity of the cloth, but most people—when they hear the
story and see the evidence—come to know as well as I do that this
is the tablecloth of the Last Supper, the very cloth depicted in so
many famous paintings, including Leonardo da Vinci's, the very
tablecloth over which Christ broke that bread and poured that wine.

I want to say right here: as an insurance investigator, I had many
years experience with and exposure to frauds, some of them silly,
some of them so well constructed as to seem genuine. We had homi-

cides made to look like drunk driving and a bad curve; we had grand larcenies perpetrated by nephews, nieces, wives, and sons, all in cahoots with the "victim"; we had an insured Learjet go down to the bottom of Lake Michigan which upon salvage turned out to be a junked boxcar, the jet having been sold in Mexico. In my experience as a detective, I learned slowly over the years to trust nothing, nobody. It's a terrible profession, picking through death cars and the ashes of every dry cleaner's that burns up. The owner stands there hating you and you don't trust him, a guy you never met before in your life. The twelve years I worked for Specific Claims in Ann Arbor were hard years on me, and they destroyed my faith in the human race.

And when I went to Italy with the Art Guild and I found, well, I was offered, this piece of white cloth, I saw my chance to turn my life around. I do not now speak nor have I ever spoken Italian, but I could see from the ardor in the man's eyes that he too had recovered his faith and he wanted me to take care of this sacred emblem in a way that he, working in his brother's restaurant, could never do. I paid him, left the Art Guild Renaissance trip early, flew back to Ann Arbor, and quit my job, and I have been sharing my good fortune ever since.

Enough about me. Let me show you my tablecloth.

As you can see, it's a large one: six foot five by twenty-three feet. We have had it all chemically analyzed and I want to share our findings with you tonight. The cloth itself is one piece, constructed of rough linen, approximately fourteen threads per inch, woven on a hand loom. X-rays have revealed thirteen place settings, most of them three-piece settings of an iron clay material, which means there were over forty dishes on the table and possibly fifty, depending on how many carafes of wine were out.

This is where Christ sat. We know this not only from historical and artistic record, but also from the fact that this one space, this seat of honor, is unmarked. Under the spectrometer all the other places have revealed breadcrumbs, spilled wine, palm prints (the oil of the human hand), in one place elbow prints (someone, possibly James the Lesser, had his sleeves rolled up), but Christ's place is clean. He not only was a careful eater, he probably didn't have that much to eat, knowing what he knew.

Examination has also revealed some shocking new evidence: *the apostles didn't all sit on one side of the table.* Three of the places, including the place where Judas Iscariot sat, were opposite Jesus. So: sorry, Leonardo, thanks for giving us all their faces, but the truth has three backs to the camera. We suspect that Judas sat opposite Jesus for the reasons that science has supplied. In fact, science, the ultimate detective, has unraveled the whole story of the Last Supper from this humble tablecloth.

Listen: *it was a nervous dinner.* We know this from the number of wineglass rings in the cloth itself. The men were picking up their glasses and setting them down more frequently than simply for drinking. They were playing with their glasses as if they were chess pieces.

These people would have been nervous for a number of reasons. None of the thirteen men in that room (with the possible exception of Jesus, who somehow knew the host) had ever eaten there before. Imagine it, you go to a new city, find a man carrying a pitcher of water down the street as Jesus had instructed you, and *ask him to have you* to Passover Dinner. It's an upstairs room with a limited view. Your host, whoever he is, doesn't eat with you. It is a strange setup. So, you're nervous. You sit there. You'd tap your glass too, maybe as many as seventy times, like Andrew, who sat here, did.

Then during dinner, your leader starts in on some topics which any one of us might think inappropriate for the supper table. Instead of the usual reaffirming and pleasant messages, the conversation is full of hostile assertions, statements of doom and gloom. Jesus says, "Verily I say unto you, that one of you shall betray me." Try that at home sometime, see if somebody doesn't spill the wine. Which, our spectrometer shows, every one of the twelve disciples did, the largest spill being here, where Judas sat. In addition, traces of breadcrumbs were found here, as we found everywhere, but these were partially decomposed via the starch-splitting enzymes found in human saliva, so we know almost certainly that Mr. Iscariot, almost two thousand years before the Heimlich Maneuver, choked on his bread when Jesus said that. We don't know who patted him on the back.

There is another large spill here (thirty-six square centimeters), and we theorize that Peter was still sitting when Jesus told him he would deny Jesus thrice before dawn. From the shape of the spill, something like a banana, it seems that Peter stood to protest, and dragged his glass with him.

Other evidence in this sacred cloth suggests that besides bread and wine, the attendees at the Last Supper enjoyed a light salad with rich vinegar and some kind of noodle dish. There was no fish. The wine was a seasoned, full-bodied red wine, which our analysis has revealed to be a California wine. This last bit of evidence has given the skeptics great joy, but I've got news for you. That it is a California wine does not mean that this is not the Tablecloth of Turin; it simply means that civilization in California is older than some people now think.

When I look at this magnificent cloth and see its amazing tale of love and faith and betrayal written for all to see in wine, bread, and prints of human hands, I'm suddenly made glad again that I went to Turin last fall with the Art Guild, that I met Antony Cuppolini in his brother's restaurant, and that for some strange reason known only to God, Antony made me caretaker of this, the beautiful Tablecloth of Turin.

A KIND OF FLYING

B Y OUR wedding day, Brady had heard the word *luck* two hundred times. Everybody had advice, especially her sister Linda, who claimed to be "wise to me." Linda had wisdom. She was two years older and had wisely married a serviceman, Butch Kistleburg, whose status as a GI in the army guaranteed them a life of travel and adventure. They were going to see the world. If Brady married me, Linda told everybody, she would see nothing but the inside of my carpet store.

Linda didn't like my plans for the ceremony. She thought that letting my best man, Bobby Thorson, sing "El Paso" was a diabolical mistake. "'El Paso,'" she said. "Why would you sing that at a wedding in Stevens Point, Wisconsin?" I told her: because I liked the song, I'm a sucker for a story, and because it was a love song, and because there *wasn't* a song called "Stevens Point."

"Well," she said that day so long ago, "that is no way to wedded bliss."

I wasn't used to thinking of things in terms of bliss, and I had no response for her. I had been thinking of the great phrase from the song that goes " . . . maybe tomorrow a bullet may find me . . ." and I was once again recommitted to the musical part of the program.

What raised *all* the stakes was what Brady did with the cake. She was a photographer even then and had had a show that spring in the Stevens Point Art Barn, a hilarious series of eye-tricks that everyone thought were double exposures: toy soldiers patrolling bathroom sinks and cowboys in refrigerators. Her family was pleased by what they saw as a useful hobby, but the exhibition of photographs had generally confused them.

When Brady picked up the wedding cake the morning we were wed, it stunned her, just the size of it made her grab her camera. She and Linda had taken Clover Lane, by the Gee place, and Brady pictured it all: the cake in the foreground and the church in the background, side by side.

When Brady pulled over near the cottonwoods a quarter mile from the church, Linda was not amused. She stayed in the car. Brady set the wedding cake in the middle of the road, backed up forty feet, lay down on the hardtop there, and in the rangefinder she saw the image she wanted: the bride and the groom on top of the three-tiered cake looking like they were about to step over onto the roof of the First Congregational Church. We still have the photograph. And when you see it, you always hear the next part of the story.

Linda screamed. Brady, her eye to the viewfinder, thought a truck was coming, that she was a second away from being run over on her wedding day. But it wasn't a truck. Linda had screamed at two birds. Two crows, who had been browsing the fenceline, wheeled down and fell upon the cake, amazed to find the sweetest thing in the history of Clover Lane, and before Brady could run forward and prevent it, she saw the groom plucked from his footing, ankle deep in frosting, and rise—in the beak of the shiny black bird—up into the June-blue sky.

"Man oh man oh man," Linda said that day to Brady. "That is a bad deal. That," she said, squinting at the two crows, who were drifting across Old Man Gee's alfalfa, one of them with the groom in his beak, "is a definite message." Then Linda, who had no surplus affection for me, went on to say several other things which Brady has been good enough, all these years, to keep to herself.

When Bobby Thorson and I reached the church, Linda came out as we were unloading his guitar and said smugly, "Glen, we're missing the groom."

Someone called the bakery, but it was too late for a replacement, almost one o'clock. I dug through Brady's car and found some of her guys: an Indian from Fort Apache with his hatchet raised in a nonmatrimonial gesture; the Mummy, a translucent yellow; a kneeling green soldier, his eye to his rifle; and a little blue frogman with movable arms and legs. I was getting married in fifteen minutes.

The ceremony was rich. Linda read some Emily Dickinson; my brother read some Robert Service; and then Bobby Thorson sang "El Paso," a song about the intensities of love and a song which seemed to bewilder much of the congregation.

When Brady came up the aisle on her father's arm, she looked like an angel, her face blanched by seriousness and—I found out later—fear of evil omens. At the altar she whispered to me, "Do you believe in symbols?" Thinking she was referring to the rings, I said, "Of course, more than ever!" Her face nearly broke. I can still see her mouth quiver.

Linda didn't let up. During the reception when we were cutting the cake, Brady lifted the frogman from the top and Linda grabbed her hand: "Don't you ever lick frosting from any man's feet."

I wanted to say, "They're flippers, Linda," but I held my tongue.

THAT WAS twenty years ago this week. So much has happened. I've spent a thousand hours on my knees carpeting the rooms and halls and stairways of Stevens Point. Brady and I now have three boys who are good boys, but who—I expect—will not go into the carpet business. Brady has worked hard at her art. She is finished with her new book, *Obelisks*, which took her around the world twice photographing monuments. She's a wry woman with a sense of humor as long as a country road. Though she's done the traveling and I've stayed at home, whenever she sees any bird winging away, she says to me: *There you go.*

And she may be kind of right with that one. There have been times when I've ached to drop it all and fly away with Brady. I've cursed the sound of airplanes overhead and then when she comes home with her camera case and dirty laundry, I've flown to her—and she to me. You find out day after day in a good life that your family is the journey.

And now Linda's oldest, Trina, is getting married. We're having a big family party here in Stevens Point. Butch and Linda have all come north for a couple of weeks. Butch has done well; he's a lieutenant colonel. He's stationed at Fort Bliss and they all seem to like El Paso.

Trina came into the store yesterday pretending to look at carpet. People find out you're married for twenty years, they ask advice. What would I know? I'm just her uncle and I've done what I could. For years I laid carpet so my wife could be a photographer, and now she'll be a photographer so I can retire and coach baseball. Life lies before us like some new thing.

It's quiet in the store today. I can count sparrows on the wire across the road. My advice! She smiled yesterday when I told her. Just get married. Have a friend sing your favorite song at the wedding. Marriage, she said, what is it? Well, I said, it's not life on a cake. It's a bird taking your head in his beak and you walk the sky. It's marriage. Sometimes it pinches like a bird's mouth, but it's definitely flying, it's definitely a kind of flying.

THE SUMMER OF
VINTAGE CLOTHING

R UTH WAS dressing for Vicky's party when Carl came home
and told her he had lost the turkey. She lowered both ends
of her necklace and looked at him. She thought: Of course you did.
It was a big moment there in the bedroom, Ruth sitting on the bed,
Carl standing before her, frowning in concentration, his palms out,
and before he could shift his weight or begin anything, she saw him
as if for the first time, her husband, a handsome man who had been
bright and clever and who was still a good lawyer, but who was, as
he stood pantomiming what he might have done with the smoked
turkey for Vicky's party, a man who had spent years growing vague.

Carl thought hard. "I'm in Canyon Market off of Foothill . . ."

"Can you help me with this?" Ruth handed him the necklace. It
was a string of small copper disks which they had purchased on last
year's trip to the Yucatán. Carl looked at it now as if it were a puzzle, and Ruth could see his mind was somewhere else.

Carl had been her mainstay; at one time she had counted on him.
But now he was gone, lost in another battle with Gerver, totally pre-
occupied with his own stress. He came home these days and *did
TV*—smoking his cigars, shoes on the couch—that being his phrase

as he raised a hand to quiet whatever question she might ask: "Not now, honey, okay? I'm doing TV here, do you see?" On the screen a man would be pressing both fists into his eyes trying to think on *The Family Feud, things at a wedding shower.* And after doing TV, Carl came to bed and wanted to mount her like a moment's information, a newsbreak. There had been times like this before in this marriage, and as soon as Carl or Gerver relented, changed their memos, shook hands, he would be back for a while and she could rely on him again. Now Ruth sat on the bed and looked at Carl as he tried to figure out why he had a necklace in his hands.

But it was her son Sean, a boy best described by the ridiculous phrase "the apple of her eye," who had Ruth most upset. It was what she had heard him say. He'd always been interesting and funny and companionable, a friend in the house really, willing to talk at night sometimes if there was popcorn or ice cream and Carl was asleep on the couch. They'd watch TV together and comment on the characters, and Sean was always surprising her with his observations. "You can tell the total mental state of a person by watching him in the left-turn lane," and during love scenes he'd point at the screen and say, "It's some kind of bonding maneuver, as far as I can tell." Sometimes he would remove his sleeping father's shoes and say, "Dad, you've got to learn to respect the furniture." And sometimes it was Ruth who slept on the couch, or feigned sleep, lying deeply in the cushions to hear Sean tell Carl about the track coach or the debate trip. Those nights covered her like a blanket and she could feel the soft electricity of it in the backs of her legs, too much and not enough at the same time, these men, talking.

This was the summer of vintage clothing. Sean and his friend David were into old clothes. They'd raid the Deseret Industries thrift shops and come home in three-piece suits and wide silk ties hand-painted with animals and birds. Sean mowed the lawn in vests and the two boys played tennis in pleated trousers. It was Ruth's joy to see the two of them on lounge chairs in the backyard like two bare-foot bankers, their ties loosened in the sun. Eventually they'd carefully disrobe, hanging their garments on the pool furniture until the baggy trousers came off revealing their swimsuits, and they'd dive into the blue water.

Lately there had been a third in this game, Dorie, also a sopho-more at Suburban, a girl Ruth liked, though it was unclear whose friend she was. David was smoother, more confident and gregarious, but Sean was tall and—the only word Ruth could think of—pretty in a Ricky Nelson kind of way. Dorie was over two or three times a week in flowered skirts and billowy blouses looking like something prime for a country weekend, sometimes a blue or beige suit, the jacket and tight skirt making her look ready to go off to the office. "This hat," Dorie would say. "Fifty cents." And she'd turn to show the large straw hat, its band a colorful wrap of red silk.

Mostly Ruth wasn't included. She watched the three young peo-ple from her kitchen window. They tuned the radio to KOY, a sta-tion that played only music from the forties and fifties, Patti Page, Robert Goulet, Glenn Miller, Tony Bennett; it was hilarious. Ruth's friend Vicky stood with her one day at the sink watching the young people and said, "I love coming over here. It makes me feel so *young*." That day at the window, Vicky had said, "They think they're in a movie. I remember it, the feeling. You sit around with your fin-gers under your chin waiting for someone to ask you what's the mat-ter. It's the age of loveliness. Everything is terribly important and terribly lovely."

The women watched Dorie stand and slowly unbutton the front of her blouse and place it on the back of her chair. She moved to the pool's edge and stood for a dive. Vicky said, "Who is that?" Dorie swam in a sleek one-piece that showed her more woman than Ruth would have imagined.

Your son is fifteen, Ruth thought. He is fifteen this summer and you are the iced-tea lady now. In three years he'll be gone. And she was the iced-tea lady, kidding them about their getups as she set the large plastic tumblers on the small tables by the pool. They can't even see me, she thought, I'm just the source of iced tea. Sometimes she hummed along with the ridiculous music. She watched them from her window with nothing as much as pure feeling, three beautiful kids in the sunshine, dressed for the forties.

It was vintage everything, really. The word itself came out almost too often. David would appear at their door in a brown suit two sizes too large and wave a videocassette, saying, "This is a classic. This is vintage Karloff." The young people watched old films in the den, black-and-white horror films, and lounged so deeply in the furniture it was as if they were hiding. When Ruth came through the room from time to time, she looked for clues about who was with whom, but the alliances were never clear. Some days Dorie lay out on the couch like an actress, the boys in the two big chairs, some days she sat with David there, and then some days she sat on the floor in front of Sean's chair. Ruth would watch for a moment, the Mummy stepping heavily through the open terrace doors or Dracula opening his caped arms and turning into a bat. She liked having the kids around the house, though they couldn't see her, but she could tell things were changing. The nights Sean would go down to David's for dinner or a movie, she would work at her desk, pretend to, and then double-check the porch light. It was hard to read. She wasn't used to this new thing, waiting for her son to return.

And then, of course, something snapped. Last night as Ruth was rinsing her serving tray, she heard through her open window her son talking to David in the blue night of the backyard. Over the humming of the pool filter pump, Sean was speaking, his voice printed on her life forever, and she heard the words before she had a chance to disbelieve them: "Yeah," she heard him say. "She is such a cunt." Ruth felt her elbows take fire and weaken, and she put down the tray in her hands.

"OKAY, OKAY," Carl went on. "I can get this." But he wasn't talking about the necklace. "I spoke to the butcher and he said that it would be a minute, then I ran into Vicky." Carl had forgotten about the necklace in his hand and was gesturing, setting up imaginary places in the grocery store. He was being logical and retracing his steps. "And she said something about something . . ."

"She said she'd see us tonight at the party and that we're going to meet her new boyfriend, the Texan." Ruth took the necklace back from him and tried to fasten it again.

"Right. That's it." Then Carl looked at her with surprise. "And she said Tom Gerver's coming. His wife is one of your accounts? Something."

"That's right."

Carl shook off the distance and said, "Okay, so the butcher handed me the bag over the counter." Carl hoisted the imaginary bag. "And when I went up front to check out I found I didn't have any cash. . . ." Here Carl thrust his hands into his pockets until he fished out a paper slip. "So I put it on Visa." He paused and read the slip very slowly: "Smoked turkey: thirty-four forty-four."

"What's the program?" Sean said, dropping a shoulder against their doorway. He was wearing a brown suit vest over a white T-shirt. His trousers were cinched tight around his narrow waist, but they still sagged. "Who's feeding you guys tonight?"

Ruth had avoided him since last night, and now with the sound of his voice she felt her heart contract. "We'll be at Vicky's," she said carefully. "What are your plans?"

Sean took two steps to Ruth and lifted the necklace from her hands. Deftly he dipped it around her neck and had it fastened before she could move.

Carl was still in the grocery store. "There was a girl behind me with a new baby, and," Carl turned to where she would have stood, "I helped her."

"I'll be here," Sean said. "David and Dorie may come over."

"And I took the baby." Now Carl's hands were really full. "It was raining . . . her car was next to mine." Carl seemed to be reading off the ceiling. "She opened the door—it's a two-door—and I put the baby in his car seat in the back."

"Dad, you are such a hero."

"And . . . I . . ." Carl dropped his arms and sat on the bed. "God,

I don't know. I drove home. I don't know where it is. I lost the turkey."

"Want me to check the car?"

"No, I've been through it six times."

"It doesn't matter," Ruth said, feeling her neck stiffen. "Call the market and ask them to set aside another. We'll pick it up on the way. Get dressed, Carl. Let's go meet Vicky's friend."

When she stood, Sean said, "You look good, Mom. A little modern, but good. David thinks you're a babe." Ruth left the room. She could hear the men talking behind her.

THE THEME of the party, Ruth had forgotten, was tequila. There were trays of Shooters and Sunrises and every plate on the buffet had a little card attached that read Tequila something or other, "Tequila Fettucine," "Tequila Jamboree." It was still raining lightly and Vicky's house was crowded with dozens of people. Vicky brought a man over and introduced Ruth and Carl. His name was actually Bo and he was from Houston or near there and he did something with land. Ruth noted Bo's thin mustache, something you rarely saw anymore, something a man does on purpose. A black line along the top of his lip.

As Ruth and Carl laid out their tray, Vicky stuck a little sign, "Tequila Turkey," on the platter. She handed Ruth a sweet Sunrise, which puckered Ruth's mouth. "Battery acid," Vicky said, pointing to the hinge of her jaw. "They give you a little sizzle right there, don't they? Battery acid. You get it from chocolate and beer too." Vicky looked at Ruth and asked, "What's the matter?"

"Nothing. Something. Somebody in our house is fifteen."

"Who? Carl?"

"Funny. We're *doing* growth at our house," Carl said. "You can feel the limits groaning."

Ruth looked at her husband and thought, How would you know?

Tom Gerver came up behind Carl and nodded at Ruth as a greeting. He took Carl by the arm, leading him into the other room, which Ruth could only interpret as a good sign.

"Is Sean still dressing for dinner?" Vicky asked.

Ruth nodded, aware she didn't want to talk about it really. There was something too personal about it, this summer. A moment later Vicky pointed to where Bo was making drinks at the bar table. "So, how do you like him?"

"He seems quite . . . manly."

Vicky smiled. "Don't you hate it," she said. "If it weren't for that trait, they'd be all right. Actually he's a nice guy. A little too willing to please. *Very* considerate. Very . . . in bed it's this and that for three hours. Newly divorced men are like that."

Vicky went over and escorted him into the party. Throughout the evening as Ruth drifted through the rooms, a lot of her friends commented on how tall Sean was now, and there were some funny things said about his costumes, divided between those who thought he had decided to run for office and those who thought he was going into the ministry. Everyone said the word *fifteen* wistfully. "Fifteen," one older woman said. "Wonderful fifteen. It's the first time you'd like to sell them."

Ruth relished being alone at the party, not engaging in long discussions, just wandering from room to room. Several people complimented her on her necklace and she had a feeling she hadn't had in a long time—since parties at her sorority house—that something was going to happen next.

The rain let up sometime after eleven and as groups of people began to venture out onto the back deck, Ruth searched the house for Carl. The doors and windows were open and the fresh cool air seemed like fall. She found him flat on his back in the wet side yard, side by side with his buddy Tom Gerver, both of them absolutely drunk. From the position of their bodies, flung out and imbedded in the grass, it looked as if they had fallen from an airplane.

"Hi honey," Carl said. "Tom and I were taking a break."

As she helped Carl up, Tom said, "You're a good woman, Ruth." He rose to an elbow and said with drunken sincerity, "I'm sorry about your turkey."

Ruth didn't care that Carl was so far gone or that she'd have to drive home. She'd driven him home before and she was relieved that he seemed to have made peace with Tom. When they were in the car, he was chatty. "What's bugging you about Sean?" he asked. "I like his girlfriend." He folded his arms, then finding they didn't fit, refolded them. They were waiting to turn left onto their street.

"How does he know about necklaces?"

"What?" Carl looked at her.

"There's something to know about necklaces," she said.

"What is it? What is there?" Carl pointed down the empty roadway, "You can turn now, Ruth. There's nobody coming."

Ruth measured the turn with exaggerated care. "She's not his girlfriend," she said.

AT HOME the house was empty though the television was on. Ruth stood and watched it for a moment—a high-rise building was burning. Carl slumped through the room, his eyes half shut, waving both palms at her and going straight to bed. Ruth sat down and slipped off her shoes. On television now, two blond men smeared with camouflage grease in sleeveless T-shirts, carrying automatic weapons, detonators, and a strange sphere, entered an elevator. This is where Sean would say to her, "Those are the bad guys, Mom." It was one of their jokes—the way she had always talked to him as a child when he watched television. Ruth watched the screen. She had distinctly heard him say it, "She's such a cunt." Several of the upper stories of the building exploded, spraying fans of white sparks into the night.

Leaving the television on, Ruth went into the kitchen and made herself a scotch and water. She wandered back through the house, every room, straightening things in the dark, her desk—so clean already—Sean's bed—neat too—in a room so clearly still a boy's, the walls all athletes and animals, his first debate trophy on the shelf (Carl's phrase, "Your *first*"). In the glowing dark she touched the dish of change on his bureau and then suddenly became self-conscious, her face warm, as if she'd been going through his pockets, and she moved into the hallway and then to the front of the house, making sure again that the porch light was on.

Back in the dark kitchen, she poured another short splash of scotch and went through the French doors onto the pool deck. It was fresh outdoors after the recent rain and she could smell the wet cement as it dried in the night and she could hear the clacking of the palm fronds above the neighbor's yard. She walked out around the pool and sat on the side of the diving board. From here her dark yard and house seemed vast, another landscape. Shapes slowly emerged, the lumps of towels, the deck tables, Sean's suit jacket on the back of a chair.

When she heard the laugh, she felt it as something sharp in her chest and then she heard it again, an alto note that could not be suppressed, and the warmth spread down her arms. "Sean?" she said, her voice strange, reedy, and then louder: "Sean?" Now she couldn't hear anything in the mix of the pool pump, the palm fronds' dry whispers. "Sean?" She couldn't see anything in the dark reflections of the water or the windows of the house and she realized she couldn't move either, she couldn't get up right now or walk to the house, it was the strangest feeling and it wouldn't let her speak again either. And for a moment in the liquid night she was that still, not calm, but not panicked either, just kept there by the weight of the two sounds she'd heard and known about all along.

Beneath her she saw the water ripple and heard it lapping at the tile in a new way, then the surface broke in a dark oval which became a face, silver under hair as black and varnished as a movie star's from the twenties. She didn't recognize him at first, his face, until he reached for the side of the pool and she saw his wrist and forearm.

"Sean?"

"Yeah. Mom, hi. Party over?" His voice was thick, husky, a whisper.

"Is that David?" Ruth looked out into the dark where she knew Dorie hid in the water.

"No, he just left," Sean said. He was treading water, staying away from her.

"It's after midnight, Sean."

"Really. Okay."

Ruth now heard Dorie's body rise from the water, the short rush of water in the far dark, and before her son's next plaintive "Mom?"—a word so saturated with pleading that she found it almost repulsive—the light in the kitchen went on around the shape of her husband. The light fell in a cartoonish square across the patio and Ruth saw Dorie stand casually as if to meet it, so casually it hurt, and drop the towel the way she would if alone after a shower, her body here only white, her arms, her high breasts white, as she lifted her shift over her head and began to wriggle into it.

"Mom?" her son said again from the water.

But coming out of the house like a figure in a horror film now, in an old pair of pajama bottoms and carrying a liter bottle of Perrier, was her husband, and he said, "Ruth? Ruth? I put it in her car." He became a dark shadow before her. He didn't know his son drifted in the water at his feet nor was he aware of the girl dressing behind him—who now knelt and busily worked at her shoes.

Ruth said nothing and then she said, "Carl."

"It's raining in the parking lot. Do you see, I know what happened." He gestured with the bottle of water and his free hand.

"When the girl flopped the front seat forward so I could reach in and put the baby in the car seat—see it? It's raining. The ground is wet. I put the bag on the floor there behind the front seat."

There was movement behind Carl and Ruth saw Dorie slip out the side gate. She could see beneath her in the water, like some creature, Sean, his white eyes, in a scene that was now only black-and-white. She stood up.

"Hey," Carl said. "Is that Sean?"

And Ruth felt then the whole world take hold and her heart, her body flood with wonder. And even though she tried, she couldn't stop from taking half a step back like an actress in a bad film, her hands raised in defense, in denial, as her eyes actually widened. She saw it; she saw it all. She saw these strangers. It was stark and clear. And she had been brought here from some other place at this point in her life, forty years of age, to live with them.

PLAN B FOR
THE MIDDLE CLASS

E VERYBODY'S THREE. Harry has just turned three and
Ricky won't be four until August, and all I want to do is get
Katie in bed. The theme for the spring is sand. It is everywhere. The
boys carry it around in their pockets until it pulls their pants down.
We don't even notice the sandy trails through the house anymore,
and when the two three-year-olds come in for lunch, they squirm
in their seats until each lifts a scoop of sand onto the table beside
his grilled cheese sandwich. They will not eat until there is sand on
the table.

Right now they are both well into their sandwiches and I watch
Katie pour milk and move about the kitchen. I can hear the uneven
flicker of sand filtering onto the floor and the sound is magnified by
my throat-dry lust. I am trying to restrain myself from going up
behind Katie and fondling her breasts. I can sense she's got an eye on
me anyway. This sweet hollow call of desire has been growing for
months, it seems, years, perhaps it too is three. It's rich. It's as crazy
as a song. Just the touch of her sleeve can set me off. Katie brushes
the hair off her forehead and looks at me again: "What?" she says.

I turn back into the living room and ask the guy who is fixing the

VCR how it's going. He's a house-call guy out of the Nickel Ads. He's young and bald and wearing white overalls. The VCR is out of its shell in four big components on the floor.

"There's a lot of sand in here, buddy," he tells me.

"I know," I say, and he looks up at me for an explanation. "It's been sandy."

"Well," he says, measuring it out like medicine and going back to the pieces of the VCR, "that's hard on the heads. You're going to wear your heads out with sand."

I nod as if to say I understand, I stand corrected, I hear and receive his scolding gratefully, I couldn't agree more. We'll do better.

The truth is that if my parents weren't flying in to be with the kids, I would have poured another cup of sand into the mechanism myself. It has served up a limited repertoire in the two years we've had it. The only movies we see are *Dumbo, Land of the Lost, More Dinosaurs,* and *Using Your Cuisinart.* After two hundred viewings I became numb to *Dumbo,* which is an ardent feminist film. *Dumbo* has no father, the circus workmen drink away their pay, the Ringmaster is a blustering fool, and the only good man is a mouse. *Land of the Lost* is the hokiest video in the country, drawn from an old television series about a family who take the wrong turn on a raft trip and end up in another world, a world full of dinosaurs, cavemen, the whole show. *More Dinosaurs* and *Using Your Cuisinart* are documentaries.

After dinner every night while I run bathwater, Katie cleans up in the kitchen, and Harry and Rick sop up one of these cinema classics. Harry sits there naked—as he is naked at the lunch table right now—and watches the television through his binoculars. Harry is a naked child all of the time. You can tie his shoes one minute and the next find them along with his shirt et cetera on the front step. But he is never without his binoculars. He holds the big end to his eyes, so things must appear way out there. Other people have told us about their children who resented and avoided clothing, so the fact that Harry is always naked doesn't bother us too much yet. However, his drifting through the house with those glasses held to his face can be disconcerting.

Ricky, on the other hand, isn't interested in his binoculars. He has become, like so many American preschoolers, an absolute paleontologist. He knows all the dinosaurs and all of their cousins. Katie has kept up with all of this, which is no small task, since they've changed all the names and half the theories since we were in school. Except the triceratops; there is still a triceratops.

From time to time, I'll stop on the way home from work and rent a movie, *Body Heat,* or *An Officer and a Gentleman,* figuring we'll watch something with a little sex in it after the boys are in bed and then I'll reach for Katie and we've had a wonderful life that way— one thing leads sweetly to another. But we never see the films. By the time the kids are down, we're shot. The videos stay in their cases on top of the console. Once we tried to watch *Siesta* in the morning while the kids were in the sandbox. Well, that's no good. That's not right. You can't watch movies in the morning.

And now my parents are coming, so they can watch *Land of the Lost.* They haven't seen it yet. They haven't heard Marshall's line as the characters look around at their jungle home: "I think we're in another world."

Back in the kitchen, Harry smiles at me and puts the large end of his binoculars to his face. He is looking at a full glass of milk that appears to be fifty yards away.

"Boys," I start, "while we're gone and Grandma and Grandpa are here, do not put sand in the television."

Ricky can't hear me. He is full face into his sandwich, all business, his hands working more and more of it into his mouth. Little naked Harry turns and looks at me with his binoculars. "Dad, Dad," he says. I wait for him to finish. I must look like I'm up here ten stories.

And, in fact, I feel remote, my little family way below, another life, another world. I've lost my job. It crumbled under me and now I'm off balance. Perhaps I'm falling, waiting as in a dream to hit the ground, waiting certainly to tell Katie.

"Dad, I got a big one," Harry says, gesturing to the milk and knocking the glass completely over in a quick splash. Katie is there in a second with a sponge almost as if she could sense it coming, the way a good infielder moves to the ball when he sees the bat swing, and the mess which I thought would be major, milk and sand, is nothing in a moment. Rick hasn't stopped eating. When Katie bends down for the last pickup, I can't stop myself, I run my hand across her arched back, and it is then I feel the first pang of something else, an itch, my rash. My jock rash is coming back. I adjust my shorts and scratch myself.

"That's lovely," Katie says, watching me. She sits down with the boys. "No sand," she says, giving each a look in the eye. "No sand in the television."

WHEN I was seventeen, I played varsity baseball for Union High School and I developed my first case of this rash, the case for the record books. There could have been many causes. Just being seventeen is what it was. And wet jocks. You take kids seventeen and make them wear wet jockstraps to play baseball, they'll get something. Jock rash seems the most harmless consequence. The school supplied socks, jocks, and T-shirts, and several times that spring the clothes dryer by the locker room was busted, and we'd take the field against Claremont or Mountain in damp straps. At first I noticed a slight burning and then the visible rash, and then being seventeen and busy, I neglected it the whole term, until I couldn't ignore it anymore. My friend Ryan McBride had the locker next to mine in the team locker room, and one night after a game I lifted the leg of my boxer shorts—we all wore boxer shorts that year—and asked him, "You got any of this?"

"Holy shit, Lew," he said. "You've got a royal case of jock itch. Come here, Baker, look at Lew's crotch!"

At the time, I didn't know that he meant I had it for life. In fact, at the time it didn't sound too bad. It sounded like a kind of compliment: Hey, Lewis, you're a man. Something like that.

It was something to see: a raised red rash running out on each leg in an area about the size of a hand, so tender that the hem of my boxer shorts felt like wire. Nights I would douse it with medicated powder and wake up with my heart beating in the raw flesh. There was no help. Finally my mother asked me what—in heaven—was the matter. I was so desperate I showed her. She wrinkled her nose and called Dr. Wilson, making an appointment for after graduation that I would never have to keep.

THE VIDEO guy is done. He used a little hand-held vacuum cleaner for a while at the end and then snapped the facing back on the VCR and shut his tools. He hands me the ticket: ninety-six dollars. It's worth it. I'm not going to squawk now. In twenty-four hours Katie and I will be in bed in our room at the Royal Hawaiian while in Arizona my parents watch *More Dinosaurs*. Ninety-six dollars is cheap.

"See, boys," I say, "Mr. Waldren"—I read his name from the receipt as I write the check—"has fixed our television. The boys don't want to put sand in the machine, do they, Mr. Waldren."

Mr. Waldren takes the check and folds it into his overalls pocket. He looks up at me and simply says, "Why would they want to do that?"

WHEN I was nine years old, I started reading the newspaper, the comics, the puzzles, and "Ask Andy." My mother would fold the paper to the right page and hand it to me. She encouraged literacy in her household, this farmgirl valedictorian from a Nebraska high school. She always completed the crossword, except for a few easy four- and five-letter words, which I was expected to do, and I remember learning forever the name of the Elbe River in Germany, which appeared with disturbing frequency in the *Salt Lake City Tribune*. But it was "Ask Andy" which really challenged me. "What Do Pandas Eat?" would be the headline, and then in small print after the two-column answer (bamboo shoots, ten pounds a day)

would be some kid's name and the fact that she had won a set of
encyclopedias for asking about pandas. It seemed obvious that I
could do better than the panda question, and I began sending questions to Andy.

My first, I remember, was based on the fact that pandas are related
to raccoons. "What Do Raccoons Eat?" I followed that with three
other questions about raccoons. "Where Do Raccoons Live?" "Why
Do Raccoons Have Masks?" "How Did the Raccoon Get Its Name?"
I became, in fact, the fourth-grade expert on raccoons, which my
teacher Mrs. Talbot thought was just fine, but Andy did not
acknowledge my questions. From North American mammals, I went
on to magnetism and sent in a series of bewildering questions about
the very essence of matter and its fundamental behavior. Andy was
unimpressed. It is not a good thing for an elementary school pupil
to send off questions in the mail and get nothing in return, and my
mother tried to ease the sting by praising my queries (she typed
them) and defending Andy in his difficult work. "He gets lots of letters, honey." Nevertheless, I let Andy go. I stopped reading his column. I just filled in the crossword puzzles with my mother's help
and took up clipping "Gasoline Alley."

That summer was Little League and YMCA Camp, and it was at
camp months later that I struck on the idea that had been waiting
for me. I saw it, I felt it just like Moon Mullins with a light bulb over
his head. I mean, I felt the physical shock of having a radical
thought. Actually, it happened on our cabin's overnight up the
Soapstone Creek. Our counselor, Michael Overholt, a college student and botanical genius, was off collecting and pressing ferns for
his collection, and the other campers and myself were having a con-
test. We were gathered around one huge Douglas Fir (flat needles),
seeing who could pee furthest up the trunk. It was there, leaning
backward marking the tree, that I saw the concept that sent me back
to "Ask Andy" for the last time.

The rest of camp went by in a blur as I waited to get home and
write my letter. I remember falling off a horse on our trail ride, mak-

ing a black-and-yellow key chain with boondoggle in crafts, and
spending most of capture-the-flag in jail. It was all irrelevant to me.
I had seen the future.

As was her custom, my mother typed my letter for me. I had to
print it first, as always, and though I could tell she didn't think it was
a brilliant question, she didn't say anything, just moved to the typewriter (a bad sign) and had me look up the word "urinate," which
wasn't much of a task once she let me know it began with a *u*. "Dear
Ask Andy, When I urinate, why does it stay in a stream instead of
spraying all over the place?" It was my longest letter to Andy, more
than twice as long as anything about raccoons, and my mother did
say, as she typed the envelope, that its length might hurt it.

I didn't care. It was a great question. And during the next year,
fifth grade, I read "Ask Andy" every day. It was a big year for the
planets, space in general, with secondary themes of reptiles and min-
eralogy. There was almost no anatomy or hydrology. It didn't really
hurt my feelings. I remember thinking as the spring came that year
and baseball started up again: It's okay. No wonder he didn't print
my question. *He doesn't know.*

My mother bought a set of *The Book of Knowledge* that year and
would buy a set of *Britannica*s the next. There wasn't anything in
either about my question, and after a while I got into the mysteries
of art, studying all the jungles of Rousseau, the stark dramas of
Goya, and then settling on the romantic Delacroix. I would stare at
"Liberty Guiding the People" for hours at a time in *The Book of
Knowledge*. Her blouse is torn down, as you know, but it isn't a
moment for niceties. If she stopped to cover herself, the battle could
be lost. I was in the sixth grade by then and I found the painting
compelling. I couldn't get her courage and nudity into my head at
the same time, and burned with curiosity about such things. But it
came to me from time to time as I'd write ELBE in the crossword puzzles, which my mother was leaving more and more blank for me to
do: I'd stumped Andy. I had this picture of some guy who looked
like Mr. Drubay, my arithmetic teacher, standing in his little office

which was stacked high with envelopes of questions as he looked out the window at a big city and scratched his head. He wasn't happy. There were probably a lot of things he didn't know, things he would never know. I feel that way more and more myself. He probably worried about being fair giving out the encyclopedias. So I ended that year thinking about that confused guy in his office and staring at Liberty's beautiful breasts amid all the damage and the danger. I'd stumped Andy. All I could think was: If there were an answer for every question, what kind of world would it be?

I AM told that one of my strengths as "Zoo Lewis," in my column "Animals Unlimited," is the patience I display toward obvious questions. In my eleven years I've received four Press Service Awards for the column, "for making the obvious interesting and the complex understandable." I enjoy my work, sure, and most of the questions I receive are extraordinarily good, germane, challenging, and lead naturally to interesting columns. People are always surprised that the armadillo crosses a river by walking across the bottom, that the gnu can run so fast, that the marten is so small. Beyond the fun stuff— the "Where does 'playing 'possum' come from?" or "How are porcupines romantic?"—there are a lot of unanswerably weird letters about feathers and fur and the death of pets. I answer all my mail. I say "I don't know" sometimes in the letters. I have even answered all of the hate mail I've had in the last six months about the evolution problem, even though I use a photocopied form for those. It's not a surprise that I answer letters; Andy never wrote back to me.

THE BOYS and I go to the airport to pick up my parents. Walking with my sons through the terminal is like magic for me, because I am a man with a secret. My parents are flying in from Michigan to stay with the boys for a week while Katie and I go to Hawaii. I'll have to spend one day with my old prof Sorenson in his research center at the university taking notes for an article on his first panda and then half of another at the Kapiolani Zoo, looking at their arrangements for the creature, but the rest of the time Katie and I will be having sexual intercourse with short breaks to eat. And I will figure a way to tell her I've been fired. This will be our first trip away from the boys, and as I noted, everybody is three. It has been like three years in space, the four of us in a capsule circling and circling in the dark. Every time there is a lull, someone floats by in your face. "Hi, Dad."

Katie and I moved our sex life later and later into the night, until it was being conducted with one of us half asleep, and then we tried the mornings, but the boys have always risen first and crawled in with us. Then we bought the VCR and used it to lure them into the living room mornings for twenty minutes of Chip and Dale cartoons while we touched very quietly in our bedroom and listened for little feet. That ploy actually worked pretty well for a while, and then we became guilty about using the TV that way.

We moved into the shower. That was always good, but it was difficult to hear in there and more than once we saw a small pink figure leaning against the frosted-glass shower doors. It was enough to take the starch out of things. Then a terrible thing happened: we became pragmatic about it. Interrupted once, we would shrug and smile at each other, rinse off, and start the day. Can I even explain how sad it made me to watch Katie pull on her clothing?

But now, I have a secret. I am one revolution of the earth away from the most astonishing sex carnival ever staged by two married people.

This is what I tell myself. And I believe it, but there's more. Though Katie hasn't said anything, I suspect she knows I'm not Zoo Lewis anymore. Cracroft told me I was history on Tuesday and then he's called and tried to be helpful twenty times. The syndicate is dropping the column. We both know why, but they cite numbers. I'm down to fifty-two papers from over a hundred and seventy. The papers are dropping the column. The *Blade*, the *Register*, the *Courier*, the *Post*. They can't handle the backlash. I'm too political. Maybe I am. It is no longer possible to write cute pieces about the dolphin, the mandrill, the Asian elephant. But this all started with four pieces on simple amphibians and what one of my hate-mail correspondents called "creeping evolutio-environmental liberal bullshit." Cracroft says *no problem,* most of the papers will do reruns of old columns for six months, and that should give me enough time to come up with some freelance stuff of a more "general nature" and maybe pitch a book.

Zoo Lewis bites the dust. Maybe he should. I was getting cranky. I've enjoyed it more than I planned to, and only one other time was there trouble: after I wrote an appreciation of the wolf, a very bright, misunderstood creature who mates for life. We got two pounds of mail from Montana and lost the *Star* and the *Ledger.*

Cracroft is a good guy. I don't blame Cracroft. He called and said I could keep my modem. He said, "I'm sorry, Lewis. Your work is good. It may just be time to shake up the feature page."

"What should I do?" I asked him. We've known each other for ten years.

"You're good," he said. "Go to plan B."

I smiled and thanked him for the modem. Plan B. Zoo Lewis *was* plan B. I was going to be a veterinarian. I was going to doctor animals, but I couldn't because of the allergies—they tried to kill me more than once. We can't even have a dog or a cat or a ferret. We can have fish in a tank, but I don't want fish. I couldn't be a vet, so I became a journalist. I'm in plan B. And it's not working.

AT THE gate, I am surprised. When my parents emerge, I have to look twice. It's not that I don't recognize them; it is that I recognize them too well. They haven't changed in a year. Why don't they look older? My mother wears her sure-of-herself grin, having gone out into the world once again and found herself still every bit the match for it. The interactions of men and women have always amused her. "Society," she used to tell me, "is not quite finished. Don't *ever* fret and stew about your place in it."

My father comes forward beside her, carrying his small valise in which there will be four or five pads of blue-lined graph paper already bearing the beginnings of several letters and drawings. He will have seen something from the window of the plane, where he always sits, that has struck him as worthy of improvement and he will have begun the plans. He works on half a dozen projects at a time. When he retired from General Motors four years ago, the grid pads just continued. He has fourteen obscure patents and is always working on two or three more in far-flung fields: a design for a safety fence for horse racing; a design for pressure tanks containing viscous liquids; a tennis racket grip. He writes me every week on the beautiful paper describing his projects and his current concerns. Most recently he's been considering the rules and statistics of baseball and has in mind several revisions. I watch my father approach with his easy stride and calm smile and I am paralyzed. He doesn't look older at all. He looks, and this has my mouth open, *just like me.* It took them almost forty years, but my genes have jelled. No wonder my three-year-old sons leap away, weaving through the travelers, to grab the hands of my mother and my father.

When I join them, my mother has already pulled two dinosaurs out of her bag and awarded one to each of the boys. I kiss my mother and when I step back she runs her hand up over my ear through the white in my hair and smiles. My father hugs me, letting his hand stay across my shoulder as he always has since my Little League days. Ricky has examined his toy, feeling the snout and counting the claws, and finding it authentic, he is very pleased. "Isn't it great?" I say to him. "A brontosaurus."

"Dad," Ricky corrects me. "It's not."

"It's an allosaurus," my mother says. I look at her and she gives me the look she's always had for me, the sweet, chiding challenge: *You can catch up if you'd like. None of this is beyond you.* But I'm not so sure. It may be beyond me, and if not, I'm not sure I want to catch up. It no longer surprises me that everyone is ahead of me. My parents are keeping up on dinosaurs.

AT HOME, my father helps me start the barbecue and we stand on the patio in the early dark. He is drinking one of Katie's margaritas and looking around at the sky as if listening for something.

"We won't have a night like this until June," he says.

"I know. February is a bonus here. June is a hundred and ten." I am arranging the chicken pieces on the hot grill. I'd like to tell my father about what is happening, that my job is over, but there is really no need. He knows already. My mother let it slip on the phone that my column wasn't running in the *Journal* anymore. My parents have always been mind readers. He can tell that change is at hand by the way I use the tongs on the chicken. This mode of communication is actually a comfort. It spares our talking like people on television.

Years ago, I called home the night I knew I was leaving veterinarian school. I was in the hospital in Denver and when my mother answered she said, "It's your allergies, isn't it, Lewis? Are you in the hospital right now?"

Ricky comes out and loops an arm around my father's leg. "Granpa, Granpa, Granpa," he says and points at the chicken sizzling on the grill. "The barbecue is very hot. You must be very careful."

Ricky's head falls against my father's leg and as my father cups the little boy's head, I know how it feels. The two stand in that kind of hug and watch me as I begin to turn the chicken. This is who I am, some guy with a spatula at twilight. I write about animals. I won't get the big adventures, page-one stuff; I've stood on a lot of patios with my father and I'll stand on quite a few with my son. That is what I'll get.

Later, in our bedroom, Harry is helping Katie pack. She's got both big suitcases open on the floor and Harry sits in one with his binoculars. He's emptied my shaving kit and is sorting through the goodies. I reach down and try to find my razor. "I already put it on the bureau," Katie says. "Do you want your Hawaiian shirt?"

"What's the protocol? I don't think you take your Hawaiian shirt to Hawaii, do you?" It's a turquoise shirt with little red and white guitars and orchids printed all over it.

"If you don't take it, we may buy another."

"Take it," I say. "Let's take it."

Harry has pulled the lid down now and he's inside the suitcase. In twenty minutes, when my mother has taken Rick in to bed and read him a book and he's flopped over on his stomach aggressively for sleep, I will come back in here and find Harry asleep in my suitcase and carry him to bed.

Of course, when you have children, all your bedtimes come back to you. Not all at once, but from night to night, pieces of your earliest nights appear. It will be the sound of a sheet or the feel of a blanket and the dark in the corner or the way the light from the hall falls on the far wall and there you are being carried to bed by someone who must have been your father or there is your mother with her hand in your hair and your head on the pillow. Some nights I lie in their room with the kids and listen to their nursery-rhyme tapes and I listen to them as they swim in the sheets, Ricky diving down first into sleep, the same way he eats, hungrily, no sense wasting time, and Harry as he turns sideways on his back and then kicks the wall softly with his heels as his blinking grows longer and longer and then his eyes shut for good and I hear the motor of his breath even out in a perfect sine curve.

When Katie comes to bed it is just about midnight. I've been listening to some guy on Larry King's radio show talk about the economy. He is advising people to keep gold under their mattresses. Katie hits the pillow with a blow-out sigh, throwing her right arm up over her eyes. "Are we actually going on a trip?" she says. "Are we going to sleep for four days or what."

"Depends on what you mean."

She turns her head my way and smiles. "You monkey. 'The coast is clear.'" That's the line we've used for fifteen years. Petting in her front room, one or two o'clock in the morning, I was always whispering: "The coast is clear." Once on her dining-room floor as close to putting something on the permanent record as we'd ever been, everybody's pants to the knees, brains full of fire, we heard her father

ten feet away in the kitchen drawing a glass of water. And now we'd
been living like that again. It makes a person dizzy.

The length of her body is the simple answer to what I am missing. It's an odd sensation to have something in your arms and to still
be yearning for it and you lie there and feel the yearning subside
slowly as the actual woman rises along your neck, chest, legs. We are
drifting against each other now. Sex is the raft, but sleep is the ocean
and the waves are coming up. Katie's mouth is on my ear and her
breath is plaintive and warm, a faint and rhythmic moan, and I pull
her up so that I can press the tops of my feet into her arches. I run
my hands along her bare back and down across her ribs and feel the
two dimples in her hip and my only thought is the same thought I've
had a thousand times: I don't remember this—I don't remember this
at all. Katie sits up and places her warm legs on each side of me, her
breasts falling forward in the motion, and as she lifts herself ever so
slightly in a way that is the exact synonym for losing my breath, we
see something.

There is a faint movement in our room, and Katie ducks back to
my chest. There is someone in our doorway. It is a little guy without
any clothes on. He has a pair of binoculars.

WHO CAN remember sex? Who can call it to mind with the sensate
vividness of actuality? I sit in the window when we lift off from Los
Angeles. Katie sits in the middle and next to her a high school kid
with a good blitz of pimples across his forehead. Katie speaks to him
and I see he has braces. Beneath us I see the margin of the Pacific fall
away. I can see all the way up to the Santa Monica Pier and the
uneven white strip of sand separates the crawling blue sea from the
brown urban grid of the city. We have just left something behind.
We have now been released from mainland considerations. Tonight
Harry is going to pad west in his bare feet, looking for us with his
glasses, but the surf is going to stop him. He'll be mad for a moment
at the Pacific Ocean, it's a big one, but then he'll turn and go back
to his room.

I love to fly. I always sit in the window and press the corner of my forehead against the plastic glass. I can feel the little bumps in my skull which are full of ideas and I move my head slightly. It kind of hurts in a nice way. Today my skull is full of sex. I'm trying to remember sex. I don't even try to resist by making notes for Sorenson or looking at the magazine, *Inflight*. The fact that I have lost my job and may lose our house, the Buick, the VCR, seems to have sharpened everything, and I feel edgy, alive. The sun is clipping through my window and falls in a square on my wrists and lap. I hear the stewardess come by, her clothing whispering, and I glimpse her tight maroon skirt, seamless and perfect as it passes.

I've always loved to look at women, what is that, terrible? There are moments I harbor in memory: buying my first sport coat on my own downtown in Salt Lake City at Mednicks, the tall young woman helping me, taking the coat back to the counter and then bending down and writing the slips as her white silk blouse fell open like doors of a cathedral and her breasts were revealed to me hanging there in the cool dark, draped in white undergarments as delicate and complicated as certain music. Of course, it happens all the time. When I buy a boatload of groceries at Safeway, the girl asks for identification for my check and then she bends to check the name and numbers. Who would look away from this healthy and dextrous checker, her cleavage sweet as milk. It's as if once she has my driver's license and is certain of who I am, she feels free to show me her breasts. I think of it and it makes buying food magical. And there have been times more raw, when driving down the hot highways I would look down into the Chevelle next to me in the jam, cars from here to heaven, and see her, some weary brunette in a skirt, legs spread, one knee cocked against the door so that the air conditioning ran into the open maw along her bare leg all gooseflesh and pin-feather right into the damp crux of my imagination.

NOW, IN an airliner with my wife fallen into a book and the jolly boy next to her gnashing peanuts, I suck at a gin and tonic and roll my forehead against the window. Below it is all sea now, and I feel the sleepy discomfort of an erection or half an erection, some vaguely pleasant stretching, and I shift in my seat belt, and I smile. My face feels sleepy and stiff and the smile feels like some kind of little exercise. This is immaturity. This is total regression. I think. I'm half asleep and I'm remembering Ryan McBride.

WHEN WE finally got to high school, Rye and I found the information about sex vague and imprecise. We'd been promised in the rumor and legend of junior high something more explicit. We'd heard everything. We'd heard about girls fighting in the parking lot, one girl's bra used to choke her if not to death then into acute brain damage. We'd heard about "heavy petting," which is exactly the kind of phrase that made Rye spit with rage. "Oh, it's heavy," he'd say. "Which is the heavy part?"

We were a little ready to rip the veil off anything vaguely masquerading as the unknown. We wanted to know. And it really got to Rye that people used the same phrases for everything.

"Doing it," they'd say. So-and-so were *doing it.*

"Totally bogus," Rye told me when we heard that about our old pal Paula Swinton and student body vice president Jeff Wild. "How could two words be more wrong? *Doing? Doing?*" he'd rant, his arms presenting the words to me in circles. "Doing?" He'd shake his head and say sadly, "It? Doing *it*? Paula and Jeff are doing *it*? What is it, one thing? Done one way? I mean, is it?" Rye would let his shoulders droop. Rye was a funny guy. He had a way, a campy way with his body. One shrug could get a room to laugh, and he'd been elected as student body secretary, the first boy ever to hold the office, on his reputation as a character. Standing there at his locker looking hurt in his green-and-gray class sweater, he mugged for me and went on, "Hey, Lewis, Lewis, Lewis. This is high school. This," he waved his book at the teeming corridor, "is secondary education." We started off for class and he put his arm over my shoulders and leaned on me. He whispered, "I had expected more. Paula and Jeff. *Please.* This place is letting me down."

And as an antidote for the ambiguity in which we floated, Rye became known, our junior and then senior year, as the guy who defined "heavy petting." "It's an ugly thing to see and if I were you I wouldn't look" was the first line of his credo as it appeared on blackboards and in graffiti in the stairwells. It closed: "It takes place below the waist." He said it as a student executive club meeting was breaking up, but it was noted on the blackboard in advanced English. In three weeks the phrase "takes place" could get a laugh in any sophomore class. A high school, we learned, is a three-story brick building with a jillion hormones and one trophy case.

He'd fall in step behind some junior in tight white Levi's, her rear bobbing like a searchlight, and he'd lean to me and say, "What is this feeling? The biological urge toward procreation of the species?" Then he'd elbow me and answer the question: "Nah."

His great and lasting fame derived, however, from planning the graduation party on Black Rock Beach and from his thesis: "Eleven," which postulated that there were eleven different kinds of erections. I can remember these things with a clarity that quiets me.

Katie has put her book on her lap and her head against my arm. It is sweetly warm here now, sunny with the kind of sleep that closes your eyes from the bottom up. The plane rides the white shell of air over the ocean, splitting silence into broomstraws, and I interlace my fingers carefully so as not to disturb my wife Katie. If you think I don't love her, you're not catching on. I close my eyes in the bright rushing world. I move my lips. So, what is this, more than it should be? I don't know. The truth: I'm praying.

The next: it doesn't last long. I move my lips carefully around the few important things I have to say and then use the bundle of my ten fingers to adjust the knob in my trousers. The walrus has a genuine bone in its penis that ranges in length between ten and twenty inches. The bone is an evolutionary device that is a great help in cold water. Eskimos save these bones, called "ooziks," for good luck. A sperm whale's penis, when erect, is nearly fifteen feet in length. The grizzly bear, more closely related to man, has erections that average four inches and require greater willing or unwilling cooperation from a mate. My watch tells me I've had this tumescence half an hour. It's the kind of erection Ryan used to call number three, the kind you get about ten in the morning in third period, a wonderful extension that makes you slide down in your seat and stretch your legs. It's related to number one, the one you wake up with, stiff as a clothespin. Number two was what? It was also a morning deal, the one that comes up between class, pointed down, trapped in your shorts pointing at five o'clock. Number two was the one you used your chemistry book to straighten out. What were the others? Eleven. We laughed our heads off, but we all knew he was right. There are eleven, minimum.

I remember the larky randiness of those days and my decision finally to push the point with a girl named Cheryl Lockwood at the graduation party. I wasn't really out of the mainstream in high school, most of our class were virgins, but I'd had a couple of relationships that had just dried up and blown away and I couldn't figure it out. I worried a little, I remember, about being unqualified for the real world of men and women. Who doesn't? My parents, of course, could read my mind, but I could not read theirs. I lived in a kind of dread that my father would take me aside one evening or my mother would try to open the topic. As it was, we lived an uneasy truce. If we were watching television at night together and there was a kissing scene, I would always leave the room, glass of water, homework, something. I was out of there.

Cheryl Lockwood was a cutie. I wasn't going with Cheryl, a smart-looking girl with short brown hair and a nice bosom, but she was my chemistry partner, and whenever we talked, we flirted. Her favorite phrase was "What you going to do, huh? Huh?" It was all smile-smile stuff, but the undercurrent was there. The way we flirted was that I would tell her she had to put on some weight and she would moan about it, *oh, no, no,* like that, and then we'd light the Bunsen burner and melt something down. When I think of her I still smell sulfur.

My decision to make serious moves on her was a result of our being sent to the principal's office together for staining Mr. Welch's hands. Our teacher, Mr. Welch, of course, deserved it, because he understood chemistry and wasn't that willing or able to let the rest of us in on the secret. He was a terrible teacher. We did learn that sodium nitrate stains human skin, however, and we spread a thin layer on our counter just before asking him over to explain something about liquid sulfur. The next day his palms were gray and he sent me and then Cheryl (because she laughed) to the office.

On the way down there I was a little high, you know, from being kicked out of class and the halls were empty and there was Cheryl in step with me and we were kind of bumping together and I said, "There is something so sexy about empty hallways, don't you think?" I put my arm around her shoulder and she put her arm around my waist and squeezed, saying, "Absolutely. What are you going to do about it?" And I said, "I'm going to get you alone at the graduation party and have my way with you." She squeezed me tighter and said, "Good. I hope you enjoy it as much as I plan to." We met with Mr. Gonzalez, the principal, and he tried to be mad about what we had done to Mr. Welsh, but he had a little trouble.

And that was that. Cheryl and I didn't flirt for the last two weeks of school. I didn't try anything because I didn't want to break the spell. We had made some kind of deal that day in the hallway and we both knew it.

WE LAND in Honolulu. I'm on the wrong side of the plane to see Waikiki, but I look down and see the water change, the seven layers of turquoise. When the wheels touch down, the plane bumps once in a soft, unreal way, and instead of thinking *we're really here,* I think: This seems unreal. And nothing that will happen for hours will dissuade me.

Our cab driver, for instance, is the same guy who took us to the airport in Phoenix. I lean back sleepily in the car and feel the strange air, moist and full of orchids and exhaust, and I see the back of his head. He must be working two shifts. He lets us off in the circular drive of the Royal Hawaiian and here the air wants to wake us, sweet with salt, in the dappled shady imbroglio of trees. I give the driver a big tip. He's going to need it to get back to Arizona by dawn. Here it is full afternoon, sunny but broken, and Katie stops me amid our suitcases on the steps of the hotel and kisses me. Just a little kiss. What am I going to do, make more of it than it is? No, some woman kisses you on an island.

When we register, there are two messages—one from Sorenson at the university, the other from Katie's friend from Tokyo, Mikki. While Katie makes the arrangement for our rental car, I step back from the majestic registration counter, smooth as marble and big as a boat. The wide Persian runners down the lobby's arcade are four inches thick. Down at the end through the glass atrium, I can see the lawn and a cluster of umbrellas around the bar, and further—through the palms—just a wedge of the fake blue sea. Katie takes my arm and says, "Let's go up and make our calls."

I smile as the boy bumps our old luggage into the elevator because I am thinking of Harry in my suitcase. He could be in there right now. You take your children everywhere.

I call Sorenson and he says to forget the zoo, to come directly to the university. He says to come *now* and gives me directions. In the tropical heat, I can feel my rash. Kate and I are in the room, fourth floor, and she has opened the shutters onto the beach and I can see a thousand bodies at their ease. The large catamaran nods in the sand in front of the hotel, its large green-and-white sail seems the flag of health. I ask a few questions, but Sorenson says, "We'll talk. I'll fill you in when you get up here." I can smell something wrong.

Katie has heard me on the phone. There is no need for us to talk. I'll be back later. "Are you okay?" I ask. "You're going to see Mikki?"

"I'll call her, meet her for a drink this afternoon."

It should be now that I bring it out—I lost my job—tell her. I can't do it. I'd end up defending something. I've still got six months' pay, residuals. She'd rail against the forces that have got me fired. I'd say something generous about the situation. I don't have it to be generous. Something crawled out of the sea two hundred million years ago, took a breath, and liked it. That guy has lost me my job.

I take a deep breath and then another, trying not to sigh, and take Katie's hand. "Let's kiss in front of the window," I say. "Be part of this place." When she comes to me in the sunlight, we kiss like two people in a movie, and I realize her arms are the reason I have a neck, an evolutionary device.

Then when I open my suitcase to grab a new shirt and find my powder, Harry's not in there. But the boys have left me a souvenir. I find the rental videocassette case and open it. *The Land of the Lost.* Harry's done a little packing for me. There's going to be a late fee on this classic.

AT SORENSON'S lab there's a little confusion. I take my bag and notes in our rental Toyota up the hill to the university and find his block building hidden among the million-year-old trees behind a little cemetery.

"The bear isn't here," he tells me.

"You moved it."

"No. It hasn't exactly arrived." Sorenson was one of my professors at Stanford and now, like everyone else, he's not getting any older. He's still got all his hair; he isn't any heavier; and he's still wearing the same wire-rims. It confuses me that I'm the same age as all these old guys. As always when things are working out, he seems unconcerned, peaceful. I think he was in physics before zoology, and he found out how fast the universe is expanding. It cooled him out about all the small stuff.

"Where is the panda, Phil?" I say. "Should we go see it?"

"There's a guy coming." He smiles. "He wants to meet Zoo Lewis."

I feel the plane ride humming in my sinuses. I sit on one of the metal stools. "There's a guy coming?"

"Right."

"Phil. Whose panda is this?"

Sorenson smiles and pours us each a cup of thick laboratory coffee. I'm glad to be here even if he's being mysterious. He got me my first assistant editorship right after I left veterinary school. He was the second one I called from the hospital after the allergy attack, and like my parents, he wasn't surprised.

Sorenson sips his coffee. "The Bible boys, did they get you yet?" He grins. It's a great grin and it makes me grin while I nod.

"They did."

"You started writing about the mammalian orders."

"The primates."

"Men are more closely related to tree sloths than are squirrels."

"Not in some newspapers," I say. We're about to laugh. "I lost the column. I'm going to do a piece on this panda and then free-lance for a while. I'm going to plan C." It feels good to level with someone. "The bad part is I had one hundred and seventy-five papers; I was syndicated. We bought a house."

"You've done some wonderful stuff, besides the newspaper deal," Sorenson says. "You can write anything you want."

A Hawaiian kid comes in, dressed like we used to dress in graduate school, a long-sleeved white oxford-cloth shirt, khakis, white tennis shoes. "Mr. Sakakida is here," he tells Sorenson.

"Ah," Sorenson says dramatically. "Mr. Sakakida. You're on, Lewis. Good luck. Just go with Johnny."

The campus is as green as one of Rousseau's paintings and quiet as a dream. The young people we pass all carry books and whisper together. Johnny doesn't know who Sakakida is, except that he is the person Sorenson has been talking to on the phone for two months. Johnny calls him "the panda man." As we walk along it bothers me that I can identify so few of the trees, they all seem like ancient, outsize houseplants, grand and succulent, fit for dinosaurs. On a dirt path we cross through a shallow ravine, and in the thick shade we come up behind a huge pagoda.

"You can find the lab, right?" Johnny asks. He's stopped. He points off to his right. "It's just up there." He starts to move off. "Go around. The panda man should be out there."

There is a huge plum Mercedes with tinted windows parked on

the gravel drive in front of the pagoda. As I start up the steps of the building, the passenger door of the Mercedes swings open and a tall oriental man in a gray suit steps out. He's wearing gold wire-rim sunglasses and he's smiling like mad.

"Dr. Wesley," he says with satisfaction.

"Mr. Sakakida?" I say and we shake hands and he bows. He waves at something in the shadows down the lane.

"We are very happy about this," he says. He's Japanese, his accent is clear. "We are glad an expert such as yourself is helping. We hope everything is fine. We are happy to help the people of Hawaii and the people of the United States of America." He bows again and goes back and steps into his car and closes the door and I watch it roll silently off through the trees.

I didn't even ask him a question. Before I can move, a new white Ford van appears and stops before me. Now I realize I can smell the cedar incense floating out of the pagoda. The driver of the van is all business. He's a large Hawaiian in a faded yellow Primo T-shirt. He wings open the van's rear doors and wants me to examine the contents.

In a slatted wooden crate there is a giant panda.

"Well," the guy says. "Are you taking delivery here?"

The bear isn't moving, and I crawl in the van. As soon as I do, I feel my pulse in my cheekbones; my face is swelling shut. She's alive—though I can tell by the overpowering smell and the matted hair that she's been in this box too long. There's hair everywhere.

"No," I say, and I can hear my allergies shutting my head down. "Drive me up the hill."

On the way back to the lab, my nose begins to run, voluminously. My face has begun to itch. My eyes are slits and I am breathing through my mouth. Allergies. That's okay by me; this is a giant panda. I feel the first excitement, but I can tell by my rasping breath that I am going to need a shot.

When we arrive at the lab, Sorenson and Johnny are ready. They've got the large cage prepared and all the equipment is clean and laid out. Sorenson takes the clipboard from my driver and then hands it to me. "You've got to sign," he says. "It'll be all right."

I sign the sheet and the driver leaves in the van.

"Heavens," Sorenson says to me. "Look at your face. Johnny, call Dr. Morris."

But when Sorenson sees the bear for the first time, he smiles. It may be dying, but it is something to see. His panda. Even my enthusiam is rekindled and when he asks me if I had any trouble, I simply say, "I met your Mr. Sakakida."

"But you're okay?" Sorenson says.

"I'm okay."

We sneak the panda in through his loading area on a gurney and start the procedures. She's shedding hair like an old doll. We take a pulse and draw blood and Sorenson and the kid start to clean her up. Old Sorenson can't get close enough. He's right in there, another phenomenon.

Ten minutes later, Dr. Morris arrives. He's a well-dressed Hawaiian with a beautiful black leather medical bag. He asks about my allergies, pries open my eyes to check my pupils, takes my blood pressure, and gives me two shots, a small one in the arm and a large one in the hip. By this time, Sorenson has finished the first set of procedures and shows Dr. Morris his prize, making the doctor promise not to tell anyone about the bear.

IT'S DARK. I remember to call Katie. She's not in the room and I leave a message at the desk. There is still a lot to do tonight. We weigh the panda and Sorenson checks her nose, teeth, skin tone. He won't have the blood results until tomorrow, so I shake Sorenson's hand. We've all scrubbed and the panda is sleeping in her new cage.

"In a year, she'll have her own quad in the zoo."

"If she makes it through the night."

"Thanks, Lewis," he says. "I appreciate this."

"Who's Sakakida?" I ask.

"An importer."

"What's his real name?"

"I don't know."

"Yes you do." I stand up. "But you've got your bear." My rash now is a sharp itch. "And now I'm going to drive back to the hotel, and you will call me tomorrow so we can all go to a sumptuous dinner, your treat."

Sorenson comes to me at the door and takes my hand. "Lewis, she's going to thrive." He's high on having this animal here and his happiness makes me smile too. "You know it, Lewis. She's going to thrive."

I love his enthusiasm. I love old Sorenson really. He's been the author of so much of the good that's happened to me. As I drive back to the hotel, the world seems full of possibility again. All the lights are on in Waikiki, ten thousand hotel windows, and the streets swarm with parties of two, four, and six, polished and sunburned and looking for dinner.

At the Royal Hawaiian, I get out on the circular drive and give the keys to the attendant, who eyes me strangely. My face is still a little swollen and I smell like bear. I smell a lot like bear. It doesn't matter. In fact, it's wonderful. The hotel seems the very edifice of romance, glittering in the night, and I can hear drums. It's seven P.M. local time.

There is a phone message. The note reads: Dearest Lewis—I've gone with Mikki over to Kaneohe to see her parents. They leave tomorrow morning. Be back at ten or eleven. *The coast is clear*—wait and see. Love, K.

I thank the concierge and hand him back Katie's messages. I step back to the center of the lobby to read my note again. It's okay. It feels like a little present. I'm tired. I fold it into my pocket.

Going upstairs is a mistake. One person in a hotel room at this point in my life is a mistake. Especially with the drums: pum-pum-pum. But I quickly shower and powder up my rash, which is slightly bigger and real angry. I dress in a pair of light khakis with my sandals and Hawaiian shirt. But I can't go out the door with that shirt on. It's too nutty. My head is almost back to normal. There are some splotches of red, but the swelling has subsided. But this shirt. So I throw a blue blazer over it and look pretty good—like the ne'er-do-well son of the local gentry.

In the elevator, I'm thinking of a riddle Ricky asked me last week: Why did the young pencil call "Yoo hoo"? Answer: Because his mommy was in the forest. It suddenly makes perfect sense to me. His mommy was in the forest. I need a drink. I'll have a civilized cocktail and Katie will come back.

From the lobby, when I open the door, the drums blast me, sucking up all the air. Boom. Boom-boom. Boom. Boom-boom. Boom. Two big drums like that in the torchlight. There are, I notice immediately, no little drums. No tambourines. No maracas. Two big drums. Boom. Boom. Boom. Boom. It makes you duck, this noise. I walk to the cabana in step, boom—boom—boom—boom, leaning against the percussion, in fact, and grab on to the bar. I can feel the drums in my chest against the wood.

Behind me under the torchlight on the lawn, the island dance show is full swing. Six big guys in leafy skirts are stomping up and down and juggling torches. It's a big show, everything's big. There are no small guys. Then the women come out and they're big too. The bartender, another guy in a Hawaiian shirt and a pencil behind his ear, is at my elbow and I order a mai tai. The women are doing something I can only describe as the hula and their hips are swinging in astounding figure eights. Their movement is mesmerizing. It is something one should call a feat. I stare at the woman nearest me and all I can do is wonder at the axle of her pelvis, how it could bear such radical and smooth leverage.

The little bar patio is only half full, so I take my drink over to one of the perimeter tables and sip the rum. There is a purple blossom in my drink as well, which I eat. I watch as the women vibrate double-time for a couple of minutes and then promenade off. Everyone applauds, even the people across the lawn inside the luau room. Next to me two young women in sleeveless summer dresses are drinking large red drinks, and on their table is a line of six little drink umbrellas and a little bouquet of wet orchids. Two lawyers from Houston is my guess. "Is that something, or what?" one of the women says to me. I smile and nod. The torchlight flares unevenly and I think I need more torches in my life. More torches and more ocean and more beaches. I can feel the pressures in my head shifting. The cocktail waitress in her green sarong slips by and I order another mai tai.

IT WAS Ryan McBride's idea to have the graduation party at Black Rock Beach on the Great Salt Lake. It was a weird idea, because in those days the Great Salt Lake was different than it is today. In the old days it was a strange and superlative place. It was the saltiest body of water on earth. It was saltier than the Dead Sea and it was six times saltier than the ocean. It was famous for salt. The mineral content was so high that bathers bobbed like corks on the surface and there were several famous postcards that showed five or six people sitting in the water as if on easy chairs. Through several years the Great Salt Lake, which was hundreds of square miles, was as salty as water can get. In twelfth-grade chemistry, before things got bad, we had studied the way salt would precipitate up an anchor rope, climbing like frost two or three feet above the surface of the water.

The lake itself sat in the broad desolate alkali desert dish twenty miles west of Salt Lake. There were few amenities, just an access road which left tourists on the half-mile-wide beach among the swarming brine flies. At Black Rock Beach there was a magnificent wooden pier which stood like a ruin high and dry, hundreds of yards from the then receding waters of the great salty lake. From time to time, some misguided soul would set up his hot dog stand near the pier and lose money all summer long.

Years before, of course, in the thirties and forties, the water had been high and there had been a famous resort on the water: Saltair, where trainloads of citizens could spend the day riding rides, bobbing in the water, and then dancing until after midnight. It had been abandoned and burned down before I was born. But when we graduated from high school the shores of the Great Salt Lake were the most forbidding place I'd ever seen on this planet. It was a vast, treeless, forlorn place smelling of brine, and even as my classmates began to park their shiny cars on that shore and climb out in their graduation clothes, bright and new and calling to each other in the twilight, it could have doubled for a tragic Martian landscape peopled by teenagers from Earth.

Cheryl Lockwood had written in my yearbook, under her picture in the Ski Club: " . . . And what are you going to do about it? Love and *expectations,* Cheryl." Something major was going to happen, I could tell, and I took her aside at the yearbook-signing party the night before graduation, placing my hand way up under her arm and marching her outside the gym and all the way to the thirty-yard line on the football field where, I'll say, I kissed her, but in fact I started to talk to her, saying only, "Meet me at the party tomorrow, and come alone." Whereupon she kissed me and then we twisted closer and kissed again like two doomed lovers under the five-story backside of our high school looming above us, the clock's ponderous lighted face tragic and remote and, as always, six hours ahead.

Graduation day was graduation day, of course, elevated and strange, perceived primarily in the stomach, I remember. At lunch, which I ate alone in our empty kitchen in a house that was already seeming someone else's, my mother sat down with me for just a minute and said, "Oh my, the last sad meal at home for the Porcupine." (Union's symbol was the Porcupine.) "And tuna fish at that. Graduation is such sweet sorrow, Lewis," she went on, "but I want you to know that even after you graduate and you begin to wrestle with life's big problems . . ." She was grinning in her omniscient way.

"Mom, I'm eating here, okay? Could we maybe talk later?"

She was having a wonderful time, but I was sweating that maybe she knew somehow that I'd been dreaming about the way Cheryl Lockwood had felt against my chest and planning the way things were going to go tonight late at the Great Salt Lake. After years of living in dank and cloudy ambiguity, I was going to find something out tonight with Cheryl. Promises had been made. We were going to *do it*. And here I was with my mother. I held my sandwich to my face like a veil.

"Lewis, Lewis," she said. "You're on your way and tomorrow you'll be out in the real world." She stood and came around the table, casually checking my forehead for fever. "But I'll still be your mama." She laughed softly. "Remember that," she said and went off to other errands.

That afternoon Rye picked me up in his huge Oldsmobile as always, but it was utterly different. We went to Ketchum's Lumber and filled the trunk with a load of free warped odd bits for the bonfire and then we cruised west on the old highway, which was rippled with ten thousand tar patches. Three carloads of classmates met us at Black Rock Beach in the afternoon sunlight and after we'd dumped all the wood, Rye stepped back and took it all in. "This, my friends, is *serious,*" he said. At first we all thought he was speaking about the ugly pile of wood, but then he spread his arms to take in the wasteland. "Congratulations on your impending graduation from high school in America. Your first responsibilities as graduates will be to meet me here right after dark for an extended pagan ritual." He nodded sagely and rolled his eyes. "Bring a date."

It was probably out there on the sour ragged edge of the saltiest lake on earth that I felt the rules change. I was watching Ryan entertain the troops for a minute before we climbed back in his car and headed for town and graduation. I remember looking back at the city spread on the mountains twenty miles away. There was still a good amount of snow on the peaks, even in June, and the houses on the hills looked like the remnants of someone else's life. Oh, the feeling was enough to close my callow throat, scary and delicious.

On the way back to town, I wanted to talk. I wanted to ask Ryan, whom I had known for years, if he felt it too. But we didn't talk that way. There had been lots of times that spring as I climbed in the old

Oldsmobile when I'd wanted to say, "These are the electric nights, right? Can you feel it? What is going on?" We were seniors on the baseball team, and State Street had been granted to us, the new kings. We went out almost every night in Ryan's car that spring, and the nights were just full, the way May can pack a night when you're seventeen, which is so different from being sixteen. The nights were sweet and long and then suddenly, after cruising State and grabbing a cheeseburger at the Breeze Inn and maybe a Coke for the road, I was being dropped off in the new cool dark and even my old house looked beautiful to me too. Oh god, what nights. Something was going to happen, but I didn't know what it was, and I took the not knowing as my just being seventeen.

THE DRUMS stop. The air descends in a hum and I look up and see the dancers rearranging themselves for the torch dance. The patio is now full and two young couples are standing behind my table watching the show. The men have navy haircuts and wear new Hawaiian shirts. The drummers are moving their drums to each side of the raised platform now, and I take it as a cue and stand up, offering the honeymooners my table.

"I've been sitting too long," I say, waving them in. It's the truth: my rash is at me like fire ants and I'm happy to stand and shake things out. When I turn for the waitress, one of the women at the next table catches my eye and motions me to a chair.

"You can sit with us," she says. "This is a good part. We saw it last night." So I sit down with the two women and have another mai tai, which I know is in the margins of my limit, because I've just decided it is the best drink possible and I plan to drink them always and always.

I'm wrong about the women, I can tell immediately. They're not from Houston and they're not lawyers. By the stack of wrecked umbrellas and orchids I can only tell that they've each had four of the large red drinks. They are in their early thirties and both wear wedding rings. Before I can properly introduce myself or find out exactly who they are, the drums explode again, and so we all smile at each other and watch the show.

I haven't seen the torch dance for a long time, but it only takes a moment for me to decide that it is my favorite dance in the history of dance and I'm going to watch it every chance I get. It's the one where the big guy comes out and sits on the flaming barrel. He's wearing a huge leaf skirt, made of real leaves with some kind of oil on them that prevents them from burning, and he sits on the flames with the drums beating and then he rises and the flames shoot right back out again and then he sits down a little longer on the flames and then he finally gets up and the flames still flare and then with the bom-bom-bom of the drums he stands at the edge of the platform, smoke rising from his skirt and sweat shimmering across his forehead.

I can feel myself sweating, and the woman nearer to me says as a kind of whisper, "Don't do it again." She's talking to him, but the dancer moves back behind the flaming barrel and this time kind of attacks it, hopping up and sitting down securely on the flames, looking left and right. The woman next to me says now, "Get up. Oh, get up." It is real concern. As I hear it I recognize the midwest in her voice. Indiana. We exchange looks and raise our eyebrows and then turn back to the stage, where, after another fifteen seconds, the man jumps off the incinerator and reveals that he has put out the flames. The crowd applauds like crazy, clapping and clapping. There is great relief in this ovation. The show is over. The man takes a deep bow, and a large white smoke cloud rises from his skirt.

"Where on earth would they dream up a dance like that?" the woman across from me says.

"You guys are sisters, aren't you?" I say.

"Yvonne," says the one next to me, putting her hand on her chest. She's younger than her sister and her hair is lighter. "And this is Clare."

"I'm Lewis," I say. "And you are both from Indiana."

"Iowa," Yvonne says. "Dubuque."

"And you're here doing research on native dances."

"We're on vacation," Clare says. "We're on a two-week vacation from winter." She's a severe and pretty woman who looks a little starved. Her attention is given to the two couples at the next table.

"And are you on vacation?" Yvonne asks me.

"Yes," I say. "I'm doing a little work, but mainly my wife and I are on our first vacation from the kids."

The hotel's combo has set up in the gazebo and has begun playing. I signal the waitress again and order us all another drink.

"Is she here?" Yvonne asks.

"No. Not yet. She's off seeing friends tonight."

When the drinks arrive, the women take a moment to drain their old ones and then hand the glasses to the waitress. Simultaneously, they withdraw the little umbrellas from the daiquiris and line them up with the others. Our table looks like a miniature Shanghai street scene. I raise my glass. "A toast I've never ever made before," I say. "To Dubuque."

Yvonne touches my glass, but Clare is lost to the newlyweds. "Clare?" I say, motioning with my glass. She looks at me blankly and then her face ripples and dissolves. She's crying. She's folded her face into her hands and is crying over her big red drink.

I look to Yvonne: "Oh, my god, I'm sorry . . ."

"Let's dance," Yvonne says, and she's lifted me away from the table. The band is playing a series of Elton John's greatest hits, right now it's "Daniel," and Yvonne and I bumble into a loose embrace at the edge of the group of dancers and she tells me the story. The sisters are both widows. Their husbands, two brothers, were killed in a grain-elevator explosion in May. It has been a terrible time, especially for Clare. "You can understand," Yvonne tells me as the song ends. "She can't shake it. It's right here." Yvonne holds her hand in front of her face. "I'm going to be okay, but Clare, Clare is still hurting."

As she gives me all this news, I feel my buzz change. The high drunken feeling from the mai tais shifts now, and though I know I'm still mildly drunk because I think Elton John is the greatest musician that ever lived and I make a plan to listen to him all the time when we get home, I feel heavier, more controlled. I check my watch: ten minutes after eleven.

"I'll dance with her," I tell Yvonne.

"You could try."

Back at our table, Clare has finished crying and is sipping her drink through the straw while she watches the foursome next door come back from dancing. They bump into chairs and laugh. I sit and extend my forearms onto the table as if I had big news. "Listen," I say, "Do you guys know the difference between diplodocus and an allosaurus?"

Yvonne's being a good sport and shakes her head no, but Clare gives me that flat, open-eyed look that means she's going to cry again.

"Clare," I say too loudly. "Shall we dance?"

Yvonne stands and helps Clare scoot around. Now the band is presenting a middle-of-the-road version of "Your Song," and when I take Clare into my arms, I feel her stiffen. Out of the corner of my eye I can see the corner of her eye, and the way we are arranged it feels like close combat, like dancing with your enemy.

There are times in my life, perhaps too many times, when I feel utterly unqualified for the present moment. I had that feeling when I looked up from the examination table in veterinary school and saw the faces of my classmates looking at my ballooning face as I wheezed once and passed out. I feel this way now with Clare when the song ends and we haven't said word one and I am very ready to get back to my mai tai, the greatest drink on the island, but she doesn't move. She doesn't take her arm from my shoulder or her other from my hand. She stands stock still. I do too. There are other couples milling, embracing, so we're not really a spectacle, but the heat rises in my face anyway and I think: Of course, this is perfect. An unemployed journalist from Arizona who has been up for twenty hours is dancing on the patio of the Royal Hawaiian Hotel with a young widow from Dubuque. What will you do now?

The band kicks into a slow jazz number and Clare starts to lead. She's a good dancer, really, steady and right on the music. I pull back for a moment and say, "You know what I do? I work with pandas." She gives me a scary appraising look and I add, "Panda bears. I was a writer."

"That's okay," she says. "You'll be okay."

But when we fall together after that interchange, the whole dynamic scatters. Clare adjusts herself, hitching her arm around my neck further, and drawing her body against mine.

"Vonnie told you about Frank and Allen, didn't she."

"Yes," I say. Clare grips me at the neck. We won't be talking anymore. I can feel her against me like a drumbeat and I simply dance. Slowly. It is one of the closest embraces I have ever engaged in in public. She is pulled up so that our ears are almost touching and I can feel—with every step—the lean hardness of her body. The keyboard player is leading the combo through "Feelings" now, milking the vacant maudlin song to the limit. I look over and see Yvonne at our table and she gives me a brave nod: *Good for you, keep it up.* Clare and I have tightened things right up and now I can feel her pubic bone bruising against me with every move, intentionally, but I don't give way. She's using it to search my pelvis the way an impatient woman roots her purse for keys, and then she's found it, and hungrily she stays right on the beam. The other dancers seem oblivious to our humping; this is the age of dirty dancing or whatever, so I close my eyes and follow as she tilts frankly into me, pressuring me up to nine o'clock and then quickly to eleven. This would be the right time for Katie to show up, of course, and I could explain how I was comforting the sisters. The other couples have fallen into two-armed embraces, but Clare and I keep our clasped hands out in a classic ballroom pose, perhaps a trifle low, while our hips work like two guys tunneling out of prison.

MY FATHER told me a few things about sex. A person remembers these scenes. It was one of those nights when I was going out and I was reading *Time* magazine in the living room waiting for Ryan to honk. My father always wore plaid shirts after work with the sleeves rolled and his pencils in the pocket. He was a practical man who everywhere he went had a pencil, and though I may be more reticent than he is mostly, I am just like him with that pencil. He was an engineer and he took that approach.

"Let's talk about sex for a minute," he said. I remember he didn't say "What do you know about sex?" or "What do you want to know about sex?" No, we were in this together. We were going to talk about sex for a moment. "I'm sure that you understand the technical principles involved," he said. "The guiding physical laws of sexual intercourse between a man and a woman are very simple. You know how the man is designed, and a woman is constructed in a complementary fashion in terms of the location of the vagina and its angle. These things are obvious. What isn't as obvious to students of anatomy and sex is another essential principle of engineering." Here he asked a question: "Do you know what that principle is?"

"No, sir, I don't."

"That principle is *cooperation*. These things are all designed to facilitate sexual intercourse, but without the element of cooperation, it won't work the way it is intended. The results will be all wrong. Cooperation is the most complex concept about sex. You're going to hear a lot about love and responsibility in the next few years. Just remember they are simply part of this idea of cooperation." He stood up. "This isn't a great talk, but it's ten times what any of your pals are going to get from their dads. You'll be all right. There's no hurry."

Ryan McBride had another approach. He was still a virgin too, but when he heard that Cheryl Lockwood was meeting me at the party, he became all wisdom. "You want something to happen, right?" he told me on the way to the party graduation night. I was floating in a new freedom, still seeing myself cross the podium an hour before to pick up my diploma. I marched down the aisle, where my father stepped out and put his arm around me. He was stuffing his paper and pencil into his jacket pocket, for he had designed yet another thing—a more efficient way of distributing the diplomas without losing the sense of ceremony. His arm still around my shoulder, we walked outside the gym, where my mother in a pretty blue silk dress was waiting under the leafy campus sycamores. He and Mom were going out to dinner, and Mom smiled and said, "Welcome to the real world, where tomorrow morning bright and early we're going to weed the garden. So don't stay out too late." She kissed me on the cheek and added, "Congratulations."

Then I was in the Oldsmobile with Ryan, both of us jerking around changing clothes as he drove around the west side, picking up the big boxes of hot dogs, the bags of buns, the eight cases of soda, and the three cases of Coors from his uncle's garage, and then striking out on the old highway toward the lake. It was like rocket travel, our ship breaking clear of civilization, and slipping further and further into the wasteland void, carrying enough hot dogs for the rest of our lives. The sun had set and it was June: the earth glowed beneath us. Ryan was hollering theory. "If," Ryan pounded his right hand into the seat between us, "you want something to happen tonight with Cheryl, then you need to be realistic about how it would happen, and you know," he was growing gradually louder, beating the seat with each phrase, "that you are not going to do anything. Do you hear me? You know and I know that you are not going to do anything. You are not going to make one move. So. Listen to me. The secret is: let things *get out of control!*" I reached over and righted the steering wheel so we moved back onto the paved roadway. "So listen. Just do this. Horse around." He saw my face and said, "That's right, just horse around. Dance, bump, push, shove, touch, touch, touch. Horse around until you can let her know . . . that you're aroused. That's all it takes." Ryan had stopped pounding now and he had both hands on the wheel, but he was emphasizing his theme by turning to me after every sentence and squinting. "Once a girl feels she has aroused you, she's obligated. Girls are responsible people. They're not like guys. If they feel they've caused something, they take care of it." I squinted back at him and nodded, but I was full of questions, wondering if what he said was true and wondering—if push actually came to shove that night with Cheryl—what I would do.

IN THE middle of the next dance, Clare and I turn so I can see our table through the other dancers and I see something odd. Yvonne is talking to a pretty dark-haired woman whom I recognize as Katie. My wife is sitting with Yvonne and they are talking like classmates, and then Yvonne points at us and Katie looks, catches my eye, and waves. Clare and I are still slow-dancing, ignoring the rock beat of "Jambalaya," locked together in a pelvic clinch that has me up under the waistband of my undershorts, pain and pleasure, while she bumps and clings, her pubic bone like a blade cutting a new road in the wilderness as she breathes short and sharp against my neck. Around us the dancers are twisting and hopping, and we must look oddly stationary to my wife. I smile and nod at Katie, lift my hand from Clare's back and waggle a short wave, but as I do I feel Clare grip me as if I was going to drop her out a window and I hear air in her teeth once, twice, and she rises against me softly now and falls, and then the grip is gone and she is floating loosely in my arms. She relaxes and pulls back and when I look in her face she is contorting and rolling her eyes, clearing them the way people do who wear contact lenses, her forehead corrugating. Finally she sees me watching her. "What?" she says, averting her face. "So, what do you do with pandas?"

At the table Yvonne stands and says to Katie, "This is my sister, Clare." Katie shakes her hand and we all sit down.

"We've been dancing," I say. "You missed the torch dancers." The waitress appears and busily clears the table, deftly setting a glass of wine in front of Katie. I see the other women aren't having any more. As I settle in my chair my rash flares.

"We've had a nice talk," Yvonne says to me.

"How long have you been married?" Clare asks.

"Fourteen years."

"That's wonderful," Clare says. She smiles at me. She's being sincere. "That is really wonderful." When she stands, she seems very tall. She goes on, "Well, Vonnie, I don't know about you, but this farm girl is up too late."

The sisters depart, each giving me a handshake out of a business manual, Yvonne clasping my hand in both of hers and saying, "You've been so kind."

For a moment I consider beginning an explanation, but it would start, "Their husbands . . ." and I let it go. I feel a simple relief at being alive and I just smile at Katie.

WE AREN'T fully out of the lift when I take Katie in my arms and we kiss. "This is great," she says, as we amble down the carpeted hall in a four-legged embrace, turning, and pressing into each other. "This is hungry kissing, do you know that? Remember?" She's up against me again, her arms cinch. "Hungry kissing?"

We undress before we remember to close the door, I'm not kidding, and then in the bed, she rolls a naked leg onto me and I tell her the story of the day, not telling her about Dr. Morris and his shots. The whole time I'm telling the tale, we're moving with each other and from time to time she reaches down and checks the progress of this erection, the twelfth kind, and when she does that our moving rechecks itself and changes gear. This is what storytelling should be, this is the kind of attention narrative desires.

I bring the day right up to the torch dance and stop. Katie pulls me over onto her now and says, "You know, I've never seen you dance before. I've never seen you dance with another woman."

Now this next part, the bodies roll, their design made manifest, and there is achieved a radical connection. I'm not talking about souls. Who can tell about this stuff? Not me. You're there, you are both in something, something carnal and vaporish at once. Your mouths cock half a turn and you sense the total lock. You're transferring brains here; your spine glows. You go to heaven and right through, there's no stopping. What do you call it? Fucking? Not quite right here, this original touch, the firmament. My credo: you enter and she takes you in. This is personal. This is cooperation. Who can live to tell about it? You cooperate until you're married cell to cell, until all words flash away in the dark.

We roll apart, seizing onto our pillows as if they were life preservers. After a moment, Katie places the backs of her fingers on my cheek. She says, "I've got to go to sleep." She smiles and her eyes close. "Don't worry about the column. You don't need it. You're a writer. There are a million things to do."

MORNINGS, MANY early mornings, the boys will climb onto our bed—how many times have I been bounced awake?—and either sit on my head and talk to Katie or fish from the foot, casting my robe sash into the icy waters beneath us. They have phenomenal luck always, hoisting dozens of large fish, reptiles, and other treasures from the sea and immediately offering them to us to eat. I lie there as Ricky wedges a piece of graham cracker in my mouth, saying, "Have some fish, Dad. Really. These are good." Katie is sanguine about all this as she sits in the pillows and asks Ricky for a little lemon with her fish and Ricky pantomimes the lemon. Harry keeps a lookout on the prow, his inverted binoculars showing the doorway out there somewhere on the edge of the lost world.

If I don't eat my fish right away, Katie says to me, "Hey, Dad, get with the program. These guys are fishermen. Come on. It's better than being nomadic wanderers." What can I say? It is one of mankind's oldest struggles: life on a boat. Two guys want to fish in the open air. One guy wants to feel his wife's bare thigh under the warm covers and fish later.

NOW IN our bed in the Royal Hawaiian Hotel, I can feel my wife descending in sleep. I can almost feel her falling away into night. She goes deeper with every breath. But I am full of allergy medicine and mai tais. I swing my legs out of bed and go to the window. Things are quiet all along the shore.

ON BLACK Rock Beach twenty years ago I thought I was going to blunder across one if not all of the sexual frontiers. The scene was set, and I was ready. Night came on like the first night on earth, the sunset blistering the surface of the Great Salt Lake with the same wincing flash that it spread across the west desert sky, a flare that took our eyes and then chilled in a minute, replaced by the charcoal shadow of the planet.

Ryan lit the gas-soaked pile of lumber with a paper rolled in a ribbon which he told everyone was his diploma, and our little fire ripped into the dark. We had four sawhorse tables of food and drinks, and some guys had set up two large speakers in the back of a pickup and the flat sandy wilderness rang with Bobby Vee, the Four Seasons, Del Shannon, the Beatles, Dick and DeeDee, Roy Orbison, the Coasters, Johnny Mathis, the Boxtops, Richie Valens, the Shirelles, Andy Williams, Dion, and occasionally some wise guy would slip in Gene Autry or the Mormon Tabernacle Choir. Ryan kept the beer in the open trunk of his Olds. I remember how beautiful and illicit it looked in there, a tub of gold cans in silver ice. I thought: This is it, we're going to drink beer. I'd had a few, most of them with my father on the days when we'd poured the patio or leveled the yard, but this was different, this was a tub of gold cans on silver ice at the edge of the known world.

It was a hundred teenagers goofing around and dancing in the perimeter of a small fire by the wide margin of a big lake. And though we had miles of open space, no one wandered far from the fire. A couple might go for a walk, but there was something about knowing that there was *nothing* down that beach, nothing along the five hundred miles of coastline, not a thing, that sent them back quickly to the circle of light.

For the first hour, I manned the barbecue, blackening the hot dogs just right and then stacking them to one side of the grill. This was the real world, I remembered. Hot dogs were a hard sell. I saw Cheryl Lockwood as soon as she arrived with three other girls. Many of the girls, including Cheryl, wore their white graduation dresses and they stood in the firelight like princesses, their beauty heightened by the raw, malodorous kingdom. When they danced, and I watched Cheryl dance with a series of my friends, it was confounding that such untouchable womanhood could surf, pony, jerk. One by one they retreated to cars and changed into bermudas or Levi's and returned as the girls we knew, and the dancing became even more animated, even in the sand, as "Runaround Sue" beat into the night.

Not long after she returned in a pair of cutoff Levi's and a red football jersey, Cheryl came over to the grill. I saw she had a beer in her hand. She poked at the black papery skin of the hot dogs, finally pinching one and picking it up and examining it. "Do I dare? Who's the cook around here?"

I looked at her: "Dare."

"Dare *you*. You gonna cook all night?"

"No, Ryan'll be here in a minute."

"Good," she said and she leaned over and kissed me lightly. "Good. Then what you gonna do?" She smiled and walked back to the dancers.

I could see my old friends Georgia Morris and Paula Swinton. Paula leaned against the handsome Jeff Wild with whom she was supposedly "doing it," and Georgia had been going with an older guy for two years. He was twenty-five or something. Those girls didn't even know who I was anymore.

Ryan finally emerged from the tangle of parked cars where he had been goofing off with most of the baseball team. They were into the beer real good, and he brought me a can.

"You're a good guy," he said, trading it for the spatula. "Good luck."

I took my beer and walked off a little ways and then I walked way out, down the beach four hundred yards. No one was out there. I wanted to see it all for a moment, the party. I cracked the beer and took a sip. The firelight in everybody's hair and off the corners of the cars made it look like a little village in a big dark void. The dimensions were all vast. I seemed real small. I always seemed real small. I started to walk back. In a world so indifferent and illimitable, it was time to horse around with Cheryl Lockwood.

I found her sitting on the hood of a car, and we danced ten dances in a row, fast and slow. She was looking at me every time I looked at her. During the slow dances I bumped her when I could and tried to let her know that I dared. It was when we went back behind the cars to grab another beer that we started kissing. She guided me around and onto the trunk of someone's Thunderbird and we grappled there for half an hour or so, until we'd exhausted the possibilities of such a place. I had her bra undone, a loose holster in her shirt, and she had both hands in my back pockets.

It was then that she whispered, "Let's go swimming." When we stood, I was kind of dizzy, but we wended among all the cars and then we sprinted down the beach faster than I'd ever run before. Half a mile from the party, we stopped and kissed again, starting right in all over, but she pulled away and simply took off her clothing. I could barely hear "The Duke of Earl" across the sand, and then I stripped and headed out for the water hand in hand with Cheryl. It was an extraordinarily shallow lake and it took us a long time to get knee deep. When we did, she came against my naked body and I felt the contours of a naked woman for the first time. Behind her I could see the supine form of Antelope Island lying like an alligator two miles away. Then she turned and pulled me deeper in the water, saying something odd, something I've never forgotten. "Lewis," she said, her voice naked too, "I'm giving you the big green light."

And that was what I was thinking of—that this is really it: we were going all the way—when the water rose up my thighs and in a sudden dip, the warm water washed over my genitals and we were in up to our waists. Cheryl let go of my hand and sat backward in the sea, bobbing back up, arms, breasts, knees, and thighs. It was quite a vision.

It took about three seconds for me to realize what was happening and I felt it first as an odd spasm of chill up my back and then as a flash of heat across my forehead and sweat and then the final thing, the real thing, as the salt bit into my crotch like acid. There was no air. The pain rose way over my head like smoke. My jock rash was almost ninety square inches of raw skin counting both legs and my scrotum. The pain was like no pain. It was a quick unrelenting pressure on my temples, and I went out.

I lost the next five minutes, but whatever happened I give a lot of credit to a nakeds eventeen-year-old virgin named Cheryl Lockwood, who floated me back to the shallows where I woke looking into her face. I can still summon a brief glimpse of the outline of her breasts in the starlight as I spat salt water and tried to recover. So she saved my life, but I further credit her with saving the last slivers of my ego by not commenting on what had happened. She could so easily have said a dozen things about what this guy did when confronted with the big green light. When I sat up, the pain had become a real thing, a flaring heartbeat in my balls, that had me breathing through my teeth all the way back to the party. Our wet hair and damp clothing were huge hits at the bonfire, but because it was late and there had been worse behavior by others, it was bearable. Later, much later, when everyone was gone and Ryan and I threw the larger bits of debris into his trunk, I told him the truth: I'd failed.

"It means nothing," he told me and then he went on in a way that reminded me of why he was my best friend. "You went out after dark and passed out in the Great Salt Lake. Come on, who can do that?"

IT'S MUCH later into the night and I'm in the beautiful men's room off the lobby of the Royal Hawaiian Hotel washing my hands and singing Roy Orbison's "Crying" at about six on the ten scale and it sounds pretty good. The walls are black marble in which you can see your shadow and they polish the song so that it reverberates mournfully. This is, without doubt, the best song I've ever heard.

Although Katie has parachuted into sleep, the day won't abandon me, and I have toured the grounds, walked up to the Outrigger for a drink, and returned to the hotel for a nightcap before coming in here. It is just a minute after two A.M.

"That I'd been cry-i-ing
O-ver you . . ."

A big Hawaiian guy comes in and stands at the urinal, but I can't stop myself. I'm drying my hands and I must finish the song: the killer rhyme of *understand* and *touch of your hand* before all the "cry-ings." The guy stands at the sink and I recognize him as the torch dancer, my hero. He washes his hands with gusto and does the last few "cry-ings" with me. When we stop, I am as sad as I've been in ten years. All animals are sad after sex. This is a magnificent men's room. Our reflections stand ten feet deep in the marble like two sad visitors from the dead. The man points at me fraternally and says with great conviction: "Roy Orbison was a giant." He leaves.

My Hawaiian shirt is limp with sweat and I look like a guy who is just a little old to be a playboy. I consider doing "Only the Lonely," but it's clear that I do not have the stamina. I haul my sport coat straight and walk back out into the night. The bar is empty now, the bartender stands talking on the telephone, folding the last bar towel. I walk past the cabana through the little garden and down the cement steps to the beach. The light here is weird, the sand glowing and the sea simply a slick black space. Down along Waikiki, the hotels glimmer like ships awaiting departure. I pass the large catamaran.

"Dancing with the widows," I say aloud. I'm not really drunk anymore, but I'm still unmoored enough to talk out loud. I'm through singing, I think. Two women whose husbands have been blown to ashes. I picture it, a warm still spring afternoon, the air full and quiet, one brother sweeping the cement floor of the empty tower, the other straightening a bent hinge in the metal door when the dust trembled and fused and it all blew. The air turning white in a dust flash as big as the town had ever seen, thumping the sides of

things for two miles, and afterward only the smoking hole, a few
chunks of concrete coming down six blocks away, the one brother's
pickup cartwheeling across the rail spur, blown like a wind-twisted
section of the sports pages beneath a twenty-story fist-cloud of grain
dust. And the men themselves, where would they be? the broom? the
hammer?

I take a deep breath, my nose swollen with the mai tais, and
gather the late sea smell, mixed with the damp odors of Katie, hotel
soap, and—faintly—the panda. I step into the surf. These aren't
great sandals. I never met a pair of shoes that couldn't be improved
by the Pacific Ocean. The waves here are all tamed, and lip in at
about four inches. The surf sucks at my heels in the sand. Some
lucky tourist is going to look out his balcony and spot a guy in a blue
blazer in the ocean and call the police hoping to thwart a suicide. I'd
better back out.

I walk back ten feet and then just sit suddenly in the wet sand.
The waves can still wash up over my waist and as they do I feel the
sure mild tonic of salt on my crotch and it makes me smile. "No, he's
just drunk, dear," the tourist is saying to his wife. "Look, he's on an
elbow in the surf."

Actually it's a wet journalist, some guy who wanted to his teeth to
be a veterinarian, but whose allergies nearly killed him in a routine
dissection a month into his first semester, and now he's lost his column and received a bushel of hate mail from the fundamentalists,
people not highly evolved enough to know when *i* comes before *e,*
letters that hurt regardless of the spelling.

Oh the water feels good sloshing through my trousers. I can tell
I'm getting better: the rash will be gone by Wednesday. "Go to plan
B," Cracroft had said. It makes me smile. I was already on plan B—
or was it C? What a deal. How could I not smile? What would stop
me there, half in the ocean, from smiling? Plan B. A person could go
through the alphabet. With a little gumption and some love, a person could go through every single letter of the alphabet.

LIFE IN a body is the life for me. That night, coming home from my high school graduation party at Black Rock Beach, Rye and I sang songs. Do you see, we sang. I'm not kidding. We sang this and that and a marathon version of "Graduation Day," by the Lettermen, that went on and on as we made up verses until my street and Rye pulled up to the curb. We crooned the ending until our voices cracked. We sang. I plan on doing it again. Rye pointed at me when I opened the door to get out and said, "Here we go. Good luck, Chief. First night in the real world."

Inside, the house was dark and quiet, everyone in bed. I spent some time sitting in a wedge of light in front of the open fridge making and eating eight or nine rolled ham deals, putting different fillings in the ham each time: pickles, cheese, macaroni. I had failed with Cheryl. I had failed. I felt sad. What I felt was a kind of forlorn that when my mother saw it on my face she would say, "My aren't we a sick chick?" I was a sick chick.

But when I finally went upstairs is when something happened. I'd left my salty shoes on the patio. At the top step, I heard a noise. It was a laugh, my mother's laugh, but I didn't know it was a laugh at that moment. I mean, I thought it might have been a cough or some other noise, but then I went by their room and the door was open and I saw my mother's bare leg in the pale light from the window, the curve of her flank as she rolled, and I went right into my room without stopping and then my heart kicked in and I heard the sound again and I realized it was a kind of laughter. Well, I know all about it now, don't I? This is an easy place from which to know things, a hundred years later a million miles at sea, but then I didn't know and something slammed my chest in such a way that I knew I wasn't going to be able to sleep. I'd graduated from high school, do you see, some sick chick with no sure sense of self, but as I stood at my window for the next four hours until finally some birds began to chitter and the gray light began, a new feeling rose in me. My parents were lovers. Oh sure, oh sure. I know all about it. I knew all about it then, I thought. But the idea killed me. It clobbered me. It filled me with capacity. I didn't have the words for it, nor did I know exactly what it was, but I was certain to my soul that I had the capacity for it. I had grown up in a house with two adults who were lovers. Like wolves or swans, they had mated for life. Years later, I would too. I stood there at the window until my elbows filled with sand and I was heavy with sleep. I could see two neighbor kids walking down the alley. One had a stick and was swinging it against the fences. They were up early, the first sun orange in their hair, and they owned the day. I would give them this one. Through the stunning blue air, I could see the houses of our neighborhood floating away from me. Do you see? That was the first time my heart brimmed. The world was real.

From

THE

HOTEL

EDEN

THE HOTEL EDEN

THAT YEAR the place we would go after hours was the Hotel Eden. It had a cozy little bar in the parlor with three tiny tables and four stools at the counter. You had to walk sideways to get around, and it had a low ceiling and thick old carpets, but it had a roomy feeling and it became absolutely grand when Porter was there. Over the course of the spring he told us a hundred stories in the Eden and changed things for us.

The barman was a young Scot named Norris who seemed neither glad nor annoyed when we'd come in around midnight after closing down one of the pubs, the Black Swan or the Lamb and Flag or the forty others we saw that cold spring. Pub hours then were eleven o'clock last call, and drink up by eleven-fifteen. Porter would set his empty pint glass on the whatever bar and say to Allison and me, "The Eden then?" He'd bike over, regardless of where we were, out on the Isle of Dogs or up in Hampstead, and Allison would get us a cab.

Norris would have the little curtain pulled down above the bar, a translucent yellow sheet that said, "Residents Only." He drew it down every night at eleven; hotels could serve late to their guests. Porter had done some favor for the manager of the Hotel Eden when he'd come to London years before, and he had privileges. They became in a sense our privileges too, though—as you shall see—I was only in the Eden alone on one occasion. The curtain just touched your forehead if you sat at the bar.

We often arrived ahead of Porter, and Norris would set us up with pints of lager, saying always, "Hello, miss," when he placed Allison's glass. The Eden didn't have bitter. I remember the room as always being empty when we'd arrive, and it was a bit of a mystery at first as to why Norris was still even open. But there were times when there was a guest or two, a man or a man and a woman, having a brandy at one of the tables. We were quiet too, talking about Allison's research at the museum—she had a year in London to work on her doctorate in Art History. But it was all airy, because we were really just waiting for Porter. It was as if we weren't substantial enough to hold down our stools, and then Porter would come in, packing his riding gloves into his helmet, running a hand through his thick black hair, saying, "Right enough, Norris, let's commence then, you gloomy Northlander," and gravity would be restored. His magnetism was tangible, and we'd wait for him to speak. When he had the pint of lager in his hand, he'd turn to Allison and say something that would start the rest of the night.

One night, he lifted his glass and said, "Found a body today." Then he drank.

Allison leaned in: "A dead man?"

"Dead as Keats and naked as Byron." We waited for him to go on. His was the voice of experience, the world, the things that year that I wanted so much.

"Where?" I asked.

"Under the terrace at the Pilot."

"The place on the river?" Allison asked. He'd taken us walking through the Isle of Dogs after we'd first met and we'd stopped at half a dozen pubs which backed onto the Thames.

"Right, lady. Spoiled my lunch, he did, floating under there like that."

Allison was lit by this news. We both were. And there it was: the night kicked in at any hour, no matter how late. When Porter arrived, things *commenced.* We both leaned closer. Porter, though he'd just sucked the top off his pint, called Norris for another, and the evening was launched.

We always stayed until Porter leaned back and said, "It's a night then." He didn't have an accent to us, being American, but he had the idiom and he had the way of putting his whole hand around a glass and of speaking over the top of a pint with the smallest line of froth on his upper lip, something manly really, something you'd never correct or try to touch off him, that was something to us I can only describe as being *real.* He'd been at Hilman College years before Allison and me, and he knew Professor Mills and all the old staff and he'd even been there the night of the Lake Dorm Fire, the most famous thing about Hilman really, next to Professor Mills, I suppose. I spent a hundred hours with him in the Eden that spring, like Allison, twelve inches across that little round table or huddled as we were at the bar, and I memorized Porter really, his face, the smooth tan of red veins running up under his eyes, as if he'd stood too close to some special fire, and his white teeth, which he showed you it seemed for a purpose. His nose had been broken years ago. We played did you know so-and-so until Allison, who was still a member of Lake Sorority, brought up the fire.

"Oh yes," he said. "I was there. What's the legend grown to now? A hundred ghosts?"

"Six," Allison laughed. "There's always been six."

"Always," he protested. "You make it sound ancient. Hey, I was there. February." Then he added with authority and precision: "Fifteen years ago."

"Someone had stopped the doors with something; the six girls couldn't get out."

Porter drew on his beer and looked at me. "Hockey sticks. It was a bundle of hockey sticks through the door handles."

"That's right."

"Oh." He looked from me to Allison. "It was awful. A cold night at Hilman, and you know, it could get cold, ten degrees, old snow on the ground hard as plastic, and the colossal inferno. From the quad you could see the trapped figures bumping into the glass doors. A group of us came up from town, the Villager had just closed, you ever drink there?"

"It's now a cappuccino place," Allison said. "The Blue Dish."

"Ah, the old Villager was a capital dive. That bar could tell some tales. It's where I met our Professor Mills. Anyway, they closed at one, and when I stepped out into the winter night, there was this ethereal light pulsing from the campus like a heartbeat, and you had to go. There was no choice. I knew right away it was Lake, fully engaged, as they say, a fire like no other, trying to tear a hole in the world." Allison and I were mesmerized, and he finished: "It singed the sycamores back to Dobbs Street, and that's where a group of us stood. It hurt to look. In the explosive light, I could see figures come to the glass, they looked like fish."

When he'd finish talking like that, telling this story or that—he'd found a downed ultralight plane in the Cotswolds once on a walking tour and had had to secure the pilot's compound leg fracture—Allison and I would be unable to move. It was a spell. It's that simple. You see, we were graduate students and we weren't used to this type of thing. I'd tell you what we were used to but it all seems to drop out of memory like the bottom of a wet cardboard box. We were used to nothing: to weeks at the library at Hilman in Wisconsin and then some vacation road trips with nothing but forced high jinx and a beach. There was always one of our friends, my roommate or Allison's roommate, who would either read Dylan Thomas aloud all the way to Florida and then refuse to leave the car or get absolutely drunk for a week and try to show everyone his or her genitals as part of a discussion of our place in the universe. We were Americans and we knew it. I was twenty-three and Allison was twenty-four. We hadn't done anything, we were scholars. I'd finished my master's degree in meteorology at Northern near Hilman and was doing what—nothing. Allison got her grant. Going to England was a big deal for us. She was going to do her research at the British Museum. I was going to cool out and do London. Then we met Porter.

Allison's mentor at Hilman, the famous Professor Julie Mills, had given us some telephone numbers, and after we found a flat in Hampstead and after Allison had established a routine with her work, we called the first guy. His name was Roger Ardreprice, the assistant curator of Keats's House, and he had us meet him over there as things were closing up one cold March night. He was a smug little guy who gave us his card right away and walked with both hands in his jacket pockets and finished all his sentences with "well um um." We walked over to the High Street and then down to the Pearl of India with him talking about Professor Mills, whom he called Julie. Evidently he'd met other of her students in former years, and he assumed his role as host of all of London with a kind of jaded enthusiasm; it was clear he'd seen our kind before. It was at the long dinner that we met two other people who had studied at Hilman with the famous Professor Julie Mills. One was a quiet well-dressed woman named Sarah Garrison who worked at the Tate, and the other was a thirtyish man in a green windbreaker who came late, said hello, and then ate in the back at a table by the kitchen door with two turbaned men who evidently were the chefs. This was Porter.

Of course, we didn't talk to him until afterward. Roger Ardreprice ran a long dinner which was half reverential shoptalk about Julie Mills and half sage advice about life in London, primarily about things to avoid. Roger had a practiced world-weary smile which he played all night, even condescending to Sarah Garrison, who seemed to me to be a real nice woman. It was a relief when we finally adjourned sometime after eleven and stepped from the close spicy room onto the cold sidewalk. Sarah took a cab and Roger headed down for his tube stop, and so Allison and I had the walk up the hill. I remember the night well, the penetrating cold wind, our steps past all the shops we would eventually memorize: the newsdealer, the kabob stand, the cheese shop, the Rosslyn Arms. We were a week in London and the glow was very much on everything, even a chilly night after a strange dinner. Then like a phantom, a figure came suddenly from behind us and banked against the curb, a man on a bicycle. He pulled the goggles off his head and said, "Enough curry with Captain Prig then?" He grinned the most beguiling grin, the corners of his mouth puckered. "Want a pint?"

"It's after hours," I said.

"This is the most interesting city in the world," he said. "Certainly we can find a pint." He stopped a cab and spoke to the driver and herded us inside, saying, "See you in nineteen minutes."

And so we were delivered to the Hotel Eden. That first night we waited in front on the four long white stone steps until we saw him turn onto the street, all business on his bicycle, nineteen minutes later. "Yes, indeed," he said, dismounting and taking a deep breath through his nose as if sensing something near. "The promise of lager. Which one of you studied with Julie Mills?"

Allison said, "I did. I do. I finish next year."

"Nice woman," he said as he pulled open the old glass door of the hotel. "I slept with her all my senior year." Then he turned to us as if apologizing. "But we were never in love. Let's have that straight."

I thought Allison was going to be sick after that news. Professor Mills was widely revered, a heroine, a goddess, certainly someone who would have a wing of the museum named after her someday. Then we went into the little room and met Norris and he drew three beautiful pints of lager, gold in glass, and set them before us.

"Why'd you eat with the cooks?" Allison asked Porter.

"That's the owner and his brother," Porter said. His face was ruddy in the half-light of the bar. "They're Sikhs. Do you know about the Sikhs?"

We shook our heads no.

"Don't mess with them. They're merciless. Literally. The man who sat at my right has killed three people."

I nodded at him, flattered that he thought I'd mess with anyone at all, let alone a bearded man in a turban.

"I'm doing a story on their code." Porter drank deeply from his glass. "Besides, your Mr. Roger Ardreprice, Esquire, has no surplus love for me." He smiled. "And you . . ." He turned his glorious smile to Allison, and reached out and took her shiny brown hair in his hand. "You're certainly a Lake. We'll have to get you a tortoiseshell clip for that Lake hair." Lake was the prime sorority at Hilman. "What brings you to London besides the footsteps of our Miss Mills?—who founded Lake, of course, a thousand years ago."

Allison talked a little about the Egyptian influence on the Victorians, but it was halfhearted, the way all academic talk is in a pub, and my little story about my degree in meteorology felt absolutely silly. I had nothing to say to this man, and I wanted something. I wanted to warn him about something with an exacting and savage code, but there was nothing. I wasn't going to say what I had said to my uncle at a graduation party, "I got good grades."

But Porter turned to me, and I can still feel it like a light, his attention, and he said, with a kind of respect, "The weather. Oh that's very fine. The weather," he turned to me and then back to Allison, "and art. That is absolutely formidable." He wasn't kidding. It was the first time in the seven months since I'd graduated that I felt I studied something real, and the feeling was good. I felt our life in London assume a new dimension, and I called for another round.

That was the way we'd see him; he would turn up. We'd go four, five days with Allison working at the museum and me tramping London like a tourist, which I absolutely was, doing only a smattering of research, and then there'd be a one-pound note stapled to a page torn from the map book *London A to Z* in our mailbox with the name of a pub and an hour scribbled on it. The Flask, Highgate, 9 P.M., or Old Plover, on the river, 7. And we'd go. He would have seen the Prince at Trafalgar Square or stopped a fight in Hyde Park and there'd be a bandage across his nose to prove it. He was a character, and I realize now we'd never met one. I'd known some guys in the dorms who would do crazy things drunk on the weekend, but I'd never met anybody in my life who had done and seen so much. He was out in the world, and it all called to me.

He took us to the Irish pubs in Kilburn, all the lights on, everyone scared of a suitcase bomb, the men sitting against the wall in their black suits drinking Guinness. We went to three different pubs, all well lit and quiet, and Porter told us not to talk too loud or laugh too loud or do anything that might set off these powder kegs. "Although there's no real danger," he added, pointing at Allison's L.L.Bean boots. "They're not going to harm an American schoolgirl. And such a beautiful member of the Lake."

Maybe harm was part of the deal, the attraction, I know it probably was for me. I'd spend two days straight doing some of my feeble research, charting rainfall (London has exactly fifteen rain days per month, year-round), and then, with my shoulders cramping and my fingers stained with the wacky English marking pens we bought, I'd be at the Eden bent over a pint looking into Porter's fine face and it would all go away. He showed up early in March with his arm in a sling and a thrilling scrape across his left cheekbone. Someone had opened a car door on him as he'd biked home one night. The gravel tracks where he'd hit the road made a bright fan under his eye. His grin seemed magnified that night under our concern.

"Nothing," he said of it. "The worst is I can't ride for a week. It puts me in the tube with all the rest of you wankers." He laughed. "Say, Norris," he called. "Is there any beer in here?" I saw Allison's face, the worry there, and knew she was a goner. And I was a goner too. I'd never had a scratch on my body. Porter was too much, and I knew that this is the way I did it, had crushes, and I'd fallen for two or three people before: Professor Cummins, my thesis chair, with his black bowl of hair and bright blue eyes, a cartoon face really, but he'd traveled the world and in his own words been rained on in ninety-nine countries; and Julie Mills, who worked so closely with Allison. I'd met her five or six times at receptions and such, and her intensity, the way she set her hand below my shoulder when speaking to me as if to steady me for the news to come, and the way there was a clear second between each of her words, these things printed themselves on me, and I tried them out with no success. I tried everything and had little success generating any conviction that I might find a personality for me.

And now Allison kidded me when we'd have tea somewhere or a plowman's platter in a pub: "You don't have to try Porter's frown when you ask for a pint," she'd say. "This isn't the Eden." And I'd taken certain idiomatic inflections from Porter's accent, and when they'd slip out, Allison would turn to me, alert to it. I would have stopped it if I could. I started being assertive and making predictions, the way Porter did. We'd gone to Southwark one night, and after a few at a dive called Old Tricks, we'd stood at the curb afterward, arm in arm in the chill, and he'd said, "Calm enough now," and he'd scanned the low apartment buildings on the square, "but this will all be in flames in two years. Put it in your calendar." And when I got that way with Allison, even making a categorical statement about being late for the tube or forgetting the umbrella, she'd say, "Put it in your calendar, mate." I always smiled at these times and tried to shrug them off. She was right, after all. But I also knew she'd fallen too. She didn't pick up the posture or the walk, but Allison was in love with this character too.

One night in March, he met us at the Eden with a plan. I was a meteorologist, wasn't I? It was key for a truly global understanding of the weather for me to visit the north Scottish coast and see the effects of the Gulf Stream firsthand. "Think of it, Mark," he said, his face lit by the glass of beer. "The Gulf Stream. All that water roiling against the coast of Mexico, warming in the equatorial sun, then spooling out around the corner of Florida and up across the Atlantic four thousand miles still warm as it pets the forehead of Scotland. It's absolutely tropical. Palm trees. We better get up there."

Well, I didn't have anything to do. I was on hold, taking a year off we called it sometimes, and I looked at Allison there in the Eden. She raised her eyebrows at me, throwing me the ball, and smiled. Her hair was back in the new brown clip Porter had given her. "Sounds too good to pass up," she said. "Mark's ready for an adventure."

"Capital," Porter said. "I'll arrange train tickets. We'll leave Wednesday."

Allison and I talked about it in our flat. It was chilly all the time, and we'd get in the bed sometimes in the early afternoon and talk and maybe have a snack, some cheese and bread with some Whitbred from a canister. She came home early from the museum the Tuesday before I was to leave with Porter. There was a troubled look on her face. She undressed and got in beside me. "Well," she said. "Ready for your adventure?" Her face was strange, serious and fragile, and she put her head into my shoulder and held me.

"Hey, don't worry," I said. The part of her sweet hair was against my mouth. "You've got the people at the museum if you need anything, and if something came up you could always call Roger Ardreprice." I patted the naked hollow of her back to let her know that I had been kidding with that last, but she didn't move. "Hey," I said, trying to sit up to look her in the eyes, comfort her, but she pushed me back, burrowed in.

PORTER AND I left London in the late afternoon and clacked through the industrial corridor of the city until just before the early dark the fields began to open and hedgerows grow farther apart. Porter had arrived late for the train and kicked his feet up on the opposite seat, saying, "Sorry, mate, but I've got the ticket right here." He withdrew a glass jar from his pack and examined it. "Not a leak. Tight and dry." He held the jar like a trophy and smiled at me his gorgeous smile. "Dry martinis, and we're going to get *very* tight." Then he unwrapped two white china coffee cups and handed me one. There was a little gold crown on each cup, the blue date in Roman numerals MCMLIII. He saw me examining the beautiful cup and said, "From the coronation. But there are no saucers and—in the finest tradition of the empire—no ice."

Well, I was thrilled. Here I was rambling north in a foreign country, every mile was farther north in Britain than I'd ever been, etc., and Porter was dropping a fat green olive in my cup and covering it with silver vodka. "This is real," I said aloud, and I felt satisfied at how it felt.

"To Norris," I said, making the first toast, "and the Eden, hoping they're happy tonight."

"Agreed," Porter said, drinking. "But happy's not the word, mate. Norris is pleased, but never happy. He's been a good friend to me, these English years."

"We love him," I said, speaking easily hearing the "we," Allison entering the sentence as a natural thing. It was true. We'd often remarked as we'd caught the tube back to Hampstead or as we'd headed toward the Eden that Norris was wonderful. In fact he was one of eight people we knew by name in that great world city.

"Allison seems a dear girl." Porter said. It was a strange thing, like a violation, the two of us talking about her.

"She's great," I said, simply holding place.

"Women." Porter raised his cup. "The great unknowable."

I thought about Allison, missing her in a different way. We were tender people, that is, *kids*, and our only separations had been play ones, vacations when she'd go home to her folks and I'd go home to my folks, and then we moved in together after graduating with no fanfare, tenderly, a boy and a girl who were smart and well-meaning. Our big adventure was going off to England together, which everyone we knew and our families thought was a wonderful idea, and who knows what anybody meant by that, and really, who knows what we meant at such a young age, what we were about. We were lovers, but that term would have embarrassed us, and there are no other words which come close to the way we were. We liked each other a lot, that's it. We both knew it. We were waiting for something to happen, something to do with age and the world that would tell us if we were qualified, if we were in love, the real love. And here I was on a train with a stranger, each mile sending me farther from her into a dark night in a foreign country. I thought about her in the

quilts of our small bed in Hampstead. The first martini was working, and it had made me large: I was a man on a train far from home.

We got drunk. Porter grinned a lot and I actually made him giggle a few times with my witty remarks. The vodka evidently made
me very clever. About nine o'clock we went up to the club car, a little snack bar, and bought some Scotch eggs. This was real life, I
could feel it. I'd had a glimpse of it from time to time with Porter,
but now here we were.

One long afternoon after we'd first met him, he took us on a walk
through the Isle of Dogs. He'd had us meet him at the Bridge &
Beacon near the foot of London Bridge and we'd spent the rest of the
day tramping the industrial borough of the Isle. The pubs were hidden among all the fenced construction storage lots and warehouses.
We'd walk a quarter mile down a street with steel sheeting on both
sides and then down a little alley would be the entry to the Bowsprit
or the Sea Lion or the Roman Arch, places that had been selling
drinks for three hundred years while the roads outside, while everything outside, changed. They all had a dock and an entry off the
Thames. For us it was enchanting, this lost world at once rough,
crude, and romantic. Two steps down under a huge varnished beam
into a long room of polished walnut and brass lamps, like the captain's quarters on a ship, we'd follow Porter and sit by the window
where the river spread beneath us. He'd call the barman by name and
order three pints. I mean, we loved this stuff. We were on the inside.

"Do you know the opening of *Heart of Darkness?*" he asked. We'd
never read it. "Right here," he said, sweeping his hand at the window. "At anchor here on a sloop in the sea reach of the Thames."
And then he'd pull the paperback from his pocket and read the first
two pages. "Geez, that makes a man thirsty, eh, Mark?" He'd bump
me and we'd drink up.

It was a long tour. We left the London Bridge sometime after five
and didn't cross under the river in the tunnel at Greenwich until
almost eleven. I remember scurrying through the long tiled corridor
far beneath the river behind Porter as he dragged us along in a hurry

because the pubs were going to close and we'd miss the last train back to Hampstead. We were all full of beer and Allison and I were dislocated, a feeling I got used to and came to like, as we came out into the bright cold air and saw the *Cutty Sark* moored there. This was life, it seemed to me, and I ran into the Red Cloak on Porter's footsteps. I was bursting and so pleased to be headed for the men's when he took my arm and pulled me to the bar. "Let's have a pint first, just to savor the night," he said. I wasn't standing upright, having walked with a bladder cramp for half a mile, and now the pain and pressure were blinding. I gripped the glass and met his smile. Allison came out of the ladies' and came over. "Are we being macho or just self-destructive?" she said.

"We're playing through the pain," Porter said. "We're seeing if the Buddhists are right with their wheel of desire and misery." I could barely hear him; there was a rushing in my ears, a cataract of steady noise. Disaster was imminent. Porter took a big slug of the bitter, and I mirrored his action. We swallowed and put down the glasses. "Excuse me," he said. "Think I'll hit the loo." And he strolled slowly into the men's. A blurred moment later I stood beside him at the huge urinals, dizzy and reclaimed. "We made it, mate," he said. "Now we've got to pound down a thousand beers and catch the train."

It had been a strange season in London for me. It was all new and as they say exciting, but I couldn't figure out what any of it meant. Now on the train to the north coast with Porter, I actually felt like somebody else who had never had my life, because as I saw it, my life—high school, college, Allison—hadn't taught me anything. For the first time I didn't give a shit about what happened next. The little play dance of cause and effect, be a good student, was all gone.

"You're not married," I said. It seemed late on a train and you could talk like that.

He looked at me. "It's not clear," he said. "In the eyes of men or the eyes of God?" I must have been looking serious, because he added, "No. I'm not married. Nearly happened once, but no, it was the timing, and now I've got plenty to do."

"Oh," I said.

"It was a girl at Hilman," he said. "I'd have done it too, but it got away from us. There's a time for it and you can wait too long." He pointed at me. "You and Allison talking about it?"

"No, not really. I mean, I don't know. I guess we are, kind of, being over here together. But we've never talked about it really." Now he was just smiling at me, the kid. That's what I wanted to say: hey, I'm a kid here; I'm too young. I'm too young for anything.

Porter drank. He was the first person I'd met who drank heavily and didn't make a mess. When the guys in the dorm drank the way he did every night we saw him, you wouldn't see them for three days. "Well, just remember there's a time and if it gets away, it's gone. Be alert." It sounded so true what he said. I'd never had a talk like this on a train and it all sounded true. It had weight. I wondered if the time had come and gone. I thought about Allison at thirty or forty, teaching art history at Holyoke or someplace. She'd be married to someone else, a man who appeared to be older than she, some guy with a thin gray beard.

"How do you know if the time is right or if the time is coming up? How do you know about this timing?" I held out my beautiful white coffee cup, and Porter carefully filled it with the silver liquid. My future seemed vast, unchartable. "Whose fault was it when you lost this girl?"

Porter rolled his head to look at me. He looked serious. "Hers. Mine. She could have fixed it." He gave me a dire, ironic look. "And then it was too late."

"What was her name?"

"It's no longer important."

"Was she a Lake?"

The window with the cabin lights dimmed was a dreamy plate of our faint reflection torn up by all the white and yellow lights of industrial lots and truck parks. "Yeah," he said. "They all were. She wore her hair like Allison does and she looked that way." He had grown wistful and turned quickly to me with a grin. "Oh, hell, they all look that way when they're twenty-two." After a while, Porter sat up and again topped my cup with vodka.

In Edinburgh, we had to change trains. It was just before dawn, and I felt torn up by all the drinking. Porter walked me across to our connection, the train for Cape Wrath, and he went off—for some reason—to the stationmaster's office. Checking on something. He was going to make a few calls and then we'd be off again, north to the coast. I'd wanted to call Allison, but what would I say? I missed her? It was true, but it sounded like kid stuff somehow. It bothered me that there was nothing appropriate to say, nothing fitting, and the days themselves felt like they didn't fit, like I was waiting to grow into them. I sat sulking on the train in Edinburgh station. I was sure—that is, I suspected—that there was something wrong with me. I hadn't seen a fire or found a body or stopped a fight or *been* in one, really, nor could I say what was going to happen, because I could not read any of the signs. I wanted with all my teeth for something real to claim me. Anyway, that's as close as I can say it.

When Porter came back I could see him striding down the platform in the gray light like a man with a purpose. He didn't seem very drunk. He had a blue package under his arm. "Oh, matey, bad luck," he said, sitting opposite me in our new compartment. It was an older train, everything carpet and tassels and wood in remarkably good condition. It was like a time warp I was in, sitting there drunk while Porter told me he was going back to London. "Have to." He tapped the package. "They've overnighted all the data and I've got to compose the piece by tomorrow." He shook my hand heartily. "Wish me luck. And good luck to you. You'll love Cape Wrath. I once saw a submarine there off the coast. Good luck to you and your Gulf Stream." He smiled oddly with that last, a surreal look, I thought from my depth or height, distance anyway, and he was gone.

Well, I couldn't think. For a while I worked my face with my hands, carefully hoping that such a reasonable gesture might wake me, help me get a grip. But even after the train moved and then moved again, gaining momentum now, I was blank. Outside now the world was gray and green, the misting precipitation cutting the visibility to five hundred feet. This was part of a typical spring low pressure that would engulf all of Great Britain for a week. I didn't really know if I wanted to go on alone, but then I didn't know where I was going. I didn't know if I wanted to get off the train, because I didn't really know why I was on the train in the first place. I felt a little sick, a kind of shocky jangling that would resolve itself into nausea but not for about an hour, and so I put my feet on the opposite seat, closed my eyes, and waited.

Porter had been to our flat once. It was the day I had gone to the Royal Weather Offices in London, and when I came back, he and Allison were drinking our Whitbred at the tiny table. The place was a bed-sitter, too small for three people. I sat on the bed, but even so every time one of us moved the other two had to shift. Evidently Porter had come to invite us to some funky bar, the last mod pub off Piccadilly, he said. Allison's face was rosy in the close room. I told them about my day, the tour I'd taken, and Porter got me talking about El Niño, and I got a little carried away, I guess. I mean, I knew this stuff. But I remember them exchanging glances and smiling. I was smiling too, and I remember being happy waving my arms around as the great cycles of the English climate.

Now I felt every ripple of every steel track as it connected to the one before it, and I knew with increasing certainty that I was going to be sick. But there was something more than all the drink rising in me. Something was wrong. I was used to that feeling, that is, that things were not exactly as I expected, but this was something else. That blue package that Porter had carried back. I'd seen it all night, the corner of it, sticking out of the blown zipper of his leather valise. He'd had it all along. What was he talking about?

It was like that for forty minutes, my stomach roiling steadily, until we stopped at Pitlochry. When I stood up, I felt the whole chemistry seize, and I limped to the loo and after a band of sweat burst onto my forehead, I was sick, voluminously sick, and then I was better, that is, just stricken not poisoned. My head felt empty. I hurried to the platform and wrangled with the telephone until I was able to reach Roger Ardreprice. I had tried Allison at home and at the museum, and then I called Roger at work and a woman answered the phone: "Keats's House."

"Listen," I started after he'd come to the phone. Then I didn't know what to say. Why was I calling? "Listen," I said again. "I'm uneasy about something. . . ."

"Where are you calling from?" he asked.

"I'm in Scotland. I'm in someplace, Pitlochry. Porter and I were going north to the coast."

"Porter, oh, for god's sakes, you didn't get tangled up with Porter, did you? What's he got you doing? I should have said something."

The phone box was close, airless, and I pressed the red-paned door open with my foot. "He's been great, but . . ."

"Oh my, this is bad news. Porter, for your information, probably started the Lake fire. He was tried for it, you know. He is bloody bad news. You keep yourself and that young woman away from him. Especially the girl. What's her name?"

I set my forehead against one of the glass panes of the phone booth and breathed through my mouth deeply two or three times. "Allison," I said.

"Right," Roger Ardreprice said from London. "Don't let him at her."

I couldn't hear very well now, a kind of static had set up in my head, and I set the phone back on the cradle.

The return train was a lesson in sanity. I felt the whole time that I would go crazy the next minute, and this powerful about-to-explode feeling finally became a granite rock which I held on my lap with my traveling case. I thought if I could sit still, everything would be all right. As the afternoon failed, I sat perfectly still through the maddening countryside, across the bridges and rivers of Great Britain with my body feeling distant and infirm in the waxy shadow of my hangover. Big decisions, I learned that day, are made in the body, and my body recoiled at the thought of Porter.

From King's Cross I took a cab to the museum. I didn't care about the expense. It was odd then, being in a hurry for the first time that spring, impatient with the old city, which now seemed just a place in my way. Allison wasn't there. I called home. No answer. I checked in the Museum Pub, where we'd had lunch a dozen times; those lunches all seemed a long time ago. I grabbed another taxi and went home. Our narrow flat seemed like a bittersweet joke: what children lived here? The light rain had followed me south, as I knew it would, and in the mist I walked up to the High Street and had a doner kebab. It tasted good and I ate it as I drifted down to the tube stop. There was no hurry now. Rumbling through the Underground in the yellow light, I let my shoulders roll with the train. Everyone looked tired, hungover, ready for therapy.

I'd never been to the Hotel Eden alone, and in the new dark in the quiet rain, I stood a moment and took it in. It was frankly just a sad old four-story white building, the two columns on each side of the doors peeling as they had for years on end. Norris was inside alone, and I took a pint of lager from him and sat at one of the little tables. The beer nailed me back in place. I was worn out and spent, but I was through being sick. I had another pint as I watched Norris move in the back bar. It would be three hours before Allison and Porter came in from wherever they were, and then I would tell them all about my trip to Scotland. It would be my first story.

KEITH

THEY WERE lab partners. It was that simple, how they met. She was *the* Barbara Anderson, president of half the school offices and queen of the rest. He was Keith Zetterstrom, a character, an oddball, a *Z*. His name was called last. The spring of their senior year at their equipment drawer she spoke to him for the first time in all their grades together: "Are you my lab partner?"

He spread the gear on the counter for the inventory and looked at her. "Yes, I am," he said. "I haven't lied to you this far, and I'm not going to start now."

After school Barbara Anderson met her boyfriend, Brian Woodworth, in the parking lot. They had twin red scooters because Brian had given her one at Christmas. "That guy," Barbara said, pointing to where Keith stood in the bus line, "is my lab partner."

"Who is he?" Brian said.

Keith was the window, wallpaper, woodwork. He'd been there for years and they'd never seen him. This was complicated because for years he was short and then he grew tall. And then he grew a long black slash of hair and now he had a crewcut. He was hard to see, hard to fix in one's vision.

The experiments in chemistry that spring concerned states of matter, and Barbara and Keith worked well together, quietly and methodically testing the elements.

"You're Barbara Anderson," he said finally as they waited for a beaker to boil. "We were on the same kickball team in fourth grade and I stood behind you in the sixth-grade Christmas play. I was a Russian soldier."

Barbara Anderson did not know what to say to these things. She couldn't remember the sixth-grade play . . . and fourth grade? So she said, "What are you doing after graduation?"

"The sky's the limit," he said. "And you are going off to Brown University."

"How did you know that?"

"The list has been posted for weeks."

"Oh. Right. Well, I may go to Brown and I may stay here and go to the university with my boyfriend."

Their mixture boiled and Keith poured some off into a cooling tray. "So what do you do?" he asked her.

Barbara eyed him. She was used to classmates having curiosity about her, and she had developed a pleasant condescension, but Keith had her off guard.

"What do you mean?"

"On a date with Brian, your boyfriend. What do you do?"

"Lots of things. We play miniature golf."

"You go on your scooters and play miniature golf."

"Yes."

"Is there a windmill?"

"Yes, there's a windmill. Why do you ask? What are you getting at?"

"Who wins? The golf."

"Brian," Barbara said. "He does."

BARBARA SHOWED the note to Trish, her best friend.

REASONS YOU SHOULD GO WITH ME

A. You are my lab partner.
B. Just to see. (You too, even Barbara Anderson, contain the same restless germ of curiosity that all humanity possesses, a trait that has led us out of the complacency of our dark caves into the bright world where we invented bowling—among other things.)
C. It's not a "date."

"Great," Trish said. "We certainly believe this! But, girl, who wants to graduate without a night out with a bald whatever. And I don't think he's going to ravish you—against your will, that is. Go for it. We'll tell Brian that you're staying at my house."

KEITH DROVE a Chevy pickup, forest-green, and when Barbara climbed in, she asked, "Why don't you drive this to school?"

"There's a bus. I love the bus. Have you ever been on one?"

"Not a school bus."

"Oh, try it," he said. "Try it. It's so big and it doesn't drop you off right at your house."

"You're weird."

"Why? Oh, does the bus go right to your house? Come on, does it? But you've got to admit they're big, and that yellow paint job? Show me that somewhere else, I dare you. Fasten your seat belt, let's go."

The evening went like this: Keith turned onto Bloomfield, the broad business avenue that stretched from near the airport all the way back to the university, and he told her, "I want you to point out your least favorite building on this street."

"So we're not going bowling?"

"No, we're saving that. I thought we'd just get a little something to eat. So, keep your eyes open. Any places you can't stand?" By the time they reached the airport, Barbara had pointed out four she thought were ugly. When they turned around, Keith added: "Now, your final choice, please. And not someplace you just don't like. We're looking for genuine aversion."

Barbara selected a five-story metal building near downtown, with a simple marquee above the main doors that read INSURANCE.

"Excellent," Keith said as he swung the pickup to the curb. He began unloading his truck. "This is truly garish. The architect here is now serving time."

"This is where my father used to work."

Keith paused, his arms full of equipment. "When . . ."

"When he divorced my mom. His office was right up there." She pointed. "I hate driving by this place."

"Good," Keith said with renewed conviction. "Come over here and sit down. Have a Coke."

Barbara sat in a chaise lounge that Keith had set on the floodlit front lawn next to a folding table. He handed her a Coke. "We're eating here?"

"Yes, miss," he said, toting over the cooler and the little propane stove. "It's rustic but traditional: cheese omelets and hash brown potatoes. Sliced tomatoes for a salad with choice of dressing, and— for dessert—ice cream. On the way home, of course." Keith poured some oil into the frying pan. "There is nothing like a meal to alter the chemistry of a place."

On the way home, they did indeed stop for ice cream, and Barbara asked him: "Wasn't your hair long last year, like in your face and down like this?" She swept her hand past his eye.

"It was."

"Why is it so short now?"

Keith ran his hand back over his head. "Seasonal cut. Summer's a-coming in. I want to lead the way."

IT WAS an odd week for Barbara. She actually did feel different about the insurance building as she drove her scooter by it on the way to school. When Trish found out about dinner, she said, "That was you! I saw your spread as we headed down to Barney's. You were like camped out, right?"

Wonder spread on Barbara's face as she thought it over. "Yeah, it was cool. He cooked."

"Right. But please, I've known a lot of guys who cook and they were some of the slickest. *High School Confidential* says: 'There are three million seductions and only one goal.'"

"You're a cynic."

"Cynicism is a useful survival skill."

IN CHEMISTRY, it was sulfur. Liquid, solid, and gas. The hallways of the chemistry annex smelled like rotten eggs and jokes abounded. Barbara winced through the white wispy smoke as Keith stirred the melting sulfur nuggets.

"This is awful," Barbara said.

"This is wonderful," Keith said. "This is the exact smell that greets sinners at the gates of hell. They think it's awful; here we get to enjoy it for free."

Barbara looked at him. "My lab partner is a certifiable . . ."

"Your lab partner will meet you tonight at seven o'clock."

"Keith," she said, taking the stir stick from him and prodding the undissolved sulfur, "I'm dating Brian. Remember?"

"Good for you," he said. "Now tell me something I don't know. Listen: I'll pick you up at seven. This isn't a date. This isn't dinner. This is errands. I'm serious. Necessary errands—for your friends."

Barbara Anderson rolled her eyes.

"You'll be home by nine. Young Mr. Brian can scoot by then. I mean it." Keith leaned toward her, the streams of baking acrid sulfur rising past his face. "I'm not lying to you."

WHEN SHE got to the truck that night, Keith asked her, "What did you tell Brian?"

"I told him I had errands at my aunt's and to come by at ten for a little while."

"That's awfully late on a school night."

"Keith."

"I mean, why didn't you tell him you'd be with me for two hours?" He looked at her. "I have trouble lending credibility to a relationship that is almost one year old and one in which one of the members has given another an actual full-size, roadworthy motor vehicle, and yet it remains a relationship in which one of the members lies to the other when she plans to spend two hours with her lab partner, a person with whom she has inhaled the very vapors of hell."

"Stop the truck, Keith. I'm getting out."

"And miss bowling? And miss the search for bowling balls?"

Half an hour later they were in Veteran's Thrift, reading the bowling balls. They'd already bought five at Desert Industry Thrift Shops and the Salvation Army store. Keith's rule was it had to be less than two dollars. They already had PATTY for Trish, BETSY and KIM for two more of Barbara's friends, an initialled ball B.R. for Brian even though his last name was Woodworth ("Puzzle him," Keith said. "Make him guess"), and WALT for their chemistry teacher, Mr. Walter Miles. They found three more in the bins in Veteran's Thrift, one marked SKIP, one marked COSMO ("A must," Keith said), and a brilliant green ball, run deeply with hypnotic swirls, which had no name at all.

Barbara was touring the wide shelves of used appliances, toys, and kitchen utensils. "Where do they get all this stuff?"

"You've never been in a secondhand store before, have you?"

"No. Look at all this stuff. This is a quarter?" She held up a large plastic tray with the Beatles' pictures on it.

"That," Keith said, taking it from her and placing it in the cart with their bowling balls, "came from the home of a fan of the first magnitude. Oh, it's a sad story. It's enough to say that this is here tonight because of Yoko Ono." Keith's attention was taken by a large trophy, standing among the dozen other trophies on the top shelf. "Whoa," he said, pulling it down. It was huge, over three feet tall: six golden columns, ascending from a white marble base to a silver obelisk, framed by two embossed silver wreaths, and topped by a silver woman on a rearing motorcycle. The inscription on the base read: WIDOWMAKER HILL CLIMB—FIRST PLACE 1987. Keith held it out to show Barbara, like a man holding a huge bottle of aspirin in a television commercial. "But this is another story altogether." He placed it reverently in the basket.

"And that would be?"

"No time. You've got to get back and meet Brian, a person who doesn't know where you are." Keith led her to the checkout. He was quiet all the way to the truck. He placed the balls carefully in the cardboard boxes in the truck bed and then set the huge trophy between them on the seat.

"You don't know where this trophy came from."

Keith put a finger to his lips—*Shhhh*—and started the truck and headed to Barbara's house. After several blocks of silence, Barbara folded her arms. "It's a tragic, tragic story," he said in a low voice. "I mean, this girl was a golden girl, an angel, the light in everybody's life."

"Do I want to hear this tragic story?"

"She was a wonder. Straight A's, with an A plus in chemistry. The girl could do no wrong. And then," Keith looked at Barbara, "she got involved with motorcycles."

"Is this her on top of the trophy?"

"The very girl." Keith nodded grimly. "Oh, it started innocently enough with a little red motor scooter, a toy really, and she could be seen running errands for the Ladies' Society and other charities every Saturday and Sunday when she wasn't home studying." Keith turned to Barbara, moving the trophy forward so he could see her. "I should add here that her fine academic standing got her into Brown University, where she was going that fateful fall." Keith laid the trophy back. "When her thirst for speed grew and grew, breaking over her good common sense like a tidal wave, sending her into the arms of a twelve-hundred-cc Harley-Davidson, one of the most powerful two-wheeled vehicles in the history of mankind." They turned onto

Barbara's street, and suddenly Barbara ducked, her head against Keith's knee.

"Drive by," she whispered. "Just keep going."

"What?" Keith said. "If I do that Brian won't see you." Keith could see Brian leaning against his scooter in the driveway. "Is that guy always early?"

Keith turned the next corner, and Barbara sat up and opened her door. "I'll go down the alley."

"Cool," Keith said. "So you sneak down the alley to meet your boyfriend? Pretty sexy."

She gave him a look.

"Okay, have fun. But there's one last thing, partner. I'll pick you up at four to deliver these bowling balls."

"Four?"

"Four A.M. Brian will be gone, won't he?"

"Keith."

"It's not a date. We've got to finish this program, right?"

Barbara looked over at Brian and quickly back at Keith as she opened the truck door. "Okay, but meet me at the corner. There," she pointed, "by the postbox."

SHE WAS there. The streets of the suburbs were dark and quiet, everything in its place, sleeping, but Barbara Anderson stood in the humming lamplight, hugging her elbows. It was eerily quiet and she could hear Keith coming for two or three blocks before he turned onto her street. He had the heater on in the truck, and when she climbed in he handed her a blue cardigan, which she quickly buttoned up. "Four A.M.," she said, rubbing her hands over the air vent. "Now this is weird out here."

"Yeah," Keith said. "Four o'clock makes it a different planet. I recommend it. But bring a sweater." He looked at her. "You look real sleepy," he said. "You look good. This is the face you ought to bring to school."

Barbara looked at Keith and smiled. "No makeup, okay? It's four

A.M." His face looked tired, and in the pale dash lights, with his short, short hair he looked more like a child, a little boy. "What do we do?"

"We give each of these babies," Keith nodded back at the bowling balls in the truck bed, "a new home."

They delivered the balls, placing them carefully on the porches of their friends, including Trish and Brian, and then they spent half an hour finding Mr. Miles's house, which was across town, a tan split-level. Keith handed Barbara the ball marked WALT and made her walk it up to the front porch. When she returned to the truck, Keith said, "Years from now you'll be able to say, 'When I was seventeen I put a bowling ball on my chemistry's teacher's front porch.'"

"His name was Walt," Barbara added.

At five-thirty, as the first gray light rose, Barbara Anderson and Keith walked into Jewel's Café carrying the last two balls: the green beauty and COSMO. Jewel's was the oldest café in the city, an all-night diner full of mailmen. "So," Barbara said, as they slid into one of the huge maroon booths, "who gets these last two?" She was radiant now, fully awake, and energized by the new day.

The waitress appeared and they ordered Round-the-World omelettes, hash browns, juice, milk, coffee, and wheat muffins, and Barbara ate with gusto, looking up halfway through. "So, where next?" She saw his plate. "Hey, you're not eating."

Keith looked odd, his face milky, his eyes gray. "This food is full of the exact amino acids to have a certifiably chemical day," he said. "I'll get around to it."

But he never did. He pushed his plate to the side and turned the place mat over and began to write on it.

"Are you feeling all right?" Barbara said.

"I'm okay."

She tilted her head at him skeptically.

"Hey. I'm okay. I haven't lied to you this far. Why would I start now? You know I'm okay, don't you? Well? Don't you think I'm okay?"

She looked at him and said quietly: "You're okay."

He showed her the note he had written:

Dear Waitress: My girlfriend and I are from rival families—different sides of the tracks, races, creeds, colors, and zip codes, and if they found out we had been out bowling all night, they would banish us to prison schools on separate planets. Please, please find a good home for our only bowling balls. Our enormous sadness is only mitigated by the fact that we know you'll take care of them.

With sweet sorrow—COSMO

In the truck, Barbara said, "Mitigated?"

"Always leave them something to look up."

"You're sick, aren't you?" she said.

"You look good in that sweater," he said. When she started to remove it, he added, "Don't. I'll get it after class, in just," he looked at his watch, "two hours and twenty minutes."

BUT HE wasn't there. He wasn't there all week. The class did experiments with oxidation and Mr. Miles spent two days explaining and diagramming rust. On Friday, Mr. Miles worked with Barbara on the experiments and she asked him what was wrong with Keith. "I'm not sure," her teacher told her. "But I think he's on medication."

Barbara had a tennis match on Tuesday afternoon at school, and Brian picked her up and drove her home. Usually he came in for an hour or so on these school days and they made out a little and raided the fridge, but for the first time she begged off, claiming homework, kissing him on the cheek and running into her house. But on Friday, during her away match at Viewmont, she felt odd again. She knew Brian was in the stands. When she walked off the court after the match it was nearly dark and Brian was waiting. She gave Trish her rackets and Barbara climbed on Brian's scooter without a word. "You weren't that bad," he said. "Viewmont always has a good team."

"Brian, let's just go home."

"You want to stop at Swenson's, get something to eat?"

"No."

So Brian started his scooter and drove them home. Barbara could tell by the way he was driving that he was mad, and it confused her: she felt strangely glad about it. She didn't want to invite him in, let him grope her on the couch. She held on as he took the corners too fast and slipped through the stop signs, but all the way home she didn't put her chin on his shoulder.

At her house, she got the scene she'd been expecting. "Just what is the matter with you?" Brian said. For some reason when he'd gone to kiss her, she'd averted her face. Her heart burned with pleasure and shame. She was going to make up a lie about tennis, but then just said, "Oh Brian. Just leave me alone for a while, will you? Just go home."

Inside, she couldn't settle down. She didn't shower or change clothes. She sat in the dark of her room for a while and then, using only the tiny spot of her desk lamp, she copied her chemistry notes for the week and called Trish.

It was midnight when Trish picked her up quietly by the mailbox on the corner. Trish was smoking one of her Marlboros and blowing smoke into the windshield. She said, "*High School Confidential,* Part Five: Young Barbara Anderson, still in her foxy tennis clothes, and her old friend Trish meet again at midnight, cruise the Strip, pick up two young men with tattoos, and are never seen alive again. Is that it? Count me in."

"Not quite. It goes like this: two sultry babes, one of whom has just been a royal bitch to her boyfriend for no reason, drive to 1147 Fairmont to drop off the week's chemistry notes."

"That would be Keith Zetterstrom's address, I'd guess." Trish said.

"He's my lab partner."

"Of course he is," Trish said.

"He missed all last week. Mr. Miles told me that Keith's on medication."

"Oh my god!" Trish clamped the steering wheel. "He's got cancer. That's that scary hairdo. He's sick."

"No he doesn't. I checked the college lists. He's going to Dickinson."

"Not for long, honey. I should have known this." Trish inhaled and blew smoke thoughtfully out of the side of her mouth. "Bald kids in high school without earrings have got cancer."

KEITH WAS in class the following Monday for the chemistry exam: sulfur and rust. After class, Barbara Anderson took him by the arm and led him to her locker. "Thanks for the notes, partner," he said. "They were absolutely chemical. I aced the quiz."

"You were sick last week."

"Last week." He pondered. "Oh, you mean because I wasn't here. What do you do, come every day? I just couldn't; it would take away the something special I feel for this place. I like to come from time to time and keep the dew on the rose, so to speak."

"I know what's the matter with you."

"Good for you, Barbara Anderson. And I know what's the matter with you too; sounds like a promising relationship."

Barbara pulled his folded sweater from the locker and handed it to him. As she did, Brian came up and said to them both: "Oh, I see." He started to walk away.

"Brian," Keith said. "Listen. You don't see. I'm not a threat to you. How could I be a threat to you? Think about it." Brian stood, his eyes narrowed. Keith went on: "Barbara's not stupid. What am I going to do, trick her? I'm her lab partner in chemistry. Relax." Keith went to Brian and took his hand, shook it. "I'm serious, Woodworth."

Brian stood for a moment longer until Barbara said, "I'll see you at lunch," and then he backed and disappeared down the hall. When he was gone, Barbara said, "*Are* you tricking me?"

"I don't know. Something's going on. I'm a little confused."

"You're confused. Who are you? Where have you been, Keith Zetterstrom? I've been going to school with you all these years and I've never even seen you and then we're delivering bowling balls together and now you're sick. Where were you last year? What are you doing? What are you going to do next year?"

"Last year I got a C in Spanish with Mrs. Whitehead. It was gruesome. This year is somewhat worse, with a few exceptions, and all in all, I'd say the sky is the limit." Keith took her wrist. "Quote me on that."

Barbara took a sharp breath through her nose and quietly began to cry.

"Oh, let's not," Keith said, pushing a handkerchief into her hand. "Here. Think of this." He moved her back against the wall, out of the way of students passing by. "If I was having a good year, I might never have spoken to you. Extreme times require extreme solutions. I went all those years sitting in the back and then I had to get sick to start talking. Now that's something, isn't it? Besides, I've got a plan. I'll pick you up at nine. Listen: bring your pajamas and a robe."

Barbara looked at him over the handkerchief.

"Hey. Trust me. You were the one who was crying. I'll see you at nine o'clock. This will cheer you up."

THE HOSPITAL was on the hill, and Keith parked in the farthest corner of the vast parking lot, one hundred yards from the nearest car. Beneath them in the dark night, the city teemed and shimmered, a million lights.

"It looks like a city on another planet," Barbara Anderson said as she stepped out of the truck.

"It does, indeed," Keith said, grabbing his bag. "Now if we only knew if the residents are friendly." He took her arm. "And now I'm going to cheer you up. I'm going to take you in that building," Keith pointed at the huge hospital, lit like an ocean liner in the night, "and buy you a package of gum."

They changed clothes in the fifth-floor restrooms and met in the hallway, in pajamas and robes, and stuffed their street clothes into Barbara's tennis bag.

"Oh, I feel better already," Barbara said.

"Now take my arm like this," Keith moved next to her and placed her hand above his elbow, "and look down like this." He put his chin on his chest. Barbara tried it. "No, not such a sad face, more serious, be strong. Good. Now walk just like this, little stab steps, real slow."

They started down the hallway, creeping along one side. "How far is it?" Barbara said. People passed them walking quietly in groups of two or three. It was the end of visiting hours. "A hundred yards to the elevators and down three floors, then out a hundred more. Keep your face down."

"Are people looking at us?"

"Well, yes. They've never seen a braver couple. And they've never seen such chemical pajamas. What are those little deals, lambs?"

They continued along the windows, through the lobby and down the elevator, in which they stood side by side, their four hands clasped together, while they were looking at their tennis shoes. The other people in the car gave them room out of respect. The main hall was worse, thick with people, everyone going five miles an hour faster than Barbara and Keith, who shuffled along whispering.

In the gift shop, finally, they parted the waters. The small room was crowded, but the people stepped aside and Keith and Barbara stood right at the counter. "A package of chewing gum, please," Keith said.

"Which kind?" said the candy striper.

"Sugarless. My sister and I want our teeth to last forever."

THEY RAN to the truck, leaping and swinging their arms. Keith threw the bag containing their clothes into the truck bed and climbed into the cab. Barbara climbed in, laughing, and Keith said, "Come on, face the facts: you feel better! You're cured!" And she slid across the seat meaning to hug him but it changed for both of them and they kissed. She pulled him to her side and they kissed again, one of her arms around his neck and one of her hands on his face. They fell into a spin there in the truck, eyes closed, holding on to each other in their pajamas, her robe open, their heads against the backseat, kissing. Barbara shifted and Keith sat up; the look they exchanged held. Below them the city's lights flickered. Barbara cupped her hand carefully on the top of Keith's bald scalp. She pulled him forward and they kissed. When she looked in his eyes again she knew what was going to happen, and it was a powerful feeling that gave her strange new certainty as she went for his mouth again.

There were other moments that surfaced in the truck in the night above the ancient city. Something Keith did, his hand reminded her of Brian, and then that thought vanished as they were beyond Brian in a moment. Later, well beyond even her notions of what to do and what not to do, lathered and breathing as if in toil, she heard herself say, "Yes." She said that several times.

SHE LOOKED for Keith everywhere, catching glimpses of his head, his shoulder, in the hallways. In chemistry they didn't talk; there were final reports, no need to work together. Finally, three days before graduation, they stood side by side cleaning out their chemistry equipment locker, waiting for Mr. Miles to check them off. Keith's manner was what? Easy, too confident, too neutral. He seemed to take up too much space in the room. She hated the way he kept his face blank and open, as if fishing for the first remark. She held off, feeling the restraint as a physical pang. Mr. Miles inventoried their cupboard and asked for their keys. He had a large ring of thirty or forty of the thin brass keys. Keith handed his to Mr. Miles and then Barbara Anderson found her key in the side of her purse and handed it to the teacher. She hated relinquishing the key; it was the only thing she had that meant she would see Keith, and now with it gone something opened in her and it hurt in a way she'd never hurt before. Keith turned to her and seeing something in her face, shrugged and said, "The end of chemistry as we know it. Which isn't really very well."

"Who are you?" Barbara said, her voice a kind of surprise to her. "You're so glib. Such a little actor." Mr. Miles looked up from his check sheet and several students turned toward them. Barbara was speaking loudly; she couldn't help it. "What are you doing to me? If you ask me this is a pretty chickenshit good-bye." Everyone was looking at her. Then her face would not work at all, the tears coming from some hot place, and Barbara Anderson walked from the room.

Keith hadn't moved. Mr. Miles looked at Keith, alarmed. Keith whispered: "Don't worry, Mr. Miles. She was addressing her remarks to me."

THERE WAS one more scene. The night before graduation, while her classmates met in the bright, noisy gym for the yearbook-signing party, Barbara drove out to the airport and met Keith where he said he'd be: at the last gate, H-17. There on an empty stretch of maroon carpet in front of three large banks of seats full of travelers, he was waiting. He handed her a pretty green canvas valise and an empty paper ticket sleeve.

"You can't even talk as yourself," she said. "You always need a setting. Now we're pretending I'm going somewhere?"

He looked serious tonight, weary. There were gray shadows under his eyes. "You wanted a goodbye scene," he said. "I tried not to do this."

"It's all a joke," she said. "You joke all the time."

"You know what my counselor said?" He smiled thinly as if glad to give her this point. "He said that this is a phase, that I'll stop joking soon." Their eyes met and the look held again. "Come here," he said. She stepped close to him. He put his hand on her elbow. "You want a farewell speech. Okay, here you go. You better call Brian and get your scooter back. Tell him I tricked you. Wake up, lady. Get real. I just wanted to see if I could give Barbara Anderson a whirl. And I did. It was selfish, okay? I just screwed you around a little. You said it yourself: it was a joke. That's my speech. How was it?"

"You didn't screw me around, Keith. You didn't give me a whirl." Barbara moved his hand and then put her arms around his neck so she could speak in his ear. She could see some of the people watching them. "You made love to me, Keith. It wasn't a joke. You made love to me and I met you tonight to say—good for you. Extreme times require extreme solutions." She was whispering as they stood alone on that carpet in their embrace. "I wondered how it was going to happen, but you were a surprise. Way to go. What did you think? That I wanted to go off to college an eighteen-year-old virgin? That pajama bit was great; I'll remember it." Now people were deplaning, entering the gate area and streaming around the young couple. Barbara felt Keith begin to tremble, and she closed her eyes. "It wasn't a joke. There's this: I made love to you too. You were there, remember? I'm glad for it." She pulled back slightly and found his lips. For a moment she was keenly aware of the public scene they were making, but that disappeared and they twisted tighter and were just there, kissing. She had dropped the valise and when the mock ticket slipped from her fingers behind his neck, a young woman in a business suit knelt and retrieved it and tapped Barbara on the hand. Barbara clutched the ticket and dropped her head to Keith's chest.

"I remember," he said. "My memory is aces."

"Tell me, Keith," she said. "What are these people thinking? Make something up."

"No need. They've got it right. That's why we came out here. They think we're saying goodbye."

SIMPLY PUT, that was the last time Barbara Anderson saw Keith Zetterstrom. That fall when she arrived in Providence for her freshman year at Brown, there was one package waiting for her, a large trophy topped by a girl on a motorcycle. She had seen it before. She kept it in her dorm window, where it was visible four stories from the ground, and she told her roommates that it meant a lot to her, that it represented a lot of fun and hard work but her goal had been to win the Widowmaker Hill Climb, and once she had done that, she sold her bikes and gave up her motorcycles forever.

THE PRISONER OF
BLUESTONE

T HERE WAS a camera. Mr. Ruckelbar was helping load the
crushed sedan onto DiPaulo's tow truck when an old Nikon
camera fell from the gashed trunkwell and hit him on the shoulder.
At first he thought it was a rock or a taillight assembly; things had
fallen on him before as he and DiPaulo had wrestled the ruined vehicles onto the tiltbed of DiPaulo's big custom Ford, and of course
DiPaulo wasn't there to be hit. He had a bad back and was in the cab
working the hydraulics and calling, "Good? Are we good yet?"

"Whoa, that's enough!" he called. Now Ruckelbar would have to
clamber up and set the chains. DiPaulo, he thought, the wrecker
with the bad back.

It was a thick gray twilight in the last week of October, chilly now
with the sun gone. This vehicle had been out back for too long. The
end of summer was always bad. After the Labor Day weekend, he
always took in a couple cars. He stored them out in a fenced lot
behind his Sunoco station, getting twenty dollars a week until the
insurance paperwork was completed, all of them the same really,
totaled and sold to DiPaulo, who took them out to Junk World, his

four acres of damaged vehicles near Torrington. Ruckelbar was glad to see this silver Saab go. It had been weird having the kid almost every afternoon since it had arrived, sitting out in the crushed thing full of leaves and beads of glass, just sitting there until dark sometimes, then walking back toward town along the two-lane without a proper jacket, some boy, the brother he said he was, some kid you didn't need sitting in a totaled Saab, some skinny kid maybe fourteen years old.

Ruckelbar cinched the final chain hitch and climbed down. "What'd you get?" It was DiPaulo. The small old man had limped back in the new dark and had picked the camera up. "This has got to be worth something."

"It's that kid's. It was his sister's car."

DiPaulo handed him back the camera. "That kid. That kid doesn't need to see this. I'd chuck it in the river before I let him see it. He's nutty enough." DiPaulo shook his head. "What's he going to do when he sees the car is finally gone?"

"Lord knows," Ruckelbar said. "Maybe he'll find someplace else to go."

"Well, that car's been here a long time, summer's over, and that camera," DiPaulo poked it with one of his short stained fingers, "is long gone to everybody. Let you leave the sleeping dogs asleep. Just put it in a drawer. You listen to your old pal. Your father would." DiPaulo took Ruckelbar's shoulder in his hand for a second. "See you. I'll be back Wednesday for that van. You take care." The little old man turned one more time and pointed at Ruckelbar. "And for god's sakes, don't tell that kid where this car is going."

DiPaulo had known Ruckelbar's father, "for a thousand years before you came along," he'd say, and Ruckelbar could remember DiPaulo saying "Leave sleeping dogs asleep" throughout the years in friendly arguments every time there was some sort of cash windfall. The elder Ruckelbar would smile and say that DiPaulo should have been a tax attorney.

After DiPaulo left, Ruckelbar rolled the wooden desk chair back inside the office of the Sunoco station and locked up. The building was a local landmark really, such an old little stone edifice painted blue, sitting all alone out on Route 21, where the woods had grown up around it and made it appear a hut in a fairy tale, with two gas pumps. The Bluestone everyone called it, and it was used to mark the quarry turnoff; "four miles past the Bluestone." It certainly marked Ruckelbar's life, was his life. He had met Clare at a community bonfire at the Quarry Meadows when she was still a student at Woodbine Prep, and above there at the Upper Quarry, remote and private, one night a year later she had helped him undo both of them in his father's truck and urgently had begun a sex life that wouldn't last five years.

Ruckelbar was a sophomore at the University of Massachusetts when his father had a heart attack in the station that March and died sitting up against the wall in the single-bay garage. Ruckelbar was twenty and when he came home it would stick. Clare was back from Sarah Lawrence that summer, and it was all right for a while, even good, the way anything can be good when you're young. It was fun having a service station, and after closing they'd go to the pubs beyond the blue-collar town of Garse, roadhouses that are all gone now. It was thrilling for Clare to sit in his pickup, the station truck, the same truck in which she arched herself against him at Upper Quarry and the same truck he drives now, as he rocked the huge set of keys in the latch of Bluestone and then extracted them and turned to her for a night. But she didn't think he was serious about it. He was to be an engineer; his father had said as much, and then another year passed, his mother now ill, while he ran the place all winter, plowing the snow from around the station with a blade on the old truck that his father had welded himself. When spring came it was a done deal. The wild iris and the dogwoods burst from every seam in the earth and the world changed for Ruckelbar, his sense of autonomy and worth, and he knew he was here for life. Even by the time they married, Clare had had enough. When she saw that the little baby girl she had the next year gave her no leverage with him, she stopped coming out with box lunches and avoided driving by the place even when she had to drive to Garse going by way of Tipton, which added four miles to the trip. She let him know that she didn't want to hear about Bluestone in her house and that he was to leave his overalls at the station, his boots in the garage, and he was to shower in the basement.

He'd gone along with this somehow, gone along without an angry word, without many words at all, the separate bedroom in the nice house in Corbett, and now after nearly twenty years, it was their way. After the loss of Clare and then the loss of the memory of her in his truck and in his bed came the loss of his daughter, which he also just allowed. Clare had her at home and Clare was determined that Marjorie should understand the essential elements of disappointment, and the lessons started with his name. Now, at seventeen, Marjorie was a day student at Woodbine, the prep school in Corbett, and her name was Marjorie Bar, shortened Clare said for convenience and for her career, whatever it would be. And Ruckelbar had let that happen too. He could fix any feature of any automobile, truck, or element of farm equipment, but he could not fix this.

AT HOME after a silent dinner with Clare, he broke the rule about talking about the station and told her that DiPaulo had picked up the car, the one the boy had been sitting in every day for weeks. She didn't like DiPaulo—he'd always been part of the way her life had betrayed her—and she let her eyes lift in disgust and then asked about the boy, "What did he do?" They were clearing the supper dishes. Marjorie ate dinner at school and arrived home after the evening study hall. It was queer that Clare should ask a question, and Ruckelbar, who hadn't intended his comment to begin a conversation, was surprised and not sure of how he should answer.

"He sat in the car. In the driver's seat."

This stopped Clare midstep and she held her dishes still. "All day?"

"He came after school and walked home after dark." It was the most Ruckelbar had spoken about the station in his kitchen for five or six years. Clare resumed sorting out the silverware and wiping up. Ruckelbar realized he wanted to ask Clare what to do about the camera. "Do you remember the accident?" he asked. "The girl?"

"If it's the same girl. The three young people from Garse. She was a tramp. They were killed on Labor Day or just before. They went off the quarry road."

Ruckelbar, who hadn't seen the papers, had known about the accident, of course. The police tow truck driver had told him about the three students, and the vehicle was crushed in so radical a fashion anyone could see it had fallen some distance onto the rock. Clare seemed to know more about it, something she'd read or heard, but Ruckelbar didn't know how to ask, and in a moment the chance was lost.

"Who's a tramp?" Marjorie entered the kitchen, putting her bookbag on a chair.

"Your father has some lowlife living in a car."

Ruckelbar looked at her.

"Any pie?" Marjorie asked her mother. Clare extracted a pumpkin pie from the fridge. Under the plastic wrap, it was uncut, one of Clare's fresh pumpkin pies. Ruckelbar looked at it, just a pie, and he stopped slipping. He'd already exited the room in his head, and he came back. "I'd like a piece of that pie, too, Clare. If I could please."

"You didn't get any?" Marjorie said. "You must really smell like gasoline tonight." She was actually trying to be light.

"He's not a lowlife, Clare," he said to her as she set a wedge of pie before him and dropped a fork onto the table. Even Marjorie, who had silently sided with her mother every time she'd had the chance, looked up in surprise at Clare. "It's the boy whose sister was killed last summer."

"Sheila Morton," Marjorie said.

"The tramp," Clare said.

Ruckelbar took a bite of pie. He was going to stay right here. This was the scene he'd drifted away from a thousand times. They were talking.

"She was not a tramp," he said. "This boy is a nice boy."

"He's disturbed," Clare said. "God, going out there to sit in the car?"

"Sheila was a slut," Marjorie said. "Everybody knew that."

The moment had gone very strange for all of them together like this in the kitchen. An ordinary night would have found Ruckelbar in the garage or his bedroom, Marjorie on the phone, and Clare at the television. They all felt the vague uncertainty of having the rules shift. No one would leave and no one knew how it would end; this was all new.

"She was, Dad," Marjorie said, setting Ruckelbar back in his chair with the word "Dad," which in its disuse had become monumental, naked and direct. They all heard it. Marjorie went on, "She put out, okay? One of those guys was from Woodbine. What do you think they were doing? They were headed for the Upper Quarry. It's where the sluts go. You don't try that road unless you're going to put out."

Ruckelbar had stopped eating the pie. He put down his fork and turned: Clare was gone.

A SUNNY Saturday in New England the last day in October: Ruckelbar lives for days like these, maybe this day in particular, the sun even at noon fallen away hard, but the lever of heat still there, though more than half the leaves are down and they skirl across Route 21 and pool against the banks of old grass. Ruckelbar sits in his old wooden office chair, which he pulls out front on days just like this, the whole scene a throwback to any fall afternoon thirty years ago, that being Clare's word, "throwback," but for now he's free in what feels like the very last late sunlight of the year. It's Halloween, he remembers; tonight they turn their clocks back. It doesn't matter. For now, he's simply going to sit in the place which has become the place he belongs, a place where he is closest to being happy, no, pleased he never moved, pleased to have this place paid for and not be running the Citgo in town chasing in circles regardless of the money, pleased to have the only station in the twelve miles of Route 21 between Garse and Corbett, nothing to look at across the street but trees rolling away toward Little Bear Mountain. Ruckelbar won't make fifty dollars the whole day and he simply leans back in the sunshine, pleased to have his tools put away and the bay swept and the office neat, just pleased to have the afternoon. As he sits and lifts his face to the old sun, he feels it and he's surprised that there is something else now, something new swimming underneath the ease he always feels at Bluestone, something about last night, and he tries to dismiss it but it will not be dismissed. It took years to achieve this separate peace and now something is coming undone.

Last night Ruckelbar had gone to Clare's room. After Marjorie had finished her pie and left the kitchen, her dishes on the table still, he'd sat as their talk played again in his head, burning there like a mistake. He hadn't known the Morton girl and in defending her he'd let his wife be injured. But he felt good about it somehow, that he had protested, and his mind had opened in the realization that something in him had been killed when they'd changed Marjorie's name, and he'd hated himself for not protesting then, but he knew too that he'd always just gone along. He lifted the two plates from the table and then put them down where they were. He went to Marjorie where she talked on the phone in the den and he stood before her until she put her palm over the speaker and said, annoyed, "What?" He said, "Get off the phone and go put your dishes away. Now." He said it in such a way that she spoke quickly into the telephone and hung up. Before she could rise, he added, "I think you should watch your language around your mother; I'm sure you didn't please her tonight in speaking so freely. She's worked hard to raise you correctly and you disappointed her."

"You started it," Marjorie said.

"Stop," he said. "You apologize to her tomorrow. It will mean a lot to her. You're everything she's got." Ruckelbar wanted to touch his daughter, put his hand on her cheek, but he didn't move, and in a moment Marjorie left the room. He had not done it too many times to reach out now, and besides, his hands, he always knew, were never really clean.

Ruckelbar went upstairs and knocked at his wife's door and then, surprising himself, went into the dark room. She was in bed and he sat beside her, but could do no more. He knew she was awake and he willed himself to put his arm around her, but he could not, pulling his fists up instead to his face and smelling in his knuckles all the scents of Bluestone.

IN THE early afternoon, a Chevy Two convertible pulls in to the gas pumps. At first Ruckelbar thinks it is two nuns, but when the two women get out laughing in their full black dresses, he sees they are gotten up as witches. One puts her tall black hat on and pulls a broom from the backseat ready to mug for any passing cars. Ruckelbar steps over. The bareheaded witch is switching on the pump. "Let me get that for you," he offers. "You'll smell like gasoline at your party."

"Great," the girl says. They are both about his daughter's age. "What are you going to be?" she asks him.

"This is it," Ruckelbar says, indicating his gray overall.

"Okay," the other witch says, "so what are you, the Prisoner of Bluestone?" They laugh and Ruckelbar has to laugh there in the sunshine. Girls. His daughter would not believe that he laughed with these girls; there'd be no way to explain it to her. The valve clicks off and he replaces the nozzle. As he does, the broom witch takes it from him and holds it as if to gas the broom.

"This, get this," she says. "Let's get out your camera, Paul." She's read his name in the patch. The other witch has grabbed her broom now and poses with her friend. Hearing his name and their laughter elates him and without hesitation, as if he'd planned it, he ducks into the station and retrieves the Nikon camera. He takes their picture there, two tall witches in the sunshine, and as he does, a passing car honks a salute. One of the witches steps out now seeing the bright blue station as if for the first time and says, "What is this, a movie set? I love it that you actually sell gas." She throws her broom and hat back into the car. The other girl, the driver, reaches deep into her costume, here and there, to find her money. She has some difficulty. Her hat falls off and Ruckelbar holds it for her, finally exchanging it for the nine dollars she pays him.

"Happy Halloween," she says, getting into the car. "I like your outfit. I hope they come to let you out someday."

The other girl has been at the car's radio and a song that Ruckelbar seems to remember rises around them. As the girls begin to pull away, she calls, "You can use that picture in your advertising!" And she throws him a flamboyant kiss.

All day long the traffic is desultory, five cars an hour pass Bluestone, the sound they make on Route 21 is a sound Ruckelbar knows by heart. He knows the trucks from the cars and he knows the high whine of the school buses. He knows if someone is speeding and he can tell if a car's intention is to slow and turn in. Just before sunset he hears that sound and a little white Ford Escort coasts into the gravel yard of the station, parking to one side. There is something odd about it and Ruckelbar thinks it is more costumes, two people, one wrapped like the Mummy, but then he sees it is a rental, and when the man and the woman get out and the man has the head bandage, he knows it is the owners of the Dodge van come to get whatever they'd left inside. People come the week after an accident and get their stuff. He stands and waves at the young people and then goes to unlock the chainlink gate, trying not to look at the man's head, which is swollen crazily over the unbandaged eye.

The woman strides directly for the van as Ruckelbar says, "Take your time, I don't close until six. No rush."

The woman calls from where she's slid open the side door of the van, "Bring the basket, Jerry. It's in the back."

So now it's Ruckelbar bending into the little Ford and extracting a huge plastic laundry basket because the man Jerry says he's not supposed to bend over until the swelling subsides in a week. "I have to sleep sitting up." Jerry's about thirty, his skull absolutely out of whack, a wrong-way oval, the skin on his exposed forehead about to split, shiny and yellow. Ruckelbar can smell the varnish of liquor on his breath. When he pulls the basket from the small backseat to hand it to Jerry, the young man has already wandered out back.

Ruckelbar takes the basket around to the open side of the van and offers it there, but the woman is on her knees on the middle seat bent into the far back, trying to untangle the straps of a collapsed child seat. Her cotton shift is drawn up so that her bare thighs are visible to him. Her underpants are a shiny satin blue and the configuration of her white thighs and the way they meet in the blue fabric seem a disembodied mystery to Ruckelbar. Ruckelbar looks away and steps back onto the moist yellow grid of grass where the Saab sat for eight weeks. He can hear the woman now, a soft sucking, and he knows she is weeping. He sets the basket there in the twilight and he walks back to the office. He is lit and shaken; he feels as he did when the witch said his name. On his way he hears Jerry break the mirror assembly from the van door and he turns to watch the young man throw it into the woods and then spin to the ground and grab his head.

Out front the sun is gone, the day is gone, it feels nothing but late. The daylight seems used, thin, good for nothing. He carries his chair back into the office and there in the new gloom is the boy, arms folded, leaning against the counter.

"You scared me," Ruckelbar says. "Hello." He sets the chair behind his steel desk and switches on the office fluorescents. He's lost for a moment and simply adds, "How are you?"

"Where's my sister's car?" the boy asks. He looks different close like this in the flat light; he's taller and younger, his pale face run with freckles. He's wearing a red plaid shirt unbuttoned over a faded black T-shirt.

"The insurance company came and got it. It was theirs." The boy takes this in and makes a face that says he understands. "Remember, I told you about this a couple of weeks ago?" The boy nods at him and then turns to the big window and looks out. His eyes are roaming and Ruckelbar sees the desperation.

The camera sits on the old steel desk, and in a second Ruckelbar decides what to do; if the boy recognizes it, he'll give it to him. Otherwise, he'll let this sleeping dog be. It feels like a good decision, but Ruckelbar is floating in a new world, he can tell. They can hear the loud voices outside, the man and the woman in the back, and Ruckelbar switches on the exterior lights.

"Where would the insurance take that car?"

"I don't know," Ruckelbar says.

"Would they fix it?"

"Probably part it out," Ruckelbar says. "They don't fix them anymore, many of them."

"It had been a good car for Sheila," the boy says. "Better than any of her friends had."

"I hear good things about the Saab," Ruckelbar says. "You want a Coke, something, candy bar?"

"I don't know why I'm out here now," the boy says. Their reflections have come up in the big windows. Ruckelbar drops quarters in the round-shouldered soda machine, another throwback, and opens the door for the boy to choose. "Root beer," the boy says, extracting the bottle.

"You live in Garse?" Ruckelbar asks him.

"Yeah," the boy says. His eyes are still wide, darting, and Ruckelbar can see the rim of moisture. The world outside is now set still on the pivot point of light, the glow of the station lights running into the air out over the road through the trees all the way to the even wash of silver along the horizon of Little Bear Mountain, and above the mountain like two huge ghosts floats the mirror image of the two of them. The leaves lie still. Standing by the door Ruckelbar can feel the air falling from the dark heavens, a faint chill falling from infinity. Tomorrow night it will be dark an hour earlier.

Now Ruckelbar hears the woman's voice from outside, around the building, a cry of some sort, and then the rental Escort does a short circle in the gravel in front of the Sunoco pumps and rips dust into the new dusk as it mounts Route 21 headed for Corbett. Ruckelbar and the boy have stepped outside. They watch the car disappear, turning on its lights after a few seconds on the pavement.

"There's a bonfire at the quarry tonight," Ruckelbar says. "Garse does it. You going?"

"We'd have gone with Sheila. She liked that stuff; she liked Halloween." The boy follows him back inside.

"You want a ride home?" Ruckelbar says, knowing instantly that it is the wrong thing to say, the offer of sympathy battering the boy over the brink, and now the boy stands crying stiffly, chin down, his arms crossed tighter than anything in the world. Ruckelbar's heart heaves; he knows about this, about living in his silent house where a kind word would have broken him.

They stand that way, as if after an explosion, not knowing what to do; all the surprises in the room have been used up. Everything that happens now will be work. Ruckelbar is particularly out of ideas; he's not used to having anyone in the office for longer than it takes to make change. His father sometimes sat in here and chewed the fat with his cronies, DiPaulo and others, but Ruckelbar has never done it. He doesn't have any cronies. Now he doesn't know what to do. Ruckelbar points at the boy. "You go ahead, get the truck, bring it around front." He hands the boy his keys. The boy looks at him, so he goes on. "It's all right. You do it. You know my truck." With it dark now, Ruckelbar can see himself in the front window, a man in overalls. He's scared. It feels like something else could happen. He reaches for the phone and calls Clare, which he doesn't do three times a year. "Clare," he says, "I'm bringing somebody home who needs a warm meal. We're coming. It's not something we can talk over. We'll be about fifteen minutes, okay, honey? Did you hear me? Can you put on some of your tea?" He has never said anything like this to Clare in his life. The only people who are ever in their house are Clare's sister every other year and a few of Marjorie's friends who stand in the entry a minute or two.

"Paul," she says, and his name again jolts Ruckelbar. She goes on, "Marjorie spoke to me."

"I'm glad for that, Clare."

"She's a good girl, Paul."

"Yes, she is."

There is a pause and then Clare adds the last. "She misses her father. She said that today." Ruckelbar draws a quick breath and sees his truck like a ghost ship drift up front in the window. He lifts a hand to the boy in the truck. What he sees is a figure caught in the old yellow glass, a man in there. Ruckelbar thought everything was settled so long ago.

He turns off the light before he can see what the image will do, and he grabs his keys and the camera. Outside, the boy has slid to the passenger side. When Ruckelbar climbs in the boy says, in a new voice, easy and relaxed, "Nice truck. It's in good shape."

"It's a '62," Ruckelbar says. "My dad's truck. If you park them inside and change the oil every twenty-five hundred miles, they keep." He puts the camera on the seat. "This was in your sister's car."

The boy picks it up. "Cool," he says, hefting it. "This is a weird place," the boy says. "Who painted it blue?"

Ruckelbar is now in gear on the hardtop of Route 21. He looks back at Bluestone once, a little building in the dark. "My father did," he says.

ZANDUCE AT SECOND

B Y HIS thirty-third birthday, a gray May day which found
him having a warm cup of spice tea on the terrace of the
Bay-side Inn in Annapolis, Maryland, with Carol Ann Menager, a
nineteen-year-old woman he had hired out of the Bethesda Hilton
Turntable Lounge at eleven o'clock that morning, Eddie Zanduce
had killed eleven people and had that reputation, was famous for
killing people, really the most famous killer of the day, his photograph in the sports section every week or so and somewhere in the
article the phrase "eleven people" or "eleven fatalities"—in fact, the
word *eleven* now had that association first, the number of the dead—
and in all the major league baseball parks his full name could be
heard every game day in some comment, the gist of which would be
"Popcorn and beer for ten-fifty, that's bad, but just be glad Eddie
Zanduce isn't here, for he'd kill you for sure," and the vendors would
slide the beer across the counter and say, "Watch out for Eddie,"
which had come to supplant "Here you go," or "Have a nice day,"
in conversations even away from the parks. Everywhere he was that
famous. Even this young woman, who has been working out of the
Hilton for the past eight months not reading the papers and only
watching as much TV as one might watch in rented rooms in the
early afternoon or late evening, not really news hours, even she

knows his name, though she can't remember why she knows it and she finally asks him, her brow a furrow, "Eddie Zanduce? Are you on television? An actor?" And he smiles, raising the room-service teacup, but it's not a real smile. It is the placeholder expression he's been using for four years now since he first hit a baseball into the stands and it struck and killed a college sophomore, a young man, the papers were quick to point out, who was a straight-A student majoring in chemistry, and it is the kind of smile that makes him look nothing but old, a person who has seen it all and is now waiting for it all to be over. And in his old man's way he is patient through the next part, a talk he has had with many people all around the country, letting them know that he is simply Eddie Zanduce, the third baseman for the Orioles who has killed several people with foul balls. It has been a pernicious series of accidents really, though he won't say that.

She already knows she's not there for sex, after an hour she can tell by the manner, the face, and he has a beautiful actor's face which has been stunned with a kind of ruin by his bad luck and the weight of bearing responsibility for what he has done as an athlete. He's in the second thousand afternoons of this new life and the loneliness seems to have a physical gravity; he's hired her because it would have been impossible not to. He's hired her to survive the afternoon.

The day has been a walk through the tony shopping district in Annapolis, where he has bought her a red cotton sweater with tortiseshell buttons. It is a perfect sweater for May, and it looks wonderful as she holds it before her; she has short brunette hair, shiny as a schoolgirl's, which he realizes she may be. Then a walk along the pier, just a walk, no talking. She doesn't because he doesn't, and early on such outings, she always follows the man's lead. Later, the fresh salad lunch from room service and the tea. She explores the suite, poking her head into the bright bathroom, the nicest bathroom in any hotel she's been in during her brief career. There's a hair dryer, a robe, a fridge, and a phone. The shower is also a steamroom and the tub is a vast marble dish. There is a little city of lotions and sham-

poos. She smiles and he says, Please, feel free. Then he lies on the
bed while she showers and dresses; he likes to watch her dress, but
that too is different because he lies there imagining a family scene,
the young wife busy with her grooming, not immodest in her naked-
ness, her undergarments on the bed like something sweet and familiar. The tea was her idea when he told her she could have anything
at all; and she saw he was one of the odd ones, there were so many
odd ones anymore willing to pay for something she's never fully
understood, and she's taken the not understanding as just being part
of it, her job, men and women, life. She's known lots of people who
didn't understand what they were doing; her parents, for example.
Her decision to go to work this way was based on her vision of simply fucking men for money, but the months have been more wearing than she could have foreseen with all the chatter and the
posturing, some men who only want to mope or weep all through
their massage, others who want to walk ahead of her into two or
three nightspots and then yell at her later in some bedroom at the
Embassy Suites, too many who want her to tell them about some
other bastard who has abused her or broken her heart. But here this
Eddie Zanduce just drinks his tea with his old man's smile as he
watches the stormy summer weather as if it were a home movie.
They've been through it all already and he has said simply without
pretension: No, that's all right. We won't be doing that, but you can
shower later. I'll have you in town by five-thirty.

THE ELEVEN people Eddie Zanduce has killed have been properly
eulogized, the irony in the demise of each celebrated in the tabloid
press, the potentials of their lives properly inflated, and their fame—
brief though it may have been—certainly far beyond any which
might have accompanied their natural passing, and so they needn't
be listed here and made flesh again. They each float in the head of
Eddie Zanduce in his every movement, though he has never said so,
or acknowledged his burden in any public way, and it has become a
kind of poor form now even in the press corps, a group not known

for any form, good or bad, to bring it up. After the seventh person, a girl of nine who had gone with her four cousins to see the Orioles play New York over a year ago, and was removed from all earthly joy and worry by Eddie Zanduce's powerhouse line drive pulled foul into the seats behind third, the sportswriters dropped the whole story, letting it fall on page one of the second section: news. And even now after games, the five or six reporters who bother to come into the clubhouse—the Orioles are having a lackluster start, and have all but relinquished even a shot at the pennant—give Eddie Zanduce's locker a wide berth. Through it all, he has said one thing only, and that eleven times: "I'm sorry; this is terrible." When asked after the third fatality, a retired school principal who was unable to see and avoid the sharp shot of one of Eddie Zanduce's foul balls, if the unfortunate accidents might make him consider leaving the game, he said, "No."

And he became so stoic in the eyes of the press and they painted him that way that there was a general wonder at how he could stand it having the eleven innocent people dead by his hand and they said things like "It would be hard on me" and "I couldn't take it." And so they marveled darkly at his ability to appear in his uniform, take the field at all, dive right when the hit required it and glove the ball, scrambling to his knees in time to make the throw either to first or to second if there was a chance for a double play. They noted that his batting slump worsened, and now he's gone weeks in the new season without a hit, but he plays because he's steady in the field and he can fill the stands. His face was the object of great scrutiny for expression, a scowl or a grin, because much could have been made of such a look. And when he was at the plate, standing in the box awaiting the pitch, his bat held rigid and ready off his right shoulder as if for business, this business and nothing else, the cameras went in on his face, his eyes, which were simply inscrutable to the nation of baseball fans.

And now, at thirty-three he lies on the queen-size bed of the Bayside Inn, his fingers twined behind his head, as he watches Carol

Ann Menager come dripping into the room, her hair partially in a towel, her nineteen-year-old body a rose-and-pale pattern of the female form, five years away from any visible wear and tear from the vocation she has chosen. She warms him appearing this way, naked and ready to chat as she reaches for her lavender bra and puts it of all her clothing on first, simply as convenience, and the sight of her there bare and comfortable makes him feel the thing he has been missing: befriended.

"But you feel bad about it, right?" Carol Ann says. "It must hurt you to know what has happened."

"I do," he says, "I do. I feel as badly about it all as I should."

And now Carol Ann stops briefly, one leg in her lavender panties, and now she quickly pulls them up and says, "I don't know what you mean."

"I only mean what I said and nothing more," Eddie Zanduce says. "What was the worst?"

He still reclines and answers: "They are all equally bad."

"The little girl?"

Eddie Zanduce draws a deep breath there on the bed and then speaks: "The little girl, whose name was Victoria Tuttle, and the tourist from Austria, whose name was Heinrich Vence, and the Toronto Blue Jay, a man in a costume named William Dirsk, who was standing on the home dugout when my line drive broke his sternum. And the eight others all equally unlikely and horrible, all equally bad. In fact, eleven isn't really worse than one for me, because I maxed out on one. It doesn't double with two. My capacity for such feelings, I found out, is limited. And I am full."

Carol Ann Menager sits on the bed and buttons her new sweater. There is no hurry in her actions. She is thinking. "And if you killed someone tonight?"

Here Eddie Zanduce turns to her, his head rolling in the cradle of his hands, and smiles the smile he's been using all day, though it hasn't worn thin. "I wouldn't like that," he says. "Although it has been shown to me that I am fully capable of such a thing."

"Is it bad luck to talk about?"

"I don't believe in luck, bad or good." He warms his smile one more time for her and says, "I'm glad you came today. I wouldn't have ordered the tea." He swings his legs to sit up. "And the sweater, well, it looks very nice. We'll drive back when you're ready."

ON THE drive north Carol Ann Menager says one thing that stays with Eddie Zanduce after he drops her at her little blue Geo in the Hilton parking lot and after he has dressed and played three innings of baseball before a crowd of twenty-four thousand, the stadium a third full under low clouds this early in the season with the Orioles going ho-hum and school not out yet, and she says it like so much she has said in the six hours he has known her—right out of the blue as they cruise north from Annapolis on Route 2 in his thick silver Mercedes, a car he thinks nothing of and can afford not to think of, under the low sullen skies that bless and begrudge the very springtime hedgerows the car speeds past. It had all come to her as she'd assembled herself an hour before; and it is so different from what she's imagined, in fact, she'd paused while drying herself with the lush towel in the Bayside Inn, her foot on the edge of the tub, and she'd looked at the ceiling where a heavy raft of clouds crossed the domed skylight, and one hand on the towel against herself, she'd seen Eddie Zanduce so differently than she had thought. For one thing he wasn't married and playing the dark game that some men did, putting themselves closer and closer to the edge of their lives until something went over, and he wasn't simply off, the men who tried to own her for the three hundred dollars and then didn't touch her, and he wasn't cruel in the other more overt ways, nor was he turned so tight that to enjoy a cup of tea over the marina with a hooker was anything sexual, nor was she young enough to be his daughter, just none of it, but she could see that he had made his pact with the random killings he initiated at the plate in baseball parks and the agreement left him nothing but the long series of empty afternoons.

"You want to know why I became a hooker?" she asks.

"Not really," he says. He drives the way other men drive when there are things on their minds, but his mind, she knows, has but one thing in it—eleven times. "You have your reasons. I respect them. I think you should be careful and do what you choose."

"You didn't even see me," she says. "You don't even know who's in the car with you."

He doesn't answer. He says. "I'll have you back by five-thirty."

"A lot of men want to know why I would do such a thing. They call me young and beautiful and talented and ready for the world and many other things that any person in any walk of life would take as a compliment. And I make it my challenge, the only one after survive, to answer them all differently. Are you listening?"

Eddie Zanduce drives.

"Some of them I tell that I hate the work but enjoy the money; they like that because—to a man—it's true of them. Some I tell I love the work and would do it for free; and they like that because they're all boys. Everybody else gets a complicated story with a mother and a father and a boyfriend or two, sometimes an ex-husband, sometimes a child who is sometimes a girl and sometimes a boy, and we end up nodding over our coffees or our brandies or whatever we're talking over, and we smile at the wisdom of time, because there is nothing else to do but for them to agree with me or simply hear and nod and then smile, I do tell good stories, and that smile is the same smile you've been giving yourself all day. If you had your life figured out any better than I do, it would have been a different day back at your sailboat motel. Sorry to go on, because it doesn't matter, but I'll tell you the truth; what can it hurt, right? You're a killer. I'm just a whore. I'm a whore because I don't care, and because I don't care it's a perfect job. I don't see anybody else doing any better. Show me somebody who's got a grip, just one person. Survive. That's my motto. And then tell stories. What should I do, trot out to the community college and prepare for my future as a medical doctor? I don't think so."

Eddie Zanduce looks at the young woman. Her eyes are deeper, darker, near tears. "You are beautiful," he says. "I'm sorry if the day wasn't to your liking."

She has been treated one hundred ways, but not this way, not with this delicate diffidence, and she is surprised that it stings. She's been hurt and neglected and ignored and made to feel invisible, but this is different, somehow this is personal. "The day was fine. I just wish you'd seen me."

For some reason, Eddie Zanduce responds to this: "I don't see people. It's not what I do. I can't afford it." Having said it, he immediately regrets how true it sounds to him. Why is he talking to her? "I'm tired," he adds, and he is tired—of it all. He regrets his decision to have company, purchase it, because it has turned out to be what he wanted so long, and something about this girl has crossed into his view. She is smart and pretty and—he hates this—he does feel bad she's a hooker.

And then she says the haunting thing, the advice that he will carry into the game later that night. "Why don't you try to do it?" He looks at her as she finishes. "You've killed these people on accident. What if you tried? Could you kill somebody on purpose?"

At five twenty-five after driving the last forty minutes in a silence like the silence in the center of the rolling earth, Eddie Zanduce pulls into the Hilton lot and Carol Ann Menager says, "Right up there." When he stops the car, she steps out and says to him, "I'll be at the game. Thanks for the tea."

AND NOW at two and one, a count he loves, Eddie Zanduce steps out of the box, self-conscious in a way he hasn't been for years and years and can't figure out until he ticks upon it: she's here somewhere, taking the night off to catch a baseball game or else with a trick who even now would be charmed by her unaffected love for a night in the park, the two of them laughing like teenagers over popcorn, and now she'd be pointing down at Eddie, saying, "There, that's the guy." Eddie Zanduce listens to the low murmur of twenty-four thousand people who have chosen to attend tonight's game knowing he would be here, here at bat, which was a place from which he could harm them irreparably, for he has done it eleven times before. The announcers have handled it the same after the fourth death, a young lawyer taken by a hooked line shot, the ball shattering his occipital bone the final beat in a scene he'd watched every moment of from the tock! of the bat—when the ball was so small, a dot which grew through its unreliable one-second arc into a huge white spheroid of five ounces entering his face, and what the announcers began to say then was some version of "Please be alert, ladies and gentlemen, coming to the ballpark implies responsibility. That ball is likely to go absolutely anywhere." But everybody knows this. Every single soul, even the twenty Japanese businessmen not five days out of Osaka know about Eddie Zanduce, and their boxes behind first base titter and moan, even the four babies in arms not one of them five months old spread throughout the house know about the killer at the plate, as do the people sitting behind the babies disgusted at the parents for risking such a thing, and the drunks, a dozen people swimming that abyss as Eddie taps his cleats, they know, even one in his stuporous sleep, his head collapsed on his chest as if offering it up, knows that Eddie could kill any one of them tonight. The number eleven hovers everywhere as does the number twelve waiting to be written. It is already printed on a best-selling T-shirt, and there are others, "I'll be 12th," and "Take Me 12th!" and "NEXT," and many others, all on T-shirts which Eddie Zanduce could read in any crowd in any city in which the Orioles took the field. When he played baseball, when he was listed on the starting roster—where he'd been for seven years—the crowd was doubled. People came as they'd come out tonight on a chilly cloudy night in Baltimore, a night that should have seen ten thousand maybe, more likely eight, they flocked to the ballpark, crammed themselves into sold-out games or sat out—as tonight—in questionable weather as if they were asking to be twelfth, as if their lives were fully worthy of being interrupted, as if—like right now with

Eddie stepping back into the batter's box—they were asking, Take me next, hit me, I have come here to be killed.

Eddie Zanduce remembers Carol Ann Menager in the car. He hoists his bat and says, "I'm going to kill one of you now."

"What's that, Eddie?"

Caulkins, the Minnesota catcher, has heard his threat, but it means nothing to Eddie, and he says that: "Nothing. Just something I'm going to do." He says this stepping back into the batter's box and lifts his bat up to the ready. Things are in place. And as if enacting the foretold, he slices the first pitch, savagely shaving it short into the first-base seats, the kind of ugly truncated liner that has only damage as its intent, and adrenaline pricks the twenty-four thousand hearts sitting in that dangerous circle, but after a beat that allows the gasp to subside, a catch-breath really that is merely overture for a scream, two young men in blue Maryland sweatshirts leap above the crowd there above first base and one waves his old brown mitt in which it is clear there is a baseball. They hug and hop up and down for a moment as the crowd witnesses it all sitting silent as the members of a scared congregation and then a roar begins which is like laughter in church and it rides on the night air, filling the stadium.

"I'll be damned," Caulkins declares, standing mask off behind Eddie Zanduce. "He caught that ball, Eddie."

Those words are etched in Eddie Zanduce's mind as he steps again up to the plate. He caught the ball. He looks across at the young men but they have sat down, dissolved, leaving a girl standing behind them in a red sweater who smiles at him widely and rises once on her toes and waves a little wave that says, "I knew it. I just knew it." She is alone standing there waving. Eddie thinks that: she's come alone.

The next pitch comes in fat and high and as Eddie Zanduce swings and connects he pictures this ball streaming down the line uninterrupted, too fast to be caught, a flash off the cranium of a man draining his beer at the very second a plate of bone carves into his brain and the lights go out. The real ball though snaps on a sharp hop over the third baseman, staying in fair territory for a double. Eddie Zanduce stands on second. There is a great cheering; he may be a killer but he is on the home team and he's driven in the first run of the ballgame. His first hit in this month of May. And Eddie Zanduce has a feeling he hasn't had for four years since it all began, since the weather in his life changed for good, and what he feels is anger. He can taste the dry anger in his mouth and it tastes good. He smiles and he knows the cameras are on him but he can't help himself he is so pleased to be angry, and the view he has now of the crowd behind the plate, three tiers of them, lifts him to a new feeling that he locks on in a second: he hates them. He hates them all so much that the rich feeling floods through his brain like nectar and his smile wants to close his eyes. He is transported by hatred, exulted, drenched. He leads off second, so on edge and pissed off he feels he's going to fly with this intoxicating hatred, and he smiles that different smile, the challenge and the glee, and he feels his heart beating in his neck and arms, hot here in the center of the world. It's a feeling you'd like to explain to someone after the game. He plans to. He's got two more at bats tonight, the gall rises in his throat like life itself, and he is going to kill somebody—or let them know he was trying.

WHAT WE
WANTED TO DO

W HAT WE wanted to do was spill boiling oil onto the
heads of our enemies as they attempted to bang down
the gates of our village, but, as everyone now knows, we had some
problems, primarily technical problems, that prevented us from
doing what we wanted to do the way we had hoped to do it. What
we're asking for today is another chance.

There has been so much media attention to this boiling oil issue
that it is time to clear the air. There is a great deal of pressure to dismantle the system we have in place and bring the oil down off the
roof. Even though there isn't much left. This would be a mistake.
Yes, there were problems last month during the Visigoth raid, but as
I will note, these are easily remedied.

From its inception I have been intimately involved in the boiling
oil project—research, development, physical deployment. I also happened to be team leader on the roof last month when we had occasion to try the system during the Visigoth attack, about which so
much has been written.

(It was not an "entirely successful" sortie, as I will show. The
Visigoths, about two dozen, did penetrate the city and rape and

plunder for several hours, but *there was no pillaging.* And make no questions about it—they now know we have oil on the roof and several of them are going to think twice before battering down our door again. I'm not saying it may not happen, but when it does, they know we'll be ready.)

First, the very concept of oil on the roof upset so many of our villagers. Granted, it is exotic, but all great ideas seem strange at first. When our researchers realized we could position a cauldron two hundred feet directly above our main portals, they began to see the possibilities of the greatest strategic defense system in the history of mankind.

The cauldron was expensive. We all knew a good defense was going to be costly. The cauldron was manufactured locally after procuring copper and brass from our mines, and it took—as is common knowledge—two years to complete. It is a beautiful thing capable of holding one hundred and ten gallons of oil. What we could not foresee was the expense and delay of building an armature. Well, of course, it's not enough to have a big pot, pretty as it may be; how are you going to pour its hot contents on your enemies? The construction of an adequate superstructure for the apparatus required dear time: another year during which the Huns and the Exogoths were raiding our village almost weekly. Let me ask you to remember that era—was that any fun?

I want to emphasize that we were committed to this program—and we remain committed. But at every turn we've met problems that our researchers could not—regardless of their intelligence and intuition—have foreseen. For instance: how were we to get a nineteen-hundred-pound brass cauldron onto the roof? When had such a question been asked before? And at each of these impossible challenges, our boiling oil teams have come up with solutions. The cauldron was raised to the roof by means of a custom-designed net and hoist including a rope four inches in diameter which was woven on the spot under less than ideal conditions as the Retrogoths and the Niligoths plundered our village almost incessantly during the cauldron's four-month ascent. To our great and everlasting credit, we did not drop the pot. The superstructure for the pouring device was dropped once, but it was easily repaired on-site, two hundred feet above the village steps.

That was quite a moment, and I remember it well. Standing on the roof by that gleaming symbol of our impending safety, a bright brass (and a few lesser metals) beacon to the world that we were not going to take it anymore. The wind carried up to us the cries of villagers being carried away by either the Maxigoths or the Minigoths, it was hard to tell. But there we stood, and as I felt the wind in my hair and watched the sporadic procession of home furnishings being carried out of our violated gates, I knew we were perched on the edge of a new epoch.

Well, there was some excitement; we began at once. We started a fire under the cauldron and knew we would all soon be safe. At that point I made a mistake, which I now readily admit. In the utter ebullience of the moment I called down—I did not "scream maniacally" as was reported—I called down that *it would not be long*, and I probably shouldn't have, because it may have led some of our citizenry to lower their guard. It was a mistake. I admit it. There were, as we found out almost immediately, still some bugs to be worked out of the program. For instance, there had never been a fire on top of the entry tower before, and yes, as everyone is aware, we had to spend more time than we really wanted containing the blaze, fueled as it was by the fresh high winds and the tower's wooden shingles. But I hasten to add that the damage was moderate, as moderate as a four-hour fire could be, and the billowing black smoke surely gave further intruders lurking in the hills pause as they considered finding any spoils in our ashes!

But throughout this relentless series of setbacks, pitfalls, and rooftop fires, there has been a hard core of us absolutely dedicated to doing what we wanted to do, and that was to splash scalding oil onto intruders as they pried or battered yet again at our old damaged gates. To us a little fire on the rooftop was of no consequence, a fribble, a tiny obstacle to be stepped over with an easy stride. Were we tired? Were we dirty? Were some of us burned and cranky? No matter! We were committed. And so the next day, the first quiet day we'd had in this village in months, that same sooty cadre stood in the warm ashes high above the entry steps and tried again. We knew— as we know right now—that our enemies are manifold and voracious and generally rude and persistent, and we wanted to be ready.

But tell me this: where does one find out how soon before an enemy attack to put the oil on to boil? Does anyone know? Let me assure you it is not in any book! We were writing the book!

We were vigilant. We squinted at the horizon all day long. And when we first saw the dust in the foothills we refired our cauldron, using wood which had been elevated through the night in woven baskets. Even speaking about it here today, I can feel the excitement stirring in my heart. The orange flames licked the sides of the brass container hungrily as if in concert with our own desperate desire for security and revenge. In the distance I could see the phalanx of Visigoths marching toward us like a warship through a sea of dust, and in my soul I pitied them and the end toward which they so steadfastly hastened. They seemed the very incarnation of mistake, their dreams of a day abusing our friends and families and of petty arsony and lewd public behavior about to be extinguished in one gorgeous wash of searing oil! I was beside myself.

It is important to know now that everyone on the roof that day exhibited orderly and methodical behavior. There was professional conduct of the first magnitude. There was no wild screaming or cursing or even the kind of sarcastic chuckling which you might expect in those about to enjoy a well-deserved and long-delayed victory. The problems of the day were not attributable to inappropriate deportment. My staff was good. It was when the Visigoths had approached close enough that we could see their cruel eyes and we could read the savage and misspelled tattoos that I realized our error. At that time I put my hand on the smooth side of our beautiful cauldron and found it only vaguely warm. Lukewarm. Tepid.

We had not known then what we now know. *We need to put the oil on sooner.*

It was my decision and my decision alone to do what we did, and that was to pour the warm oil on our enemies as they milled about the front gates, hammering at it with their truncheons.

Now this is where my report diverges from so many of the popular accounts. We have heard it said that the warm oil served as a stimulant to the attack that followed, the attack I alluded to earlier in which the criminal activity seemed even more animated than usual in the minds of some of our townspeople. Let me say first: I was an eyewitness. I gave the order to pour the oil and I witnessed its descent. I am happy and proud to report that the oil hit its target with an accuracy and completeness I could have only dreamed of. We got them all. There was oil everywhere. We soaked them, we coated them, we covered them in a lustrous layer of oil. Unfortunately, as everyone knows, it was only warm. Their immediate reaction was also what I had hoped for: surprise and panic. This, however, lasted about one second. Then several of them looked up into my face and began waving their fists in what I could only take as a tribute. And then, yes, they did become quite agitated anew, recommencing their assault on the weary planks of our patchwork gates. Some have said that they were on the verge of abandoning their attack before the oil was cast upon them, which I assure you is not true.

As to the attack that followed, it was no different in magnitude or intensity from any of the dozens we suffer every year. It may have seemed more odd or extreme since the perpetrators were greasy and thereby more offensive, and they did take every stick of furniture left in the village, including the pews from the church, every chair in the great hall, and four milking stools, the last four, from the dairy.

But I for one am simply tired of hearing about the slippery stain on the village steps. Yes, there is a bit of a mess, and yes, some of it seems to be permanent. My team removed what they could with salt and talc all this week. All I'll say now is watch your step as you come and go; in my mind it's a small inconvenience to pay for a perfect weapon system.

So, we've had our trial run. We gathered a lot of data. And you all know we'll be ready next time. We are going to get to do what we wanted to do. We will vex and repel our enemies with boiling oil. In the meantime, who needs furniture? We have a project! We need the determination not to lose the dream, and we need a lot of firewood. They will come again. You know it and I know it, and let's simply commit ourselves to making sure that the oil, when it falls, is very hot.

THE CHROMIUM HOOK

JACK CRAMBLE

EVERYBODY KNOWS this, that we pulled in the driveway and I found the hook when I went around to Jill's door. It was caught in the door handle, hanging there like I don't know what. I didn't know what it was at first, but when Jill got out she knew, and she started screaming, for which I don't blame her. Her father came out and made like where had we been and did we know it was almost one o'clock. He's a good guy, but under real pressure, I guess, since his wife had her troubles. Anyway, he looks at the hook, and then he looks Jill over real good, suspicious-like, like we'd been up to something, which we definitely had not. We had been, as everybody knows, up at Conversation Point with our debate files, and the time got away from us. I was helping her with her arguments, asking questions, like that, things like, "What are the drawbacks of an international nuclear-test-ban treaty?" And she would fish around in her file box and try to find the answer. Her one shot at college is the debate team, and their big meet with Northwoods was a week from that Saturday. It was Mr. Royaltuber who called the police, and the word got out.

JILL ROYALTUBER

IT WAS the scaredest I've ever been, and when I think of how close that homicidal maniac came to getting us and doing whatever he was going to do with that big vicious hook, my blood runs cold. Jack was really brave. He wanted to get out of the car after we heard the first noises, the scrapings, and see what it was, but I wouldn't let him. Sometimes boys just don't have any sense. We'd already heard about the escaped homicidal maniac on the radio. They'd interrupted *Wild Johnny Hateras's Top Twenty Country Countdown* with the news bulletin that some one-armed madman had escaped the loony bin on Demon Hill and was sort of armed and dangerous. And of course Discussion Point is right there by the iron fence of the nuthouse. We had gone up to Discussion Point to work through some problems I'd been having since my mom left, and Jack was talking to me about being strong and saying he'd be there for me and not to get too depressed and to look on the sunny side of things, that Mom was better off in the hospital—she certainly seemed happier. So Jack was being that thing, supportive, which I love. A boyfriend who is captain of football is one thing, and a boyfriend who is captain of football and supportive is another. But I kept him from getting out of the car after we heard the noises. The wind had come up a little and it was dark as dark, and I said, "Let's just get out of here." Jack wasn't afraid. He wanted to stay. But I told him it was late, and then we heard the scratching closer, against the car, and it felt like it was right on my bare spine. "Pull out!" I yelled, and he gunned the engine of his Ford—it's a wonderful car, which he did all the work on—and we headed for home.

DR. STEWART NARKENPIE, DIRECTOR, THE SPINARD PSYCHIATRIC INSTITUTE

IT IS NOT a loony bin. It is not a nuthouse or a funny farm. It's not even an insane asylum. It is, as I've been telling everyone in this community for the twenty-two years I've lived here, the Spinard Psychiatric Institute, a center for the treatment of psychological disorders. It is a medical hospital, the building and grounds of which occupy just under two hundred acres on the top of Decatur Hill, and it employs thirty-eight citizens from the lovely town of Griggs, including Mr. Howard Lugdrum, who was injured seriously in last week's incident. I have spoken to the Rotary Club once a year for forever, as well as to the Lions and the Elks and the Junior Achievement and the graduating class of the high school and the Vocational Outreach in the Griggs Middle School, explaining what we do and how we do it and that the Spinard Psychiatric Institute is not a loony bin or any other kind of bin, and I am not getting through. It is not a bin! Even though a large portion of our community has had family and friends enter the Institute as patients only to be returned to the community after treatment in better shape than before, and even though most everybody has visited the grounds—if not for personal reasons, then certainly at our annual Community Picnic on the South Lawn—there still persists this incurable sense that once you pass under the Spinard stone arch you are entering the twilight zone. Yes, we do have a big iron fence, because some of our patients get confused and could possibly wander away, and yes, the buildings, some of them, have bars over the windows for the safety of our patients, and some of our patients wear restraints when out-of-doors, but they are dangerous to no one but themselves. I cannot say how weary I am of setting the record straight. It is not a nuthouse, and I am not a mad scientist. We don't have any mad scientists, mad professors, or mad doctors. No one's mad. We don't use that term. We do have some disturbed patients, but we're treating them, and there is a chance—with rest counseling, and medication—that they will get better. We do not perform operations except as they become medically necessary. We had an appendectomy last fall. We do not operate on the brain. We do not—as the high school paper suggests regularly—do brain transplants, dissections, or enlargements. Most recently I had to speak with Wild Johnny Hateras at KGRG, the radio station in Griggs, about the prank news bulletin on Halloween, which is just the kind of thing that keeps any understanding between the Institute and the town in tatters and is responsible, I think, for the harm resulting from last Saturday's incident, about which we've heard so much.

MR. HOWARD LUGDRUM

IT HURT. Don't you think that hurt? Everybody talks about the kids: oh, they were scared, they were frightened and nervous, oh, they were terrified. Well, think about it—had two trespassers yanked off *their* prosthesis? In the course of doing their job, were either of *them* pulled from their feet and dragged till an arm came off, and left there tumbling in the dirt? As it turns out, I was lucky I was wearing my simple hook and the straps broke; if I'd been wearing my regular armature, those two little criminals would have dragged me to death, and we'd have murder here instead of reckless endangerment.

ROD BUDDAROCK

IF ANYBODY, one person, says anything, one thing, about my buddy Jack Cramble being up there at Passion Point to do anything, one thing, besides help little Jill Royaltuber with family problems, such as they are, I'll find that person and use his lying butt to wipe up Main Street. I'm not joking here. I know Jack from being co-captain of football, and I know what I'm saying. Of course, he could have come to the team party out at the Landing, but here was a girl who had some troubles and he was there to help. There's been a lot of talk about what they were really doing. Jack made that crack about debate, which was too bad, because he couldn't get within two miles of the debate team—I'm a better debater than Jack and Jill put together—but he only said that to protect Jill's reputation, such as it is. She's a nice girl, but a little confused. It was only last year that her mom went bonkers, and Jill herself went a little nuts about that time, but she is no slut. If anybody, one person, says anything about Jill Royaltuber being a wide-mouthed, round-heeled slut, I'll find that person and trouble will certainly rain down upon his or her head like hot shit from Mars.

MR. HOWARD LUGDRUM

I'D SEEN the car before. It's a two-door Ford, blue and white. There are five or six cars I see there by our north fence in the pine grove. They bring their girlfriends up from town in the good weather, and we find the empty beer bottles and condoms. The kids call it Passion Point. We had a timed light system there until a few years ago, but the Environmental Protection Agency asked us to dismantle it because of the Weaver's bat, a protected species that hunts there at night. The deal about the parking is that the grove is our property and we stand liable for any harm. Two kids climb in the backseat of some old clunker with a faulty exhaust and the Institute would be sued until the thirteenth of never. I mean, these are kids at night in old cars. What we've done is put the grove on the watchman's tour, and one of us takes the big flashlight and shines it on a few bare butts every night of the week. Until last week, it's been kind of funny—I mean, you see some white rear end hop up, and then the cars start up and wheel out like scurrying rats. Once interrupted, they don't come back. Until the next night. Like I said, these are kids.

I'm in charge of the buildings and grounds at the Institute, and I like my work there; it's been a good place to me.

SHERIFF CURTIS MANSARACK

THE MOST frequently asked question is "When you bust a beer bust, do you keep the beer?" For Pete's sake. Every weekend I roust one or two of these high school beer parties, most often on the hill or down at Ander's Landing. Sometimes, though, there'll be a complaint and I'll be called to a private residence. A lot of these kids know me by now, and they know that about eleven-thirty old Sheriff Mansarack will slip up in his cruiser and flash the lights long enough for every drunk sophomore to run into the bushes so that I can cite the two or three seniors too drunk to flee.

I was in the middle of such a raid last Saturday night, Halloween, a night when I know for a sure fact that there is going to be trouble, and I got the call from Oleena Weenz, our dispatcher. There had been, in her words, a "vicious assault by a pervert," and she directed me to the address on Eider Street where I found Mr. Rick Royaltuber and the two young people and heard the story. I knew the boy, Jack Cramble, and had seen him play football earlier that night when Griggs beat Bark City, and I was kind of surprised that he wasn't down with the rest of the team drinking beer at the Landing. I also knew Mr. Royaltuber, as I had taken the call when his wife went off the deep end a year ago. When a guy helps you subdue his wife and pries her fingers off a rusty pair of kitchen scissors while you hold her kicking and screaming on your lap on the front porch in front of all the neighborhood, you remember him. That was a bad deal, embarrassing for me to get caught off guard. I mean, she looked normal. I hadn't seen the scissors. And it was bad for old Royaltuber too, with her shrieking out about him porking what's-her-name, the wife of old Dr. Dizzy up at the loony bin, and rattling those scissors at us. Hey, sometimes kitchen tools are the worst. And she was strong.

Anyway, I spoke to Mr. Royaltuber and I saw the hook there on the car door. It was a regular artificial arm, straps and all, one of them torn, and it scared me too. I mean, when that thing came off, it had to hurt. I took the report, but it wasn't all in line, and to tell the truth neither was the front of the Royaltuber girl's shirt. She was misbuttoned the way you are after putting away your playthings in a hurry.

The Cramble boy kept at me to get back up there right away before the pervert got somebody else, saying things like Wasn't I the sheriff? Wasn't I supposed to do something? Well, I could see *he* wanted to do something, something that had been interrupted up at Passion Point, so I just told them all it was going to be all right, which it was, and I headed back to the Landing, where I was able to run off about ten kids and confiscate a case and a half of Castle Moat, which is not my favorite, but it'll do.

MR. HOWARD LUGDRUM

I NEVER married. Years ago, after my accident, I changed my plans about a career in tennis and went up to college near Brippert and got into their vocational-ed program in hotel management.

I was pretty numbed out after Cassie's family moved who knows where. This is a long time ago now. Her girlfriend Maggie Rayne hung around with me for a while, and then I think she saw the limits of a man with one hand and moved on. Her father was a professor at the medical school, and I was clearly outclassed. So, anyway, I never married. I didn't realize the torch was still lit—or really how alive I could feel—until I saw Cassie again a year ago, when she was carried up here kicking and screaming, spitting and cursing, her eyes red and her hair wild, the most beautiful thing I've seen in, let's see, seventeen years.

MRS. MARGARET RAYNE NARKENPIE

I HAD not planned on a mountaintop in Bushville. I had not actually thought I would—after seven years of graduate study and three years at the Highborn Academy—find myself banished to the left-hand districts of Forsaken Acres, dressing for dinner at the macaroni-and-cheese outlet, opting for the creamed tuna on special nights. I had lived in a wasteland as a girl, and I thought I was through with it. Let's just say, for the sake of argument, that marrying the highest-ranking doctor in my father's finest class, a tall, good-looking psychiatrist of sterling promise who could have written his ticket anywhere in the civilized world, I was expecting to live in a place where there was more than one Quicky Freeze and a Video Hut. I had dared to think London, New York, even Albuquerque. I had not imagined Griggs. My husband—who has his Institute and his staff and his many duties and all his important vision for psychiatric health care—can't even see Griggs. So, the way I live here and whom I associate with in this outpost of desolation is, it would seem to me, my business.

Mr. Royaltuber handles all the television and monitor maintenance and repair for the Spinard Institute. He has also helped us with the satellite dish and the cable connections we use at home. He's a nice man, and I have lunch with him from time to time. We've become, under the circumstances and in this barren place, friends. I met his wife only once, when I was at his home. It was less than pleasant.

MR. WILD JOHNNY HATERAS, RADIO PERSONALITY, KGRG

IF ANYBODY pretends to be hurt or surprised by our little prank, they're bad actors. Everybody in this burg knows what we do on Halloween with the "important news bulletin" and the hook. We've been doing it since I started spinning platters here twelve years ago. Nick goes out and slips a dozen of the phony hooks on car doors, and then I interrupt the program with my announcement about the maniac. I think of it as our little annual contribution to birth control, all those kids jumping up when I cut into "Unchained Melody" with my homicide-and-hook news brief. When we started, we used those plastic hooks from the costume shop in Orpenhook, but, sad to say, gang, it's impossible to scare anybody anymore with a plastic hook. Don't tell *me* the world's a better place. So now we get them in Bark City, little steel hooks that at least look authentic for a few minutes. But this will probably be the last year we send Nick out with anything at all, because of the trouble up by the nuthouse, and because he's afraid of getting shot. Can you believe that? You go out on Halloween to have a little fun anymore and you run a good chance of getting plugged? Hey, Griggs, wake up, all is not well. If you can't harass the teenagers without running the risk of getting killed, this town is in trouble.

MRS. CASSIE ROYALTUBER

IT'S FUNNY what people think. You try to put a pair of kitchen scissors in the doctor's wife one afternoon and they think (a) you're crazy, or (b) you're desperately in love with your sweet husband, or (c) you caught her in bed with your husband, with whom she's been sleeping for two years, and therefore you're just slow to catch on, since everybody, absolutely everybody else in this village, which is not exactly full of geniuses, has known about the affair since the first week, or (d) that you're all three: crazy, in love, and slow to catch on.

Well, it is simply exhilarating to be liberated from (a) the slings and (b) the arrows of public opinion and to take it for what it is, which is (a) irrelevant and (b) as absolutely wrong as it can be.

Who in their right mind—which is where I find myself—would consider that the television repairman's wife might have another reason? Who would grant the past its due, the vast sweeping privilege of history and justice? Who would guess that (a) I knew Mrs. Narkenpie before she and her doctor moved to Griggs, in fact before she was Mrs. Narkenpie, when she was simply Margaret Rayne, and that (b) she was the prime reason I had been forcibly removed from my one true love so many years ago, and that (c) I had chosen those scissors not for the convenience of their being right there in the drawer but because they were appropriate—I wanted to cut her the way she cut my Howard.

And the things I screamed I screamed on purpose. How are you going to get into the loony bin unless they think you're loony?

ROD BUDDAROCK

WHAT HE does is take the beer. This seems to be his only deal as a cop, to drive around on weekends and take beer from kids. And he keeps the beer. Some kids just go ahead and buy his brand, which is the Rocary Red Ale—fifteen dollars a case at any Ale and Mail. Isn't there any crime to stop? How do you get a job like that—free car and free beer? Hey, I'll sign up. As is, I'm glad I'm a senior and out of here next spring. He comes into our Halloween party last Saturday, the same night that there's a maniac with a hook roaming all over Griggs, attacking kids, slashing at everything in sight, and he busts us, scaring everybody shitless and causing Ardeen Roster to break her nose running away in the bushes, and he writes *me* a ticket for it. Then, while some monster with one arm has practically taken over the whole town, he takes our beer, and there's still about three and a half cases of Red Pelican—which you have to drive to Orpenhook to even find—so I'm forced to live the rest of my life picturing this civic wart pounding down our Pelicans every afternoon on his deck while he dreams up his next law enforcement strategy. Life is hard on the young, man, count on it.

MR. HOWARD LUGDRUM

I'M GOING to need to get my hook back. There's a lot of work up here that requires two hands. We've got leaves to rake, tons, and a lot of other seasonal preventive maintenance—storm windows, snowplow prep work—and I can't load and deliver firewood effectively without my prosthesis. I'd appreciate its return as soon as possible.

MR. RICK ROYALTUBER

CASSIE WAS never even cranky all these years. I mean, of all people, she's the last I'd expect to crack up. It was tough to send her off. It hurt me to put her up on the hill, but there it was, we couldn't deny she'd lost control of her senses when she tried to harm Mrs. Narkenpie. How do you think I feel knowing she's up there, locked up in a nuthouse night and day, wearing a straitjacket or what-have-you. But the doctor said it was for the best, and I believe him. These things, so many of them, are beyond ordinary folks.

SHERIFF CURTIS MANSARACK

INCIDENTAL TO my call on the Royaltubers Halloween night, I had the Cramble boy pop open his trunk, and I found the following:

nylon rope, 100 yards
hammer
hatchet
power screwdriver
small grappling hook
duct tape, two rolls
canvas, 12x12
flashlights, two
pepper spray, two canisters
bolt cutters
doritos, large bag, taco-flavored

JILL ROYALTUBER

I NEVER saw his face. I never saw anything really. All I heard was some vibrations, I guess—maybe footsteps in the leaves, and then a kind of metallic clicking like scritch, scritch, and I was begging Jack to pull out, to just pull out of there. We hadn't been doing anything. Jack had hurt his hand in the game against Bark City, and I had been massaging that. We were trying to relax.

MRS. CASSIE ROYALTUBER

I LOVED Howard from Moment Number One, when we met seventeen years ago, on the night of the construction of our high school's homecoming float, which was a big ram. We were the Cragview Rams. He and I were part of the tissue brigade, two dozen kids handing Kleenex each to each in a line that ended at the chicken-wire sculpture, which slowly filled with the red, white, and blue paper. He was standing next to me and our hands touched once a second as the tissue flowed through us, my left hand, his right hand, which he would lose that spring, touch, touch, touch. He was the first tender boy I ever knew, and I was happy when he invited me to the homecoming dance. There is no need to explain every delicate step of that fall, Moment Number Two and Moment Number Three, except to say that when we gave our hearts, we gave our hearts completely, and everything else followed. It was the year I died and went to heaven for a while.

Moment Number Four I discovered that I was pregnant, and even that seemed magical, until my father found out thanks to my jealous classmate, wicked Maggie Rayne, who also told him that Howard and I always met after school in the Knopdish junkyard. And it was there, Moment Number Five, that my father found us in the rear seat of an old VW van, which had been like a haven for us, and he yanked me out onto the ground and slammed that rusty door forever, or so I thought, on my one good thing—Howard Lugdrum.

Howard, I heard, lost his arm in the "accident," and my father moved us far away, here to Griggs. The Moments now go unnumbered. Before the summer was over, young, handsome Ricky Royaltuber was coming round, and I didn't care, I did my part. I wasn't even there, and I guess I've been away a long time.

I didn't care when Maggie Rayne moved to town with her fancy doctor, and I didn't care that she went after and got Ricky. It freed me in a way. I can hardly remember who came and went in our house—Jill's friends, neighbors, boys.

But when I heard that the stars had relented and uncrossed and again lined up my way, that Howard had come to Griggs, working at this very loony bin in which I now live, I woke up, and in a major way. Afternoons, he comes in with a cup of tea, and we sit and he lets me hold it while we talk. These days are sweet days again, full of sweet moments. Even now I can see him through these bars, cleaning the windows of the van with the big circles of his left hand.

JACK CRAMBLE

I DON'T care who knows it now: I was going to spring her. Last
year, when I was a nobody from nowhere, she was the only person
in town who would listen. I was the new kid in town then, not captain of the football team, and she was always there for me. I told her
everything. It was easier and better than talking to my own folks,
and she was different, a woman, more woman than anybody I'll ever
meet again. I loved her and I loved the way she talked, putting my
problems in perspective a, b, c, or 1, 2, 3. To keep seeing her I started
dating that dipweed Jill, who has been nothing but a pain in the
neck with all her "sharing," "caring," and "daring." Such a girl. Such
a needy little girl. Just thinking about her makes my skin crawl. Let's
go up to the Point, she'd say, so she could crawl all over me. I'll tell
you flat, she knows nothing about being a real woman like her
mother. We went up there on Halloween after the game so I could
scope out the fence and the approach to Cassie's room. The plan was
for midnight. Of course, Jill jumped me when we parked, and lucky
for me the watchman came along or I'd have had to go all the way.
As it was, her pants were already to her ankles, and he got a hell of
a view of her bare ass in the window.

But it hasn't deterred me. Cassie and I are meant to be together,
that's clear, regardless of the age difference. I'm going back up there
in a night or two and busting her out. Football season's over, and it's
time to be me. My heart knows what to do, and it says, Scale the
wall, break her out!

MR. HOWARD LUGDRUM

SHE WAS here almost a year before she told me. Though I knew
instantly we'd pick up where we left off, my heart steady through the
years to the one woman I loved, Cassie waited to be sure it was still
me, I guess, that a man with one arm could be trusted. So last week

we were at tea in her room after her counseling session, and she looked at me funny and told me something amazing: I have a daughter! A daughter! Having Cassie back in my life after so long seemed almost too much for me to bear, and now . . . a child. Well, not a child but a young woman. And, Cassie told me, I could see her if I went by the north pine grove sometime after nine that night, Halloween. I'd see a blue-and-white Ford and my daughter would be in it! It was all I could do to get the afternoon hours out of the way; it was a waiting like no waiting I have ever known. My daughter! As it happened, I don't know if I saw her or not, just somebody's butt in the moonlight.

SHERIFF CURTIS MANSARACK

FALL IN Griggs is a good thing: the leaves change color and there's football and the smell of the first wood fires. Halloween's my last big chance to score a beer bust, and I almost never miss. I didn't miss this year. Every year there's a hook, sometimes more than one, and it takes a week or two for things to quiet down. I don't mind the hooks; the waxed windows are worse. I'd trade the waxed windows for two more hooks. Soon it will snow and life gets real easy: there's no cop better than old Jack Frost.

PERSON BEHIND LAST TREE IN THE TWILIGHT

AT NIGHT, as I drift through these woods, I tap my hook from time to time against my leg and the feel of the hard iron spurs me on past fence and fern, past drooping branches and the cobbed underbrush. What I need is an older-model American car parked alone in the dark, one with a grip handle I can snare. The lift handles are no good, and everything anymore has the aerodynamic lift handles. I want a '60 Fairlane or a '58 Chevrolet, a car with bench seats big enough for two young people to get comfortable and tangle up their clothing and their brain waves so that they forget the dark, the woods, the person with a hook, every Halloween, approaching through the leaves.

A NOTE ON THE TYPE

N O ALPHABET comes along full grown. A period of development is required for the individual letters to bloom and then another period for them to adjust to their place in the entire set, and sometimes this period can be a few weeks or it can be a lifetime. No quality font maker ever sat down and wrote out A to Z just like that. It doesn't happen. Getting Ray Bold right required five months, these last five months, an intense creative period for me which has included my ten-week escape from the state facilities at Windchime, Nevada, and my return here one week ago. Though I have always continued sharpening my letters while incarcerated, most of the real development of Ray Bold occurred while I was on the outside, actively eluding the authorities. There's a kind of energy in the out-of-doors, moving primarily along the sides of things, always hungry, sleeping thinly in hard places, that awakens in me the primal desire toward print.

And though Ray Bold is my best typeface and the culmination of my work in the field, I should explain it is also my last—for the reasons this note on the type will illuminate. I started this whole thing in the first place because I had been given some time at the Fort

Nippers Juvenile Facility in Colorado—two months for reckless endangerment, which is what they call Grand Theft Auto when you first start in at it, and I was rooming with Little Ricky Grudnaut, who had only just commenced his life as an arsonist by burning down all four barns in the nearby town of Ulna in a single night the previous February. Juvenile facilities, as you can imagine, are prime locations for meeting famous criminals early in their careers, and Little Ricky went on, as everyone now knows, to burn down eleven Chicken Gigundo franchise outlets before he was apprehended on fire himself in Napkin, Oklahoma, and asked to be extinguished.

But impulsive and poultry-phobic as he may have become later, Little Ricky Grudnaut gave me some valuable advice so many years ago. I'd moped around our cell for a week—it was really a kind of dorm room—staring at this and that, and he looked up from the tattoo he was etching in his forearm with an old car key. It was Satan's head, he told me, and it was pretty red, but it only looked like some big face with real bad hair—and he said, "Look, Ray, get something to do or you'll lose it. Make something up." He threw me then my first instrument, a green golf pencil he'd had hidden in his shoe.

It was there in Fort Nippers, fresh from the brutality of my own household, that I began the doodling that would evolve into these many alphabets which I've used to measure each of my unauthorized sorties from state-sponsored facilities. Little Ricky Grudnaut saw my first *R* that day and was encouraging. "It ain't the devil," he said, "but it's a start."

I HAVE decided to accept the offer of reduced charges for full disclosure of how and where I sustained my escape. In Windchime I had been sharing a cell with Bobby Lee Swinghammer, the boxer and public enemy, who had battered so many officials during his divorce proceedings last year in Carson City. Bobby Lee was not happy to have a lowly car thief in his cell and he had even less patience with my alphabets. I tried to explain to him that I wasn't simply a car thief, that I was now, in the words of the court, "an habitual criminal" (though my only crime had been to steal cars which I had been doing for years and years), and I tried to show him what I was working on with Ray Bold. Bobby Lee Swinghammer's comment was that it looked "piss plain," and it irked him so badly that he then showed me in the next few weeks some of his own lettercraft. These were primarily the initials *B* and *L* and *S* that he had worked on while on the telephone with his attorney. And they are perfect examples of what is wrong with any font that comes to life in prison.

The design is a result of too much time. I've seen them in every facility in which I have resided, these letters too cute to read, I mean flat-out baroque. Serifs on the *T*'s that weigh ten pounds; Bobby Lee had beaked serifs on his *S*'s that were big as shoes. His *B* was three-dimensional, ten feet deep, a *B* you could move into, four rooms and a bath on the first floor alone. I mean he had all afternoon while his lawyer said, "We'll see" a dozen different ways, why not do some gingerbread, some decoration? I kept my remarks to a minimum. But I've seen a lot of this, graffiti so ornate you couldn't find the letters in the words. And what all of that is about is one thing and it's *having time*. I respect it and I understand it—a lot of my colleagues have got plenty of time, and now I've got some again too, but it's a style that is just not for me.

I became a car thief because it seemed a quick and efficient way to get away from my father's fists, and I became a font maker because I was caught. After my very first arrest—I'd taken a red Firebird from in front of a 7-Eleven—in fact in my first alphabet, made with a golf pencil, I tried my hand at serification. I was thirteen and I didn't know any better. These were pretty letters. I mean, they had a kind of beauty. I filigreed the *C*'s and *G*'s and the *Q* until they looked like they were choking on lace. But what? They stood there these letters so tricked up you wouldn't take them out of the house, too much makeup, and you knew they weren't any good. For me, that is. You put a shadow line along the stem of an R and then beak the tail, it's too heavy to move.

The initials that Bobby Lee Swinghammer had been carving into the back of his hand with a Motel 6 ballpoint pen looked like monuments. You could visit them, but they were going absolutely nowhere.

And that's what I wanted in this last one, Ray Bold, a font that says "movement." I mean, I was taking it with me and I was going to use it, essentially, on the run. Bobby Lee was right: it is plain but it can travel light.

I want to make it clear right here, though Bobby Lee and I had our differences and he did on occasion pummel me about the head and upper trunk (not as hard as he could have, god knows), he is not the reason I escaped from Windchime. I have escaped, as the documents point out, eleven times from various facilities throughout this part of the west, and it was never because of any individual cellmate, though Bobby Lee was one of the most animated I've encountered. I like him as a person, and I'm pleased that his appeal is being heard and that soon he will be resuming his life as an athlete.

I walked out of Windchime because I had the chance. I found that lab coat folded over the handrail on our stairs. Then, dressed as a medical technician, with my hair parted right down the middle, I walked out of there one afternoon, carrying a clipboard I'd made myself in shop, and which is, I'll admit right here, the single most powerful accessory to any costume. You carry a clipboard, they won't mess with you.

Anyway, that windy spring day I had no idea of the direction this new alphabet would take. I knew I would begin writing; everybody knew that. I always do it. I've been doing it for more than twenty years. When my father backhanded me for the last time, I fled the place but not before making my *Ray* on his sedan with the edge of a nickel. It wasn't great, and I don't care to write with money as a rule, but it was me, my instinct for letter-craft at the very start.

I also knew I'd be spending plenty of time in the wilderness, the high desert there around Windchime and the forests as they reach into Idaho and the world beyond. I know now that, yes, landscape did have a clear effect on the development of Ray Bold, the broad clean vistas of Nevada, the residual chill those first few April nights, and the sharp chunk of flint I selected to inscribe my name on a stock tank near Popknock. That first *Ray* showed many clues about the alphabet to come: the *R* (and the *R* is very dear to me, of course) made in a single stroke (the stem bolder than the tail); the small case *a*, unclosed; and the capital *Y*, which resembles an *X*. These earmarks of early Ray Bold would be repeated again and again in my travels— the single stroke, the open letter, the imprecise armature. To me they all say one thing: energy.

I made that *Ray* just about nightfall the second night, and I was fairly sure the shepherd might have seen me cross open ground from a rocky bluff to the tank, and so, writing there in the near dark on the heavily oxidized old steel tank while I knelt on the sharp stones and breathed hard from the run (I'd had little exercise at Windchime), I was scared and happy at once, which as anyone knows are the perfect conditions under which to write your name. *Ray.* It was a beginning.

"Why do it?" they say. "You want to be famous?" It is a question so wrongheaded that it kind of hurts. Because what I do, I do for myself. Most of the time you're out there in some dumpster behind the Royal Food in Triplet or you're sitting in a culvert in Marvin or in a boxcar on a siding in Old Delphi (all places I've been) and what you make, you better make for yourself. There aren't a whole lot of people going to come along and appreciate the understated loop on your *g* or the precision of any of your descenders. I mean, that's the way I figured it. When I fell into that dumpster in Triplet I was scratched and bleeding from hurrying with a barbed-wire fence, and I sat there on the old produce looking at the metal side of that bin, and then after I'd pried a tenpenny nail from a wooden melon crate I made my *Ray*, the best I knew how, knowing only I would see it. And in poor light. I made it for myself. It existed for a moment and then I heard the dogs and I was on the run again.

There was once a week later when I took that gray LeBaron in

Marvin and it ran out of gas almost immediately, midtown, right opposite the Blue Ribbon Hardware, and I could see the town cop cruising up behind, and I took off on foot. And I can run when there's a reason, but as I run I always think, as I was thinking that day: where would I make my *Ray*? The two are linked with me: to run is to write. That day after about half a mile, I crawled into a canal duct, a square cement tube with about four inches of water running through the bottom. And with a round rock as big as a grapefruit sitting in that cold irrigation water, I did it there: *Ray*. It wasn't for the critics and it wasn't for the press. They wouldn't be along this way. It was for me. And it was as pure a *Ray* as I've ever done. I couldn't find that place today with a compass.

At times like that when you're in the heat of creation, making your mark, you don't think about hanging a hairline serif on the *Y*. It seems pretty plainly what it is: an indulgence. Form should fit function, the man said, and I'm with him.

After Marvin, that night in the water, I got sick and slept two or three days in hayfields near there. As everyone knows I moved from there to that Tuffshed I lived in near Shutout for a week getting my strength back. The reports had me eating dog food, and I'll just say to that I ate some *dog food*, dry food, I think it was Yumpup, but there were also lots of nuts and berries in the vicinity and I enjoyed them as well.

Everyone also knows about the three families I met and traveled with briefly. The German couple's story just appeared in *Der Spielplotz* and so most of Germany and Austria are familiar with me and my typeface. I hope that their tale doesn't prevent other Europeans from visiting Yellowstone and talking with Americans at the photo-vistas. I'm still amused that they thought I was a university professor (because I talked a little about my work), but on a three-state, five-month run from the law you're bound to be misunderstood. The two American families seemed to have no difficulty believing they'd fallen into the hands of an escaped felon, and though I did interrupt their vacations, I thought we all had a fine time, and I returned all of their equipment except the one blue windbreaker in good condition.

THOUGH I have decided to tell my story, I don't see how it is going to help them catch the next guy. Because those last five weeks were not typical in the least. Fortunately, by the time I arrived in Sanction, Idaho, Ray Bold was mostly complete, for I lost interest in it for a while.

Walking through that town one evening, I took a blue Country Squire station wagon, the largest car I ever stole, from the gravel lot of the Farmers' Exchange. About a quarter mile later I discovered Mrs. Kathleen McKay in the back of the vehicle among her gear. When you find a woman in the car you're stealing, there is a good chance the law will view that as kidnapping, so when Mrs. McKay called out, "Now who is driving me home?" I answered, truthfully, "Just me, Ray." And at the four-way, when she said left, I turned left.

Now it is an odd thing to meet a widow in that way, and the month that followed, five weeks really, were odd too, and I'm just getting the handle on it now. Mrs. McKay's main interests were in painting pictures with oil paints and in fixing up the farm. Her place was 105 acres five miles out of Sanction and the house was very fine, being block and two stories with a steep metal snow roof. Her husband had farmed the little place, she said, but not very well. He had been a Mormon from a fine string of them, but he was a drinker and they'd had no children, and so the church, she said, had not been too sorry to let them go.

She told me all this while making my bed in the little outbuilding by the barn, and when she finished, she said, "Now I'm glad you're here, Ray. And I hope tomorrow you could help me repair the culvert."

I had thought it would be painting the barn, which was a grand building, faded but not peeling, or mowing the acres and acres of weeds, which I could see were full of rabbits. But no, it was replacing the culvert in the road to the house. It was generally collapsed along its length and rusted through in two big places. It was a hard crossing for any vehicle. Looking at it, I didn't really know where to start. I'd hid in plenty of culverts, mostly larger than this one, which was a thirty-inch corrugated-steel tube, but I'd never replaced one. The first thing, I started her old tractor, an International, and chained up to the ruined culvert and ripped it out of the ground like I don't know what. I mean, it was a satisfying start, and I'll just tell you right out, I was involved.

I trenched the throughway with a shovel, good work that took two days, and then I laid her shiny new culvert in there pretty as a piece of jewelry. I set it solid and then buried the thing and packed the road again so that there wasn't a hump, there wasn't a bump, there wasn't a ripple as you crossed. I spent an extra day dredging the ditch, but that was gilding the lily, and I was just showing off.

And you know what: she paid me with a pie. I'm not joking. I parked the tractor and hung up the shovel and on the way back to my room, she met me in the dooryard like some picture out of the *Farmer's Almanac*, which there were plenty of lying around, and she handed me an apple pie in a glass dish. It was warm and swollen up so the seams on the crosshatch piecrust were steaming.

Well, I don't know, but this was a little different period for old Ray. I already had this good feather bed in the old tack room and the smell of leather and the summer evenings, and now I had had six days of good work where I had been the boss and I had a glass pie dish in my hands in the open air of Idaho. What I'm saying here is that I was affected. All of this had affected me.

To tell the truth, kindness was a new thing. My father was a crude man who never hesitated to push a child to the ground. As a cop in the town of Brown River he was not amused to have a son who was a thief. And my mother had more than she could handle with five kids and preferred to travel with the Red Cross from flood to fire across the plains. And so, all these years, I've been a loner and happy at it I thought, until Mrs. McKay showed me her apple pie. Such a surprise, that tenderness. I had heard of such things before, but I honestly didn't think I was the type.

I ate the pie and that affected me, two warm pieces, and then I ate a piece cool in the morning for breakfast along with Mrs. McKay's coffee sitting over her checked tablecloth in the main house as another day came up to get the world, and I was affected further. I'm not making excuses, these are facts. When I stood up to go out and commence the mowing, Mrs. McKay said it could wait a couple of days. How'd she say it? Like this: "Ray, I believe that could wait a day or two."

And that was that. It was three days when I came out of that house again; it didn't really make any difference to those weeds. I moved into the main house. I can barely talk about it except to say these were decent days to me. I rode a tractor through the sunny fields of Idaho, mowing, slowing from time to time to let the rabbits run ahead of the blades. And in the evenings there was washing up and hot meals and Mrs. McKay. The whole time, I mean every minute of every day of all five weeks, I never made a *Ray*. And this is a place with all that barnwood and a metal silo. I didn't scratch a letter big or small, and there were plenty of good places. Do you hear me? I'd lost the desire.

But, in the meantime I was a farmer, I guess, or a hired hand, something. I did take an interest in Mrs. McKay's paintings, which were portraits, I suppose, portraits of farmers in shirtsleeves and overalls, that kind of thing. They were good paintings in my opinion, I mean, you could tell what they were, and she had some twenty of the things on her sunporch, where she painted. She didn't paint any of the farmers' wives or animals or like that, but I could see her orange tractor in the back of three or four of the pictures. I like that, the real touches. A tractor way out behind some guy in a painting, say only three inches tall, adds a lot to it for me, especially when it is a tractor I know pretty well.

Mrs. McKay showed some of these portraits at the fair each year and had ribbons in her book. At night on that screen porch listening to the crickets and hearing the moths bump against the screens, I'd be sitting side by side with her looking at the scrapbook. I'd be tired and she would smell nice. I see now that I was in a kind of spell, as I said, I was affected. Times I sensed I was far gone, but could do nothing about it.

One night, for example, she turned to me in the bed and asked, "What is it you were in jail for, Ray? Were you a car thief?"

I wasn't even surprised by this and I answered with the truth, which is the way I've always answered questions. "Yes," I said. "I took a lot of cars. And I was caught for it."

"Why did you?"

"I took the first one to run away. I was young, a boy, and I liked having it, and as soon as I could I took another. And it became a habit for me. I've taken a lot of cars I didn't especially want or need. It's been my life in a way, right until the other week when I took your car, though I would have been just as pleased to walk or hitchhike." I had already told her that first day that I had been headed for Yellowstone National Park, though I didn't tell her I was planning on making *Ray*s all over the damn place.

After a while that night in the bed she just said, "I see." And she said it sweetly, sleepily, and I took it for what it was.

WELL, THIS dream doesn't last long. Five weeks is just a minute, really, and things began to shift in the final days. For one thing I came to understand that I was the person Mrs. McKay was painting now by the fact of the cut fields in the background. The face wasn't right, but maybe that's okay, because my face isn't right. In real life it's a little thin, off-center. She'd corrected that, which is her privilege as an artist, and further she'd put a dreamy look on the guy's face, which I suppose is a real nod toward accuracy.

"Are these your other men?" I asked her one night after supper. We'd spoken frankly from the outset and there was no need to change now, even though I had uncomfortable feelings about her artwork; it affected me now by making me sad. And I knew what was going on though I could not help myself. I could not go out in the yard and steal her car again and pick up my plans where I'd dropped them. I'll say it because I know it was true, I was beyond

affected, I was in love with Mrs. McKay. I could tell because I was
just full of hard wonder, a feeling I understood was jealously. I mean
there were almost two dozen paintings out there on the porch.

But my question hit a wrong note. Mrs. McKay looked at me
while she figured out what I was asking and then her face kind of
folded and she went up to bed. I didn't think as it was happening
to say I was sorry, though I was sorry in a second, sorrier really for
that remark than for any of the two hundred forty or so vehicles I
had taken, the inconvenience and damage that had often accompanied their disappearance. What followed was my worst night, I'd
say. I'm a car thief and I am not used to hurting people's feelings. If
I hurt their feelings, I'm not usually there to be part of it. And I
cared for Mrs. McKay in a way that was strange to me too. I sat
there until sunrise when I printed a little apology on a piece of
paper, squaring the letters in a way that felt quite odd, but they
were legible, which is what I was after: "I'm sorry for being a fool.
Please forgive me. Love, Ray." I made the Ray in cursive, something
I've done only three or four times in my whole life. Then I went out
to paint the barn.

It was midmorning when I turned from where I stood high on
that ladder painting the barn and saw the sheriff's two vehicles
where they were parked below me. I hadn't heard them because cars
didn't make any whump-whump crossing that new culvert. When I
saw those two Fords, I thought it would come back to me like a lost
dog—the need to run and run, and make a *Ray* around the first
hard corner. But it didn't. I looked down and saw the sheriff. There
were two kids in the other car, county deputies, and I descended the
ladder and didn't spill a drop of that paint. The sheriff greeted me
by name and I greeted him back. The men allowed me to seal the
gallon of barn red and to put my tools away. One of the kids helped
me with the ladder. None of them drew their sidearms and I appre-
ciated that.

It was as they were cuffing me that Mrs. McKay came out. She
came right up and took my arm and the men stepped back for a

moment. I will always remember her face there, so serious and pure. She said, "They were friends, Ray. Other men who have helped me keep this place together. I never gave any other man an apple pie, not even Mr. McKay." I loved her for saying that. She didn't have to. You have a woman make that kind of statement in broad daylight in front of the county officials and it's a bracing experience; it certainly braced me. I smiled there as happy as I'd been in this life. As the deputy helped me into the car, I realized that for the first time *ever* I was leaving home. I'd never really had one before.

"Save that paint," I said to Mrs. McKay. "I'll be back and finish the job." I saw her face and it has sustained me.

THEY HAD found me because I'd mowed. Think about it, you drive County Road 216 twice a week for a few years and then one day a hundred acres of milkweed, goldenrod, and what-have-you are trimmed like a city park. You'd make a phone call, which is what the sheriff had done. That's what change is, a clue.

SO, HERE I am in Windchime once again. I work at this second series of Ray Bold an hour or two a day. I can feel it evolving, that is, the font is a little more vertical than it was when I was on the outside and I'm thickening the stems. And I'm thinking it would look good with a spur serif—there's time. It doesn't have all the energy of Ray Bold I, but it's an alphabet with staying power, and it has a different purpose: it has to keep me busy for fifteen months, when I'll be going home to paint a barn and mow the fields. My days as a font maker are numbered.

My new cellmate, Victor Lee Peterson, the semi-famous archer and survivalist who extorted all that money from Harrah's in Reno recently and then put arrows in the radiators of so many state vehicles during his botched escape on horseback, has no time for my work. He leafs through the notebooks and shakes his head. He's spent three weeks now etching a target, five concentric circles on the wall, and I'll say this, he's got a steady hand and he's got a good understanding of symmetry. But, a target? He says the same thing about my letters. "The ABC's?" he said when he first saw my work. I smile at him. I kind of like him. He's an anarchist, but I think I can get through. As I said today: "Victor. You've got to treat it right. It's just the alphabet but sometimes it's all we've got."

NIGHTCAP

I WAS filing deeds, or rather, I had been filing deeds all day, and now I was taking a break to rest my head on the corner of my walnut desk and moan, when there was a knock at my door. My heart kicked in. People don't come to my office. From time to time folders are slipped under my door, but my clients don't come here. They call me and I copy something and send it to them. I'm an attorney.

Still and all, I hadn't been much of anything since Lily, the woman I loved, had—justifiably—asked me to move out three months ago. Simply, there were days of filing. I didn't moan that often, but I sat still for hours—hours I couldn't bill to anyone. I wanted Lily back, and the short of it is that I'm not going to get her back in this story. She's not even *in* this story. There's another woman in this story, and I wish I could say there's another man. But there isn't. It's me.

And now the heavy golden doorknob turned, and the woman entered. She wore a red print cowboy shirt and tight Levi's and under one arm she held a tiny maroon purse.

"Wrong room," I said. I had about four wrong rooms a week.

"Jack," she said, stepping forward. It was either not the wrong room or really the wrong room. "I'm Lynn LaMoine. Phyllis told me that if I came over there was a good chance I could talk you into going to the ball game tonight."

Well. She had me sitting down, half embarrassed about having my moaning interrupted, overheard, and her sister, Phyllis, Madame Cause-Effect, the most feared wrongful death attorney in the state, somehow knew that I was in limbo. I steered the middle road; it would be the last time. "I like baseball," I said. "But don't you have a husband?"

She nodded for a while, her mouth set. "Yeah," she said "I was married, but . . . maybe you remember Clark Dewar?"

"Sure," I said, "He's at Stover-Reynolds."

She kept nodding. "A lawyer." Then she said the thing that sealed this small chapter of my cheap fate. "Look, I just thought it might be fun to sit outside in the night and watch the game. I'm not good at being lonely. And I don't like the lessons."

It was a page from my book, and I jumped right in. "We could go to the game," I told her. "The Gulls aren't very good, but I've got an old classmate who's coach, and the park organist is worth the price of admission."

At this she smiled so that just the tips of her front teeth showed and stood on one leg so that her shape in those Levi's cut a hard curve against the door behind her. I heard myself saying, "And the beer is cold and it's not going to rain." I explained that I didn't have a car and gave her my address. As a rule I try not to view women as their parts, but—as I said—my moaning had been interrupted and the whole era has me in a hammerlock, and as Lynn turned, her backside involuntarily brought to mind a raw word from some corner of my youth: tail.

THAT NIGHT as I eased into her car I realized that this was the first time I had been in a car alone with a woman for four weeks. For a moment, nine or ten seconds, it actually felt like a date. Ten tops. Though I hadn't accomplished anything with my life so far, I was showered and shined and the water in my hair was evaporating in a promising way, and we were going to the ball game.

I looked over at Lynn in her black silky skirt and plum sweater. She looked like a lot of women today: good. I couldn't tell if this was the outfit of a woman in deep physical need or not. The outfit didn't look overtly sexual, or maybe it did but so did everything else. And then I realized that in the muggy backwash late in this sour month, I felt the faint but unmistakable physical stir of desire. I've got to admit, it was a relief. I took it as a sign of well-being, possibly good health. It was a feeling that well-directed could get me somewhere.

As we arrived, turning onto Thirteenth South under the jutting cement bleachers of Derks Field, I smiled at myself for being so simple. I glanced again at Lynn's wardrobe. You can't tell a thing anymore by the way people dress; it only helps in court. No one dresses like a prostitute these days, not even the prostitutes. And besides, in my eight-year-old Sears khakis and blanched blue Oxford-cloth shirt from an era so far bygone only the Everly Brothers would have remembered it, I looked like the person in trouble, the person in deep, inarticulate need.

IN THE ambiguity in which American ballparks exist, and they are a ragtag bunch, Derks Field is it. It is simply the loveliest garden of a small ballpark in the western United States. The stadium itself is primarily crumbling concrete poured the year I was born and named after John C. Derks, the sports editor at the *Tribune* who helped found the Pacific Coast League, Triple A Baseball, years ago. Though it could seat just over ten thousand, the average crowd these days was a scattered four hundred or so. This little Eden is situated, like most ballparks, in a kind of tough low-rent district spotted with small warehouses and storage yards for rusting heavy equipment.

As a boy I had come here and seen Dick Stuart play first base for the Bees; it was said he could hit the ball to Sugarhouse, which was about six miles into deep center. And my college team had played several games here my senior year while the campus field was being moved from behind the Medical School to Fort Douglas, and I mean Derks was a field that made you just want to take a few slides in the rich clay, dive for a liner in the lush grass.

Lynn and I parked in the back of the nearby All-Oil gas station and walked through a moderately threatening bevy of ten-year-old street kids milling outside the ticket office. When the game started, they would fan out across the street and wait to fight over foul balls, worth a buck apiece at the gate.

I love the moment of emerging into a baseball stadium, seeing all the new distance across the expanse of green grass made magical by the field lights bright in the incipient twilight. The bright cartoon colors on the ads of the home-run fence make a little carnival of their own, and above the "401 Feet" sign in straightaway center, the purple mountains of the Wasatch Front strike the sky, holding their stashes of snow like pink secrets in the last daylight.

I felt right at home. There was Midgely, the only guy who stayed with baseball from our college squad, standing on the dugout steps just like a coach is supposed to look; there were all the teenage baseball wives sitting in the box behind the dugout, their blond hair buoyant in the fresh air, their babies struggling in the lap blankets; there was the empty box that our firm bought for the season and which no one *ever* used; there beyond first in the general admission were Benito Antenna's fans, a grouping of eight or nine of the largest women in the state come to cheer their true love; and there riding the summer air like the aroma of peanuts and popcorn and cut grass were the strains of Steiner Brightenbeeker's organ cutting a quirky and satanic version of "How Much Is That Doggie in the Window?" I could see the Phantom of the Ballpark himself pounding out the melody in his little green cell, way up at the top of the bleachers next to the press box.

"What?" Lynn said, returning from a solo venture underneath the bleachers. She handed me a beer and a bag of peanuts. She had insisted on buying the tickets, too. Evidently I was being hosted at the home park tonight.

"Nothing. That guy's an old friend of mine." I pointed up at Steiner. Lynn was being real nice, I guess, but I felt a little screwy. Seeing Steiner and being in a ballpark made me think for a minute the world might want me back. He had played at our parties.

And it is my custom with people I don't know to pay my own way, at least, but as she had handed me the plastic cup, I had accepted it without protest. My financial picture precluded many old customs, even those grounded on common sense. I would keep track and pay her back sometime. Besides, early in the game, so to speak, I didn't have the sense not to become indebted to this woman.

"Don't you want a beer?" I asked her. She demurred, and retrieved a flask of what turned out to be brandy from her purse along with a silver thimble. I don't have the official word on this, but I don't think you drink brandy at the ballpark. Certain beverages are married to their sports, and I still doubt whether baseball, even the raw, imprecise nature of Triple A, had anything to do with brandy. Brandy, I thought, taking another look at my date as we stood for Steiner's version of "The Star Spangled Banner," which he sprinkled with "Yellow Submarine," brandy is the drink for quoits.

I don't know; I was being a jerk. It wasn't a first. Blame it this time on the eternal unrest that witnessing baseball creates in my breast. There you are ten yards from the field where these guys are *playing*. So close to the fun. I loved baseball. The thing I regretted most was that I hadn't pressed on and played a little minor-league ball. Midgely himself and Snyder, the coach, talked to me that last May, but I was already lost. Nixon was in the White House and baseball just didn't seem relevant activity.

That isn't my greatest regret. I regretted ten other things with equal vigor—well, twelve say. Twelve tops. One in particular. Things that I wanted not to have happened. I wanted Lily back. I wanted to locate the little gumption in my heart that would allow me to step up and go on with my life. I wanted to be fine and strong and quit the law and reach deep and write a big book that some woman on a train would crush to her breast halfway through and sigh. But I could see myself on the table at the autopsy, the doctor turning to the class and looking up from my chest cavity a little puzzled and saying, "I'm glad you're all here for this medical first. He didn't have any. There's no gumption here at all."

I took a big sip of the beer and tried to relax. Brandy's okay in a ballpark, a peccadillo; it was me that was wrong. Lynn rooting around in her big leather purse for her silver flask and smiling so sweetly under the big lights, her face that mysterious thing, varnished with red and amber and the little blue above the eyes, Lynn was just being nice. I thought that: she's just being nice. Then I had the real thought: it's a tough thing to take, this niceness, good luck.

The most prominent feature of any game at Derks is the approximate quality of the pitching. By the third inning we had seen just over a thousand pitches. These kids could throw hard, but it was the catcher who was doing all the work. The wind-up, the pitch, the catcher's violent leap and stab to prevent the ball from imbedding itself in the wire backstop. Just watching him spearing all those wild pitches hurt my knees: up down up down.

I started in, as I always do, explaining the game to Lynn, the fine points. What the different stances indicated about the batters; why the outfielders shifted; how the third baseman is supposed to move to cover the return throw after a move to first. Being a frustrated player, like every other man in America, I wanted to show my skill.

After a few more beers, I settled down. The air cooled, the mountains dimmed, the bright infield rose in the light. I leaned back and just tried to unravel. I listened to Steiner's music, now the theme song from *Exodus*, and I could faintly hear his fans singing, "This land is mine, God gave this land to me . . ." Steiner made me smile. He played what he wanted, when he wanted. In nine innings you could hear lots of Chopin and Liszt, Beethoven, Bartok, and Lennon. He'd play show tunes and commercial jingles. He played lots of rock and roll, and I once heard his version of *An American in Paris* that lasted an inning and a half. He refused to look out and witness the sport that transpired below him. He had met complaints that he didn't get into the spirit of the thing by playing the heady five-note preamble to "Charge!" one night seventy times in a row, until not only was no one calling "Charge!" at the punch line, but the riff had acquired a tangible repulsion in the ears of the management (next door in the press box), and they were quick to have it banished forever. As long as the air was full of organ music, they were happy.

When Steiner did condescend and play "Take Me Out to the Ball Game," he did it in a medley with "In-A-Gadda-Da-Vida" by Iron Butterfly and "Sympathy for the Devil" by the Rolling Stones. The result, obviously, was an incantation for demon worship which his fans loved. And his fans, a group of ten or twelve young kids, done punk, sat below the organ loft with their backs to the game, bobbing their orange heads to Steiner's urgent melodies. This also mollified the management's attitude toward Steiner: the dozen general admission tickets he sold to his groupies alone.

As the game progressed through a series of walks, steals, over-throws, and passed balls, Lynn sipped her brandy and chattered about being out, how fresh it was, how her husband had only taken her to stockholders' meetings, how she didn't really know what to say (that got me a little; shades of actual dating), how being divorced was so different from what she supposed, not really any fun, and how grateful she was that I had agreed to come.

I held it all off. "Come on, this is great. This is baseball."

"Phyllis said you liked baseball."

I didn't lie: "Phyllis is a shrewd cookie."

"She's a good lawyer, but her husband is a shit too." Lynn tossed back her drink. "You know, Jack, I honestly didn't know anything about marriage when I married my husband. I mean anything." Lynn sipped her brandy. "Clark came back from his mission and he seemed so ready, we just did it. What a deal. He told me later, this is much later, in counseling that he'd spent a lot of time on his mission planning, you know, our sex life. I mean, planning it out. It was awful." She lifted her tiny cup again, tossing back the rest of the drink.

"But," she began again, extending the word to two syllables, "divorce is worse. I don't like being alone. At all. But it's more than that." She looked into my face. "It's just . . . different. Hard." I saw her put her teeth in her lip on the last word, and she closed her eyes. When they opened again, she printed up a smile and showed me the flask. "Are you sure you wouldn't like any?"

"No," I said, kicking back my chair and standing. "I'll get another beer. Be right back."

Under the grandstand, I stood in the beer line and tried to pretend she hadn't shown me her cards. A friend of mine who has had more than his share of difficulty with women not his wife, especially young women not his wife, real young women, called each episode a "scrape." That's a good call. I'd had scrapes too. My second year in law school I took Lisa Krinkel (now Lisa Krink, media person) on a day trip to the mountains. We had a picnic on the Provo River, and I used my skills as a fire-tender and picnic host, along with the accessories of sunshine and red wine, to lull us both into a nifty last-couple-on-earth reverie as we boarded my old car in the brief twilight and headed for home. As always, I hadn't really done anything, except some woody wooing, ten kisses and fingers run along her arm; after all—though I might pretend differently for a day—I was going with Lily by then. Lisa and I pretended differently all the way home. I remember thinking: What are you doing, Jack? But Lisa Krinkel against me in the front seat kept running her fingernails across my chest in a chilling wave down to my belt buckle, untucking my shirt in the dark and using those fingernails lightly on my stomach, her mouth on my neck, warm, wet, warm, wet, until my eyes began to rattle. Finally, I pulled into the wide gravel turnout by the Mountain Meadow Café and told her either to stop it or deliver.

I wish I could remember exactly how I'd said that. It was probably something like: "Listen, we'd better not keep that up because it could lead to something really terrible which we both would regret forever and ever." But as a man, you can say that in such an anguished way, twisting in the seat obviously in the agonizing throes of acute arousal, a thing—you want her to know—so fully consuming and omnivorous that no woman (even the one who created this monstrous lust) could understand. You writhe, breathing melodramatic plumes of air. You roll your eyes and adjust your trousers like an animal that would be better off in every way put out of its misery. And, as I had hoped, Lisa Krinkel did put me out of my misery with a sudden startling thrust of her hand and then another minute of those electric fingernails and some heavy suction on my neck.

Then the strangest thing happened. When she was finished with my handkerchief, she asked me if we could pray. Well, that took me by surprise. I was just clasping my belt, but I clasped my hands humble as a schoolboy while she prayed aloud primarily to be delivered from evil, which was something I too hoped to be delivered from, but I sensed the prayer wasn't wholly for me as she sprinkled it liberally with her boyfriend's name: Tod. She went on there in the front seat for twenty minutes. I mean if prayers work, then this one was adequate. That little "Tod" every minute or so kept me alert right to the *amen*. We mounted the roadway and drove on in the dark. It had all changed. Now it seemed real late and it seemed a lot like driving my sister home from her date with Tod. Later I started seeing her on television, where she was a reporter for Channel 3, and it was real strange. Her hair was different, of course, blond, a professional requirement, and her name was different, *Krink*, for some reason, and I could barely remember if I had once had a scrape with this woman (including a couple of four-day nail scratches), if she was a part of my history at all. I mean, watching the news some nights it seemed impossible that I had ever prayed with Lisa Krink.

One of the primary cowardly acts of the late twentieth century is standing beneath the bleachers finishing a new beer before buying another and joining your date. I stood there in the archway, smacking my shoes in a little puddle of water on the cement floor, and tossed back the last of my beer. How lost can you be? The water was from an evaporative cooler mounted up in the locker-room window. It had been dripping steadily onto the floor for a decade. Amazing.

I could fix that float seal in ten minutes. I'd done it at our house when Lily and I first moved in. And yet, I stood out of sight wondering how I was going to fix anything else. I bought another beer and went out to join Lynn. Just because you're born into the open world doesn't mean you're not going to have to hide sometimes.

Lynn looked at me with frank relief. I could read it. She thought I had left. I probably should have, but you can't leave a woman alone on this side of town, regardless of how bad the baseball gets.

The quality of Triple A baseball is always strained. I could try to explain all the reasons, but there are too many to mention. It is not just a factor of skill or experience, because some of the most dextrous nineteen-year-olds in the universe took the field at the top of every inning along with two or three seasoned vets, guys about to be thirty who had seen action a year or two in the majors. No, it wasn't ability. The problem came most aptly under the title "attitude," and that attitude is best defined as "not giving a shit." It's exacerbated by the fact that not one game in a dozen got a headline and three paragraphs in the *Register* and none of the games were televised. And who—given the times—is going to leave his feet to stop a hot grounder down the line if his efforts are not going to be on TV?

Night fell softly over the lighted ballpark, unlike the dozens of flies that pelted into the outfield. The game bore on and on, both squads using every pitcher in the inventory, and Midgely and the other coach getting as much exercise as anyone by lifting their right and then their left arms to indicate which hurler should file forward next. The pitchers themselves marched quietly from the bull pen to the mound and then twenty pitches later to the dugout and then (we supposed) to the showers. By the time the game ended, after eleven (final score 21 to 16), there were at least four relievers who had showered, shaved, and dressed and were already home in bed.

In an economy measure, the ballpark lights were switched off the minute the last out, a force at second, was completed, and as the afterimage of the field burned out on our eyeballs, we could hear the players swearing as they bumbled around trying to pick their ways into the dugout. Lynn and I fell together and she took my arm so I could lead us stumbling out of the darkened stadium. It was kind of nice right there, a woman on my arm for a purpose, the whole world dark, and through it all the organ music, Steiner Brightenbeeker's mournful version of "Ghost Riders in the Sky." Outside, under the streetlights, the three dozen other souls who had stuck it out all nine innings dispersed, and Lynn and I crossed the street to her car. I looked back at the park. Above the parapet I could see Steiner's cigarette glowing up there in space. I pointed him out to Lynn and started to tell her that I had learned a lot from him, but it didn't come out right. He had always been adamant about his art. He was the one who told me to do something on purpose for art; to go without for it. To skip a date and write a story. That if I did, by two A.M. I'd have fifteen pages and be flying. I couldn't exactly explain it to her, so I just mentioned that he had done the music for the one play I'd ever written a thousand years ago and let it go at that.

At the car we could still hear the song. Steiner would play another hour for his fierce little coterie. The Phantom of the Ballpark.

Lynn and I went to her apartment in Sugarhouse for a nightcap. Now that's a word. Like *cocktail*, which I rarely use, it implies certain protocol. It sounds at first like you are supposed to drink it and get tired, take a few sips and yawn politely and then go to your room. A nightcap. I asked for a beer.

Her apartment was furnished somewhat like the interior of a refrigerator in white plastic and stainless steel, but the sofa was a relatively comfortable amorphous thing that seemed to say, "I'm not really furniture. I'm just waiting here for the future."

The only thing I knew for sure about a nightcap was that there was a moment when the woman said, "Do you mind if I slip into something more comfortable?" I was flipping quickly through the possible replies to such a question when Lynn came back with a pilsner glass full of Beck's for me and a small snifter of brandy for herself. She did not ask if she could slip into something more com-

fortable; instead she just sat by me in the couch or sofa, that thing,
and put her knee up on the seat and her right hand on my shoulder.
For a moment then, it was nifty as a picture. I thought: Hey, no
problem, a nightcap. This is easy.

"How's your nightcap?" I asked Lynn. We hadn't really talked
much in the car or parking it in the basement or riding the elevator
to her floor or waiting for her to find her keys and I didn't know how
we were doing anymore. Isn't that funny? You see a friend playing
the organ in the dark, and you fall asleep at the wheel. I sipped the
beer and I had no idea of what to say or do next.

"I love baseball," she breathed at me. She smelled nice, of brandy
and a new little scent, something with a European city in the name
of it, and her hand on my shoulder felt good, and I realized, as anyone realizes when he hears a woman tell him a lie when she knows
it is a lie and that he is going to know it is a lie and that the rules
have been changed or removed and that frankly, he should now do
anything he wants to, it's going to be all right. He's not going to get
slapped or told, "You fool, what are you doing!" It's a realization that
sets the adrenaline on you, your heart, your knees, and I sat there
unable to move for a moment as the blood beat my corpuscles open.

When I did move, it was to reach for her, slowly, because that's the
best moment, the reach, and I pulled her over toward me to kiss her,
but she came with the gesture a little too fully and rolled over on top
of me, setting her brandy skillfully on the floor as her mouth closed
on mine.

It had been a while for this cowboy, but even so, she didn't quite
feel right in my arms. Her body was not the body that I was used to,
that I associated with such pleasures, and her movements too had an
alien rhythm which I didn't at first fully appreciate. I was still being
dizzied by these special effects when she started in earnest. It wasn't
a moment until we were in a genuine thumping sofa rodeo, she on
top of me, riding for the prize. My head had been crooked into the
corner, stuffed into a spine-threatening pressure seal, and Lynn was
bent (right word here) on tamping me further into the furniture. She

did pause in her frenzy at one point, arch up, and pull her skirt free, bunching it at her waist. It was so frankly a practical matter, and her rosy face shone with such businesslike determination, that it gave me a new feeling: fear. Supine on that couch device, I suddenly felt like I was at the dentist. How do these things turn on us? How does something we seem to want, something we lean toward, instantly grow fangs and offer to bite our heads off?

I remember Midgely at the plate during a college game, going after what he thought was the fattest fastball he'd ever seen. It was a slow screwball, and when it broke midway through his swing and took him in the throat, he looked betrayed. He was out for a week. He couldn't talk above a whisper until after graduation. And right now I was midswing with Lynn, and I could tell something ugly was going to happen.

Meanwhile, with one halfhearted hand on her ass and the other massaging the sidewall of her breast, I was also thinking: You don't want to be rude. You don't want to stand, if you could, and heave her off and run for the door. With her panties tangled to her knees like that she'd likely take a tumble and put the corner of something into her brain. There you are visiting her in the hospital, coma day 183, the room stuffed with bushels of the flowers you've brought over the last six months, and you're saying to her sister Phyllis, the most ardent wrongful-death attorney in the history of the world, "Nightcap. We'd had a nightcap."

No, you can't leave. It's a nightcap, and you've got to do your part. You may know you're in trouble, but you've got to stay.

A moment later, Lynn peaked. Her writhing quadrupled suddenly and she went into an extended knee-squeeze seizure, a move I think I had first witnessed on *Big Time Wrestling*, and then she softened with a sigh, and said to me in her new voice, breathy and smiling, a whisper really, "What do you want?"

It's a great question, right? Even when it is misintended as it was here. It was meant here as the perfect overture to sexual compliance, but my answers marched right on by that and lined up. What do I want? *I want my life back. I want to see a chiropractor. I want baseball to be what it used to be.*

But I said, "How about another beer? I should be going soon, but I could use another beer."

When she left the room, shaking her skirt down and then stepping insouciantly out of her underpants, I had a chance to gather my assertiveness. I would tell her I was sorry, but not to call me again. I would tell her I wasn't ready for this mentally or physically. I would tell her simply, Don't be mad, but we're not right for each other *in any way.*

When Lynn reappeared with my beer, I sucked it down quietly and kissing her, took my ambivalent leave. The most assertive thing I said was that I would walk home, that I needed the air. Oh, it was sad out there in the air, walking along the dark streets. Why is it so hard to do things on purpose? I felt I had some principles, why wouldn't they apply? Why couldn't I use one like the right instrument and fix something? Don't answer.

I walked the two miles back to the corner where I used to live, the lost Ghost Mansion. It was as dark as a dark house in a horror film. Was the woman I loved asleep in there? I turned and started down the hill toward my apartment. Oh, I was separated all right, and none of the pieces were big enough to be good for anything. I said Lily's name and made one quiet resolution: no more nightcaps. At all.

DR. SLIME

THIS IS about the night Betsy told me she was leaving, the night that marked the end of a pretty screwy time all around. Everyone I knew was trying to be an artist, or really was an artist on some scale, and this was in Utah, so you can imagine the scale. Betsy had been almost making a living for several years as a singer, local work for advertising agencies and TV and radio, and my brother Mitchell, who loved her and with whom she lived, was an actor and model for television ads and local theater and whatever movie work came to town. I mean these were people who had consciously said, "I'm going to be an artist no matter what," and that seemed kind of crazy and therefore lovable because it is more interesting than anything nine to five, and I found myself taking care of them from time to time over a three-year period, sponsoring meals and paying their rent two or three times a year, and hanging out with them generally, because I am a regular person, which put me in awe of their refusal to cope with daily duties, and I'll just say it here, rather than let it sneak in later and have you think I'm a vile snake: I came to develop, after the first few months of catching midnight suppers after Mitch's shows and lunches downtown with Betsy after her auditions or after she'd recorded some commercial or other, a condition that anyone in my regular shoes would have developed, I mean not a strange or evil condition, but a profound condition nevertheless, and the condition that I bore night and day was that I was deeply and irrevocably in love with Betsy, my brother's lover, though as you will see it netted me nothing more than a sour and broken heart, broken as regular hearts can be broken, which I probably deserved, no, certainly deserved, and a condition regardless of its magnitude that allowed me to do the noble, the right thing, as you will also see, since I think I acted with grace or at least minor dexterity under such pressure.

I am not an artist. I am a baker for a major supermarket chain and it is work I enjoy more than I should perhaps, but I am dependent on my effort yielding tangible results, and at the end of my shift I go home tired and smelling good. On the day I'm talking about here I came home to my apartment about six A.M. having baked three flights of AUNT DOROTHY's turnovers all night—apple, peach, and raisin—I am AUNT DOROTHY—and found an envelope under the door containing fifteen twenties, the three hundred dollars that Mitch owed me. The note read "THERE IS MORE WHERE THIS CAME FROM. M." Every time he paid me back, this same note was enclosed. It meant that he had found work. His last gig for a smoked-meat ad paid him eight hundred dollars a day for four days, the only work he had in seven months. Mitch was feast or famine.

I put the money in the utility drawer in the kitchen; I would be lending it to him again. I didn't know what it was this time, but Betsy had called a couple of times this week worried, asking about him, what he was doing. He had a big bruise on his neck, and a slug of capsules, unidentifiable multicolored capsules, had begun appearing in the apartment.

"He's an actor," I told her. This is what I used to tell our parents when they would worry. It was a line, I had learned, that was the good news and the bad news at once.

"Yeah, well, I want to know what part beats him up and has him carting drugs."

I wanted to say: So do I, that no-good, erratic beast. Why don't you just drop him and fall into this baker's bed, where you'll be coated in frosting and treated like a goddess. I'll put you on a cake; I'll strew your path with powdered sugar and tender feathers of my piecrusts, for which I am known throughout the Intermountain West.

I said: "Don't worry, Betsy, I'll help you find out."

IT WAS that night that she came over to my place on her scooter about seven o'clock and told me she knew something and asked me would I help her, which meant Just Shut Up and Get on the Back. She wore an arresting costume, a red silk shirt printed with little guitars and a pair of bright blue trousers that bloomed at the knees and then fixed tight at the ankle cuff. I scanned her and said, "What decade are we preparing for?"

"Forties," she said, locking up. "Or nineties. You ready? Have you eaten?" I had only been on that red scooter two or three times and found it a terrible and exquisite form of transportation, and the one legitimate opportunity this baker had for putting his hands on the woman who quickened his yeasty heart, in other words, Betsy, my brother's lover, his paramour, his girlfriend, his, his, his.

We took the machine south on State Street. It was exhilarating to be in the rushing air, but the lane changes and a few of the stops made me feel even more tentative than I already did. I held Betsy's waist gingerly, so that at the light on Ninth, she turned and said, "Doug, this is a scooter, hold on for god's sakes. We're friends. Don't start acting like a goddamned man." And she clamped my hands onto her sides firmly, my fingers on the top of her hipbones.

That was good, because it made me feel comfortable resting my chin on her shoulder too, as half a joke, and I could feel her smiling as we passed under the streetlights. But the joke was on me, nuzzling a woman of the future, who was I kidding? She smelled fresh, only a little like bread, and though I didn't know it, this was the very apex of my romantic career.

We passed through the rough darkness on Thirty-third South and

could see the huge trucks working under lights removing the toxic
waste dump where Vitro Processors had been, and then on the rough
neon edge of West Valley City, Betsy pulled into Apollo Burger
Number Two, a good Greek place. When we stopped I felt the air
come up around my face in a little heat. I quickly sidestepped into
the bathroom to adjust myself in my underwear; at some point in
the close float out here, holding Betsy, my body had begun acting
like *a goddamned man.*

We ate pastrami burgers and drank cold milk sitting at a sticky
picnic table in front of the establishment. It wasn't eight o'clock yet
and Betsy assured me we had plenty of time. She knew where we
were going because she had asked the driver of the van who had
pulled up at their apartment two hours ago. He had come in looking for Mitchell and had told her: Granger High School, eight
o'clock. She knew something else, but wasn't telling me.

"He's got to stop taking these stupid nickel-and-dime jobs," she
said, as she made a tight ball of her burger wrapper.

"All work has its own dignity," I said—it was one of Mitch's lines.

"Bullshit, it's exploitation. I'm through with it."

"You're not going to sing anymore?"

She stood and threw the paper into a barrel. "I didn't say that."

On the scooter again, I didn't nuzzle. The dinner and the little lesson had taken the spirit out of it for me. I just squinted into the
wind and held on. Thirty-fifth South widened into a thick avenue of
shopping plazas separated by angry little knots of fast-food joints.
Betsy maneuvered us a mile or two and then turned left through a
tire outlet parking lot and around a large brick building that I
thought was a JC Penney but turned out to be Granger High. We
cruised through the parking lot, which was full, and she leaned the
scooter against the building. The little marquee above the entrance
read: *Welcome Freshmen,* and then below: *Friday, Mack's Mat
Matches, 8:00 P.M.*

We stood in a little line of casually dressed Americans at the door
and paid four-fifty each for a red ticket which let us into the

crowded gymnasium. A vague whomp-whomp we'd been hearing in the hall turned out to be two beefy characters in a raised wrestling ring in the center of the gym slamming each other to the mat.

"Wrestling," I said to Betsy as she led me through the crowd, searching for seats.

"Looks like it."

I followed her, stepping on people's feet all the way across the humid room. There were many family clusters encircled by children standing on the folding chairs and then couples of slumming yuppies, the guy in bright penny loafers and a pastel Lacoste shirt, and sprinkled everywhere small gangs of teenagers in T-shirts waving placards which displayed misspelled death threats toward some of the athletes.

Betsy and I ended up sitting well in the corner of the gym right in the middle of a boiling fan club for the Proud Brothers. Two chubby girls next to me wore Proud Brothers Fan Club T-shirts in canary yellow (the official color) and on the front of each was a drawing of a wrestler's face. The whole club (twelve or so fifteen-year-olds, boys and girls) was hot. They were red in the face and still screaming. Over in the ring, one man would hoist the other aloft and half our neighbors would squeal with vengeful delight, the other half would gasp in horror, and then, after twirling his victim a moment, the wrestler would hurl his opponent to the mat and ka-bang! the whole room would bounce, and the Proud Brothers Fan Club would explode. The noise wanted to tear your hair out. Finally, I noticed that one of the participants had entangled the other's head in the ropes thoroughly and was prancing around the ring in a victory dance. The man in the ropes hung there, his tongue visible thirty rows back, certainly dead. The referee threw up the winner's hands, the bell gonged about twenty times, and the Proud Brothers Fan Club screamed one last time, and the whole gym lapsed into a wonderfully reassuring version of simple crowd noise.

The two girls beside me had fallen into a sisterly embrace, one consoling the other. One girl, her face awash in sweat and tears, peered over her friends' shoulders at me. "Were those the Proud Brothers?" I asked her.

She squeezed her eyes shut in misery and nodded. Her friend turned around to me fully in an odd shoulder-back posture and pulled her T-shirt down tight in what I thought was a gesture meant to display her nubby little breasts, but then she pointed beneath the distorted portrait on the shirtfront to the name below: TOM. Her friend, the bereaved, stood and showed me her breasts too, which were much larger and still heaving from the residual sobs so much that it was difficult to recognize the face on her shirt as human, but I finally read the name underneath: TIM.

"And it was Tim who was just killed?" I asked. She collapsed into her friend's arms again.

Betsy nudged me sharply. "What'd you say to her?" She tapped my arm with her knuckle. "You're going to get arrested. These are children."

By now they had carried the body of one brother away and the other brother had finished his prancing, and the announcer, a little guy in a tux, crawled into the ring with a bullhorn.

"Ladies and gentlemen . . ." he began and before he had finished rolling *gen-tull-mn* out of his mouth, Betsy turned to me and I to her, the same word on our lips: "Mitch!"

We both sat up straight and watched this guy very carefully. It was Mitchell all right, but they had him in a pompadour toupee, a thin mustache, and chrome-frame glasses. What gave him away was his voice and arrow posture and the way he held his chin up like William Tell. He had a good minor strut going around the ring, blasting his phrases in awkward, dramatic little crescendoes at the audience. "*Wee are pleeezd! Tooo pree-zent! A No! Holds! Barred! Un-Ree-Strik-Ted! Marr-eeed Cupples! Tag-Team-Match! Fee-chur-ring Two Dy-nam-ic Du-os! Bobbie and Robbie Hansen! Ver-sus. Mario and Isabella Delsandro!*"

Evidently these were two new dynamic duos, because the crowd was quiet for a moment as people twisted in their seats or stood up to evaluate the contestants. And both couples looked good. Bobbie and Robbie Hansen, I never did find out which was which, were a beefy though not unattractive blond couple who wore matching blue satin wrestling suits. The Delsandros were very handsome people indeed. Mario nodded his beautiful full hairdo at the fans for a moment before dropping his robe and revealing red tights. But it was Isabella who decided the evening. She also had curly black hair and a shiny red suit, but when she waved at the audience, they quieted further. There were some gasps. The girls next to me actually covered their mouths with their hands; I hadn't seen that in real life ever. This was the deal: there was a tuft of hair under each of her arms. It was alien enough for this crowd. Mormon women shave under their arms; it's doctrine. The booing started a second later and when the bell sounded, the fans had made their choice.

When Mitchell ducked out of the ring, Betsy said, "Announcer. That's not bad."

"They've got him up like Sammy Davis, Jr."

"But," she added, "where does an announcer get a black eye?"

I was having trouble taking my eyes from the voluptuous Mrs. Delsandro, who now as the *unclean woman* was getting her ears booed off.

"You're right," I said. "We better stay around, find out what he's up to."

I won't detail the match (or the one after it featuring the snake and the steel cage), but in a sophisticated turn of fate, the Delsandros won. I bounced in my chair the whole forty minutes watching Robbie and Bobbie have at the luckless Mario and Isabella. They were pummeled, tossed, and generously bent. Then, late in the match, Robbie or Bobbie (Mr. Hansen) was torturing Mrs. Delsandro, twisting her arm, gouging her eyes, rendering her weaker and weaker. Mr. Delsandro paced and wept in his corner, pulling his hair out, praying to god, and generally making manifest my very feelings for the woman in the ring. Finally Mr. Hansen climbed on the turnstile and leapt on the woozy woman, smashing her to the mat.

He was going for the pin. He lay across Mrs. Delsandro this way and that, maneuvering cruelly, but every time the referee would slap the mat twice, she'd squirm away. Robbie Hansen or Bobbie Hansen, whatever his name was, was relentless. Mr. Mario Delsandro prayed in his corner of the ring. Evidently his prayers were answered, because about the tenth time the referee slapped the mat twice, Isabella Delsandro bucked and threw Mr. Hansen clear and in a second she was on him. It was such a relief, half the fans cheered.

What she did next sealed the Hansens' fate. She whomped him a good one with a knee drop and then ducked and hoisted him aloft, belly to heaven, in a refreshing spinal stretch. Well, it took the crowd, who thought they were rooting for the home team, less than a second to spot Mr. Hansen as a sick individual. His blue satin shorts bulged precisely with the outline of his skewered erection, and Mrs. Delsandro toured him once around the ring for all to see and then dropped him casually on his head. By now they were urging her, in loud and certain terms, to kill Mr. Hansen. Wrestling is one thing. Transgressing the limits of a family show is entirely another. I heard cries which included the phrases *decapitate, assassinate*, and *put him to sleep.*

She responded by giving him the Norwegian Fish Slap, the Ecuadoran Neck Burn, and the Tap Dance of Death, and then, before tagging her wonderful husband, she stood over the prostrate and slithering Mr. Hansen, her legs apart, her hands on her hips, and she raised her chin triumphantly and laughed. Oh god, it was passion, it was opera, it was giving me the sweats.

When Mario Delsandro leaped into the ring, he swept up his beautiful dark wife and kissed her fully on the mouth. The crowd sang! Mr. Hansen thought he would use the opportunity to crawl away home, but no! Still in the middle of the most significant kiss I've ever witnessed in person, Mr. Delsandro stepped squarely in the middle of Mr. Hansen's back and pressed him flat.

There was never any hope for Mr. Hansen anyway. Among the spectators of his rude tumescence was his wife, Robbie or Bobbie,

Mrs. Hansen, and she stood at her corner, her arms crossed as if for the final time, and sneered at him with all her might. Mario Delsandro took his time punishing Mr. Hansen: the German Ear Press, the Thunder Heel Spike, the Prisoner of War, the Ugandan Skull Popper, and the complicated and difficult-to-execute Underbelly Body Mortgage. A few times, early in this parade of torture, Mr. Hansen actually crawled away and reached his corner, where Mr. Delsandro would find him a second later, pleading with his wife to tag him, please tag him, save his life. She refused. At one point while he was begging her for help, she actually turned her back and called to the audience, "Is there a lawyer in the house?" No one responded. The attorneys present realized that to get in between two wrestlers would probably be a mistake.

After taking his revenge plus penalty and interest, Mr. Delsandro tagged the missus, and she danced in and pinned the comatose Mr. Hansen with one finger. The Delsandros kissed and were swept away by the adoring crowd. Mrs. Hansen stalked off. There was a good chance she was already a widow, but the crowd was on its feet and I couldn't see what ever happened to her husband, Mr. Hansen, Robbie or Bobbie.

Mitchell announced the next match, using the same snake oil school of entertaining, which was about right, because, as I said, it involved a snake and a steel cage and five dark men in turbans.

When that carnage was cleared, we found out what we wanted to know. Another announcer, a round man dressed in a black suit carrying what looked like a Bible in his hand, climbed into the ring and introduced the final match of the evening, a grudge match, a match between good and evil if there ever was one, a match important to the very futures of our children, et cetera, et cetera, and here to defend us is David Bright, our brightest star!

Ka-lank! The lights went out. Betsy grabbed my arm. "David Bright?" she said. "Mitch is David Bright?"

"Come to save us all."

An odd noise picked across the top of the room and then

exploded into a version of "Onward Christian Soldiers" so loud most people ducked. A razor-edge spotlight flashed on, circling the room once, and then focusing on a crowded corner. In it appeared a phalanx of brown-shirted security guards, all women, marching onward through the teeming crowd. When the entourage reached the ring, we heard the announcer say, "Ladies and gentlemen: David Bright! Our Brightest Star!" And the lights went on and a blond athlete stepped into the ring. He raised his arms once and then took several ministeps to the center of the ring, where he lowered his head in what was supposed to be prayer and bathed in the tumult.

"That's not Mitch." I squinted. "Is it?"

"No," Betsy said. "Look at that guy. There's a lot of praying at these wrestling matches. Is it legal?"

When the crowd slowed a bit and David Bright had gone to his corner and begun a series of simple stretches, the announcer started to speak again. He said, "And his opponent . . ." and couldn't get another word out for all the booing.

I sat down and pulled Betsy to her chair. We looked at each other in that maelstrom of noise. It was a throaty, threatening roar that was certainly made in the jungles when men first began to socialize.

"I think we're about to see Mitch." I told her.

"It sounds as if we're about to see him killed."

"We'll be able to tell by his theme song."

The announcer had continued garbling in the catcalls, and then the lights went out and the spot shot down, circling, and then the sound system blared static and by the first three notes of the song that followed I knew we were in trouble. It was "White Rabbit" by Jefferson Airplane. The spot fixed on the other corner of the room, and here came a Hell's Angel in a sleeveless black leather jacket, swatting his motorcycle cap at the fans, *get your hands off*. Well, it was a big guy, a large hairy Hell's Angel, a perfect Hell's Angel in my opinion, because, it was not my brother Mitchell, and Betsy knew that too, because we exchanged grateful and relieved looks. However, when the Angel reached the ring, he didn't climb up, but bent down and this dirty, skinny person in a red satin robe who had been behind him stepped on the Hell's Angel's back and entered the bright lights of the ring. This guy was Mitchell.

This guy put his face right into all the booing as if it were the sweetest wind on earth. This guy moved slowly, confidently, like Hotspur, which I saw Mitchell play at the Cellar Theater, and he reached into the roomy pockets of his red satin robe and threw handfuls of something at the crowds.

"What's that?" I asked the Proud Brothers fan beside me. The cheerful chubby girl had been my source of information all night.

"Drugs," she said. "He always tries to give drugs to the kids."

I could see pills being thrown back into the ring.

Mitchell was laughing.

The announcer closed down his diatribe, which no one could hear, and then yelled, pointing at Mitchell: "*Dr. Slime!*" The booing now tripled, which gave Mitchell such joy he reached down and scooped up a handful of capsules and ate them, grinning.

The bell sounded and Mitchell was still in his robe. David Bright had come forward to wrestle, but Mitchell waved a hand at him, *just a minute*, and poured something on the back of his hand and then snorted it, blowing the residue at the fans. He laughed again, a demented laugh, just like Mephistopheles, which I saw him play at the University Playhouse, coiled his robe, forgot something, unrolled it, removed a syringe, laughed, threw the syringe at the fans, rerolled his robe, and threw it in David Bright's face. David was so surprised by the unfair play that my brother, Dr. Slime, was able to deliver the illegal Elbow Drill to his kidneys. Then while David staggered around on his knees in a daze, removing the robe from his head, Dr. Slime strutted around the ring eating drugs off the mat and waggling his tongue and eyes at those at ringside. From time to time, he'd stop chewing and kick David Bright about the face. The crowd was pissed off. They had rushed the ring and now stood ten deep in the apron. Mitchell could have walked out onto their faces.

He was milking it. I'd seen him do this one other time, in *Macbeth*, running the soliloquies to twice their ordinary length because he sensed an audience with a high tolerance for anguish. Now he knelt and took something from his sock and then snorted it. He leaped in frenzied drug-induced craziness, lest anyone forget he was a maniac, a drug fiend. He whacked the woozy David Bright rapid-fire karate-like blows. He was a whirling dervish.

Then while David Bright still tried to shake off his drubbing and climb to his feet, something happened to Dr. Slime. Something chemical. He kicked David Bright, knocking him down, and raised his arms, his fingers clenched together in (what my female neighbor told me was) his signature attack, the Crashing Bong, and prepared to bring it down on David Bright, ending a promising career. Then Dr. Slime stopped. There he was, mid-ring, his arms up as if holding a fifty-pound hammer, and he froze. Then, of course, he began vibrating, shaking himself out of the pose, his head trembling sickeningly like a tambourine, his hands fluttering full-speed. He began to jerk, drool, and grunt.

His demise couldn't have come at a worse time. David Bright, our brightest star, suddenly came to and stood up. He looked mad. The rest of the match took ten seconds. David Bright, who must have outweighed Mitchell by sixty pounds, picked him up like a rag doll, sorting through his limbs like a burglar, finally grabbing his heels and beginning to spin him around and around like the slingshot that other David used.

Betsy was on my arm with both her hands and when David Bright let go of Mitchell and Mitchell left the ring and sailed off into the dark, she screamed and jumped on my back to see where he landed. We couldn't see a thing.

The crowd was delighted and David Bright took three or four polite bows, curtsies really, and humbly descended from the light. Betsy was screaming her head off: "You beasts! You fucking animals! I'll kill you all!" Things like that. Things that I would have loved to hear her cry for me.

I was crazy to go find Mitchell or his body or who was responsible for this heinous mayhem and file felony charges, suit, something, but Betsy was broken down, screaming into my shirt by now, and I

held her and said *There there*, which is stupid, but I was so glad to
have anything to say that I said it over and over.

The auditorium emptied and finally we ended up sitting, worn
out, in our seats in the empty corner of the room. My good friend
the Proud Brothers fan disappeared and then returned with two yellow T-shirts and gave them to me. "Here," she said. "Glad to meet
you. You two are welcome to the club if you can make it next
Friday."

I looked down at Betsy, her face wrecked, and I felt my own blood
awash with the little chemicals of fear and anger. And love.

"You got the right spirit," the girl said and turned to leave.

We couldn't find Mitchell. We went back through both of the
entrances the wrestlers had used, finally running into the school janitor, who simply said, "They don't stay around not one second. They
get right in the motor home." He left us alone in the dark corridor.

"Why would he do this?" she said. "Why would he get hooked up
with these sleazoid sadists?" She was as beautiful as worried girls get
late at night in an empty school.

"I don't know."

"Well, find out!" She said this as an angry order, and then caught
herself and smiled. "We've got to talk to him, get him out of this."

"Save him," I said.

"What are you saying?" She tilted her head, focusing on me.

"Nothing." Then I decided to go on. "It's just . . . Betsy, I saw him
strutting around that ring, playing that crowd."

"And?"

"And: he loved it."

Betsy folded her arms. "He loved having his neck broken."

I wanted to say, Listen, Betsy, it's art. It's all worth it. I had some
new information on this subject, having witnessed the Delsandros
wrestle, having witnessed their soaring struggle, and having had my
heart in their hands, I was a new convert, but what could I say,
some guy who is Aunt Dorothy every night in a bakery? I said,
"Let's not fight."

She shook her head at me a minute, a phrase in body language that seemed to mean *you pathetic man.* And then we prowled the vacant corridors of Granger High School for a while, from time to time calling, "Mitchell!"

We went into the second-floor girls' room, because we could see the light under the door, and inside she turned to me and said, "Oh hell." It was a four-stall affair, primarily public-school gray with plenty of places to put your sanitary napkins. I could see the back of Betsy's beautiful head in the mirror. There was an old guy standing next to her and when I spoke I realized he was a screwed-up baker out of town for a night with his brother's girlfriend. He looked in serious need of a blood transfusion, exercise, good news.

"Dr. Slime?" I said to the stalls.

"What a night," Betsy said. "It doesn't matter. He's gone." She leaned against the counter and folded her arms. "He told me I should tell you my news."

"Good, okay," I said, leaning against the counter too and folding my arms. We stood like that, like two girlfriends in the girls' room.

"I'm going to L.A. Next week. I have some interviews with agents and two auditions."

"Auditions?" I said. I am a baker. It is not my job to catch on quickly. I looked at her face. She was as beautiful as any movie actress; with her mouth set as it was now and the soft wash of freckles across her nose and her pale hair up in braids, she looked twenty. She was smart and she could sing. "You're going to L.A. You're not coming back here."

"No, I guess I'm not," she said.

"Does Mitchell know?"

"Mitchell knows."

"How hurt is he?"

"That would be a stupid question, wouldn't it, Doug? Don't you think?"

I took my stupid question and the great load of other stupid questions forming in my ordinary skull out of the girls' room and through the dark hallways of Granger High and out into the great sad night. The parking lot was empty and I stood by the red scooter as if it were a shrine to the woman I loved, I ached for, in other words Betsy, who now walked toward me across the pavement, and who now, I realized, wasn't exactly my brother's lover anymore, a notion that gave me an odd shiver. I was as confused as bakers get to be.

"How certain are these things you've got out there?"

"How certain? How certain is my staying here, singing jingles for the next ten years? Come on, Doug: I want to be a singer." She mounted the scooter and waited.

"You are a singer, Betsy. The best. I love your singing. And so, this is your move, right?"

She nodded.

"And it's worth Mitchell?"

She started the machine and the blue exhaust began to roil up into the night. It wasn't a real question and she was right not to answer. Through the raining flux of emotions, worry about Mitchell, love for Betsy, the answer had descended on me like a ton of meringue. I knew the answer. *It was worth it.* It's funny about how the world changes and how art can turn the wheel. I had seen the Delsandros and I had seen my brother, a talented person, an artist, fly through the air to where I knew not, but I knew it was worth it. To be thrown that way in front of two thousand people, well, I'd never done it and I never would, but I know that Mitchell even as he squirmed through the terrific arc of his flight thought it was worth it. That's what art is, perhaps, the look I had seen on his face.

Is this clear? I was annoyed to my baker's bones at these two people and I wanted them to be mine forever. But they were both flying and I was proud of that too. I then climbed on behind my lost love, a woman who sings like an angel and drives a scooter like the devil, that is, Betsy, and I kissed her cheek. Just a little kiss. I wasn't trying anything. "Let us go then," I said, "and see if we can find our close friend Dr. Slime."

DOWN THE GREEN RIVER

W E WERE fine. We were holding on to a fine day on the fine Green River in the mountains of Utah five hours from Salt Lake with the sun out and Toby already fishing, when his mother, Glenna, said, "We're sinking." She had been a pain in the ass since dawn. I wanted nothing more than to argue, prove her wrong, but I couldn't because there was real water in the bottom of the raft. You're supposed to leave your troubles behind when you float a river, but given our histories, that was a fat chance.

We were that strange thing: old friends. I'd known Glenna since college; she had been Lily's roommate and there was a time when we were close as close. She had been an ally in my quest for Lily. We'd had a thousand coffees at their kitchen table and she'd counseled and coached me, been a friend. Then after college she had married my pal Warren, which had been her mistake, and I had not married Lily, which had recently (twenty-two days ago) become mine. Warren had not been good to Glenna. His specialty was young women and he used his position as editor of the *Register* to sharpen it. She had grown embittered to say the least, and I wanted now simply to cut that deal—old friends or not—call her a sour unlikable bitch and get on with the day my way; if I had known that she was going to be the photographer for the news story I was writing, I'd have stayed in town.

She had her suitcase—something that has no business even near a raft—balanced on the side tube, and she held her camera case aloft in the other hand. It was dripping. The suitcase made me mad. I was just mad. Glenna had been to Lily's wedding a month (twenty-two days) ago. She had talked to Lily. Now I could see the water over the tops of her shoes in the deep spaces where she stood. It was not common to tear a raft on the gravel, but it happened. I looked downriver for a landing site. The banks were both steep cutaways, but there was a perfect sandbar off to the right side, and I paddled us for it.

After the three of us dragged the raft clear of the water and unloaded the gear, spreading it out to dry, I set Toby at the downstream point with a small Mepps spinner and went back to repair the raft. Glenna was sitting on her suitcase, checking her camera. Her goddamned suitcase. Warren had assigned me the story and her the photographs. "Floating the Green"—it would run in Thursday Sports.

I was trying not to think. I had taken the job to get out of town and because I needed the money. Warren said the photographer would pick me up at four A.M., and there in the dark when I saw Glenna's '70 Seville, the same car she'd had at school, my heart clenched. We had all spent a lot of time in that car. And I knew she'd seen Lily. Twenty-two days. If I had been ready, been able to commit; if I had been thirty percent mature; if I had not assumed being more "interesting" than Lily's other dates would keep me first, then I might not have been standing on a sandbar with my teeth in my lip. Did I want to ask Glenna a few questions? Does Lily miss me? Has she said my name? Where should I send her tapes? Yes. Would I? Hey, I had a raft to fix, and as I said, I was trying not to think.

Now sitting on her suitcase on a sandbar, she stretched and reached in her bag for another Merit, which she lit and inhaled. "How'd he talk you into this one?" she said as smoke.

"He mentioned the beauty of nature." I waved up at the sunny gorge, the million facets of the exposed cliffs. "The clear air, the sweet light . . ."

"Bullshit, Jack."

"The money, which I need." I flopped the raft upside down. There were a dozen black patches of various sizes on the bottom, but I could find no new hole. Using my knife, I tested the edges of all the old patches, and, sure enough, one large one was loose. "What about you? You don't need another photo credit."

She pointed at Toby where he fished from the edge of the sand. "I'm here because you know how to do whatever it is we're going to do and you can show it to Toby in some semblance of man-to-boy goodwill and something will have been gained." She flipped the butt into the Green River. "About the rest, I could give a shit. If Warren wants me out of town so he can chase Lolita, so be it."

I bent to my work, scraping at the old patch. I peeled it off and revealed a two-inch L-shaped tear. I wiped the area down and prepared my own new patch with the repair kit while the sun dried the bottom of the raft. I didn't like that phrase *so be it*. There's gloom if not doom in that one.

And sure enough, a moment later Glenna spoke again. "Jack," she said. "Something's happening with the water." Her imprecision almost cheered me, then I looked and saw our sandbar was shrinking. Toby had reeled in and was walking back, stepping with difficulty in the soft sand.

"Jack," he said. "The water's rising."

I stood still and watched it for a moment. The clear water crawled slowly and surely up the sand. The water was rising.

"My patch isn't dry. Load everything on the raft as it is." I set the cooler and my pack on the upside-down raft and Glenna put her suitcase and Toby placed the sleeping bags and the loose stuff in a heap on the raft. She paused long enough to snap a few photographs of our disaster.

The water inched up, covering our feet, lifting at the raft.

"We're going to get wet now, aren't we?" Glenna said.

"Yes," I said. "Just hold on to the raft and we'll float it down to the gravel spit." I pointed downstream two hundred yards.

"Why is the water rising?" Toby said, laying his pole onto our gear.

"Power for Los Angeles," I told him.

"Some guy's VCR timer just kicked in so he can record *Divorce Court* while he's out playing tennis," Glenna said. "This water is cold!"

Finally enough water crept under the raft to lift it free and we walked it down into the deeper water of the fresh, cold Green River. "Jack," Glenna said, blaming me for hydroelectric power everywhere, "this fucking water is cold!"

"Just hold on," I said to Toby as the water rose toward my chin. "This will be easy."

That is when I saw the next thing, something over my shoulder, and I turned as a small yellow raft drifted swiftly by. There were four women crowded into it. They appeared to be naked.

AN HOUR later, we started again. We had clambered out of the river onto the gravel, unloaded the raft, and let the patch air-dry for thirty minutes while Toby and I chose our next series of flies, and Glenna, stripped down to her tank top and Levi's, commenced drinking cans of lemon and cherry wine coolers. Then we turned the raft over again, reloaded it, and tenderly made into the river. I immediately pieced Toby's fly rod together, attached the reel, and geared him up with a large Woolly Caddis, the kind of mothy thing that bred thickly on this part of the river. I clipped a bubble five feet from the fly so it would be easier, this early in the day, to handle. Sitting on the side of the raft, I began to organize my tackle, and I had to consciously slow myself down. My blood was rich with the free feeling I always get on a river. The sunshine angled down with its first heat of the day on my forearms as I worked, and I realized that my life was a little messy, but for now I was free. It was okay. I was now afloat in a whole different way. It was a feeling a boy has. I smiled with a little rue. Even in a life that is totally waxed, there are still stupid pleasures. It was morning, and I smiled; come on, who hasn't screwed up a life?

Toby had a sharp delivery on his cast, which we worked on for a while as the raft drifted along the smooth sunny river. He was still throwing the line, not punching it into place, but he mastered a kind of effective half-and-half with which he was able to set the fly in the swollen riffles about half the time. It was now late in the morning, but there was enough shade on the water that the fishing could still be good.

I started working the little nymph in the quiet shady pools against the mountain as we'd pass. Once, twice, drift, and back. I saw some sudden shadows and I was too quick on the one rise I had. Glenna was sitting on her awful suitcase, back against the raft tube, her arms folded, drinking her coolers, quiet as Sunday school behind her oversize dark glasses. From time to time I had to set my rod down and avert the canyon wall or a small boulder or two in the river with the paddle and center us again.

Then later in the morning Glenna took a series of photographs of Toby as he knelt and fly-cast from his end of the raft. She was able, in fact, to film his first fish, a nice twenty-inch rainbow trout which answered the caddis in an odd rocky shallow, coming out of the water to his tail, and Toby, without a scream or a giggle, worked the fish into the current and fifty yards later into our now hot boat. He was a keeper, and Toby said, finally letting his enthusiasm show, "The first one I caught from a raft, ever." I killed the fish on my knee, showing Toby how to tap it smartly behind the cranium, and put him in my creel.

"It's awfully good luck to have the first fish to be a keeper," I told him. "Now our nerves are down and we can be generous with the newcomers." Even Glenna seemed pleased watching us, as if her expectations for this sojourn were somehow being met.

I thought about the article I would write. I could have written it without coming, really. I knew the Green by the back. I would talk about the regulations (flies and lures only—no bait); I would talk about the boat launch and the fluctuating river level; I would say take along a patch kit. I would not mention anything that happened next.

The sun had straightened into noon, and the fishing had slowed considerably. I had taken two little trout from pools in the lee of two boulders, handling them with exaggerated care for Toby's information and then returning them to the water. Then, around the next bend, there was a long slow avenue of river and I found out I had been right about the four rafters. They had been nude. About a half mile down, under a sunny gray shale escarpment, there was a party in session. Eleven or twelve rafts of all sizes had been beached, and fifty or sixty people loitered in the area in a formless nude cocktail party.

"Fish this side of the raft," I said to Toby, adjusting his pole opposite the nudists. Just as I settled him, with a promise of lunkers in that lane, Glenna spotted the other rafters and determined the nature of the activity. She was working down her third wine cooler, a beverage which evoked her less subtle qualities, and she cried out, "Check this out!"

A dozen or so of these noble campers sat bare-assed on a huge fallen log along the river, nursing their beers, taking the sun, watching the river the way people wait for a bus. I heard one call out, "Raft alert! Raft ho!" There was some laughter and a stir of curiosity about our little craft as it drew closer.

I wondered what it was about the wilds that made all these young lawyers feel impelled to take off their clothing. Is it true that as soon as most folks can't see the highway anymore, they immediately disrobe? We came abreast the naked natives in an eerie slow-motion silence. They stopped drawing beer from the keg, quit conversations, stood off the log. Many turned toward us or took half a step toward the river. Glenna was leaning dangerously out of the raft on that side, another wine-cooler casualness (she was just full of wine coolers), and Toby had swiveled fully around from his fishing

duties, striking me in the ear with the tip of his rod. I lifted it from
his hands.

One bold soul strode down to the edge of the river, waggling himself in the sunshine. He lifted his cup of beer at us and called,
"Howdy! What ya doing?" Behind him, still standing against the log,
was a slender, dark-haired girl who looked a lot like Lily. She was
about as tall and had the posture. Her breasts were pure white, the
two whitest things I'd ever seen at noon on a river, a white that hurt
the eyes, and her pubic hair glinted red in the bright sunlight. Oh, I
don't need to see these things. I need to fish and have my heart start
again and be able to breathe without this weight in my chest. I could
not physically stop looking at the girl.

"The same thing you are," Glenna answered the young man.
"Fishing with worms!" She laughed a full raw laugh back in her
throat, leaning so hard on the side of the raft that a quick stream of
cold river water sloshed in. As Glenna continued staring the man
down and chortling, I thought, This is where it comes from: the
devil and the deep blue sea. I am caught, for a moment, between the
devil and the deep blue sea. I looked down into the crystal green slip
of the river; the stones shimmered and blinked, magnifying themselves in the bent waterlight.

Slowly, we slid past the naked throng. It seemed a blessing that
Glenna had not thought to take any photographs. I shifted some of
the gear out of the new bilgewater and cast one terrible glance back
at the girl and her long bare legs. The arch of her ass along that large
smooth log caught my heart like a fishhook. Toby had collapsed like
a wet shirt and was sitting on the bottom of the raft, soaking. He
bore all the signs of having been electrocuted. I doused his face in a
couple handfuls of river water to put out the expression on his face
and sat him up again with his fishing pole and a new lure, a lime-
green triple teaser which looked good enough for us to eat. I almost
had him convinced that it was still possible to fish in this world
when I heard Glenna groan and I felt the raft shift as she stood.

I cursed the pathetic confectioneer who had invented wine coolers and turned to see Glenna reach down and pull her tank top over

her head, liberating Romulus and Remus, the mammoth breasts. Shuddered by the shirt, they rippled for a moment and then settled in the fresh air.

"No topless fishing," I said to her. "Don't do that." I handed her the shirt.

She threw it in the river. "I'm not going to fish," she said back to me. Toby had put his pole down again. This river trip had become more dangerous than he'd ever dreamed. I put one hand on his shoulder to restrain him from leaping into the sweet Green River. When I felt him relax, I turned back to Glenna and her titanic nudity. It was still a day. The sun touched off the river in a bright, happy way. We fell out of the long straight stretch into a soft, meandering red canyon. It was still a day.

"Look, Glenna," I said. She had opened another wine cooler. "Look. We're going to fish. This is a raft trip and we're going to fish. It would help everything if you would take your drink and turn around and face forward. Either way, you're going to get a wicked sunburn." I moved the three plastic-covered sleeping bags in such a way as to make her a backrest. She looked at me defiantly, and then she turned her back and settled in.

It was still a day. I took the bubble off Toby's line and showed him how to troll the triple teaser. "There are fish here," I told him. "Let's go to work." I tied an oversize Royal Coachman on my line and began casting my side of the river, humming—for some reason—the Vaughn Monroe version of the ominous ballad "Ghost Riders in the Sky." I knew the words, even the yippie-ai-ais.

WE PASSED Little Hole at three o'clock and I knew things would get better. Ninety-nine percent of the rafters climb out at Little Hole and we could see two dozen big GMC pickups and campers waiting in the parking lot. We'd already passed a flotilla of Scout rafts all tethered together in a large eddy taking fly-casting lessons. It was a relief to see that they didn't have enough gear to spend the night on the river.

It had been an odd scene, all those little men in their decorated uniforms, nodding seriously into the face of their leader, a guy about my age who was standing on a rock with his flyrod, explaining the backcast. It was his face as it widened in surprise that signaled the troop to turn and observe what would be for many of them the largest breasts they would ever witness in person no matter how long they lived. Glenna had smiled easily at all of them and waved sweetly at their leader. I said nothing, but put my pole down and paddled hard downstream, just in case Glenna had really got to the guy and brought out the incipient vigilante all Scout leaders have. I didn't want to be entangled in some midstream citizen's arrest.

Anyway, it was a relief to pass Little Hole and know that we would see no more human beings until tomorrow noon when we'd land at Brown's Park and the end of the trail, so to speak.

By this time, Glenna was relaxed. She'd slowed her drinking (and her speech and about everything else) and seemed to be in a kind of happy low-grade coma, bare-breasted in the prow of our ship like some laid-back figurehead. Toby had been doing well with the triple teaser, taking three small trout, which we'd released. He handled the fish skillfully and made sure they returned to the river in good shape. I had had nothing on the Coachman, but it was not the fly's fault. I had been casting in time with "Ghost Riders in the Sky":

> Then cowboy change your ways today, (cast)
> Or with us you will ride, (cast)

and a fish would have been lucky to even catch a glimpse of its fur.

> A-trying to catch the Devil's herd (cast)
> Across these endless skies. (cast)

So there had been a little pressure, but now the long green shadows dragged themselves languorously across the clear water. It was late afternoon. We were past Little Hole. It was still a day. We dropped around two bends and were suddenly in the real wilderness, I could feel it, and I felt that little charge that the real places give me.

I had been here before, of course, many times with Lily. In the old days I thickened my favorite books in the bottom of rafts. Lily and I would leave the city Friday night, spend two days fishing scrupulously down the Green River, and drive back five hours from Brown's Park in the dark, arriving back in town in time for class with a give-away suntan and the taste of adrenaline in my mouth. My books, *The Romantic Poets, The Victorian Poets, Eons of Literature*, were all swollen and twisted, their pages still wet as I sat in class, some of them singed where I had tried to dry them by the fire. Those trips with Lily were excruciatingly one-of-a-kind ventures—the world, planet and desire, fused and we had our way with it. I remember it all. I remember great poetry roasting cheerily by the fire in some lone canyon while Lily and I lay under the stars. Those beautiful books, I still have them.

MY LINE tripped once hard and then I felt another sharp tug as my Royal Coachman snapped away in the mouth of what could only be a keeper. I set the hook and measured the tension. The trout ran. I gave him line evenly as the pressure rose, and he broke the surface, sixty yards behind us in the dark swelling river.

"Whoa!" Toby said.

"Watch your line, son," I told him. "It's the perfect time of night."

But even as I worked the trout stubbornly forward in the river, I was thinking about Lily. I'd never grown up and now fishing wasn't even the same.

THAT FISH was a keeper, a twenty-inch brown, and so were the two Toby took around the next bend as we passed under a monstrous spruce that leaned over the water. Four hills later we drifted into the narrows of Red Canyon. It was the deep middle of the everlasting summer twilight, and I cranked us over to the bank, booting the old wooden oars hard on the shallow rocky bottom. We came ashore halfway down the gorge so we could make camp. The rocky cliffs had gone coral in the purple sky and the river glowed green behind us as we unloaded the raft.

Glenna finally grabbed another T-shirt and struggled into it, something about being on land, I suppose, and said, "Oh, I gotta pee!" stepping stiffly up the sage-grown shore.

By the time she returned, the darkness had thickened, and Toby and I had a small driftwood fire going and were clearing an area for the tents. Glenna hugged herself against the fresh air coming along the river. She was a little pie-faced, but opened another wine cooler anyway. I fetched a flannel shirt from my kit and gave it to Toby, and then I settled down to the business of frying those fish. Since we were having cocktails, Glenna already reclining before the fire, I decided to take the extra time and make trout chowder.

Here's how: I retrieved my satchel of goodies, including a half pint of Old Kilroy, which is a good thing to sip if you're going to be cooking trout over an open fire while the night cools right down. In there too was a small tin of lard. You use about a tablespoon of lard for each trout, melting it in the frying pan and placing the trout in when the pan is warm, not hot. If the pan is too hot the fish will curl up and make it tricky cooking. If you don't have lard or butter, it's okay. Usually you don't. Without it you have to cook the trout slower, preventing it from sticking and burning in the pan by sprinkling in water and continuously prodding the fish around. Cut off the heads so the fish will fit into the pan. Then slice both onions you brought and let them start to cook around the fish. At the same time, fill your largest pot with water and put it on to boil. In Utah now you have to boil almost all your water. There is a good chance that someone has murdered his neighbor on instructions from god and thrown him in the creek just upstream from where you're making soup. Regardless, with a river that goes up and down eight inches twice a day, you have a lot of general cooties streaming right along. This is a good time to reach into the pack and peel open a couple cans of sardines in mustard sauce as appetizers, passing them around in the tin along with your Forest Master pocketknife, so the diners can spear a few and pass it on.

Okay, by the time your water boils, you will have fried the trout.

When they've cooled, it will be easy to bone them, starting at the tail and lifting the skeleton from each. This will leave you with a platter of trout pieces. Add a package of leek soup mix (or vegetable soup mix) to the boiling water and then a package of tomato soup mix (or mushroom soup mix) and then the fried onion and some garlic powder. Then slip the trout morsels into the hot soup and cook the whole thing for another twenty minutes while you drink whiskey and mind the fire. You want it to thicken up. Got any condensed milk? Add some powdered milk at least. Stir it occasionally. Pepper is good to add about now too. When it reaches the consistency of gumbo, break out the bowls. Serve it with hunks of bread and maybe a slab of sharp cheddar cheese thrown across the top. It's a good dinner, easier to eat in the dark than a fried trout, and it stays hot longer and contains the foods that real raftsmen need. Bitter women who have been half naked all day drinking alcoholic beverages will eat trout chowder with gusto, not talking, just sopping it up, cheese, bread, and all. Be prepared to serve seconds.

AFTER HER second bowl, her mouth still full of bread, Glenna said, "So, quite a day, eh, Jack?"

"Five good fish," I said, nodding at Toby. "Quite a day."

"No, I mean . . ."

"I know what you mean." I moved the pot of chowder off the hot ring of rocks around the fire and set it back on the sand, securing the lid. "We rescued a day from the jaws of the nudists."

The cooking had calmed me down, and I didn't want to get started with Glenna, especially since she was full of fructose and wine. Cooking, they say, uses a different part of your brain and I know which part, the good part, the part that's not wired all screwy with your twelve sorry versions of your personal history and the four jillion second guesses, backward glances, forehead-slapping embarrassments. The cooking part is clean as a cutting board and fitted accurately with close measurements and easy-to-follow instructions, which, you always know, are going to result in something edible and nourishing, over which you could make real conversation with someone, maybe someone you've known since college.

I ran the crust of my bread around the rim of my bowl and ate the last bite of chowder. It was good to be out of the raft, sitting on the ground by the fire, but I could feel there was going to be something before everybody hit the hay.

"Did you have fun, honey?" Glenna said to Toby. "Are you glad you came?"

"Yeah."

"Do you like old Jack here?"

"Aw, he's okay," I said and smiled at Toby.

"I've known Jack a long time."

"I know," Toby said.

"When did we meet, Jack?"

I broke some of the driftwood smaller in my hands and fed the fire back up. Toby had already filled the other kettle with water and I balanced it over the flames on three rocks.

"You want some coffee?" I said. I did not want to get started on the old world. We had met in the lobby of Wasatch Dorm my junior year. Glenna had come up to take my picture for the *Chronicle*. It was the Christmas of the White Album and Warren had decided I should run for class president. That afternoon she introduced me to her roommate, Lily Westerman.

"I don't think so," she said, showing me her bottle of Cabernet Lemon-Lime.

"Get your cup, Toby," I said. When I heard the boiling water cracking against the side of the kettle, I poured him a cup of hot chocolate. I fixed myself a cup of instant coffee and poured in a good lick of whiskey. Toby was standing to one side, a bright silhouette in the firelight.

"I think I'll go to bed," he said. "You guys are going to talk ancient history for a while. Dad was a big man on campus. This was during the war and he ran the paper, and Mom was the head photographer. You were all students, sort of, and Jack was going with

Lily, who was Mom's roommate, and their house was like a club in the days when things mattered." He sipped his chocolate and toasted us. He knew how smart he was. "This was years ago."

"He's older than I am."

"Oh Jack," Glenna said, suddenly looking at me with eyes as cool and sober as the night. "Everybody's older than you are. That's always been your thing. It's kind of cute—about half." She must have seen me listening too hard, because she immediately waved her hand in front of her face and said, "Jack, ignore me. I'm drunk. That's what I do now: the drunk housewife."

"I don't believe her," I told Toby.

"I don't either," he said.

"Are you mad at your mother for embarrassing you today?" Glenna said. She was slumped against a rock opposite me. Her voice was now husky from too much sun, too much wine, too much lemon-lime.

"Mom," Toby said. "I'm tired. It was a pretty wild day. Good night." And he stepped down through the sage to his tent.

Halfway in the dark, he turned. "But Mom, you know what you said to that guy today, the naked guy?"

"Yeah?"

"It wasn't right. We weren't fishing with worms. The Green River is artificial flies and lures only."

"Okay, honey."

"But it was pretty funny, given the situation." He nodded once at us. "Good night." Toby disappeared in the dark.

"He's a good kid," I said.

She nodded the way people nod when their eyes are full and to speak would be to cry.

"It's okay," I said. "It was a good day." I looked at her slumped on her suitcase, her hideous and beautiful suitcase, which seemed now simply something else trying to break my heart.

"Oh, Jack, I'm sorry. I'm so surprised by what I do, what anybody does. I guess I'm surprised any of it gets to me. If we'd just met, this would be a fun trip. If we were strangers. We're two people who know too much."

It was the worst kind of talk I'd ever heard around a campfire, and I wanted it to go away. "You're all right," I said. "You've got Toby." That, evidently, of course, was exactly the wrong thing to say and I sensed this from what I could hear in Glenna's breath. She was going to cry. The whole night seemed wrong.

I could hear a high wind in the junipers, but it was quiet in our camp. The campfire fluttered and sucked, settling down. I stared into the pink coals and watched them pulse white. I could see the bright edge of light on the cliff tip that meant in an hour the moon would break over the canyon. The other noise that came along sure as sure was the soft broken sucking of Glenna crying. She had her hand over her face in a gesture of real grief. I watched her for a moment, holding myself still. I was going to cry too, but I was going to try to wait for the moon. Finally, I went around the dying fire and sat by her.

"Hey, Glenna. Glenna," I whispered. "Did you bring any sunburn stuff?"

She shook her head no.

"Here," I said, handing her my tube of aloe. "Use this tonight. Okay? Use plenty. You surely scorched yourself." I could feel the heat from her sunburn as I sat by her.

"He's a good kid," she said.

"He's a great kid."

She shuddered and drew up in a series of short serious sobs. When that wave passed, I said, "What's the matter?" We were both speaking quietly.

She shook her head again, this time as if shaking something off. She said, "You're bright and young and you get married and you kind of always have money and then, bang-o, a thousand people later you're sunburned and eating fish in the big woods with an old friend and only the smallest part of it seems like the center of your life anymore. What's that about?"

I was beyond speaking now, lost in a widening orbit miles from our little fire. I knew she was going to go on. "There is a message, you know. From Lily. We saw her at the wedding." It had taken her all day but she had finally said Lily's name. "It's terrible, of course. We were eating cake and she came over to our table and said to tell Jack hello. So, *hello.*"

Now I had to hold her. Someone offers you that kind of last hello and whether you're camped by the river or not, you'll probably hug her, feeling her pulsing sunburn, and sit there thinking it all over for a little while. I had forever turned some corner in my life this month (twenty-two days), but I hadn't known it until Glenna said hello. Like it or not I was through being a boy.

So be it.

We sat there quietly and soon—over the steady low flash of the river—I could hear Toby, down in his tent, humming. It was something familiar, a sad ballad involving the devil's cattle and a long ride.

OXYGEN

I

N 1967, the year before the year that finally cracked the twentieth century once and for all, I had as my summer job delivering
medical oxygen in Phoenix, Arizona. I was a sophomore at the
University of Montana in Missoula, but my parents lived in
Phoenix, and my father, as a welding engineer, used his contacts to
get me a job at Ayr Oxygen Company. I started there doing what I
called dumbbell maintenance, the kind of makework assigned to
college kids. I cleared debris from the back lot, mainly crushed packing crates that had been discarded. That took a week, and on the last
day, as I was raking, I put a nail through the bottom of my foot and
had to go for a tetanus shot. Next, I whitewashed the front of the
supply store and did such a good job that I began a month of painting my way around the ten-acre plant.

These were good days for me. I was nineteen years old and this
was the hardest work I had ever done. The days were stunning,
starting hot and growing insistently hotter. My first week two of the
days had been 116. The heat was a pure physical thing, magnified
by the steel and pavement of the plant, and in that first week, I
learned what not to touch, where not to stand, and I found the

powerhouse heat simply bracing. I lost some of the winter dormitory fat and could feel myself browning and getting into shape. It felt good to pull on my Levi's and workshoes every morning (I'd tossed my tennies after the nail incident), and not to have any papers due for any class.

Of course, during this time I was living at home, that is arriving home from work sometime after six and then leaving for work sometime before seven the next morning. My parents and I had little use for each other. They were in their mid-forties then, an age I've since found out that can be oddly taxing, and besides they were in the middle of a huge career decision which would make their fortune and allow them to live the way they live now. I was nineteen, as I said, which in this country is not a real age at all, and effectively disqualifies a person for one year from meaningful relationship with any other human being.

I was having a hard ride through the one relationship I had begun during the school year. Her name was Linda Enright, a classmate, and we had made the mistake of sleeping together that spring, just once, but it wrecked absolutely everything. We were dreamy beforehand, the kind of couple who walked real close, bumping foreheads. We read each other's papers. I'm not making this up: we read poetry on the library lawn under a tree. I had met her in a huge section of Western Civilization taught by a young firebrand named Whisner, whose credo was "Western civilization is what you personally are doing." He'd defined it that way the first day of class and some wit had called out, "Then Western Civ is watching television." But Linda and I had taken it seriously, the way we took all things I guess, and we joined the Democratic Student Alliance and worked on a grape boycott, though it didn't seem that there were that many grapes to begin with in Montana that chilly spring.

And then one night in her dorm room we went ahead with it, squirming out of our clothes on her hard bed, and we did something for about a minute that changed everything. After that we weren't even the same people. She wasn't she and I wasn't I; we were two young citizens in the wrong country. I see now that a great deal of it was double- and triple-think, that is I thought she thought it was my fault and I thought that she might be right with that thought and I should be sorry and that I was sure she didn't know how sorry I was already, regret like a big burning house on the hill of my conscience, or something like that, and besides all I could think through all my sorrow and compunction was that I wanted it to happen again, soon. It was confusing. All I could remember from the incident itself was Linda stopping once and undoing my belt and saying, "Here, I'll get it."

The coolness of that practical phrase repeated in my mind after I'd said goodbye to Linda and she'd gone off to Boulder, where her summer job was working in her parents' cookie shop. I called her every Sunday from a pay phone at an Exxon station on Indian School Road, and we'd fight and if you asked me what we fought about I couldn't tell you. We both felt misunderstood. I knew I was misunderstood, because I didn't understand myself. It was a glass booth, the standard phone booth, and at five in the afternoon on a late-June Sunday the sun torched the little space into a furnace. The steel tray was too hot to fry eggs on, you'd have ruined them. It gave me little burns along my forearms. I'd slump outside the door as far as the steel cord allowed, my skin running to chills in the heat, and we'd argue until the operator came on and then I'd dump eight dollars of quarters into the blistering mechanism and go home.

The radio that summer played a strange mix, "Little Red Riding Hood," by Sam the Sham and the Pharaohs, over and over, along with songs by the Animals, even "Sky Pilot." This was not great music and I knew it at the time, but it all set me on edge. After work I'd shower and throw myself on the couch in my parents' dark and cool living room and read and sleep and watch the late movies, making a list of the titles eventually in the one notebook I was keeping.

About the third week of June, I burned myself. I'd graduated to the paint sprayer and was coating the caustic towers in the oxygen plant. These were two narrow, four-story tanks that stood beside the metal building where the oxygen was bottled. The towers were full of a viscous caustic material that air was forced through to remove nitrogen and other elements until the gas that emerged was 99 percent oxygen. I was forty feet up an extension ladder reaching right and left to spray the tops of the tanks. Beneath me was the pump station that ran the operation, a nasty tangle of motors, belts, and valving. The mistake I made was to spray where the ladder arms met the curved surface of the tank, and as I reached out then to hit the last and farthest spot, I felt the ladder slide in the new paint. Involuntarily I threw my arms straight out in a terrific hug against the superheated steel. Oddly I didn't feel the burn at first nor did I drop the spray gun. I looked down at what seemed now to be the wicked machinery of my death. It certainly would have killed me to fall. After a moment, and that's the right span here, a moment, seconds or a minute, long enough to stabilize my heartbeat and sear my cheekbone and the inside of both elbows, I slid one foot down one rung and began to descend.

All the burns were the shapes of little footballs, the one on my face a three-inch oval below my left eye, but after an hour with the doctor that afternoon, I didn't miss a day of work. They've all healed extraordinarily well, though they darken first if I'm not careful with the sun. That summer I was proud of them, the way I was proud not to have dropped the spray gun, and proud of my growing strength, of the way I'd broken in my workshoes, and proud in a strange way of my loneliness.

Where does loneliness live in the body? How many kinds of loneliness are there? Mine was the loneliness of the college student in a summer job at once very far from and very close to the thing he will become. I thought my parents were hopelessly bourgeois, my girlfriend a separate race, my body a thing of wonder and terror, and as I went through the days, my loneliness built. Where? In my heart? It didn't feel like my heart. The loneliness in me was a dryness in the back of my mouth that could not be slaked.

And what about lust, that thing that seemed to have defeated me that spring, undermined my sense of the good boy I'd been, and rinsed the sweetness from my relationship with Linda? Lust felt related to the loneliness, part of the dry, bittersweet taste in the lava-hot air. It went with me like an aura as I strode with my three burns across the paved yard of Ayr Oxygen Company, and I felt it as a certain tension in the tendons in my legs, behind the knees, a tight, wired feeling that I knew to be sexual.

THE LOADING dock at Ayr Oxygen was a huge rotting concrete slab under an old corrugated-metal roof. Mr. Mac Bonner ran the dock with two Hispanic guys that I got to know pretty well, Victor and Jesse, and they kept the place clean and well organized in a kind of military way. Industrial and medical trucks were always delivering full or empty cylinders or taking them away, and the tanks had to be lodged in neat squadrons which would not be in the way. Victor, who was the older man, taught me how to roll two cylinders at once while I walked, turning my hands on the caps and kick-turning the bottom of the rear one. As soon as I could do that, briskly moving two at a time, I was accepted there and fell into a week of work with them, loading and unloading trucks. They were quiet men who knew the code and didn't have to speak or call instructions when a truck backed in. I followed their lead.

The fascinating thing about Victor and Jesse was their lunches. I had been eating my lunch at a little patio behind the main building, alone, not talking to the five or six other employees who sat in groups at the other metal tables. I was the college kid and they were afraid of me because they knew my dad knew one of the bosses. It seemed there had been some trouble in previous summers, and so I just ate my tuna sandwiches and drank my iced tea while the sweat dried on my forehead and I pulled my wet T-shirt away from my shoulders. After I burned my face, people were friendlier, but then I was transferred up to the dock.

There were dozens of little alcoves amid the gas cylinders standing on the platform, and that is where I ate my lunches now. Victor and Jesse had milk crates and they found one for me and we'd sit out of sight up there from eleven-thirty to noon and eat. There was a certain uneasiness at first, as if they weren't sure if I should be joining them, but then Victor saw it was essentially a necessity. I wasn't going to get my lunch out of the old fridge on the dock and walk across the yard to eat with the supply people. On the dock was where I learned the meaning of *whitebread*, the way it's used now. I'd open my little bag, two tuna sandwiches and a baggie of chips, and then I'd watch the two men open their huge sacks of burritos and tacos and other items I didn't know the names of and which I've never seen since. I mean these were huge lunches that their wives had prepared, everything wrapped in white paper. No baggies. Jesse and I traded a little bit; he liked my mother's tuna. And I loved the big burritos. I was hungry and thirsty all the time and the hefty food seemed to make me well for a while. The burritos were packed with roast beef and onions and a fiery salsa rich with cilantro. During these lunches Victor would talk a little, telling me where to keep my gloves so that the drivers didn't pick them up, and where not to sit even on break.

"There was a kid here last year," he said. "Used to take his breaks right over there." He shook his head. "Right in front of the boss's window." It was cool and private sitting behind the walls of cylinders.

"He didn't stay," Jesse said. "The boss don't know you're on break."

"Come back in here," Victor said. "Or don't sit down." He smiled at me. I looked at Jesse and he shrugged and smiled too. They hadn't told the other kid where not to sit. Jesse handed me a burrito rolled in white paper. I was on the inside now; they'd taken me in.

That afternoon there was a big Linde Oxygen semi backed against the dock and we were rolling the hot cylinders off when I heard a crash. Jesse yelled from back in the dock and I saw his arms flash and Victor, who was in front of me, laid the two tanks he was rolling on the deck of the truck and jumped off the side and ran into the open yard. I saw the first rows of tanks start to tumble wildly, a chain reaction, a murderous thundering domino chase. As the cylinders fell off the dock, they cartwheeled into the air crazily, heavily tearing clods from the cement dock ledge and thudding into the tarry asphalt. A dozen plummeted onto somebody's Dodge rental car parked too close to the action. It was crushed. The noise was ponderous, painful, and the session continued through a minute until there was only one lone bank of brown nitrogen cylinders standing like a little jury on the back corner of the loading dock. The space looked strange that empty.

The yard was full of people standing back in a crescent. Then I saw Victor step forward and walk toward where I stood on the back of the semi. I still had my hands on the tanks.

He looked what? Scared, disgusted, and a little amused. "Mi amigo," he said, climbing back on the truck. "When they go like that, run away." He pointed back to where all of the employees of Ayr Oxygen Company were watching us. "Away, get it?"

"Yes, sir," I told him. "I do."

"Now you can park those," he said, tapping the cylinders in my hand. "And we'll go pick up all these others."

It took the rest of the day and still stands as the afternoon during which I lifted more weight than any other in this life. It felt a little funny setting the hundreds of cylinders back on the old pitted concrete. "They should repour this," I said to Victor as we were finishing.

"They should," he said. "But if accidents are going to follow you, a new floor won't help." I wondered if he meant that I'd been responsible for the catastrophe. I had rolled and parked a dozen tanks when things blew, but I never considered that it might have been my fault, one cockeyed tank left wobbling.

"I'm through with accidents," I told him. "Don't worry. This is my third. I'm finished."

The next day I was drafted to drive one of the two medical oxygen trucks. One of the drivers had quit and our foreman, Mac Bonner, came out onto the dock in the morning and told me to see

Nadine, who ran Medical, in her little office building out front. She was a large woman who had one speed: gruff. I was instructed in a three-minute speech to go get my commercial driver's license that afternoon and then stop by the uniform shop on Bethany Home Road and get two sets of the brown trousers and short-sleeved yellow shirts worn by the delivery people. On my way out I went by and got my lunch and saw Victor. "They want me to drive the truck. Dennis quit, I guess." This was new to me and I was still working it over in my mind; I mean, it seemed like good news.

"Dennis wouldn't last," Victor said. "We'll have the Ford loaded for you by nine."

The yellow shirt had a name oval over the heart pocket: David. And the brown pants had a crease that will outlast us all. It felt funny going to work in those clothes and when I came up to the loading dock after picking up the truck keys and my delivery list, Jesse and Victor came out of the forest of cylinders grinning. Jesse saluted. I was embarrassed and uneasy. "One of you guys take the truck," I said.

"No way, David." Victor stepped up and pulled my collar straight. "You look too good. Besides, this job needs a white guy." I looked helplessly at Jesse.

"Better you than me," he said. They had the truck loaded: two groups of ten medical blue cylinders chain-hitched into the front of the bed. They'd used the special cardboard sleeves we had for medical gas on all the tanks; these kept them from getting too beat up. These tanks were going to be in people's bedrooms. Inside each was the same oxygen as in the dinged-up green cylinders that the welding shops used.

I climbed in the truck and started it up. Victor had already told me about allowing a little more stopping time because of the load. "Here he comes, ladies," Jesse called. I could see his hand raised in the rearview mirror as I pulled onto McDowell and headed for Sun City.

At that time, Sun City was set alone in the desert, a weird theme park for retired white people, and from the beginning it gave me an eerie feeling. The streets were like toy streets, narrow and clean, running in huge circles. No cars, no garage doors open, and, of course, in the heat, no pedestrians. As I made my rounds, wheeling the hot blue tanks up the driveways and through the carpeted houses to the bedroom, uncoupling the old tank, connecting the new one, I felt peculiar. In the houses I was met by the wife or the husband and was escorted along the way. Whoever was sick was in the other room. It was all very proper. These people had come here from the midwest and the east. They had been doctors and professors and lawyers and wanted to live among their own kind. No one under twenty could reside in Sun City. When I'd made my six calls, I fled that town, heading east on old Bell Road, which in those days was miles and miles of desert and orchards, not two traffic lights all the way to Scottsdale Road.

Mr. Rensdale was the first of my customers I ever saw in bed. He lived in one of the many blocks of townhouses they were building in Scottsdale. These were compact units with two stories and a pool in the small private yard. All of Scottsdale shuddered under bulldozers that year; it was dust and construction delays, as the little town began to see the future. I rang the bell and was met by a young woman in a long silk shirt who saw me and said, "Oh, yeah. Come on in. Where's Dennis?"

I had the hot blue cylinder on the single dolly and pulled it up the step and into the dark, cool space. I had my pocket rag and wiped the wheels as soon as she shut the door. I could see her knees and they seemed to glow in the near dark. "I'm taking his route for a while," I said, standing up. I couldn't see her face, but she had a hand on one hip.

"Right," she said. "He got fired."

"I don't know about that," I said. I pointed down the hall. "Is it this way?"

"No, upstairs, first door on your right. He's awake, David." She said my name just the way you read names off shirts. Then she put her hand on my sleeve and said, "Who hit you?" My burn was still raw across my cheekbone.

"I got burned."

"Cute," she said. "They're going to love that back at . . . where?"

"University of Montana," I said.

"University of what?" she said. "There's a university there?" She cocked her head at me. I couldn't tell what she was wearing under that shirt. She smiled. "I'm kidding. I'm a snob, but I'm kidding. What year are you?"

"I'll be a junior," I said.

"I'm a senior at Penn," she said. I nodded, my mind whipping around for something clever. I didn't even know where Penn was.

"Great," I said. I started up the stairs.

"Yeah," she said, turning. "Great."

I drew the dolly up the carpeted stair carefully, my first second story, and entered the bedroom. It was dim in there, but I could see the other cylinder beside the bed and a man in the bed, awake. He was wearing pajamas, and immediately upon seeing me, he said, "Good. Open the blinds, will you?"

"Sure thing," I said, and I went around the bed and turned the miniblind wand. The Arizona day fell into the room. The young woman I'd spoken to walked out to the pool beneath me. She took her shirt off and hung it on one of the chairs. Her breasts were white in the sunlight. She set out her magazine and drink by one of the lounges and lay facedown in a shiny green bikini bottom. I only looked down for a second or less, but I could feel the image in my body.

While I was disconnecting the regulator from the old tank and setting up the new one, Mr. Rensdale introduced himself. He was a thin, handsome man with dark hair and mustache and he looked like about three or four of the actors I was seeing those nights in late movies after my parents went to bed. He wore an aspirator with the two small nostril tubes, which he removed while I changed tanks. I liked him immediately. "Yeah," he went on, "it's good you're going

back to college. Though there's a future, believe me, in this stuff."
He knocked the oxygen tank with his knuckle.

"What field are you in?" I asked him. He seemed so absolutely
worldly there, his wry eyes and his East Coast accent, and he seemed
old the way people did then, but I realize now he wasn't fifty.

"I, lad, am the owner of Rensdale Foundations, which my father
founded," his whisper was rich with humor, "and which supplies me
with more money than my fine daughters will ever be able to
spend." He turned his head toward me. "We make ladies' undergarments, lots of them."

The dolly was loaded and I was ready to go. "Do you enjoy it?
Has it been a good thing to do?"

"Oh, for chrissakes," he wheezed a kind of laugh, "give me a week
on that, will you? I didn't know this was going to be an interview.
Come after four and it's worth a martini to you, kid, and we'll do
some career counseling."

"You all set?" I said as I moved to the door.

"Set," he whispered now, rearranging his aspirator. "Oh
absolutely. Go get them, champ." He gave me a thin smile and I left.
Letting myself out of the dark downstairs, I did an odd thing. I
stood still in the house. I had talked to her right here. I saw her
breasts again in the bright light. No one knew where I was.

Of course, Elizabeth Rensdale, seeing her at the pool that way, so
casually naked, made me think of Linda and the fact that I had no
idea of what was going on. I couldn't remember her body, though,
that summer, I gave it some thought. It was worse not being a virgin, because I should have then had some information to fuel my
struggles with loneliness. I had none, except Linda's face and her
voice, *"Here, let me get it."*

From the truck I called Nadine, telling her I was finished with
Scottsdale and was heading—on schedule—to Mesa. "Did you pick
up Mr. Rensdale's walker? Over."

"No, ma'am. Over." We had to say "Over."

"Why not? You were supposed to. Over."

The heat in the early afternoon as I dropped through the river bottom and headed out to Mesa was gigantic, an enormous, unrelenting thing, and I took a kind of perverse pleasure from it. I could feel a heartbeat in my healing burns. My truck was not air-conditioned, a thing that wouldn't fly now, but then I drove with my arm out the window through the traffic of these desert towns. "I'm sorry. I didn't know. Should I go back? Over." I could see going back, surprising the girl. I wanted to see that girl again.

"It was on your sheet. Let it go this week. But let's read the sheet from now on. Over and out."

"Over and out," I said into the air, hanging up the handset.

Half the streets in Mesa were dirt, freshly bladed into the huge grid which now is paved wall to wall. I made several deliveries and ended up at the torn edge of the known world, the road just a track, a year maybe two at most from the first ripples of the growth which would swallow hundreds of miles of the desert. The house was an old block home gone to seed, the lawn dirt, the shrubs dead, the windows brown with dust and cobwebs. From the front yard I had a clear view of the Santan Mountains to the south. I was fairly sure I had a wrong address and that the property was abandoned. I knocked on the greasy door and after five minutes a stooped, red-haired old man answered. This was Gil, and I have no idea how old he was that summer, but it was as old as you get. Plus he was sick with the emphysema and liver disease. His skin, stretched tight and translucent on his gaunt body, was splattered with brown spots. On his hands several had been picked raw.

I didn't want to go into the house. This was the oddest call of my first day driving oxygen. There had been something regular about the rest of it, even the sanitized houses in Sun City, the upscale apartments in Scottsdale so new the paint hadn't dried, and the other houses I'd been to, magazines on a coffee table, a wife paying bills in the kitchen.

I pulled my dolly into the house, dark inside against the crushing daylight, and was hit by the roiling smell of dog hair and urine.

I didn't kneel to wipe the wheels. "Right in here," the old man said, leading me back into the house toward a yellow light in the small kitchen, where I could hear a radio chattering. He had his oxygen set up in the corner of the kitchen; it looked like he lived in the one room. There was a fur of fine red dust on everything, the range, the sink, except half the kitchen table where he had his things arranged, some brown vials of prescription medicine, two decks of cards, a pencil or two on a small pad, a warped issue of *Field & Stream*, a little red Bible, and a box of cough drops. In the middle of the table was a fancy painted plate, maybe a seascape, with a line of Oreos on it. I got busy changing out the tanks. You take the cardboard sleeve off, unhook the regulator, open the valve on the new tank for one second, blasting dust from the mouth, screw the regulator on it, open the pressure so it reads the same as you came, sleeve the old tank, load it up, and go. The new tank was always hot, too hot to touch from being in the sun, and it seemed wrong to leave such a hot thing in someone's bedroom. Nadine handled all the paperwork.

The cookies had scared me and I was trying to get out. Meanwhile the old man sat down at the kitchen table and started talking. "I'm Gil Benson," his speech began, "and I'm glad to see you, David. My lungs got burned in France in 1919 and it took them all these years to buckle." He spoke like so many of my customers in a hoarse whisper. "I've lived all over the world, including the three A's: Africa, Cairo, Australia, Burberry, and Alaska, Point Barrow. My favorite place was Montreal, Canada, because I was in love there and married the woman, had children. She's dead. My least favorite place is right here because of this. One of my closest friends was young Jack Kramer, the tennis player. That was many years ago. I've flown almost every plane made between the years 1938 and 1958. I don't fly anymore with all this." He indicated the oxygen equipment. "Sit down. Have a cookie."

I had my dolly ready. "I shouldn't, sir," I said. "I've got a schedule and better keep it."

"Grab that pitcher out of the fridge before you sit down. I made us some Kool-Aid. It's good."

I opened his refrigerator. Except for the Tupperware pitcher, it was empty. Nothing. I put the pitcher on the table. "I really have to go," I said. "I'll be late."

Gil lifted the container of Kool-Aid and raised it into a jittery hover above the two plastic glasses. There was going to be an accident. His hands were covered with purple scabs. I took the pitcher from him and filled the glasses.

"Sit down," he said. "I'm glad you're here, young fella." When I didn't move he said, "Really. Nadine said you were a good-looking kid." He smiled, and leaning on both hands, he sat hard into the kitchen chair. "This is your last stop today. Have a snack."

So began my visits with old Gil Benson. He was my last delivery every fourth day that summer, and as far as I could tell, I was the only one to visit his wretched house. On one occasion I placed one of the Oreos he gave me on the corner of my chair as I left and it was right there next time when I returned. Our visits became little three-part dramas: my arrival and the bustle of intrusion; the snack and his monologue; his hysteria and weeping.

The first time he reached for my wrist across the table as I was standing to get up, it scared me. Things had been going fine. He'd told me stories in an urgent voice, one story spilling into the other without a seam, because he didn't want me to interrupt. I had *I've got to go* all over my face, but he wouldn't read it. He spoke as if placing each word in the record, as if I were going to write it all down when I got home. It always started with a story of long ago, an airplane, a homemade repair, an emergency landing, a special cargo, an odd coincidence, each part told with pride, but his voice would gradually change, slide into a kind of whine as he began an escalating series of complaints about his doctors, the insurance, his children—naming each of the four and relating their indifference, petty greed, or cruelty. I nodded through all of this: I've got to go. He leaned forward and picked at the back of his hands. When he tired after forty minutes, I'd slide my chair back and he'd grab my wrist. By then I could understand his children pushing him away and moving out of state. I wanted out. But I'd stand—while he still held me—and say, "That's interesting. Save some of these cookies for next time." And then I'd move to the door, hurrying the dolly, but never fast enough to escape. Crying softly and carrying his little walker bottle of oxygen, he'd see me to the door and then out into the numbing heat to the big white pickup. He'd continue his monologue while I chained the old tank in the back and while I climbed in the cab and started the engine and then while I'd start to pull away. I cannot describe how despicable I felt doing that, gradually moving away from old Gil on that dirt lane, and when I hit the corner and turned west for the shop, I tromped it: forty-five, fifty, fifty-five, raising a thick red dust train along what would someday be Chandler Boulevard.

Backing up to the loading dock late on those days with a truck of empties, I was full of animal happiness. The sun was at its worst, blasting the sides of everything, and I moved with the measured deliberation the full day had given me. My shirt was crusted with salt, but I wasn't sweating anymore. When I bent to the metal fountain beside the dock, gulping the water, I could feel it bloom on my back and chest and come out along my hairline. Jesse or Victor would help me sort the cylinders and reload for tomorrow, or many days, everyone would be gone already except Gene, the swing man, who'd talk to me while I finished up. His comments were always about overtime, which I'd be getting if I saw him, and what was I going to do with all my money.

What I was doing was banking it all, except for pocket money and the eight dollars I spent every Sunday calling Linda Enright. I became tight and fit, my burns finally scabbed up so that by mid-July I looked like a young boxer, and I tried not to think about anything.

A terrible thing happened in my phone correspondence with Linda. We stopped fighting. We'd talk about her family; the cookie business was taking off, but her father wouldn't let her take the car.

He was stingy. I told her about my deliveries, the heat. She was looking forward to getting the fall bulletin. Was I going to major in geol-
ogy as I'd planned? As I listened to us talk, I stood and wondered:
Who are these people? The other me wanted to interrupt, to ask:
Hey, didn't we have sex? I mean, was that sexual intercourse? Isn't the
world a little different for you now? But I chatted with her. Neither
one of us mentioned other people, that is boys she might have met,
and I didn't mention Elizabeth Rensdale. I shifted my feet in the
baking phone booth and chatted. When the operator came on, I was
crazy with Linda's indifference, but unable to say anything but "Take
care, I'll call."

Meanwhile the summer assumed a regularity that was nothing but
comfort. I drove my routes: hospitals Mondays, rest homes
Tuesdays, residences the rest of the week. Sun City, Scottsdale, Mesa.
Nights I'd stay up and watch the old movies, keeping a list of titles
and great lines. It was as much of a life of the mind as I wanted.
Then it would be six A.M. and I'd have Sun City, Scottsdale, Mesa. I
was hard and brown and lost in the routine.

I was used to sitting with Gil Benson and hearing his stories,
pocketing the Oreos secretly to throw them from the truck later; I
was used to the new-carpet smell of all the little homes in Sun City,
everything clean, quiet, and polite; I was used to Elizabeth Rensdale
showing me her white breasts, posturing by the pool whenever she
knew I was upstairs with her father. By the end of July I had three
or four of her little moves memorized, the way she rolled on her
back, the way she kneaded them with oil sitting with her long legs
on each side of the lounge chair. Driving the valley those long summer days, each window of the truck a furnace, listening to
"Paperback Writer" and "Last Train to Clarksville," I delivered oxygen to the paralyzed and dying, and I felt so alive and on edge at
every moment that I could have burst. I liked the truck, hopping up
unloading the hot cylinders at each address and then driving to the
next stop. I knew what I was doing and wanted no more.

Rain broke the summer. The second week in August I woke to the first clouds in ninety days. They massed and thickened and by the time I left Sun City, it had begun, a crashing downpour. It never rains lightly in the desert. The wipers on the truck were shot with sun rot and I had to stop and charge a set at a Chevron station on the Black Canyon Freeway and then continue east toward Scottsdale, crawling along in the stunned traffic, water everywhere over the highway.

I didn't want to be late at the Rensdales'. I liked the way Elizabeth looked at me when she let me in, and I liked looking at her naked by the pool. It didn't occur to me that today would be any different until I pulled my dolly toward their door through the warm rain. I was wiping down the tank in the covered entry when she opened the door and disappeared back into the dark house. I was wet and coming into the air-conditioned house ran a chill along my sides. The blue light of the television pulsed against the darkness. When my eyes adjusted and I started backing up the stairway with the new cylinder, I saw Elizabeth sitting on the couch in the den, her knees together up under her chin, watching me. She was looking right at me. I'd never seen her like this, and she'd never looked at me before.

"This is the worst summer of my entire life," she said.

"Sorry," I said, coming down a step. "What'd you say?"

"David! Is that you?" Mr. Rensdale called from his room. His voice was a ghost. I liked him very much and it had become clear over the summer that he was not going back to Pennsylvania. He'd lost weight. His face had become even more angular and his eyes had sunken. "David."

Elizabeth Rensdale whispered across the room to me, "I don't want to be here." She closed her eyes and rocked her head. I stood the cylinder on the dolly and went over to her. I didn't like leaving it there on the carpet. It wasn't what I wanted to do. She was sitting in her underpants on the couch. "He's dying," she said to me.

"Oh," I said, trying to make it simply a place holder, let her know that I'd heard her. It was the wrong thing, but anything, even silence, would have been wrong. She put her face in her hands and lay over on the couch. I dropped to a knee and, putting my hand on her shoulder, I said, "What can I do?"

This was the secret side that I suspected from this summer. Elizabeth Rensdale put her hand on mine and turned her face to mine so slowly that I felt my heart drop a gear, grinding now heavily uphill in my chest. The rain was like a pressure on the roof.

Mr. Rensdale called my name again. Elizabeth's face on mine so close and open made it possible for me to move my hand around her back and pull her to me. It was like I knew what I was doing. I didn't take my eyes from hers when she rolled onto her back and guided me onto her. It was different in every way from what I had imagined. The dark room closed around us. Her mouth came to mine and stayed there. This wasn't education; this was need. And later, when I felt her hand on my bare ass, her heels rolling in the back of my knees, I knew it was the mirror of my cradling her in both my arms as we rocked along the edge of the couch, moving it finally halfway across the den as I pushed into her. I wish I could get this right here, but there is no chance. We stayed together for a moment afterward and my eyes opened and focused. She was still looking at me, holding me, and her look was simply serious. Her father called, "David?" from upstairs again, and I realized he must have been calling steadily. Still, we were slow to move. I stood without embarrassment and dressed, tucking my shirt in. That we were intent, that we were still rapt, made me confident in a way I'd never been. I grabbed the dolly and ascended the stairs.

Mr. Rensdale lay white and twisted in the bed. He looked the way the dying look, his face parched and sunken, the mouth a dry orifice, his eyes little spots of water. I saw him acknowledge me with a withering look, more power than you'd think could rise from such a body. I felt it a cruel scolding, and I moved in the room deliberate with shame, avoiding his eyes. The rain drummed against the window in waves. After I had changed out the tanks, I turned to him and said, "There you go."

He rolled his hand in a little flip toward the bedtable and his glass of water. His chalky mouth was in the shape of an O, and I could hear him breathing, a thin rasp. Who knows what happened in me then, because I stood in the little bedroom with Mr. Rensdale and then I just rolled the dolly and the expired tank out and down the stairs. I didn't go to him; I didn't hand him the glass of water. I burned; who would ever know what I had done?

When I opened the door downstairs on the world of rain, Elizabeth came out of the dark again, naked, to stand a foot or two away. I took her not speaking as just part of the intensity I felt and the way she stood with her arms easy at her sides was the way I felt when I'd been naked before her. We looked at each other for a moment; the rain was already at my head and the dolly and tank was between us in the narrow entry, and then something happened that sealed the way I feel about myself even today. She came up and we met beside the tank and there was no question about the way we went for each other what was going on. I pushed by the oxygen equipment and followed her onto the entry tile, then a moment later turning in adjustment so that she could climb me, get her bare back off the floor.

So the last month of that summer I began seeing Elizabeth Rensdale every day. My weekly visits to the Rensdale townhouse continued, but then I started driving out to Scottsdale nights. I told my parents I was at the library, because I wanted it to sound like a lie and have them know it was a lie. I came in after midnight; the library closed at nine. After work I'd shower and put on a clean shirt, something without my name on it, and I'd call back from the door, "Going to the library." And I knew they knew I was up to something. It was like I wanted them to challenge me, to have it out.

Elizabeth and I were hardy and focused lovers. I relished the way every night she'd meet my knock at the door and pull me into the room and then, having touched, we didn't stop. Knowing we had two hours, we used every minute of it and we became experts at each other. For me these nights were the first nights in my new life, I mean, I could tell then that there was no going back, that I had changed my life forever and I could not stop it. We never went out for a Coke, we never took a break for a glass of water, we rarely spoke. There was admiration and curiosity in my touch and affection and gratitude in hers or so I assumed, and I was pleased, even proud, at the time that there was so little need to speak. There was one time when I arrived a little early when Mr. Rensdale's nurse was still there and Elizabeth and I sat in the den watching television two feet apart on the couch, and even then we didn't speak. I forget what program was on, but Elizabeth asked me if it was okay, and I said fine and that was all we said while we waited for the nurse to leave.

On the way home with my arm out in the hot night, I drove like the young king of the desert. Looking into my car at a traffic light, other drivers could read it all on my face and the way I held my head cocked back. I was young those nights, but I was getting over it.

Meanwhile Gil Benson had begun clinging to me worse than ever and those prolonged visits were full of agony and desperation. As the Arizona monsoon season continued toward Labor Day, the rains played hell with his old red road, and many times I pulled up in the same tracks I'd left the week before. He stopped putting cookies out, which at first I took as a good sign, but then I realized that he now considered me so familiar that cookies weren't necessary. A kind of terror had inhabited him, and it was fed by the weather. Now most days I had to go west to cross the flooded Salt River at the old Mill Avenue Bridge to get to Mesa late and by the time I arrived, Gil would be on the porch, frantic. Not because of oxygen deprivation; he only needed to use the stuff nights. But I was his oxygen now, his only visitor, his only companion. I'd never had such a thing happen before and until it did I'd thought of myself as a compassionate person. I watched myself arrive at his terrible house and wheel the tank toward the door and I searched myself for compassion, the smallest shred of fellow feeling, kindness, affection, pity, but all I found was repulsion, impatience. I thought, surely I would be kind, but that was a joke, and I saw that compassion was a joke too along with fidelity and chastity and all the other notions I'd run over this summer. Words, I thought, big words. Give me the truck keys and a job to do, and the words can look out for themselves. I had no compassion for Gil Benson and that diminished over the summer. His scabby hands, the dried spittle in the ruined corners of his mouth, his crummy weeping in his stinking house. He always grabbed my wrist with both hands, and I shuffled back toward the truck. His voice, already a whisper, broke and he cried, his face a twisted ugliness which he wiped at with one hand while holding me with the other. I tried to nod and say, "You bet," and "That's too bad. I'll see you next week." But he wouldn't hear me any more than I was listening to him. His voice was so nakedly plaintive it embarrassed me. I wanted to push him down in the mud and weeds of his yard and drive away, but I never did that. What I finally did was worse.

The summer already felt nothing but old as Labor Day approached, the shadows in the afternoon gathering reach although the temperature was always 105. I could see it when I backed into the dock late every day, the banks of cylinders stark in the slanted sunlight, Victor and Jesse emerging from a world which was only black and white, sun and long shadow. The change gave me a feeling that I can only describe as anxiety. Birds flew overhead, three and four at a time, headed somewhere. There were huge banks of clouds in the sky every afternoon and after such a long season of blanched white heat, the shadows beside things seemed ominous. The cars and buildings and the massive tin roof of the loading dock were just things, but their shadows seemed like meanings. Summer, whatever it had meant, was ending. The fact that I would be going back to Montana and college in three weeks became tangible. It all felt complicated.

I sensed this all through a growing curtain of fatigue. The long hot days and the sharp extended nights with Elizabeth began to shave my energy. At first it took all the extra that I had being nineteen, and then I started to cut into the principal. I couldn't feel it mornings, which passed in a flurry, but afternoons, my back solid sweat against the seat of my truck, I felt it as a weight, my body going leaden as I drove the streets of Phoenix. Unloading became an absolute drag. I stopped jumping off the truck and started climbing down, stopped skipping up onto the dock, started walking, and every few minutes would put my hands on my waist and lean against something, the tailgate, the dock, a pillar.

"Oy, amigo," Jesse said one day late in August as I rested against the shipping desk in back of the dock. "Qué pasa?"

"Nothing but good things," I said. "How're you doing?"

He came closer and looked at my face, concerned. "You sick?"

"No, I'm great. Long day."

Victor appeared with the cargo sheet and handed me the clipboard to sign. He and Jesse exchanged glances. I looked up at them. Victor put his hand on my chin and let it drop. "Too much tail." He was speaking to Jesse. "He got the truck and forgot what I told him. Remember?" He turned to me. "Remember? Watch what you're doing." Victor took the clipboard back and tapped it against his leg. "When the tanks start to fall, run the *other* way."

A moment later as I was getting ready to move the truck, Jesse came out with his white lunch bag and gave me his leftover burrito. It was as heavy as a book and I ate it like a lesson.

But it was a hot heedless summer and I showered every night like some animal born of it, heedless and hot, and I pulled a cotton T-shirt over my ribs, combed my wet hair back, and without a word to my parents, who were wary of me now it seemed, drove to Scottsdale and buried myself in Elizabeth Rensdale.

THE SUNDAY before Labor Day, I didn't call Linda Enright. This had been my custom all these many weeks and now I was breaking it. I rousted around the house, finally raking the yard, sweeping the garage, and washing all three of the cars, before rolling onto the couch in the den and watching some of the sad, throwaway television of a summer Sunday. In each minute of the day, Linda Enright, sitting in her father's home office, which she'd described to me on the telephone many times (we always talked about where we were; I told her about my phone booth, the heat, graffiti, and passing traffic), was in my mind. I saw her there in her green sweater by her father's rolltop. We always talked about what we were wearing and she always said the green sweater, saying it innocently as if wearing the sweater that I'd helped pull over her head that night in her dorm room was of little note, a coincidence, and not the most important thing that she'd say in the whole eight-dollar call, and I'd say just Levi's and T-shirt, hoping she'd imagine the belt, the buckle, the trouble it could all be in the dark. I saw her sitting still in the afternoon shadow, maybe writing some notes in her calendar or reading, and right over there, the telephone. I lay there in my stocking feet knowing I could get up and hit the phone booth in less than ten minutes and make that phone ring, have her reach for it, but I didn't. I stared at the television screen as if this was some kind of work and I had to do it. It was the most vivid that Linda had appeared before me the entire summer. Green sweater in the study through the endless day. I let her sit there until the last sunlight rocked through the den, broke, and disappeared. I hated the television, the couch, my body which would not move. I finally got up sometime after nine and went to bed.

Elizabeth Rensdale and I kept at it. Over the Labor Day weekend, I stayed with her overnight and we worked and reworked ourselves long past satiation. She was ravenous and my appetite for her was relentless. That was how I felt it all: relentless. Moments after coming hard into her, I would begin to palm her bare hip as if dreaming and then still dreaming begin to mouth her ear and her hand would play over my genitals lightly and then move in dreamily sorting me around in the dark and we would shift to begin again. I woke from a brief nap sometime after four in the morning with Elizabeth across me, a leg between mine, her face in my neck, and I felt a heaviness in my arm as I slid it down her tight back that reminded me of what Victor had said. I was tired in a way I'd never known. My blood stilled and I could feel a pressure running in my head like sand, and still my hand descended in the dark. There was no stopping. Soon I felt her hand, as I had every night for a month, and we labored toward dawn.

In the morning, Sunday, I didn't go home, but drove way down by Ayr Oxygen Company to the Roadrunner, the truck stop there on McDowell adjacent to the freeway. It was the first day I'd ever been sore and I walked carefully to the coffee shop. I sat alone at the counter, eating eggs and bacon and toast and coffee, feeling the night tick away in every sinew the way a car cools after a long drive. It was an effort to breathe and at times I had to stop and gulp some air, adjusting myself on the counter stool. Around me it was only truck drivers who had driven all night from Los Angeles, Sacramento, Albuquerque, Salt Lake City. There was only one woman in the place, a large woman in a white waitress dress who moved up and down the counter pouring coffee. When she poured mine, I looked up at her and our eyes locked, I mean her head tipped and her face registered something I'd never seen before. If I used such words I'd call it *horror*, but I don't. My old heart bucked, I thought of my Professor Whisner and Western Civ; if it was what I was personally doing, then it was in tough shape. The gravity of the moment between the waitress and myself was such that I was certain to my toenails I'd been seen: she knew all about me.

THAT WEEK I gave Nadine my notice, reminding her that I would be leaving in ten days, mid-September, to go back to school. "Well, sonnyboy, I hope we didn't work your wheels off." She leaned back, letting me know there was more to say.

"No, ma'am. It's been a good summer."

"We think so too," she said. "Come by and I'll have your last check cut early, so we don't have to mail it."

"Thanks, Nadine." I moved to the door; I had a full day of deliveries.

"Old Gil Benson is going to miss you, I think."

"I've met a lot of nice people," I said. I wanted to deflect this and get going.

"No," she said, "you've been good to him; it's important. Some of these old guys don't have much to look forward to. He's called several times. I might as well tell you. Mr. Ayr heard about it and is writing you a little bonus."

I stepped back toward her. "What?"

"Congratulations." She smiled. "Drive carefully."

I walked slowly out to the truck. I cinched the chain hitches in the back of my Ford, securing the cylinders, climbed wearily down to the asphalt, which was already baking at half past eight, and pulled myself into the driver's seat. In the rearview mirror I could see Victor and Jesse standing in the shadows. I was tired.

Some of my customers knew I was leaving and made kind remarks or shook my hand or had their wife hand me an envelope with a twenty in it. I smiled and nodded gratefully and then turned business-like to the dolly and left. These were strange good-byes, because there was no question that we would ever see each other again. It had been a summer and I had been their oxygen guy. But there was more: I was young and they were ill. I stood in the bedroom doors in Sun City and said, "Take care," and I moved to the truck and felt something, but I couldn't even today tell you what it was. The people who didn't know, who said, "See you next week, David," I didn't correct them. I said, "See you," and I left their homes too. It all had me on edge.

The last day of my job in the summer of 1967, I drove to work under a cloud cover as thick as twilight in winter and still massing. It began to rain early and I made the quick decision to beat the Salt River flooding by hitting Mesa first and Scottsdale in the afternoon. I had known for a week that I did not want Gil Benson to be my last call for the summer, and this rain, steady but light, gave me the excuse I wanted. Of course, it was nuts to think I could get out to Mesa before the crossings were flooded. And by now, mid-September, all the drivers were wise to the monsoon and headed for the Tempe Bridge as soon as they saw overcast. The traffic was colossal, and I crept in a huge column of cars east across the river, noting it was twice as bad coming back, everyone trying to get to Phoenix for the day. My heart was only heavy, not fearful or nervous, as I edged forward. What I am saying is that I had time to think about it all, this summer, myself, and it was a powerful stew. The radio wouldn't finish a song. "Young Girl," by Gary Puckett and the

Union Gap or "Cherish," by the Association without interrupting with a traffic bulletin about crossing the river.

I imagined it raining in the hills of Boulder, Colorado, Linda Enright selling cookies in her apron in a shop with curtains, a Victorian tearoom, ten years ahead of itself as it turned out, her sturdy face with no expression telling she wasn't a virgin anymore, and that now she had been for thirty days betrayed. I thought, and this is the truth, I thought for the first time of what I was going to say *last* to Elizabeth Rensdale. I tried to imagine it, and my imagination failed. I tried again, I mean, I really tried to picture us there in the entry of the Scottsdale townhouse speaking to each other, which we had never, ever done. When I climbed from her bed the nights I'd gone to her, it was just that, climbing out, dressing, and crossing to the door. She didn't get up. This wasn't *Casablanca* or *High Noon*, or *Captain Blood*, which I had seen this summer, this was getting laid in a hot summer desert town by your father's oxygen deliveryman. There was no way to make it anything else, and it was too late as I moved through Tempe toward Mesa and Gil Benson's outpost to make it anything else. We were not going to hold each other's faces in our hands and whisper; we were not going to stand speechless in the shadows. I was going to try to get her pants off one more time and let her see me. That was it. I shifted in my truck seat and drove.

Even driving slowly, I fishtailed through the red clay along Gil's road. The rain had moved in for the day, persistent and even, and the temperature stalled and hovered at about a hundred. I thought Gil would be pleased to see me so soon in the day, because he was always glad to see me, welcomed me, but I surprised him this last Friday knocking at the door for five full minutes before he unlocked the door, looking scared. Though I had told him I would eventually be going back to college, I hadn't told him this was my last day. I didn't want any this or that, just the little visit and the drive away. I wanted to get to Scottsdale.

Shaken up like he was, things went differently. There was no chatter right off the bat, no sitting down at the table. He just moved things out of the way as I wheeled the oxygen in and changed tanks. He stood to one side, leaning against the counter. When I finished, he made no move to keep me there, so I just kept going. I wondered for a moment if he knew who I was or if he was just waking up. At the front door, I said, "There you go, good luck, Gil." His name quickened him and he came after me with short steps in his slippers.

"Well, yes," he started as always, "I wouldn't need this stuff at all if I'd stayed out of the war." And he was off and cranking. But when I went outside, he followed me into the rain. "Of course, I was strong as a horse and came back and got right with it. I mean, there wasn't any sue-the-government then. We were happy to be home. I was happy." He went on, the rain pelting us both. His slippers were all muddy.

"You gotta go," I told him. "It's wet out here." His wet skin in the flat light looked raw, the spots on his forehead brown and liquid; under his eyes the skin was purple. I'd let him get too close to the truck and he'd grabbed the door handle.

"I wasn't sick a day in my life," he said. "Not as a kid, not in the army. Ask my wife. When this came on," he patted his chest, "it came on bang! Just like that and here I am. Somewhere." His eyes, which had been looking everywhere past me, found mine and took hold. "This place!" He pointed at his ruined house. "This place!" I put my hand on his on the door handle and I knew that I wasn't going to be able to pry it off without breaking it.

Then there was a hitch in the rain, a gust of wet wind, and hail began to rattle through the yard, bouncing up from the mud, bouncing off the truck and our heads. "Let me take you back inside," I said. "Quick, Gil, let's get out of this weather." The hail stepped up a notch, a million mothballs ringing every surface. Gil Benson pulled the truck door open, and with surprising dexterity, he stepped up into the vehicle, sitting on all my paperwork. He wasn't going to budge and I hated pleading with him. I wouldn't do it. Now the hail had tripled, quadrupled, in a crashfest off the hood. I looked at Gil, shrunken and purple in the darkness of the cab; he looked like the victim of a fire.

"Well, at least we're dry in here, right?" I said. "We'll give it a minute." And that's what it took, about sixty seconds for the hail to abate, and after a couple of heavy curtains of the rain ripped across the hood as if they'd been thrown from somewhere, the world went silent and we could hear only the patter of the last faint drops. "Gil," I said. "I'm late. Let's go in." I looked at him but he did not look at me. "I've got to go." He sat still, his eyes timid, frightened, smug. It was an expression you use when you want someone to hit you.

I started the truck, hoping that would scare him, but he did not move. His eyes were still floating and it looked like he was grinning, but it wasn't a grin. I crammed the truck into gear and began to fish-tail along the road. I didn't care for that second if we went off the road; the wheels roared mud. At the corner, we slid in the wet clay across the street and stopped.

I kicked my door open and jumped down into the red mud and went around the front of the truck. When I opened his door, he did not turn or look at me, which was fine with me. I lifted Gil like a bride and he clutched me, his wet face against my face. I carried him to the weedy corner lot. He was light and bony like an old bird and I was strong and I felt strong, but I could tell this was an insult the old man didn't need. When I stood him there he would not let go, his hands clasped around my neck, and I peeled his hands apart care-fully, easily, and I folded them back toward him so he wouldn't snag me again. "Goodbye, Gil," I said. He was an old wet man alone in the desert. He did not acknowledge me.

I ran to the truck and eased ahead for traction and when I had traction, I floored it, throwing mud behind me like a rocket.

By the time I lined up for the Tempe Bridge, the sky was torn with blue vents. The Salt River was nothing but muscle, a brown torrent four feet over the river-bottom roadway. The traffic was thick. I merged and merged again and finally funneled onto the bridge and across toward Scottsdale. A ten-mile rainbow had emerged over the McDowell Mountains.

I radioed Nadine that the rain had slowed me up and I wouldn't make it back before five.

"No problem, sonnyboy," she said. "I'll leave your checks on my desk. Have you been to Scottsdale yet? Over."

"Just now," I said. "I'll hit the Rensdales' and on in. Over."

"Sonnyboy," she said. "Just pick up there. Mr. Rensdale died yesterday. Remember the portable unit, okay? And good luck at school. Stop in if you're down for Christmas break. Over."

I waited a minute to over and out to Nadine while the news subsided in me. I was on Scottsdale Road at Camelback, where I turned right. That corner will always be that radio call. "Copy. Over," I said.

I just drove. Now the sky was ripped apart the way I've learned only a western sky can be, the glacial cloud cover broken and the shreds gathering against the Superstition Mountains, the blue air a color you don't see twice a summer in the desert, icy and clear, no dust or smoke. All the construction crews in Scottsdale had given it up and the bright lumber on the sites sat dripping in the afternoon sun. They had taken the day off from changing this place.

In front of the Rensdales' townhouse I felt odd going to the door with the empty dolly. I rang the bell, and after a moment Elizabeth appeared. She was barefoot in jeans and a T-shirt, and she just looked at me. "I'm sorry about your father," I said. "This is tough." She stared at me and I held the gaze. "I mean it. I'm sorry."

She drifted back into the house. It felt for the first time strange and cumbersome to be in the dark little townhouse. She had the air-conditioning cranked way up so that I could feel the edge of a chill on my arms and neck as I pulled the dolly up the stairs to Mr. Rensdale's room. It had been taken apart a little bit, the bed stripped, our gear all standing in the corner. With Mr. Rensdale gone you could see what the room was, just a little box in the desert. Looking out the window over the pool and the two dozen tiled roofs before the edge of the Indian reservation and the sage and creosote bushes, it seemed clearly someplace to come and die. The mountains, now all rinsed by rain, were red and purple, a pretty lie.

"I'm going back Friday." Elizabeth had come into the room. "I guess I'll go back to school."

"Good," I said. "Good idea." I didn't know what I was saying. The space in my heart about returning to school was nothing but dread.

"They're going to bury him tomorrow." She sat on the bed. "Out here somewhere."

I started to say something about that, but she pointed at me. "Don't come. Just do what you do, but don't come to the funeral. You don't have to."

"I want to," I said. Her tone had hurt, made me mad.

"My mother and sister will be here tonight," she said.

"I want to," I said. I walked to the bed and put my hands on her shoulders.

"Don't."

I bent and looked into her face.

"Don't."

I went to pull her toward me to kiss her and she leaned away sharply. "Don't, David." But I followed her over onto the bed, and though she squirmed, tight as a knot, I held her beside me, adjusting her, drawing her back against me. We'd struggled in every manner, but not this. Her arms were tight cords and it took more strength than I'd ever used to pin them both against her chest while I opened my mouth on her neck and ran my other hand flat inside the front of her pants. I reached deep and she drew a sharp breath and stretched her legs out along mine, bumping at my ankles with her heels. Then she gave way and I knew I could let go of her arms. We lay still that way, nothing moving but my finger. She rocked her head back.

About a minute later she said, "What are you doing?"

"It's okay," I said.

Then she put her hand on my wrist, stopping it. "Don't," she said. "What are you doing?"

"Elizabeth," I said, kissing at her nape. "This is what we do. Don't you like it?"

She rose to an elbow and looked at me, her face rock-hard, unfamiliar. "This is what we do?" Our eyes were locked. "Is this what you came for?" She lay back and thumbed off her pants until she was naked from the waist down. "Is it?"

"Yes," I said. It was the truth and there was pleasure in saying it.

"Then go ahead. Here." She moved to the edge of the bed, a clear display. The moment had fused and I held her look and I felt seen. I felt known. I stood and undid my belt and went at her, the whole time neither of us changing expression, eyes open, though I studied her as I moved looking for a signal of the old ways, the pleasure, a lowered eyelid, the opening mouth, but none came. Her mouth was open but as a challenge to me, and her fists gripped the mattress but simply so she didn't give ground. She didn't move when I pulled away, just lay there looking at me. I remember it as the moment in this life when I was farthest from any of my feelings. I gathered the empty cylinder and the portable gear with the strangest thought: *It's going to take me twenty years to figure out who I am now.*

I could feel Elizabeth Rensdale's hatred, as I would feel it dozens of times a season for many years. It's a kind of dread for me that has become a rudder and kept me out of other troubles. That next year at school, I used it to treat Linda Enright correctly, as a gentleman, and keep my distance, though I came to know I was in love with her and had been all along. I had the chance to win her back and I did not take it. We worked together several times with the Democratic Student Alliance, and it is public record that our organization brought Robert Kennedy to the Houck Center on campus that March. Professor Whisner introduced him that night, and at the reception I shook Robert Kennedy's hand. It felt, for one beat, like Western Civilization.

THAT BAD day at the Rensdales' I descended the stair, carefully, not looking back, and I let myself out of the townhouse for the last time. The mud on the truck had dried in brown fans along the sides and rear. The late afternoon in Scottsdale had been scrubbed and hung out to dry, the air glassy and quick, the color of everything distinct, and the brown folds of the McDowell Mountains magnified and looming. It was fresh, the temperature had dropped twenty degrees, and the elongated shadows of the short new imported palms along the street printed themselves eerily in the wet lawns. Today those trees are as tall as those weird shadows. I just wanted to close this whole show down.

But as I drove through Scottsdale, block by block, west toward Camelback Mountain, I was torn by a nagging thought of Gil Benson. I shouldn't have left him out there. At a dead end by the Indian School canal I stopped and turned off the truck. The grapefruit grove there was being bladed under. Summer was over; I was supposed to be happy.

Back at Ayr Oxygen, I told Gene, the swing man, to forget it and I unloaded the truck myself. It was the one good hour of that day, one hour of straight work, lifting and rolling my empties into the ranks at the far end of the old structure. Victor and Jesse would find them tomorrow. They would be the last gas cylinders I would ever handle. I locked the truck and walked to the office in my worn-out workshoes. I found two envelopes on Nadine's desk: my check and the bonus check. It was two hundred and fifty dollars. I put them in my pocket and left my keys, pulling the door locked behind me.

I left for my junior year of college at Missoula three days later. The evening before my flight, my parents took me to dinner at a steakhouse on a mesa, a western place where they cut your tie off if you wear one. The barn-plank walls were covered with the clipped ends of ties. It was a good dinner, hearty, the baked potatoes big as melons and the charred edges of the steaks dropping off the plates. My parents were giddy, ebullient, because their business plans which had so consumed them were looking good. Every loan they'd positioned was ready; the world was right. They were proud of me, they said, working hard like this all summer away from my friends. I was changing, they said, and they could tell it was for the better.

After dinner we went back to the house and had a drink on the back terrace, which was a new thing in our lives. I didn't drink very much and I had never had a drink with my parents. My father made a toast to my success at school and then my mother made a toast to my success at school and to my success with Linda Enright, and she smiled at me, a little friendly joke, and she clinked her scotch and water against my bottle of Bud and tossed it back. "I'm serious," she said. Then she stood and threw her glass out back and we heard it shatter against the stucco wall. A moment later she hugged me and she and my father went in to bed.

I cupped my car keys and went outside. I drove the dark streets. The radio played a steady rotation of exactly the same songs heard today on every fifty-thousand-watt station in this country; every fifth song was the Supremes. I knew where I was going. Beyond the bright rough edge of the lights of Mesa I drove until the pavement ended, and then I dropped onto the red clay roads and found Gil Benson's house. It was as dark as some final place, and there was no disturbance in the dust on the front walk or in the network of spiderwebs inside the broken storm door. I knocked and called for minutes. Out back, I kicked through the debris and weeds until I found one of the back bedroom windows unlocked and I slid it open and climbed inside. In the stale heat, I knew immediately that the house was abandoned. I called Gil's name and picked my way carefully to the hall. The lights did not work, and in the kitchen when I opened the fridge, the light was out and the humid stench hit me and I closed the door. I wasn't scared, but I was something else. Standing in that dark room where I had palmed old Oreos all summer long, I now had proof, hard proof, that I had lost Gil Benson. He hadn't made it back and I couldn't wish him back.

Outside, the cooked air filled my lungs and the bright dish of Phoenix glittered to the west. I drove toward it carefully. Nothing had cooled down. In every direction the desert was being torn up, and I let the raw night rip through the open car window. At home my suitcases were packed. Some big thing was closing down in me; I'd spent the summer as someone else, someone I knew I didn't care for and I would be glad when he left town. We would see each other from time to time, but I also knew he was no friend of mine. I eased along the empty roadways trying simply to gather what was left, to think, but it was like trying to fold a big blanket alone. I kept having to start over.

ACKNOWLEDGMENTS

"Bigfoot Stole My Wife" in *Quarterly West,* University of Utah; *Sudden Fiction International,* ed. Thomas and Shapard, W. W. Norton; *Dreamers and Desperadoes,* ed. Lesley, Laurel, Bantam Doubleday Dell; *The Norton Anthology of Short Fiction,* 5th edition, ed. R. V. Cassill, W. W. Norton.

"Blazo" in *Ploughshares,* Emerson College, Boston; *A Writer's Country* ed. Schell et al., Prentice Hall; *The Norton Anthology of Contemporary Fiction,* 2nd edition, ed. R. V. Cassill and Joyce Carol Oates, W. W. Norton.

"Blood" in *McCall's*; *dadmag.com* online ed. Jonathan Black.

"The Chromium Hook" in *Harper's,* October 1995.

"DeRay" in *Gentleman's Quarterly; Best of the West, Vol. 5,* ed. Thomas and Thomas, W. W. Norton.

"Down the Green River" in *The Southern Review; Salt Lake City Magazine.*

"Dr. Slime" in *Western Humanities Review,* University of Utah.

"The Governor's Ball" in *TriQuarterly,* Northwestern University.

"Hartwell" in *Playboy; The Student Body: Short Stories About College Life,* ed. John McNally, University of Wisconsin Press.

"The Hotel Eden" in *Esquire Magazine,* May 1997.

"The H Street Sledding Record" in *Network,* Salt Lake City, Utah; *McCall's*; *Insight,* Arizona State University; *Willamette Week,* Portland, Oregon; *A Literary Christmas,* Great Contemporary Christmas Stories, ed. Lilly Golden, Atlantic Monthly Press; *New Writers of the Purple Sage,* Contemporary Western Writing, ed. Russell Martin, Viking Penguin.

"I Am Bigfoot" in *Harper's; This World (San Francisco Chronicle); Dreamers and Desperadoes,* ed. Lesley, Laurel, Bantam Doubleday Dell; *The Norton Anthology of Short Fiction,* 5th edition, ed. R. V. Cassill, W. W. Norton.

"Keith" in *Tell,* New York City; *The Peregrine Reader,* ed. Vause and Porter, Peregrine Smith; *Success Stories for the 90's,* ed. Nowman. Institute of Children's Literature, West Redding, Ct.

"A Kind of Flying" in *McCall's*; *The Wedding Cake in the Middle of the Road*, ed. Susan Stamberg and George Garrett, W. W. Norton; *Literary Cavalcade* (Scholastic Monthly); *Las Vegas Life*.

"Life Before Science" in *Fiction Network*, San Francisco.

"Max" in *Carolina Quarterly*, University of North Carolina.

"Milk" in *North American Review*, Cedar Falls; *Neo*, Salt Lake City; *The Family Therapy Networker*, Washington, D.C.; *Best American Short Stories 1987*, ed. Ann Beattie, Houghton Mifflin.

"Nightcap" in *Salt Lake City Magazine*, May 1997.

"A Note on the Type" in *Harper's*; *The Writing Path 2*, ed. Petit, University of Iowa Press.

"On the U.S.S. Fortitude" in *The New Yorker*; *Practical English Handbook*, 9th edition, ed. Watkins and Dillingham, Houghton Mifflin; *Voices Louder than Words*, ed. Bill Shore, Vintage/Random House.

"Oxygen" in *Witness*, Farmington Hills, Michigan; *American Short Stories Since 1945*, ed. John Parks, Oxford University Press.

"Phenomena" in *Writers' Forum*, University of Colorado; *Best of the West, Vol 1*, ed. James Thomas, Peregrine Smith; *Higher Elevations*, Stories from the West, ed. Blackburn and Pellow, Ohio University Press/Swallow Press.

"Plan B for the Middle Class" in *New Virginia Review*.

"The Prisoner of Bluestone" in *Gentleman's Quarterly*, April 1996.

"Santa Monica" in *Kaimana*, Honolulu, Hawaii.

"The Status Quo" in *Network*, Salt Lake City.

"The Summer of Vintage Clothing" in *Harper's*.

"Sunny Billy Day" in *Gentleman's Quarterly*; *Baseball Fantastic*, ed. W. P. Kinsella, Quarry Press; *Bottom of the Ninth*, Great Contemporary Baseball Stories, ed. John McNally, Southern Illinois University Press.

"The Tablecloth of Turin" in *Story*; *Sudden Fiction, Continued*, ed. Thomas and Shapard, W. W. Norton.

"The Time I Died" in *Carolina Quarterly*, University of North Carolina.

"What We Wanted to Do" in *Witness*, Farmington Hills, Michigan; *Harper's*; *The Best American Humor 1994*, ed. Waldocs, Simon & Schuster.

"Zanduce at Second" in *Harper's*; *Baseball Fantastic*, ed. W. P. Kinsella, Quarry Press.

Thanks to the many editors who helped bring these stories forward. A special thanks to four people: Carol Houck Smith, Bob Shacochis, Gail Hochman, and Marianne Merola.